Empty, Lifeless Space
Spread Before Sisko as He
Stepped onto the Ops Deck.

Slowly, he turned from where he stood, his gaze searching. . . .

And finding. A chair before one of the consoles slowly turned, revealing the figure that had been sitting there. An image with his face.

His voice: "I've been waiting for you." A smile formed on the face of Sisko's mirror image, his echo. "For a long time."

Sisko nodded slowly, acknowledging its existence. He knew he should have expected it.

The echo's face—Sisko's face, transformed but still the same—was an emotionless mask, cold and inhuman, divorced from all feeling.

"There can't be two of us here. That's not possible." The echo's voice came from deep inside, as though the words were the result of long brooding. "You'll have to go."

The image's hand lifted and reached for Sisko's throat. . . .

Look for STAR TREK Fiction from Pocket Books

STAR TREK
DEEP SPACE NINE®

WARPED

K.W. JETER

POCKET BOOKS
New York   London   Toronto   Sydney   Tokyo   Singapore

POCKET BOOKS, a division of Simon & Schuster Inc.
1230 Avenue of the Americas, New York, NY 10020

Copyright © 1995 by Paramount Pictures. All Rights Reserved.

STAR TREK is a Registered Trademark of Paramount Pictures.

This book is published by Pocket Books, a division of Simon & Schuster Inc., under exclusive license from Paramount Pictures.

ISBN: 0-671-56781-0

First Pocket Books paperback printing April 1996

10 9 8 7 6 5 4 3 2 1

POCKET and colophon are registered trademarks of Simon & Schuster Inc.

Printed in the U.S.A.

To Sam Ward,
Joyce Reynolds-Ward and
Lew Ward

HISTORIAN'S NOTE

This adventure takes place shortly after Kai Opaka answered the call of the Prophets, and before the events depicted in the episodes "The Homecoming," "The Circle," and "The Siege."

WYOSS

CHAPTER
1

"Look—"

A hand darted into the water, through the ribbons of green weeds streaming in the current, into the darkness between the stones smooth as black pearls. A fist came back up, with flashes of silver wriggling from either side, a clear rivulet dripping from the elbow.

Jake Sisko regarded the fish in the other boy's grasp. As before—since the first time—he was filled with both admiration and a stomach-knotting unease at the other's lightning quickness. *Too fast*, he thought. Like a knife piercing the water without even a splash. *That's not right.*

The two boys hunkered knees-to-chest on the largest rock in the middle of the creek, the yellow sun above drying the wet marks their bare feet had left behind them. The water churned white a few inches away. Jake squinted against the glare, turning his gaze toward the tall-grass fields that rolled up to the stand of trees that served as a windbreak at the crest of the hill. *Eucalyptus*, his father had called them, crushing the sickle leaves in his big hand to release their sharp, penetrating scent. Jake's father had reached up and pulled away a strip of bark—it didn't hurt the trees, this type shed the long, twisting pieces like snakeskins—and given it to him as a kind of souvenir, one that he still had dangling on the wall of his bedroom.

"Look," insisted the other boy, thrusting the captured fish in front of Jake's face. The creature's round eyes were emblems of unreasoning panic, the pink-rimmed gills fluttering wide in the strangling air. Its mouth made an idiot O, as the boy's thumb traced the seam of its belly.

Jake wanted to tell the other boy to let the fish go, to throw it back into the water, where it could disappear into the shadowed refuge downstream. But he was afraid to. Not *afraid*—Jake's spine stiffened at the edge of the traitorous thought—but held by a dark fascination, as though standing at a cliff whose rim crumbled beneath one's toes.

He didn't even know the other boy's name. But then he didn't need to.

"Aw, we've done a fish before. They're nothing special." The other boy weighed the creature's fate and found it unworthy of further consideration. He tossed it away, not even watching where it broke the water's surface and flicked out of sight. He leaned over the side of the rock, shading his eyes to hunt for something better.

Jake felt the squeezing around his heart relax. In the distance, on the creek's other side, the grasses' feathery tops parted and settled together again as a hidden shape moved below them. He knew it was the big orange tabby with battered ears that lived on the mice from the barn beyond the hill. Or the barn that had used to be over there; the sway-backed shingled roof and gaping boards, with the mounds of dusty-smelling hay and withered, ancient horse turds inside, had gradually faded away, as though pushed from existence by this little world's new commanding presence. That was probably why the cat had to roam farther afield, to find something to eat. Everything here had changed, or was about to, Jake knew.

His companion leaned closer to the shadow on the water. Jake watched, keeping his own breath still. He didn't want to do or say anything that would draw attention to the cat on its solitary, preoccupied hunt. There were things that could happen to it—things that the other boy might do—that made Jake's stomach knot up again.

"I saw something down here. . . ." The other boy muttered as his hand brushed through the green weeds. A lock of hair dark as his eyes dangled across his brow. Oddly—another thing that Jake knew wasn't right—the other boy's shoulders were dusted with freckles, like the ones on his forearms beneath sandy red hair. It seemed as if those parts were all that was left of the boy who had lived in this world before, a redhead with a snub nose and a broad, open smile. The newcomer's smile was a twisting of one corner of a thin-lipped mouth, an expression filled with amusement at what its owner had glimpsed inside Jake's heart.

"What?" Curious despite his misgivings, Jake leaned over to see. His shadow mingled with the other's, casting the water even darker. "What is it?"

The other boy stretched out, chest against the rock, so he could reach all the way down, the water swirling to the pit of his arm. Jake could see when he had caught whatever it was, from the sudden tensing of his muscles and the black spark of delight in his eyes.

Sitting back on his haunches, the other boy held up the prize. For a moment, Jake thought the wetly shining thing was just a rock, a flattish one wide as his companion's outstretched fingertips. Then he saw the stubby clawed legs poking out from the corners. A face like a crabby old man's, annoyed at his bald head being exposed to the sun, protruded from under the shell, then drew back in deep suspicion. When the scaly eyelids came partway down, it looked kind of like his friend Nog's uncle, the Ferengi innkeeper back aboard the station.

"Cool. . . ." The other boy examined the turtle as if he had never seen one before. Jake was surprised at that—the creek was full of them, either scooting about on the bottom or basking on the lower rocks in the shallows. "This could be . . . *interesting*. . . ."

Jake felt the sick feeling in his gut again, as though he were helpless to keep himself from falling into the dark eyes that looked over the turtle shell at him. Whatever happened next—like the things that had happened already—he knew he would be part of it. That his hands would be right next to the other boy's. That he would even hold, if the other let him, the little knife with the blade that jumped out when a button was pushed.

In the field beyond the creek, the barn cat had caught some small, blind thing that it had greedily torn open with its teeth and claws. The sweat on Jake's shoulders chilled, as though the sun had disappeared behind a cloud. At the horizon of his vision, he'd always before been able to see, if he stared hard enough, where this world became nothing but a wall inside another world. Now this bright earth's shadows gathered there.

He brought his gaze back to the two smaller pieces of darkness before him. The eyes regarded him; then the other boy smiled in wicked conspiracy.

"This'll be fun." The other boy reached into the pocket of his jeans and fetched out the little folding knife. "You know it will."

Jake squeezed his eyes shut, against the reflection of his own face that bounced off the sudden snap of metal in the other's hand. It didn't do any good to keep whispering to himself that nothing here was real.

But he went on saying it, anyway.

* * *

A section of bulkhead, the curved wall between the gridded floor and the overhead light panels, considered its position. *There's really no need for this*—if the bulkhead had possessed any vocal apparatus, it might have spoken the words aloud, just to hear them echo down the station's empty corridor. The bulkhead would have been able to hear that, as part of its surface, indistinguishable from the rest, served as a crude tympanic membrane, carrying the sounds of voices and footsteps—if there had been any—to the intelligence concealed within. *He must be already gone,* thought the bulkhead; it rippled like flowing water for a moment, then peeled away from the insensate metal beneath and recoalesced into the form of *Deep Space Nine's* chief of security.

Odo looked around the angle of the nearest corner, to where the passageway split into the farther reaches of the station. Now that he had resumed the humanoid appearance by which most of DS9's personnel recognized him, he could visually scan the area. Before, any transformation of his matter into an optic sensor might have given away his carefully maintained disguise.

There was no sign of the individual he had been tracking. In Odo's memory was a complete dossier on one Ahrmant Wyoss, an itinerant freight handler who had been catching occasional pickup work in the station's main docking pylon. Despite the range of computerized equipment on the dock, from overhead-tracking forklifts that could shift multi-ton reactor cores to tweezerlike micromanipulators capable of extracting the black specks of monocloned seed stock from radiation-resistant transport gel, there was still a need for the kind of sheer muscle mass that could break open a wooden packing crate from one of the low-tech trading worlds. Wyoss possessed that much, along with a heavily brooding face that to Odo indicated a chronic overindulgence in central-nervous-system depressants. That Wyoss also had enough rudimentary intelligence left to elude a tracker tinged Odo's thoughts with unease; it didn't fit with the profile he had mentally constructed of the suspect.

From behind him came the sound of a small object hitting the floor. Not startled, but in his customary state of hyperalertness, Odo turned quickly and spotted the source, a small plastoid box with a pair of dangling probe wires and a digital readout on one side. It was a sign of how thoroughly Ahrmant Wyoss had filled his thoughts, that he had forgotten the device he had brought along. He had hidden it, tucking it into a ceiling crevice, before flowing into his own molecule-thick concealment over the bulkhead segment.

He turned the device over in his hand; the numbers on the readout still corresponded to Wyoss's credit/access code. Chief of Operations O'Brien had cobbled together the device as a favor for Odo, part of the relationship of mutual back-scratching the two of them had worked out. Odo had exceeded his authority, by perhaps only a small bit, in leaning on a band of petty thieves who had been pilfering from some of the chief's outlying storage lockers, and O'Brien had in turn designed and put together this handy little gizmo. And kept quiet about it.

Odo meditatively ran his thumb across the points of the probe wires. By a strict interpretation of DS9's regulations, the device was illegal; without a written order from the station's commander, the equivalent of a planetside court order, accessing any record of an individual's financial dealings, no matter how small, was forbidden. The moral qualms Odo felt—it was his job to enforce the laws, not break them—were small, in proportion to the device's limited function: all it could do was extract the access codes and corresponding names from the data banks of the station's holosuites, giving him a record of who had used each one, and when. That had been useful in establishing a pattern of behavior for Wyoss; the suspect had spent an inordinate amount of time immersed in the artificial worlds created by one or another of the holosuites that had been installed along this passageway.

That habit alone served as an identifying quirk for Wyoss; this bank of holosuites was several levels away from the main action of the Promenade. Whenever the suspect had emerged from the detailed sensory experience for which he had programmed the suite, he'd had to trudge a long way to knock back a few synthales at Quark's emporium. That datum was still being turned over at the back of Odo's thoughts, an analogue to his slow fidgeting with the device in his hand.

An obsessive need for privacy? Odo considered that possibility, and discarded it as before. A thug like Ahrmant Wyoss wouldn't care what other people thought of his recreational activities. And besides, the interior of a holosuite, no matter what busily teeming sector its door might exit onto, was already as private as technology could devise. The only place more private would be the inside of one's own skull. Which was, of course, part of the holosuites' attraction. For himself, Odo couldn't see much of a point in that; there was rarely a moment of his life when he didn't feel essentially alone, a creature of unknown origin, separated from all others.

He pushed those thoughts aside, with no more effort than closing the lid on a box of old-fashioned still photographs and family data recordings. He had trained himself to do as much, to attend to the job at hand, whatever it might be. Everybody, he supposed, did the same; the fact that the box he carried around, tucked away in a dark corner of remembrance, held nothing but empty brooding made no difference.

Ahrmant Wyoss was somewhere else aboard the station; the sooner the suspect was located, the better. There were three corpses lying in the morgue connected to the station's central infirmary; each of them had been ripped open, from throat to bipedal lower extremities, by a honed pryblade, the folding tool that the loading docks' freight-handlers used to slice through heavy cables and lever apart stuck container seals.

Odo had seen one of the pylon crew draw the razor-edged tool out of his overalls' back pocket and flick it to full extension in his hand faster than eye could follow or thought anticipate. Two of the corpses in the morgue had been the frenzied product of one of Wyoss's coworkers, who had slit his own throat before Odo could apprehend him. The third and latest murder had been committed more discreetly, with no clue left behind, other than the rousing of the security chief's even sharper instincts, every time he had seen Wyoss skulking through the station's corridors. Something in the eyes, or rather behind them, like a worm uncoiling around the pit of a small fruit . . . That, plus the rather more concrete datum of Wyoss's pryblade being missing from the locker where he kept his other tools when he wasn't working.

Stop wasting time, Odo scolded himself. Something had kept him loitering here, long after he had ascertained that Wyoss was not in this sector. Another suspicion, as though a sense beyond sight or hearing had caught the trace of some other crime being committed.

The holosuite closest to him was one of the new ones that had been shipped on board the station and powered up. It provided him a measure of grim satisfaction to think of someone cutting into Quark's territory of salacious entertainment; the Ferengi was no doubt already fuming about this competition and how unfair it was to him. The notion of Quark's discomfiture was almost satisfying enough to outweigh the tiresome necessity of investigating and keeping an eye on the owners of the new holosuites.

At the moment, this one was occupied; he had already used O'Brien's clever device to determine that someone other than Wyoss had entered the suite, before he'd taken up his disguised surveillance. Odo reinserted the probe wires beneath the edge of the door's control panel, to obtain the exact credit/access code.

On the device's small readout panel, the numbers shifted,

held for a moment, then changed to letters. One by one, they spelled out the name SISKO.

That's odd, mused the security chief. Why would the station's commander come this far to use a holosuite, when there were the closer ones above Quark's bar.

Another letter appeared on the readout. The initial J. The access code had been that for Benjamin Sisko's son, Jake.

Odo gazed at the small mystery for a few seconds longer, then switched off the device and stowed it in his uniform pocket. A wordless concern still nagged at him, but there was no time to puzzle over it now. He turned and strode quickly toward the corridors' hub.

Just for a moment, he had felt as if someone else was there with him, another presence more human than the one with which he shared this little world. Jake looked over his shoulder, expecting—or rather, hoping—to see a door open in the horizon. Maybe his father would step across the water-smoothed rocks turning back to gray metal, reach down and take his hand as the stream thinned and disappeared, and pull him back into the narrow spaces and skyless ceilings of the real world.

He saw no one behind him; the feeling passed, replaced by the certainty of how alone he was, with no one but the other boy for company. The boy who existed nowhere else but here.

Reluctantly, Jake brought his gaze back around to his companion. The other boy's dark, lank hair fell across his brow as he studied the turtle in his hand. He poked at the side of the shell with the knifepoint, as though trying to find a hidden latch. Jake felt a hollowness at the base of his gut, a souring wad of spit beneath his tongue.

There had been a time before the other boy had shown up in this world. Now there were times when Jake wished he could go back to then, to be alone here again. And other times, when the sick, dizzy feeling inside himself grew so large that it threatened to swallow him up, when he was crazily glad that the other boy had come. That was when he knew that the things the other said were only echoes of things that had already been spoken in some dark sector of his own heart.

"You want to?" As if he had read Jake's thoughts, the other boy held the knife out to him.

Jake shook his head. "I'll just watch. This time."

The other boy's unpleasant, knowing smile broke, then disappeared as he focused his attention back to the turtle. The stumpy, scaly legs kicked in futile struggle.

He had already started remembering, and couldn't stop. To when he had first become aware of the other boy's presence here. Jake hadn't even seen him, but had found his handiwork. In the woods farther down the creek's length, the trees whose wild profusion of branches broke this world's sunlight into scattered coins. There, in the damp-smelling shadows, Jake had found a space of bare earth scraped out of the tangled roots and dead leaves. Empty except for something that lay beneath a swarm of flies, their avid buzzing like the sound of the electronic currents beneath the surfaces of this world. He'd prodded the object with his toe, the flies dispersing then settling back down upon it, and caught a glimpse of the small animal opened from beneath its small chin to between its hind legs. A cat, or what had been one, with enough of its gray tabby fur unmarked to show that it wasn't the orange prowler from the barn. Jake had stepped back from it in disgust, and had almost tripped over one of the cords, pieces of dirty frayed rope he hadn't noticed before, that looped around the trunks of the nearest trees and pulled the dead thing into a spread-eagled X on the ground.

That had been the first sign, the emblem of the other boy's arrival here. Since then, Jake had seen more things. But never without feeling sick in his gut afterward, so that now he pushed away the little knife when it was offered to him, despite the other's sneer.

He closed his eyes when he heard a tiny sound, the whisper the knife made when it cut through something soft and yielding. Not for the first time, he wished everything around him was a dream, a real dream, the kind from which he could wake when it got too scary.

She turned in the cramped space, knowing that her chance for sleep was coming to an end. Major Kira Nerys knew she could have used a lot more of it, to ease the fatigue in her bones and the mental weariness that had seemed to gather like silt behind her eyes.

There was another reason for keeping her eyes squinted shut against the flashing lights, for trying to ignore the metal-on-metal sounds that rattled down the freight shuttle's interior, and the voices of the crew members. With enough effort, she could hold on to the last fading edge of the dream that had visited her, the small comfort for which she had been grateful, as though it had been her long-dead father's kiss upon her brow. A vision of green fields rolling to a domed and spired city just in sight at the horizon; she had drifted above as though on a bed of soft winds, reaching a hand down to touch the surface of Bajor, as though her homeworld was the face of a lover whose sleep she watched in her own . . .

"Major Kira—" A voice prodded her, in synch with the jostling her shoulder received. "Sorry to disturb you—"

I just bet you are. She was awake enough to keep her thoughts from muttering aloud. The impulse to cock back her arm—her hand had already squeezed itself into a fist—and punch out whoever it was had been resisted. The dream had already faded into irretrievability, not even a memory left behind. *That's because it wasn't real,* Kira told herself as she took a deep breath of the shuttle's stifling air supply, readying herself for full consciousness. What had been shown to her wasn't even widespread on Bajor; the visit to this region had lasted nearly five days, and all she had seen had been the same scarred landscape, the crumbling pit mines and mountains of worthless extraction tailings left behind by the Cardassians, that had been there when she had first shipped off-planet to the *Deep Space Nine* station. The green processes of nature were taking a long time in softening the torn hillsides; the soil had been so depleted by its ravagers that even the toughest weeds had difficulty in taking root.

"We're going to be docking soon. . . ."

"All right." She nodded, swallowing the taste that sleep had left in her mouth, then glanced up at the crew member standing beside the cot. A kid, hardly worth displaying her anger toward, even if he had deserved it. "Thanks." She swung her feet onto the shuttle's deck and sat up. "I'll be coming forward in a minute or so."

The crew member exited, leaving her alone with the hold's other occupant, a wooden crate nearly as tall as herself. Automatically, as she had done several times already on the journey from Bajor, she reached out and tugged on the chains wrapped around the crate. The ancient, rust-specked padlocks were sealed with not only the insignia of the Bajoran provisional government, but a simpler cursive signature as well, drawn in candle wax by the fingertip of one of the senior Vedeks of the dominant Bajoran religious order. A formality, more than a security measure; any competent thief could have cut through the chains with a microtorch, rifled the crate's contents, and sealed it all back up with nothing more than a few hair-thin seams in the metal links. If the treasures inside had needed any protection—a debatable proposition; they had little other than historical value—then that had been the reason for Kira's presence: "riding shotgun," to use the old Earth phrase employed when she had been given the assignment. Though once the crate had been loaded aboard the freight shuttle, she had felt little guilt about catching up on her sleep, after the exertions of her other assignment, the confidential one, on the surface of Bajor.

Everything was in order with the crate, just as she had expected. The freight shuttle's crew members were all professionals, as much as she was; as long as their cargo wasn't leaking toxic radiation or some other hazard, they had little interest in anything other than making sure it reached its destination. Kira snapped together the collar fastening of her uniform and stood up, smoothing her hair back away from her brow.

"There's an estimated time to docking of a quarter hour." The shuttle's navigator looked over his shoulder at Kira standing behind him. "We could go ahead and beam you aboard if you're in a hurry." He shrugged. "If you want, we could have you notified as soon as your cargo is transferred onto the loading dock."

Looking past the navigator and the pilot in the next seat over, Kira could see the distant shape of *Deep Space Nine* through the port; the curved pylons hung against the starry black. She felt a slight, pseudogravitational tug at her bones, as though her body were already willing itself to be back inside the station's habitat ring, the world of metal that the instinctive parts of herself had already started to regard as home. That internal perception saddened her, as had the one at the beginning of her mission, when she had stepped onto Bajoran soil for the first time in almost a year and had realized that she had felt like an alien on her own birth planet.

She shook her head. "No, that's all right." She had carried out every detail of her mission this far; she could see through the rest. "Establish a comm link and notify Commander Sisko of my arrival. And arrange for intrastation transport of the cargo to his private office on Ops deck. I'll meet him there." She turned away and headed back to the hold.

Away from the shuttle's crew, Kira leaned her hands against the wooden crate, as though some subtle emanation from what it held might enter her soul. Inside were pieces of Bajor, remnants of one who might have been the planet's essence, as though the oceans' tides had been a single being's heart-beat . . .

She felt nothing. Eyes closed, Kira's head hung below her shoulders for a moment longer, until she gathered enough strength to push herself away from the crate.

Gettting sentimental wasn't part of your assignment. She brushed a few splinters from her palms. If the crate's contents were as dead as she sometimes felt, in her bleakest moments, her own connection to her native world to be, then that was just something she would have to deal with. For better or worse.

But for now, all of that could wait. Major Kira Nerys sat down on the edge of the cot and methodically began reviewing everything she needed to report to her commanding officer.

Suddenly, in what one of normal humanoid physiology might have termed the blink of an eye, he saw the one for whom he had been searching. Odo felt the electric rush of aroused suspicion inside himself, as though he had been capable of fine-tuning an olfactory system for himself, to catch some pheromone for incipient murder. Across the crowded Promenade, the currents of hustlers and marks mingling below the elevated walkway, he had spotted Ahrmant Wyoss.

Odo pulled himself back into the shadow of a structural pillar, to keep from being sighted in turn by his target. Total nonvisibility could have been achieved by changing his shape again, to anything from another section of bulkhead to one of the anaconda-like cables looping overhead. But with this many watching eyes in the vicinity, he was constrained; nothing would have sent an alarm through the Promenade's denizens faster than DS9's chief of security being caught so obviously spying on the sector's action.

There was another reason he wished to maintain his customary appearance. To shift in and out of a simulation of an inanimate object required precious seconds in which the atoms of his material form sought their new equilibrium with each other. Seconds that could seem long as hours, if in them he was unable to stop one of the crimes he had sworn himself to prevent. The humanoid form he had created for himself was the best combination of speed and strength he could devise, while still maintaining at least a rough resemblance to a majority of natives of the galaxy's scattered worlds. Keeping all of them unaware of how tensely coiled his muscles were, ready for sudden movement, was a deceptive skill closer to an actor's art than a policeman's.

"There you are, my dear Odo!" A familiar voice came from close beside him. "I've been looking all over for you."

He looked down from the corner of his eye; the Ferengi innkeeper's piranha grin loomed up at him. "Given the nature of your enterprises, Quark—" He craned his neck to keep the far reaches of the Promenade in view. "—you never have to wait very long for me to make an appearance. Now, do you?"

"Once again, I detect a sarcastic tone to your comments." Quark emitted a martyr's sigh. "I suppose that's the plight of the small businessman in today's universe. Always an object of suspicion, merely for cutting a few of the needless bureaucratic corners that so impede the free flow of commerce."

"Indeed." Odo gave the Ferengi just enough attention to keep the conversation alive. A constant visual scan of the Promenade while talking was so much a part of his habitual behavior—and deliberately so—that it shouldn't arouse any undue notice on the other's part. "And exactly what corners have you been cutting lately? Not watering down your synthale again, are you?"

"Cutting corners? Me? Never." Quark drew himself to his full height, bringing himself almost to Odo's shoulder. "I was speaking in *general* terms about these matters. And that synthale wasn't watered—it was an experiment, to create a *lighter, less filling* beverage for my customers."

"And at full price, of course."

Quark shrugged. "I was charging for the creativity involved." His expression soured with a deep brooding. "Your accusations are really unjust, you know—especially when you consider the unsavory nature of certain other individuals doing business around here."

That remark drew a fraction more of Odo's attention. "And who might that be?"

"Never mind. Perhaps at a later date we'll discuss these matters. Right now, I don't think you're even listening to me." Quark's puzzled gaze swung parallel to that of the security chief. "Just what is it that you find so fascinating over there?"

"It's nothing to do with you." Across the Promenade, the sweating, heavy-jawed face of Ahrmant Wyoss was still visible, his small eyes glaring beneath a brow furrowed in concentration. Odo could see, as others passed in front of the suspect, how his hands clenched into white-knuckled fists, the cords of his wrists tautening with each squeeze. Even from this far away, Odo could pick up the murderous radiation given off by the man. He glanced over at Quark. "Now might be a good time for you to go back behind your bar."

"Oh?" Quark had had similar discreet warnings before, and had learned to heed them. He took an apprehensive step back from Odo's side. "I'd appreciate it if you didn't do anything to scare the customers away. That'd be only right, considering your plans to use my premises for your little conference with Commander Sisko."

"I don't know what you're talking about." To Odo, the Ferengi's voice had started to seem like an insect buzzing around his head, one that he wished he could brush away with a stroke of a hand. "I'm not having any conference with the commander. In your establishment or anywhere else."

"But . . . I just received a communication from one of

Sisko's adjutants, asking me to reserve a private booth for two. With all the usual mandatory security screening, of course. So I just naturally assumed, what with the rather . . . *unusual* developments we've had on the station lately, that you were the other party involved."

Odo felt a familiar anger ticking upward inside him. The Ferengi's mannerism of constant hinting, of never coming right out and speaking what was on his mind, probing every word in a conversation for some possibility of gain, had driven him to the boiling point on several previous occasions. Right now, he didn't have the time to waste.

"Listen to me, Quark." He managed to keep his voice under control, his sight still trained upon his quarry across the Promenade. "I promise you that we are going to have a detailed discussion—soon. And if there's something you should have already told me about, I'll pick you up by the heels and shake you until you do so. Is that clear? In the meantime, perhaps you should go back and wipe off the table in one of your booths. Commander Sisko has, I'm sure, a great many other things on his mind beside some outbreak of prehensile-fingered sneak thieves, or whatever else it is that's troubling you so much."

The sarcasm had no effect on Quark. "I wish that's all it were." His face had clouded once more, eyes narrowing and voice filled with an uncharacteristic bitterness. "Very well. I can see that the scope of your duties doesn't include defending the principle of free enterprise against unfair competition." He turned on his heel and started toward the ramp leading down to the Promenade's main area.

With the Ferengi gone, all of Odo's attention focused again on its original target. With careful timing, each step taken when Ahrmant Wyoss's simmering gaze swung away, the security chief moved in closer.

* * *

She watched as Commander Sisko ran a hand along the edge of the wooden crate. He nodded slowly, his expression one of deep, even melancholy contemplation.

"Here are the keys, sir." Major Kira extended the small, primitive bits of metal on her palm. "For the locks."

"What's that?" Sisko turned toward her. "Oh . . . of course." He took the keys and closed his fist around them. "Do you know if there's any special procedure we should follow about breaking the seals? I did a search through all the onboard databases concerning Bajoran religious practices, but I couldn't really find anything regarding this situation."

"I don't think there's anything special you have to do, Commander." It wasn't the first time that she had to admit to gaps in knowledge of her home planet's faith, gaps that seemed to grow larger the longer she was away. "The seals are more of a formality than anything else; the elders wanted to assure us that the contents are genuine."

"There's little doubt of that, I'm afraid." Sisko pressed his fist against the wood. "I wish it were otherwise—I'd give a great deal for everything inside here to be fake." He shook his head. "You've done a good job with this assignment, Major. Just a shame that it was necessary."

Kira held her silence. The commander had spoken her feelings as well.

Inside the crate were mute bits and pieces, fragments of the past and tokens of remembrance. Of the Kai Opaka, the one who had served as the very soul of Bajor. A soul that had fled from that world, to an eternal life . . . and death.

It didn't matter now, what the Kai's choice had been. Her absence from Bajor had left an equal emptiness inside Kira. And in Commander Sisko—she could sense that, in the sad hush of his words.

Sisko pushed himself away from the crate. "I require a full debriefing from you, regarding the present political developments on Bajor. Right now, if you're up to it."

"Of course, Commander." That had been the other part of her assignment. "I can give you a quick verbal rundown if you like, then a complete written report in two shifts from now."

"Excellent. I've had Quark reserve us a security-screened booth in his establishment on the Promenade. You might find that more relaxing than this office."

Kira took a deep breath. "If you don't mind, sir—I'm not really in the mood for dealing with the crowds down there. I'm pretty tired."

"I can appreciate that, Major. However, I'm also aware of how rumors can spread from the Ops crew throughout the station. The official word is that you went to Bajor solely for the purpose of escorting these relics into our possession. If we take the time to go over your political analysis here, it may generate some speculation. Whereas a visit to Quark's will be seen as no more than some much-needed relaxation after completing your assignment."

What she really felt like was falling backward onto the bunk in her quarters and passing into dreamless sleep. The brief catnaps she had been able to grab on Bajor and in the freight shuttle's hold had been barely enough to keep her going. "Very well," she said, nodding. Inside her head, she was already sorting through and condensing her report to the barest essentials.

The details were just about ready, lined up for presentation, when she and Sisko stepped from the turbolift and onto the Promenade deck. That was when she saw the flash of metal.

He opened his eyes, even though he didn't want to. Jake had to; he had to *see*.

"Here you go—" The other boy's voice had broken through the silence Jake had tried to pull around himself. "It's your turn now."

A flash of metal, the blade of the knife—he saw it extended toward him again, glistening on the other boy's palm. The smile curled at one corner of the boy's mouth, beneath the dark eyes that watched Jake with conspiratorial delight.

He saw the other thing as well, on top of the stone the boy crouched beside; the thing that had been alive and whole when Jake had closed his eyes, and now was broken. But still alive. A jagged piece of shell had slid to the water's edge.

"Go on!" commanded the other boy, thrusting the knife's handle closer. "You know you want—"

Disgust and anger welled up inside Jake. His arm lashed out on its own, knocking the blade away, sending it spinning in the sunlight, bright silver above the creek's rippling surface.

He scrambled to his feet, his breath choking in his throat, and turned and ran. Behind him, he could hear the other boy laughing, the sky echoing with it as Jake reached his hand toward the horizon and the door to the sunless corridors that were his home.

The flash of metal stabbed his vision, as though the point of the pryblade had leapt the course of the Promenade. Even as Odo shoved the people around him aside, he knew that he had waited too long, knew that he had betrayed himself and his duty by holding back and watching. The weapon rose above Ahrmant Wyoss's head, his fist clenched rigid at its hilt; the man's eyes had opened wide and glaring now, as though the pressure of the madness inside his skull had broken through the last barrier membrane.

Someone screamed, a high wailing pitch of fright. The crowd surged back from Wyoss, the space around him expanding as the Promenade's visitors scrambled back from the naked blade. The humanoid wall in front of Odo tightened almost solid; he grabbed two different sets of shoulders and pulled them apart from each other, wedging himself through the gap and reaching ahead to drive another opening. The wave of panic had blocked his sight of Wyoss; shoving aside more bodies, he dove toward the retreating front of the crowd.

Odo saw then what had triggered Wyoss's sudden action. His own attention had been so focused on its target that he had lost track of anything else happening on the Promenade; he had only been vaguely aware of the turbolift doors opening a few meters away from Wyoss. *That was what he was waiting for,* realized Odo. *Waiting for—*

Two people had emerged from the turbolift. Talking to each other, not perceiving the outbreak of chaos their entrance had caused . . . until it was too late.

He could see who it was, see that the ones who had stepped onto the Promenade deck were Major Kira and Commander Sisko. In a distant corner of Odo's memory, there was just space enough for a microsecond flash of what Quark had told him about a booth reserved for a conference. . . .

Then there was no time at all. With his hand straining desperately forward, Odo launched himself over the last ring of bodies. Even as Commander Sisko spotted the arc of descending metal and raised his forearm to ward off the blurring stroke aimed at him.

CHAPTER
2

FOR A MOMENT, HE SAW NOTHING. ONE OF THE FIGURES BLOCKING Odo's path scrambled backward, away from the glittering pryblade in Ahrmant Wyoss's grasp, as though the weapon's curving path was about to scythe through every exposed neck on the Promenade. Odo fell onto his side, quickly rolling onto his hands and knees, and looking up in time to see a spark fly from the pryblade as it clanged against the turbolift's doorway.

Major Kira had reacted first, dropping into a crouch and using the uncoiling thrust of her shoulder to propel both herself and Commander Sisko out of the blade's path. The jarring impact of metal against metal shot through Wyoss's arm, snapping his head back, teeth clenched against the shock.

In another few seconds, before Odo could do anything to assist, it was over. Sisko rolled with the momentum that the major's thrust had given him, coming up against Wyoss's legs with enough force to stagger him against the wall. The

24

pryblade flew out of Wyoss's grasp, then skittered across the Promenade deck, as Sisko brought the butt of his palm straight up into the underside of the other man's chin. An elbow check to the abdomen dropped Wyoss writhing to his knees.

"I've got him." Odo pulled Wyoss's arms back and snapped a pair of restraints onto his wrists. He pulled the unresisting form to its feet. "Are you all right, Commander?"

Sisko brushed down the front of his uniform. He nodded, then glanced over his shoulder at Kira. "A little adrenaline overdose, Constable, but nothing serious. How about you, Major?"

"Don't worry about me." Kira glared at the man slumping from the hold Odo had on the restraints. "Who the hell is this creep, anyway?"

Odo detected an accusatory tone in Kira's voice, as though it had been his fault that the weapon had come within a few centimeters of her head. "The suspect's identity has already been established," he said stiffly. "There are a great many things about his background, and his motives, that remain the subject of an ongoing investigation."

Head lowered, Sisko peered into Wyoss's slack-jawed, semi-conscious face. "Is this connected to the, ah, *incidents* that you spoke to me about previously?"

"I'm afraid that's likely to be the case, Commander."

"I see." Sisko straightened back up. "We'll need to discuss this matter further. Have a complete report ready for me by the end of the shift."

Odo gave a quick nod in acknowledgment. "Come on—" Wyoss's head wobbled on his neck as Odo propelled him forward. "Go about your business," he barked at the circle of gawking faces. "There's nothing to see here." Leaning down, he scooped up the pryblade with his free hand. "Move along."

A path opened through the bodies, and Odo shoved the

suspect toward the security station at the other end of the Promenade.

"Now I'm the one who needs a drink." Commander Sisko managed to show a thin smile from across the booth's table. "I think that little unpleasantness drew more attention from me than I was prepared to give."

Kira nodded, rubbing her eyes. "It certainly woke me up." She tilted her head back, trying to dispel the fatigue she again felt advancing upon her. "Has there been something going on aboard the station while I was away, that I should know about?"

"Perhaps . . . though I'm not sure yet." The creases in Sisko's brow grew deeper. "I'll have to give you a briefing as soon as I've gotten some more details from Odo. Let's just say for now that our encounter out there was not the first of its kind—though it was the first where I seemed to be the target."

When she had recovered more of her mental energy, Kira knew she would have to examine the commander's troubling statement. An environment such as *Deep Space Nine* had a difficult time keeping out the galaxy's brain-sick refuse; much of the station's mission was to facilitate passage through its docking ports. Theoretically, entry could be denied to anyone posing a threat to the welfare of the station or any of its crew, but as a practical matter, there wasn't time to do more than the most cursory screening procedures. It was the age-old problem of access—and the abuse of same—in an open society. She and Odo had had discussions about it in the past, that the only way to truly secure the station would be to lock it down tight as it had been under the control of the Cardassians. And doing that alone would defeat everything the Federation was trying to accomplish here.

Determining where Odo stood on the issue had been

difficult; Kira knew that the security chief's first loyalty was to DS9 itself, the only world he had ever known, just as hers was to Bajor. In his own way, Odo was as much a patriot as she considered herself to be. Everything else came second for him, just as for herself, as she had to admit when she examined her own heart's allegiances. To know that was also to recognize a certain coldness and calculation that entered into her dealings with everyone else, who didn't share the exact same agenda—such as Commander Sisko and any other representative of the Federation's Starfleet. Maybe that was why so many other crew members saw her and Odo the same way, as rigid and uptight, steel-spined—oddly so in his case, given that he regularly reverted to a complete liquid state.

And at the same time, she knew, Odo and Sisko—and she herself as well—had to present a united front to everyone outside DS9, from the Federation authorities who could withdraw their support for the station's mission at any time, to the Cardassians who were continually sniffing around for any crack through which they could worm their way back in and reestablish their control, now that the station's true value had been revealed. A united front against all of that and more, no matter what conflicting forces might be building up inside.

Kira rubbed harder at the corner of her brow, to ease the ache that had started throbbing behind the thin wall of bone. She had promised herself not to think about all this stuff, at least not now, and again she hadn't been able to stop herself.

There had been a time when things had been easier to figure out, when there had been no question who the enemy was. When she had been fighting with the Bajoran resistance, the rule of thumb had been that if it was Cardassian, it was worth a full-strength phaser shot to the head. Her moral landscape was rendered in shades of gray now, the effect of having become, in essence, a political animal. She had already encountered fellow Bajorans who would have been happy to see her dead; how much longer until she felt the same way over every little squabble about their mutual birthright, the fate of their home planet?

How much longer—what a joke, Kira ruefully chided herself. Bajoran politics had already reached that stage. That was what she was here to talk to Commander Sisko about.

"With the compliments of the house . . ."

Another voice broke into her self-lacerating thoughts. She turned and saw a familiar grinning face as the booth's curtain was moved aside.

Quark set a tray with two synthales upon the table and tilted his head in a parody of a formal bow. "In appreciation for the fine demonstration you just gave out on the Promenade. Well done, Commander."

One of Sisko's eyebrows arched. "It was not done for the amusement of you and your patrons." He picked up the mugs and set them down in front of himself and Kira.

"What a pity, then." Quark held the tray against his chest. "If we could schedule a display like that on a regular basis, it might prove very entertaining. We could use something to draw in a few more customers."

Sisko looked across the tables to the bar. "It doesn't seem as if you're hurting for trade."

The grin disappeared, replaced by a heavy-browed scowl. "Of course, Commander, I couldn't expect *you* to be as knowledgeable about business conditions as we poor entrepreneurs have to be. Let's just say that people are finding . . . *other* means of entertainment these days."

"Please." Sisko held up his hand. "The major and I have a great many things to discuss. If you're not making the usual house percentage from your Dabo tables, I'm sure you'll find a way to rectify the situation. In the meantime . . ."

The bow was repeated, a little deeper and more obsequiously this time. "Your privacy is assured, Commander; our esteemed chief of security inspected these premises—or at least this part—not more than three shifts ago, and found nothing amiss." Quark stepped back. "Just signal if you'd like another round."

With the booth's transparent shield in place, the murmur of voices from outside was cut to dead silence. Kira took a careful sip, then pushed the mug away from herself. "It's gotten worse, Commander." She studied her hands laid flat upon the table for a moment, then looked up at him. "Much worse than we had thought it would be."

Sisko nodded slowly. "The Severalty Front?"

"Who else? But then again, I would never have thought they would be able to organize so quickly, or so effectively." The details of all that Kira had discovered during her mission were now bleakly arrayed in her thoughts. "It looks like we severely underestimated the strength of anti-Federation sentiment on Bajor. Or to put it another way, we were completely unaware of all that was being done to neutralize the separatists. And by whom it was being done."

She didn't even need to speak the name aloud. Just by looking at Benjamin Sisko, the slump of his shoulders under an invisible burden, the grim set of his face, she could see that he knew exactly the person referred to.

"It certainly bears out the wisdom of that old Earth aphorism—" The commander tapped the mug before him with a fingernail. "—that one doesn't miss the water until the well runs dry. I'm afraid that with Kai Opaka's absence, we're going to see a lot more dry wells, both here and on Bajor."

Absence, not *death*—Kira was grateful he had said it that way. She and Commander Sisko were among the handful of people who knew the exact details of the Kai's fate. A fate that, as far as other Bajorans were concerned, was the same as death. Kira had been aware, even before this mission, that an entire school of theological debate had sprung up over whether the Kai's having "answered the call of the Prophets" meant that she had suffered a corporeal death or had been transfigured to another plane of existence. Given the fervor of the disputants, it probably wouldn't have made much difference if Kira had told them that the Kai was still alive, albeit on a war-torn moon on the other side of the galaxy.

And in practical terms, the Kai's absence from Bajor, no matter what its true nature, meant a great deal. *Now we really are missing that water,* thought Kira. She and the commander had suspected for some time that Kai Opaka's influence on the simmering cauldron of Bajoran politics had been more than just that of a conciliatory spiritual presence. This just-completed mission had confirmed that all along the Kai had been working behind the scenes, deftly playing one faction off against another, pulling strings that were hardly more than spider threads, a whisper in one ear, a gentle smile of blessing that could shift a crucial vote one way or another. It had been the good fortune of Starfleet that all those delicate wiles had been expended on behalf of moving Bajor toward full membership in the Federation. The Kai had seen the future of Bajor in league with other worlds, a part of a galaxy-wide net, and not as an isolated world withdrawn into itself.

That wisdom, and all of the Kai's maneuverings behind the scenes, had given the pro-Federation forces a slim majority in the Bajoran provisional government. Given the passions of those who held contrary beliefs, it would have been impossible to have brought everyone around to the same conclusions.

"So what do you think?" The commander set his half-empty mug of synthale down. "From all that you learned this time, what would you estimate the chances are for the Severalty Front?"

Kira shook her head. "I don't know." Since the Kai's absence from Bajor, the splinter groups and factions opposed to membership in the Federation had managed to unite their efforts behind a single banner. "Who am I kidding? I *do* know.

The Front's chances are good—*real* good. As I said, we had no idea of the opposition's numbers. That's the downside of what Kai Opaka accomplished on this issue; with her doing so much that we weren't even aware of, we were lulled into believing that the anti-Federation forces were ineffective and actually decreasing in number. Now that the lid's off them, it's clear that they're a much bigger threat than we ever gave them credit for."

"I still don't understand." Sisko rapped a fist against the table in frustration. "How any of your people can oppose a process that will bring their world such benefits—"

"Commander." She felt another fatigue, older and deeper, rising inside her. "We've gone over this before. The simple truth is that those supposed benefits just haven't shown up yet, have they? This is something I was afraid of from Day One here. In order to get the Bajoran provisional government to agree to Starfleet's taking control of DS9, the benefits of eventual Federation membership had to be sold, and sold *hard* to them. And so far the Federation hasn't delivered."

"These things take time, Major. But there *will* be a tremendous expenditure of financial and technical resources upon this sector—"

"Oh, sure. As if we haven't heard that sort of thing before." She had no resistance to letting her anger out; she found herself expressing the exact same thoughts as the isolationists. "For God's sake, Commander, the Cardassians told us as much while they were stripping every leaf and speck of minerals from the planet. After what they did to us, this station and its access to the stable wormhole is the only thing of value that Bajor has left. Can you blame us—that is, can you blame the Severalty Front—for being afraid that this will be stolen from us as well?"

"Major, at one time I thought that this was just a personal trait of yours, one that I would just have to get accustomed to." Sisko's voice turned coldly formal. "But upon reflection, I find that Kai Opaka was unique in more than one way. She was the only Bajoran I ever met who had cultivated the virtue of patience."

"Patience—" Kira could barely keep herself from exploding. "Commander, we don't have time for patience. We've suffered enough."

Sisko drew himself up to full height, his shoulders broadening against the booth's upholstery. "If that's the case, then despite our earlier assessment, your world may be a long way from readiness for Federation membership and its benefits. The Bajoran government has to learn that there are limits, even for the Federation. The Federation Council has concerns other than the welfare of Bajor and its people; there are other worlds and other races who have claims—and perhaps better ones—on the Federation's attention and development resources. And more importantly, some of those worlds have a lot more experience and skill at political maneuvering than the Bajoran provisional government has shown. This is exactly the kind of struggle where patience is not just a virtue, it's a strategy. The winning strategy."

She had heard the lecture from him before. Despite her fatigue, she could feel her spine turning to steel. "Reassessment is a two-way street, Commander. If Bajor is so far down the list of the Federation's priorities, then you'd better be prepared for Bajor to take a good hard look at what it gets out of dealing with the Federation."

"I see." Sisko's voice softened. "And is that what *you* want, Major? For Bajor to go its own way?"

Inside herself, she again felt the tug, two opposite vectors of force, the division between the oldest loyalty of her heart and the new one she had assumed. "No—" She shook her head. "I wouldn't be here at *Deep Space Nine* if that were what I wanted."

"Very well." Sisko drained the last of his synthale and pushed the empty mug away from him. "You've demonstrated the depth of your commitment to the station's mission before; I have no cause to doubt you on that score. I'd like to remind you, Major—and you may regard this as a personal rather than a professional comment—that you're not the only one here who has to make a difficult choice between one path and another." He reached for the booth's security curtain, his hand stopping before drawing it aside. "I'll need a complete report on your assignment. And I mean absolutely complete: names, alliances, antagonisms, influences that we can bring to bear on different factions and individuals in the provisional government . . . everything. We're going to have to do a lot more of our own messy work from now on."

Kira watched the commander threading his way among the crowded tables, heading for the bar's exit. Her own drink sat half-finished in front of her. She lifted the mug and took a sip, the taste sharply bitter on her tongue.

The lights were off in the suite, but he could tell that someone was home. A touch upon the otherwise still molecules of air, the barely detectable sound of breathing. His son, asleep.

Sisko let the door slide shut behind him, blocking the angled fall of light from the station's corridor outside. His own shadow was swallowed by the room's darkness. He moved forward, walking with practiced ease around the low tables and chairs, and other familiar accoutrements of this small, private world. And almost immediately banged his knee against something large, heavy and unexpected.

"What the—" He bit off the exclamation of pain and surprise. The sound of the collision hadn't woken Jake. He hobbled to the nearest control panel and brought up enough light by which to see.

The object in the middle of the room was the wooden crate that Major Kira had brought back from Bajor.

He sat down heavily on the sofa, rubbing his shin. One of the Ops deck crew must have taken the initiative to have the crate transferred here from his office—or perhaps he himself had given the order; right now he couldn't remember. For a moment, he imagined that the crate had walked by itself to his quarters, like the proverbial white elephant. His heart felt leaden as he gazed at the rough wooden sides.

And that sense came without even undoing the locks and prying open the lid. He already had a good notion of the crate's contents. *Bits and pieces* . . . On old Earth and other worlds, the bones of saints had been the objects of veneration. Presumably, the crate held nothing as ghoulish as that; the Kai was still walking around with all of her bones safely tucked inside her, even though at the other end of the galaxy.

The Bajoran priests—the professional colleagues, as it were, of the Kai—had described in general terms what had been packed away in the crate. A small chest of precious woods, darker than the night sky, and inlaid with symbols formed of shining metal, that held a half-dozen or so scrolls of religious texts, hand-copied by the Kai when she had been a novice over a half-century ago. They were of no great value beyond that of remembrance of the one who had so carefully brushed the intricate characters upon the vellum leaves. Other things, even closer to perfect muteness, their animating spirit departed: a hand-carved table that had sat in a corner of the Kai's sleeping chamber, the oil lamp from the niche in the stone wall, a sequence of ear ornaments, each wrapped in feather-edged paper, each more elaborate and bejewelled than the one before, all of them signifying the mortal woman's ascent through the hierarchy of her people's faith.

Foolish veneration was discouraged by the priests; the Bajoran religion had enough wisdom to teach that only living things were sacred. There had been a time when these things would have been destroyed; but someone among Kai Opaka's remaining brethren had had the kindly—or cruel—inspiration to send them up to the *Deep Space Nine* station, as though it were the planet's attic. *So I could deal with them instead,* thought Sisko. Perhaps that was justice for his part in bringing about the Kai's fate.

If he had strength enough, he knew, it would be best for everyone if he shoved the unopened crate out one of the station's airlocks. But he knew also that he wouldn't.

Commander Benjamin Sisko felt tired and alone now, surrounded by the overlapping hollow shells of the station, and the empty regions of the cold stars beyond. The only one who had sensed the burden of command he bore was gone, as good as dead. The galaxy, or the little part of it that he carried around with him, was an emptier place without the Kai in it.

A pang of guilt penetrated his brooding. The bleak notions of *absence* and *loss* reminded him that he had barely any contact with his own son over the last few shifts. There had never seemed to be any time.

And when will there be time? He heard the question asked with the Kai's soft voice, inside his head. *You know there's only now. This time, Benjamin.*

His knee had stopped aching, enough for him to get up and hobble to the door of his son's room. The dim light from the ceiling cast his shadow across the bed.

Jake lay with his legs drawn up, a fist pressed hard against his face and eyes squeezed tight, like the image of a much younger child futilely trying to ward off bad dreams. Sisko could see that the boy's skin was shiny with sweat; he stepped into the room and laid his hand on Jake's brow, but felt no fever.

He stepped back from the bedside, his own heart more troubled than before. There was so much, in this room as well as through all of DS9, that he could do little about. Wherever Jake walked in his dreams, he was as alone there as his father was in this world.

Sisko drew the door closed, letting the child go on sleeping. If he could be here when his son awoke, perhaps that would be comfort enough.

For both of them.

CHAPTER
3

GOOD INTENTIONS PAVED THE ROAD TO A GUILTY CONSCIENCE;
which was, Benjamin Sisko had to acknowledge to himself,
one of the lesser forms of hell. It was almost mild enough to be
put out of his thoughts as he sat down for a briefing with the
station's chief of security.

"Is there something on your mind, Commander?" From the
other side of the desk, Odo peered at him with concern. "You
seem somewhat preoccupied. I could come back later, if you
wish—"

"No; no, that's all right, Constable." Sisko shook his head.
"It's nothing important; just a promise I made to myself, that
I've already broken. I meant to spend some time with my son
Jake at the beginning of this shift, before he went off to his
classes." The school started up by Keiko O'Brien, the wife of
the chief of operations, had quickly reached the level of
keeping regular hours, with both a permanent body of stu-
dents and the children of the station's long- and short-term
guests. "But he was already gone by the time I woke up."

"Ah. Family matters." As much as was possible, Odo's

masklike face revealed a brief trace of emotion. "I suppose I should count myself fortunate, that I have just one set of duties with which to concern myself."

Sisko knew better. He was well aware that the security chief's orphan status—beyond that even, Odo's singularity; there were no other known members of his species—constituted an inner vacuum that continually tugged at his thoughts. Whatever problems Sisko had with bringing up Jake in the artificial environment of DS9, he still knew that he was envied for the simple fact of having a blood relation with him.

"Be that as it may, Constable. Perhaps we should get down to business." He turned toward the computer panel sitting on the desk; the last screenful of Odo's report still showed. Sisko reached out a fingertip and blanked the words away. "This is a very distressing situation that's developed."

"It's more than that, Commander. It's intolerable." Odo's eyes readily displayed anger; now they became two hotly glaring coals. "I won't have it aboard my station."

The security chief's proprietary attitude about DS9 was, Sisko supposed, a displacement of his suppressed familial instincts. Odo reacted toward any threat to the station, any transgression of order within its precincts, as another sentient creature might have felt about one of his own flesh and blood being placed in jeopardy. That made for a zealous execution of Odo's job as the station's top police official; at the same time, the commander knew there was always the danger of Odo exceeding the restraints of the authority that had been given him. *Deep Space Nine* represented one of the frontiers of the Federation; rights could be too easily trampled on here, all for the sake of insuring the station's survival.

To his credit, Odo had always managed to stay mindful of the letter of the law. If he stepped over the line—and Sisko knew he did; it would be impossible not to, in a place like this, and still get his job done—it was still within the law's spirit. Or at least it had been so far.

"We've had murders on the station before." Odo's voice broke into the commander's reflections. "Given the nature of our operation here, the constraints that we unfortunately have to work under, the transient population constantly moving through, I suppose we have to recognize a certain inevitability of frictions arising between individuals, the chance of illicit profit through violence, and the like. Plus, with our remote location, we will attract a certain mind-set—certain *dissolute* personalities, shall we say—that somehow believes DS9 is the perfect locale for the settling of grudges and the perpetuation of vendettas." Odo took a deep breath—a simulated humanoid mannerism—in an effort to calm himself. His voice lowered as he gazed brooding at the stars visible in the office's viewport. "I've sometimes wondered if there might not be a certain psychic centrifugal force at work, by which all the disconnected elements in the universe inevitably wind up here on the fringe." He glanced back at Sisko. "It seems unlikely it could be mere coincidence that we get so many of them."

He had heard these dark musings from Odo before, generally at the end of a long, difficult shift. "Your view may be a little prejudiced, Constable. Your job forces you to concentrate on the more aberrant happenings aboard the station."

"'Aberrant' is putting it mildly. Especially with this latest series of events. 'Psychopathic' might be a better choice of words."

The security chief was right about that, Sisko admitted to himself. Odo's report on the murder epidemic that had broken out aboard DS9 had gone into distressing levels of detail.

"This Ahrmant Wyoss individual you have in custody . . . I take it he would have been our third perpetrator? That is, of course, if he had managed to land the blow he had aimed at myself and Major Kira."

"The fourth, actually," said Odo. "Though it's out of our

jurisdiction, I believe it's appropriate to count in this series the unfortunate occurrences aboard the Denebian heavy-cargo transport that disembarked from our main docking pylon some twenty cycles ago. The craft was still within primary communication distance when the violence broke out. Three people died in that episode, including the murderer by his own hand. Suicide as the termination of a psychotic rampage appears to be a significant element of the pattern."

"Which would make our Wyoss an important subject of investigation." With a touch, Sisko brought the report back onto the computer panel's screen. He began scrolling through the text. "Since Wyoss is the only one we've managed to apprehend alive. Are there any traceable connections between him and the other perpetrators?"

Odo shrugged. "Nothing definitive. Tangential factors, such as their being aboard the station during overlapping periods of time. I'm still sifting through the data, though; if I can find one element common to all of them—and one that is sufficiently close to being unique—then maybe we'll have something to work with."

"And that is, of course, that our assumption is valid that Ahrmant Wyoss is part of this series." Sisko turned toward Odo from the screen. "He didn't actually kill anyone—fortunately. Or that we know of, at least."

"If he did kill anyone, Commander, it would have to have been done since he came aboard the station. We wouldn't have allowed him entry if there had been any kind of record on him. In that sense, Wyoss is not an unknown quantity; we can track his employment history for nearly two decades. He's had a few batteries of psych tests along the way, and they don't show anything unusual. Just a run-of-the-mill itinerant laborer of marginal intelligence and skills. There are millions of them wandering between planets."

"That's something else of which we get more than our fair

share." Sisko tapped a fingernail against the words on the screen. "And you believe that you can connect this extremely ordinary individual with our little group of dead murderers?"

"Commander. He *did* take a swing at your head with an open pryblade—"

Sisko interrupted with an upheld hand. "Yes, of course; I mean with something besides that small datum." He managed a wry smile. "In my career, I've had several attempts on my life, and I've never assumed yet that they were all part of a single epidemic. They all seemed to be more of the sort of phenomenon that comes with the territory, as it were."

"In this case I believe we have indicative, if not conclusive, evidence. Ahrmant Wyoss was brought to my attention by one of his work-group supervisors, who had become alarmed by signs of a deteriorating mental condition on Wyoss's part. Specifically, an alteration in personality accompanied by verbal pronouncements of a disjointed and violent nature. A psych screening was performed on Wyoss and the results tagged and forwarded to me. I immediately noticed the similarity between the transcript of Wyoss's bizarre ramblings and the few recordings and *ex post facto* accounts of the dead murderers. For example, the comm line to the Denebian transport was inadvertently left open, and we have close to a quarter hour of that individual's comments to himself— along with some fairly gruesome sound effects—as he went about his self-appointed task. In all cases, and certainly in Wyoss's, there are common elements of an absorbing fantasy construct in which the individuals seem to be trapped. The murders themselves appear to be the result of some kind of high-level autistic functioning, in which the components of the normally perceived environment—such as other people —are seen as parts of another, completely enclosed world. And judging from the nature of the murderers' responses to those perceptions, it's not a particularly pleasant world."

Everything Odo said had been in his report; Sisko could look at the computer panel and see nearly the exact same words. Going over it this way had given him time to sort through his own thoughts on the matter.

Unfortunately, there were still not enough facts at hand on which to base a course of decision.

Sisko gazed up at the office's curved ceiling. "As long as we have this material from the murderers—and presumably more material forthcoming from our attempted murderer—we should put it through as much analysis as possible. There may be something we're overlooking. . . ."

"I quite agree, Commander. That's why I've asked Lieutenant Dax to begin a separate investigation. I've turned copies of all my records pertaining to this case over to her, and given her complete access to the prisoner Ahrmant Wyoss. She indicated that she understood the urgency attached to this matter, and has already started work on it."

"Dax?" Sisko brought his gaze back down. "But why not Dr. Bashir? I would've thought that he had more expertise in what would seem to be largely a psychological inquiry."

Odo's posture stiffened against the back of his chair. "In fact, I *did* initially approach our chief medical officer. I'm afraid, however, that Dr. Bashir was not cooperative."

He had been afraid of that. The chief medical officer was, if nothing else, a man of principle, as yet unalloyed by the compromises that a few more years of experience might bring.

"I'll speak to him." With a few taps of his finger, Sisko sent the report back to the computer's confidential archives. "In the meantime, Constable, give this matter your highest priority. Notify me at once of any new developments."

"Of course, Commander."

As soon as Odo had left the office, Sisko pushed his own chair back from the desk and stood up. He had a good notion that the chief medical officer was already waiting for him.

* * *

"Because it is, in essence, a medical problem. That's why, Commander."

Science Officer Jadzia Dax could hear the tension in Bashir's voice. The doctor only had his experience with Benjamin Sisko as a commanding officer aboard DS9 to go on; he didn't have the decades of knowing Sisko as a human being that her symbiont partner had brought to their shared consciousness. It was always easier for a Trill to view the great emotions of mere humanoid life, the angers and jealousies and other passions that loomed so large to those experiencing them, as mere epiphenomena, ripples on centuries-old seas.

A three-way conversation—or argument, at least on the part of the other two points of the triangle—had broken out in the research facility that she administered aboard the station. Commander Sisko had come upon her and Dr. Bashir, engaged in debating the ethics involved in Ahrmant Wyoss's case.

She could see that Benjamin was in danger of losing his temper, in that deceptively calm, voice-lowering manner that reasonably terrified a good number of the station's crew. But then again, Bashir's obstinacy—he was not quite the thin, pliable reed that many took him to be at first encounter—was notably evocative of that reaction in others.

"Commander—" In deference to Starfleet etiquette, she addressed him by his rank in public, rather than by the first name their long friendship allowed her to use. "I think both viewpoints can be accommodated here. There's no reason why my assisting Odo's investigation would necessarily interfere with the subject's therapeutic requirements."

"We're not talking about a 'subject' here." The steel in Sisko's voice barely softened when he replied to her. "The individual in question is charged with attempted murder. The target of Wyoss's attack was myself, DS9's most senior officer, and if he had managed to continue unapprehended, presumably he would have taken Major Kira's life as well. That puts an even more serious cast on the matter; we're dealing with what could have been a critical blow to the station's operating capability and to the ongoing execution of our mission here."

Bashir placed his hands against the lab table behind him, as though bracing himself for an anticipated stormwind. "I would like to respectfully submit that the commander may be letting his personal feelings interfere with his judgment. It would be only natural, and certainly expected by a competent psychologist, for you to be affronted by the subject's admittedly regrettable actions. That can give rise to feelings of vindictiveness on your part."

That, remarked Dax to herself, *is a rhetorical tactic that's not going to work.* One didn't need to share a centuries-old mentality to predict the negative effect the doctor's words were having.

"To be concerned about an epidemic of murder aboard this station, Dr. Bashir, can hardly be ascribed to vindictiveness." The steel had chilled to subzero temperatures. "I would be as concerned about the matter if that pryblade had been aimed at *your* head." The commander was silent for a moment, as though forcing himself to resist contemplating such an event. "Until we ascertain what's behind these events, I have to assume that something is happening which could endanger our entire onboard population. The welfare of the station takes precedence over the interests of this single individual."

Dr. Bashir didn't flinch, though Dax had detected a nervous clenching of his jaw as Sisko had spoken. "Sir, as DS9's commander, you may be able to justify that decision. But being the station's chief medical officer, I am first bound by my oaths as a doctor. The threat that you believe the station is faced with is still a matter of conjecture; your use of the word *epidemic* itself is a loose appropriation of a precise technical term—we haven't isolated a bacillus or virus that's being carried through the air ducts and is turning people into crazed murderers. I'm sorry, sir; I don't mean to indulge in a lecture on this point, but right now we don't have any basis for assuming the subject Wyoss's violent actions were necessarily connected to those previously committed, or that there will be similar acts committed by other individuals in the future."

"Waiting to see whether more murders will be committed on my watch," said Sisko drily, "is not a course of action—or *in*action—that I am going to undertake. The successful administration of a Starfleet directive is not a matter of applying strict scientific judgment. When lives are at stake, the worst-case scenario is the one which must determine our actions. When it's determined conclusively that these murders are not part of a series, and that there is no threat to the station's crew and residents, *and* to DS9's continued operations, *then* Ahrmant Wyoss's therapeutic concerns will be given the priority you evidently feel they deserve."

The argument had raged back and forth in front of Dax; now she tried to intervene. "You have to remember," she said, turning to Bashir, "that I'll be keeping an open mind in my research. What Odo may have concluded about the subject will have no bearing on my findings. It's entirely possible that I'll discover that Wyoss's actions and his mental state have absolutely nothing to do with the other murders."

Bashir appeared not to have heard her; he drew himself to full attention, his gaze locked straight into Sisko's. "Commander, I must state my continued disagreement with your decision in this matter. It is my belief as a doctor that the subject Ahrmant Wyoss should be immediately transported off-station, to the nearest Starfleet facility where he can receive the level of psychotherapeutic attention he needs."

"Your protest is noted, Doctor." Sisko's words became clipped and formal. "And my decision is unaltered."

The tension in the room abated when the door slid shut, though the commander's angry footsteps could still be heard echoing in the corridor beyond.

"Julian—" She turned toward Bashir. "Would you care to

explain to me just what it is you think you're going to accomplish with this approach? There's part of me that's known Benjamin Sisko a lot longer than you can ever hope to, and I can *assure* you that this is absolutely the wrong way to handle him."

"My, my." Bashir smiled at her. "This is a rare show of emotion from you. You're usually so calm and collected about these things." He nodded toward the door. "As a matter of fact, I think I've accomplished a great deal just now. I've got our good commander just where I want him."

She stared at him in amazement. "Then it's not Ahrmant Wyoss who needs psychotherapeutic care. It's *you.*"

"Perhaps. Since I came to DS9, there have been occasions when I thought I should have my head examined. But in the meantime, I've made sure that Wyoss will, if not immediately, at least eventually get a degree of care that I wouldn't have been able to provide him here aboard the station. You see, now Commander Sisko will bend over backward to demonstrate that he bears no hostility toward a mentally ill individual. As soon as you and Odo are finished with him, Wyoss will be shipped off to the best treatment facility that Sisko can pull the strings for." Bashir shrugged. "Otherwise, the commander might have insisted that I take care of Wyoss—you know how Sisko prefers solving all our problems on-site. And frankly, from what I've seen, this particular psychosis might be a little beyond my expertise."

Dax shook her head. "That was absolutely reprehensible of you, Julian. I find it repugnant that you would try to manipulate anyone like that—let alone a friend of mine."

"Really?" Bashir seemed genuinely surprised by her reaction. "But if it accomplishes what's best . . . surely that's all that matters . . ."

She had turned away from him, calling up a screenful of data on the lab bench's computer panel. It served to mask the annoyance she felt welling up inside her over the doctor's petty Machiavellianism. There were times, admittedly few in number, when the ballast of her symbiont's centuries of wisdom were overriden by a strong emotional reaction from her younger physical self. If she had been able to split herself down the middle, the temptation to slap Bashir's smug, self-satisfied face would have been irresistible. Or better yet, in the style of Kira Nerys that she sometimes envied, a good roundhouse punch between his eyes.

"In the first place," spoke Dax without turning around, "that's *not* all that matters. The fallacy of the ends justifying the means is a common one for the—shall we say?—less sophisticated mind to fall into. And secondly, based upon my long-standing personal knowledge of Commander Sisko, it's clear to me that you could have accomplished just as much, if not more, by being forthright with him, rather than indulging your unfortunate penchant for being overly clever."

"Oh." With that one syllable, Bashir's voice indicated a sudden state of deflation. "I merely thought that . . ." The rest of his words dwindled away.

She glanced over her shoulder, noting with satisfaction that her unexpectedly sharp comments had had the desired effect.

"Now, if you don't mind—" She tapped out a command on the computer's keyboard. "I have to work to do."

Bashir said nothing more; she heard only the sound of the lab's door sliding open, then closing. When she was alone, she could feel—almost regretfully—the spasm of annoyance subsiding, the catecholamines within her skull and the adrenaline in her bloodstream returning to their usual levels. If she had, as the old Earth saying put it, jumped down Bashir's throat, she could at least justify it on a rational basis as having been appropriate to the situation.

The question of further action was a delicate one. After a moment's consideration, she rejected the notion of relating to Benjamin any details of this conversation. It was a matter for him and Bashir to work out between themselves.

Another voice spoke within her. The ancient one, separating for a moment from the invisible, parallel course with the mind of a humanoid female that had not yet completed one life.

All phenomena are transitory, said the symbiont. *This, too.*

She almost replied aloud, but checked herself, hearing her own voice inside her head. *That's all very well in the long run. But we have to deal with these situations—and these people— at this moment.*

The symbiont was incapable of a smile or laughter, except that which her body could give to their shared existence. But she could detect, as she had before, the gentle amusement that temporal affairs evoked from it.

At this moment, came the voice, *some of these people hardly even exist.*

The process of formulating a reply, the working out of the transient and benign schizophrenia between one side of her conjunct being and the other, was interrupted when she felt the symbiont align itself once more with the thoughts of its host body. That was a sensation she had long become used to, that of becoming whole and undivided once more. Yet something more: as though currents of water in which she swam had turned their motion to hers, augmenting the smallest force of her will.

That was enough to allow her to put the unpleasant incident between the commander and Dr. Bashir firmly out of mind. In some ways, though Bashir's expertise and analytical skills would have been of considerable value, it would be easier for the time being without him around. Not all of the things she had begun monitoring were taking place inside Ahrmant Wyoss's skull. There were others, data from the various sensors arrayed in the empty, starlit space beyond DS9, deviations in readings that were so small as to be almost infinitesimal—she'd had to lower the percept thresholds on several devices to enable them to register anything at all. Just enough to form not a pattern, but the barest suggestion of one: a few scattered points on the graph she held inside her thoughts, the outline of a shape not yet visible to her. Until she knew what that meant—or whether there was anything more than just a random shifting in background radiation levels—it was best to keep the observations to herself.

She turned her attention to the computer screen. There, the smaller universe of Ahrmant Wyoss was being carefully pried apart. On the screen, rows of numbers bounced between a narrow range of values, giving her a real-time monitoring of his physiological processes. A scrolling graph of brain-wave function showed him to still be in a state of narcotized sleep, though with abnormal spikes of activity throughout the thalamocortical zones. Something was going on inside the subject's visual information processes that was connected to the hyperactive REM being picked up by the optical sensors.

He's seeing things, thought Dax. *But what?* Mere dreams, even nightmares, didn't produce such neuroanatomical storms.

She scanned past the other numbers. Respiratory functions were on the high side, but sustainable, as hormone levels whipsawed between apparent panic and anger states. As Odo had remarked to her when the subject had been transferred to her keeping, whatever world Wyoss had found himself trapped in, it was evidently not a pleasant one.

With another command, she switched the screen to a view from the overhead camera in the subject's secured isolation chamber. With clinical detachment, Dax observed the clenching of the jaw, the straining neck tendons, the feverish sweat upon the brow. Invisible energy restraints at the wrists and ankles, and a wider band across the abdomen, prevented Wyoss from injuring himself.

"Computer, give me audio on this subject." In response to her spoken command, a low guttural murmuring came from the panel's speaker. "Increase one-point-two-five decibels."

Now she could make out the words, the alternately furious and terrified monologue that seeped through Wyoss's teeth. The voice was scarcely human, a howl of anguish from the darkest, unexplored caverns of the brain stem.

"All right, that's enough." The lab's silence folded around her again. The subject's words, loosened by an injection of one of the more powerful pentathol analogues, had spoken of things that no sane person would wish to hear. But she would have to, eventually; every syllable was being picked up by the chamber's microphones and recorded in the data banks.

She blanked the screen. "Computer. I want all material from this subject indexed against the recordings logged on by the chief of security, reference tag 'Epidemic.' Give me a breakdown on all distinctive word patterns and imagery that cross-link between the recordings. Prepare a transcript with embedded back-markers."

"Processing," responded the synthesized voice.

There was nothing to do now but wait. It would take only a few minutes at most. But part of her, that had listened to the words with dread, wished it would be longer.

"I just wanted to see my dad." He gave a small shrug, as if it were nothing important. "That's all."

School was over for this shift, and Jake had come up to the Ops deck on the off chance that his father might have time for him. Perhaps they could go get something to eat—it'd been a long while since they'd had dinner together in their living quarters—or if there were only a few minutes to spare, maybe he could just sit in his father's private office behind Ops, and they could talk. Not even about the things that weighed heaviest on Jake's heart and mind, but about anything at all. He'd always thought that that made his father feel better as well.

"Sure—" The comm tech, a lieutenant who was one of Jake's favorites, glanced over her shoulder toward Commander Sisko's office. The door was partially retracted, voices drifting out from the other side. "Tell you what, I'll go see if he's busy right now. You just wait here, okay?"

Standing in the Ops entranceway, Jake watched as she slipped through the deck's low-key bustle of activity, the constant monitoring of the station's well-being. The big viewscreen was blanked at the moment, without even a scattering of distant stars beamed aboard. Though if there had been a show like that, he knew, nobody here would have had the time to pull away from their gauges and controls to take a look at it.

The comm tech had crossed over to where she could cast a surreptitious glance into the office. She caught the arm of one of the other crew members passing by; they had a quick, whispered conversation.

"I'm sorry." She had come back and leaned her head close to Jake's. "But it looks like right now's not a very good time. Your father's got an agenda full of conferences and briefings—I don't know when he's going to get through it all."

"That's okay." Jake made a stone-faced effort to conceal his disappointment. He knew that these chances had grown increasingly scarce. They were hardly worth bothering with, if they weren't something he wanted so much. He shrugged again. "I guess I'll see him later on."

"I'm sure you will." The comm tech gave him a sympathetic smile and a pat on the shoulder. "Soon as I can, I'll let him know you were here."

Jake turned and walked away without replying.

And kept walking, with no intended destination, not even watching where his footsteps along the metal-walled corridors led him.

Though when he arrived, he knew that some part inside had led him there.

Jake glanced toward the darkness at either end of the corridor. Silence; hardly anyone ever came to this sector. He had stumbled upon it by accident, in his wanderings around the station. Assured that no one was watching him, he laid the flat of his hand against the nearest door. There were three others just like it, all in a row, the entrances to a bank of holosuites. The new ones, the ones that were special; the ones that could take him to places that weren't programmed into Quark's boring old holosuites. And to one place in particular, a very special place . . .

He punched his access code into the control panel and stepped inside.

Behind him, he heard the doorway to that other world, the one with his father in it, seal shut. Squinting, he glanced up at the bright sun overhead, then started walking through the field of wind-brushed yellow grasses, the stalks parting around him like a whispering sea.

"I figured you'd be back." The other boy smiled and side-armed a small stone across the creek. The smile twisted at one corner, to signal just how much he knew. "Where else could you go?"

Jake looked away, feeling his breath tighten in his chest. Even under this false yet oddly true sun, a cold shiver ran over the skin of his arms.

CHAPTER
4

HE GRASPED THE EDGE OF THE EMPTY TRAY AND PULLED IT TOWARD himself, bringing the server's face within centimeters of his own.

"Tell me," said Odo, his gaze boring straight to the back of the startled Quark's skull. "Everything you seemed so insistent that I should know before."

Quark managed to tug the tray free and straightened up, smoothing with one hand the disarrayed lapels of his jacket. "I have absolutely no idea what you're talking about." He glanced over his shoulder, aware that other patrons of his establishment had noticed the confrontation between him and the chief of security. "Tell you *what?* Perhaps you've been working a little too hard. I don't want to suggest that you're imagining things, but—"

"Don't play coy with me, Quark." He leaned over the unordered drink, which had been deposited in front of him as a fruitless attempt at ingratiation. "Just last shift, you might as well have been welded to my elbow, the way that you were

53

tugging at me and hinting that you had some huge secret to impart. And now it's business as usual around here? You're severely trying my patience."

"Please . . . could you keep your voice down?" The Ferengi's manner became even more nervous and agitated. That was what Odo had expected; these types with an obsessive interest in other people's affairs always reacted in panic at the thought of their own being revealed. "I assure you—"

"You'll *assure* me nothing." Odo brought his voice up another notch in volume. "But you *will* expand upon those rather broad hints you were so generous with before. You seemed quite concerned about what you termed 'unusual developments'; there's apparently some negative impact on your manifold business enterprises, from certain 'unsavory characters'—though I can't imagine anyone so far gone in depravity that *you* could justifiably call them that."

"I so enjoy these witticisms of yours." Quark forced one of his sharp-pointed smiles. "Kindly and well-intentioned as I'm sure they're meant to be. But look—" He leaned closer, his words set in a conspiratorial whisper. "I've got . . . well, *business* arrangements with half the individuals in this bar. All strictly legitimate, of course."

Odo emitted a snort of disbelief.

"All right, sort of legitimate. Harmless, let's say. But these people tend to be a little on the paranoid side; they don't have the same long-standing relationship of trust with you that I do." Quark scanned the premises again, directing an even broader smile and a wave of a hand to a table ringed with scowling faces. "Be right with you." He turned back to the chief of security. "Give me a break," he pleaded. "If everyone sees the two of us having a long, intimate conversation, I could wind up going out one of the waste-disposal chutes in little pieces."

"Very well." Odo took the tray from Quark and set it down

beside the untouched synthale; his next action was to grasp the Ferengi's lapels and slam Quark down into the chair next to him. "Then my advice to you would be to talk fast."

Quark had barely enough breath for a panicky squeak. "It's the holosuites—"

"What about them? Other than the fact they represent a good percentage of your profits."

The Ferengi managed to regain some of his composure. "I run a few holosuites, true, but their value to me isn't the revenue they generate—believe me, I hardly cover my expenses on them. Rather, they're all part of my role here as host to legions of weary travelers. I've often suggested to Commander Sisko that Starfleet should consider subsidizing some of my activities here, for the sheer social value and goodwill they generate among visitors to DS9. Now, in a properly administered transit station—"

"I thought you were in a hurry."

"Yes, of course." The comment prompted another nervous survey by Quark. "You're fully aware that no matter what your own personal views might be about the morality involved in my operating the holosuites, they *are* inspected and fully licensed—by you, as a matter of fact."

"My feelings don't enter into it," said Odo sourly. "If the DS9 regulations allow you to do business in such a manner, then *I* allow it. That's all."

"But you have to admit that I run a clean operation. Some of the programming for my holosuites may be a little bit on the *risqué* side—all right, a *lot* that way—but it's all within the established guidelines for, shall we say, *adult* entertainment. There's certainly nothing in my holosuites' programming that could be considered *harmful* . . . nothing that anybody could get hurt by. . . ."

Odo peered more closely at the Ferengi. "What are you talking about?"

"The problem, my dear Odo, is that I no longer control all

of the station's holosuites; there are these new ones that have been brought on board. Now, if you and the commander were to see the wisdom of granting me an exclusive franchise . . ." A hopeful tone crept into his voice. "All right, all right; never mind." Quark began sliding off the seat. "Look, I've already stayed too long here talking to you. I've got a bar to run." He picked up the empty tray and clutched it to his chest. "It's not *my* holosuites I was referring to. They're not the problem. And that's all I can tell you right now."

Odo watched the Ferengi making his rounds among the other tables, attempting to mollify the thuggish patrons who had been casting narrow-eyed glances Quark's way.

Outside Quark's establishment, Odo moved through the crowded Promenade. There was another sector of the station that he wished to investigate.

"How's that little gadget working out? You know, the one I rigged up for you." As he crouched down with the old-fashioned manual screwdriver, DS9's chief of operations looked up at the figure standing beside him.

" 'Gadget'? Oh, yes." Odo nodded. "Quite satisfactorily, thank you. I didn't bring it with me——" He displayed his empty hands. "Otherwise, I would have been happy to demonstrate the device's efficiency."

"No need." O'Brien had gotten down on his knees, the better to apply force to a particularly stubborn panel fastening. "I'm already immodest enough about the quality of my work." He signaled with a crooked finger. "Could you point that light a little more this way? There, that's fine." With both fists clenched around the screwdriver's handle, and teeth gritted together, he strained against the reluctant bit of metal.

"Actually, I need to ask another favor of you along those lines." Odo peered around the flashlight's beam. "The device you made for me just reads out the access code of someone who's currently using a holosuite; what I require now would be something that could give me a cumulative history of a holosuite's past users. Would that be possible?"

"Sure; no problem." The screw had finally broken free, and O'Brien began backing it out. "These babies all have a log-in chip wired into the basic circuitry, so every access occasion gets recorded—you could have the times and dates, too, if you wanted." With a tiny *ping,* the screw fell out on the metal flooring. Out of habit created by years of practical engineer work, O'Brien picked up the screw and tucked it into a belt pouch before it could get lost.

"That would be most helpful."

Rubbing the small of his back, O'Brien looked over the panel. There were another sixteen fasteners to go. It would have been less work to use a power tool, but both he and Odo had agreed they didn't want anyone to know they were back here in this narrow space, and the noise might have given them away.

It had been less than half an hour ago that Odo had cornered him in his office on the engineering deck and dragooned him along on this expedition. Or "investigation," as Odo would have it. The sector in question, one of DS9's remoter and less-frequented corridors, held a row of the new holosuites. He hadn't been able to conjecture why anyone would travel all this way to use them, when there were better-maintained ones on the Promenade.

"Exactly," Odo had replied to the chief of operations' musings. "And where one finds a mystery, one must then look for a motivation."

Spoken like a real detective, O'Brien had thought. They had checked and found no one using any of the corridor's holosuites; he had then led Odo back to the normally closed-off space behind them, from which the holosuites' workings could be reached.

"Actually," continued O'Brien, "there would be a wee bit of a problem." The second of the panel's screws fell into his palm; he started on the next one. "And that'd be the same as with the other device: what you're asking for is not quite within regulations." With a raised eyebrow, he glanced up at Odo.

"Do you have a problem with that?"

"Me?" O'Brien shook his head as he stood up. Half of the screws rattled in his pocket; they had started coming along faster, the panel shifting with its own weight enough to break the seal. "But you're the policeman, remember."

Odo's expression didn't change—it never did—but his spine stiffened, as though the remark had stung him. "I'll take full responsibility for whatever consequences may ensue."

"Fine, fine; whatever." The handle of the screwdriver had grown warm and sweaty in his grip. "Tell you what. Say around the end of next shift, come around to the engineering deck when you know I'm not going to be there. If you see a package on my desk marked with the letters NT, then that's yours."

" 'NT'?"

"New toy. You'll be able to figure out how it works on your own. Ah, here we go." The final screw came free, and O'Brien slid it and the hand tool into his pocket. With his fingers braced against the flat metal, he eased the panel out and away from the wall.

"Very impressive." Odo shone the flashlight into the recess behind. "I had no idea there was quite so much inside one of these."

"You must be joking." He brushed off his palms against his uniform. "A holosuite's one of the most complicated pieces of equipment aboard the station. You'd have to go up to Ops deck and root around the multiband comm gear, the real long-distance stuff, to find anything more elaborate. Look—" He took the flashlight from Odo and used it as a pointer. "Over there you've got your miniaturized tractor-beam units; all of those have to be coordinated *exactly* with each other in order to produce even the simplest tactile sensory illusions. Same with the optical functions, the olfactory, anything where specific molecules have to be produced by the built-in replicators—" The flashlight beam skipped from one interwired module to the next. "Plus there's temperature control, and various homeostatic processes that aren't even meant to be perceived consciously, but the user would notice something was wrong if they weren't right on the money. And *all* of that has to be monitored and microadjusted in real time to interface not just with the original programming, but every move, every flick of an eyelash, that the user makes inside the chamber. So for that you need a data channel that's about big enough to run a small cruiser, and a computer node that's completely separate from the station's central unit—otherwise, if enough holosuites came on-line simultaneously, the processor drain could shut DS9 down to basic survival operations." He shook his head in admiration. "When I was back in engineering school, I tore one of these apart—a Mark One model, not anything as sophisticated as this—and believe me, I was an old man before I got it put back together."

Odo's head shake expressed a different, more rueful emotion. "It seems a pity that such ingenuity isn't put to better use. I fail to see the attraction of these devices."

"Different strokes, as they say." O'Brien smiled and clapped him on the shoulder. "Not everybody has such a rich and stimulating reality as you do."

"Hm." Odo peered into the holosuite's mazelike innards. "Right now, that reality seems somewhat discouraging. How are you going to be able to tell if this unit's been tampered with?"

That question had been the whole point of their expedition to this sector of the ship. Odo had been his usual tight-mouthed self, but O'Brien had been able to glean enough from him to know that the security chief had been tipped off about some possible alterations to these holosuites' programming banks. He had guessed on his own that the tip had come from Quark—who else? Coming from that dubious source, it might be no more than a typically sneaking maneuver to have the holosuites not under Quark's control shut down and taken off-line. Quark viewed competition as a vastly inferior state to monopoly.

"Easy enough," replied O'Brien. "If you know what you're looking for." He ducked his head below the panel opening's edge and stepped into the tight space surrounded by the different modules; he had to hold his elbows close to his sides to keep from bumping into any of them. "Should be right over . . . here." He reached outside to Odo. "Hand me that equipment bag I left over on the floor there. Thanks." From the bag he drew a small probe; numbers scrolled across its screen as he inserted the needle-like points into a socket receptor. "Tampering on holosuites was always a big worry; the problem about guarding against it is that you've got a lot of sites along the data stream that can be dinked around with. So what you've got laid over the entire assembly is what's called a web seal—there's microfilaments running from this box through every other component and back again. Poke your head in here for a moment." With his other hand, O'Brien pointed to the numbers that had stopped upon the probe's display. "See that? That's the date of the last time someone so much as laid a finger on anything in here."

"So this holosuite—and presumably the others in this sector—hasn't been tampered with."

O'Brien shrugged. "Well . . . let's not be too hasty about that conclusion." He drew another device from the equipment bag, one with the rough but serviceable appearance of his own construction. "Give me a couple more minutes."

Maneuvering through the narrow enclosure, he started tracing the almost microscopic strands of the web seal. He could feel Odo watching him as he stepped farther into the holosuite's innards.

"Those clever bastards." He had found what he had suspected would be hidden there; an LED on the device in his hand glowed red. Whoever had been in here before him merited his admiration, if only on a technical basis.

"What is it?" Odo's voice came from behind.

O'Brien emerged with a rectangular black box in his hands. "I've got to give them credit, whoever they were—that was a good clean job they did. I wouldn't have located this little number if I hadn't been able to get a decay readout on the web filament. They managed to jump a section of line, then splice this in, all without tripping the seal unit's sensors. That takes some pretty high-level skills."

Odo nodded slowly, as if already assembling a list of criteria for suspects. "How proficient would that person—or group of persons—have to be?"

"Frankly, they'd have to be as good as I am. And that's *very* good." O'Brien turned the object around in his hands. "Wonder what the hell's inside this thing. Nice, tight unit; looks like it came off a regular assembly line, and not just some kludge somebody threw together. It'll take some work to bust it open."

"How long will that take?"

"Depends. If there's an autodestruct sequence wired in, I'll have to find some way of finessing around it. That might take a shift or two. If it's clean, though, I could have it ready for Dax to start running an analysis in, oh, a couple of hours. Can't be sure until I've got it on the bench."

"Very well." Odo pointed to the black box in the chief of operations' hands. "Are there members of the engineering crew who can open up the other holosuites here and extract these things?"

"Sure." O'Brien nodded. "Once I tell them what they're looking for."

"They'll need temp security authorizations from me—I'm locking this whole sector down."

"I'll send them your way first, then."

As they turned away from the panel opening and headed for the passageway, Odo studied his companion. "Somehow . . . you knew, didn't you? That someone had tampered with that holosuite, despite the web-seal readout."

O'Brien tried to be as gentle as possible with his smile. "Perhaps you're not the only great detective on board, Constable. Didn't you notice the dust?"

Odo glanced behind himself, then back to O'Brien. "What dust?"

"Exactly—there wasn't any." He pointed to an overhead grille. "These work areas don't get the same atmospheric filtration cycles that the other sectors do. Things get pretty mucky after a while; that's why those access panels are bolted down so airtight. Whoever was in here, they were real professionals." He let his smile widen. "They cleaned up after themselves. And that's how I knew."

"Is this the article in question?" The object seemed surprisingly light in his hands. Sisko rubbed the ball of his thumb across the enameled surface. He could see the reflection of his face in it, as though it were an obsidian mirror.

"That's the casing for it," said Dax. "O'Brien didn't have any trouble getting into it—though apparently he did make the first drill hole by remote, in a bombproof chamber, just to be on the safe side." She pointed to the workbench along the laboratory's other side. "The unit's interior components are over there."

"You've completed your analysis on them?"

"For the most part. I'm afraid, Benjamin, that we'll have a difficult time determining the source of these devices. Whoever built them didn't leave a lot of clues inside."

He set the empty casing down, then looked over the carefully dismantled innards. Bright fragments of metal, the intricate tracery of microcircuits—for a moment, an irrational feeling moved at the base of his own gut, that he was looking at the disemboweled carcass of a once-living creature, one that had crept with malign rodentlike cunning into the core of the station. He pushed the disquieting thought away.

"What about its function?" Sisko picked up one of the pieces, a mute crystalline cylinder, and studied it between his thumb and forefinger. "Its effect on these altered holosuites?"

"I can give you more information on that." She stepped beside him and took the crystal away from him, replacing it in the exact ordered spot from which he had taken it. That small action held a silent reprimand, as though from an elder to a child. Which in essence it was, coming—as he knew it did—from the centuries-old symbiont inside Jadzia's torso. His ancient friend, across a gulf of so many years and aggregate lifetimes. He watched as Jadzia drew her hand away from the piece. "Unfortunately," she said, "a great deal more."

"What do you mean?"

"It's not good news, Benjamin. There are some very serious consequences to what I've found here."

"Related to the epidemic of murders?"

She nodded.

"I had a feeling that was going to be the case." Sisko leaned back against the edge of the bench. "Give me a rundown on it, then."

"Basically, the situation with the holosuites in the indicated sector is as Odo suspected; they've all been tampered with. An operations crew is currently removing the other modules identical to this one. I'll check each one of them out, but I'm confident that I'll find that they're all identical in construction and operation. The technology that's employed in these modules is a very powerful—and illicit—sensory-input technology that's usually referred to by the initials 'CI.'"

"What does that stand for?"

"'Cortical induction,'" replied Dax. "It's not anything new; it was developed shortly after the original holosuite programming modalities were devised. Actually, the relative ease with which these units were spliced into the data stream indicates that CI was originally part of the overall holosuite design, and was removed once the negative effects of CI had been discovered. The CI technology was then suppressed by the Federation authorities; the clearances necessary to do any research into the subject are almost impossible to obtain—*if* you even knew what to inquire about."

"But you know about it." Sisko gestured at the disassembled components. "You were able to almost immediately recognize this thing for what it was."

She smiled. "There are advantages to having several centuries' worth of memory. There had been some initial distribution of holosuite data; I can remember when those files were ordered back and placed under security."

Her explanation brought a raised eyebrow. "That's not done very often. The Federation scientists must have found something fairly alarming."

"A powerful technology always evokes precautions, Benjamin. One that's both powerful and uncontrollable . . ." Dax shook her head. "The Federation did the right thing in attempting to suppress CI. The murders we've had aboard the station prove that." Her hand moved slowly above the bench, as though her fingertips could read the message encoded in the carefully separated pieces. "You know how an unmodified holosuite works, Benjamin; essentially, it creates an illusory experience by presenting sensory data to the user's normal percept system, including tactile sensations through by means of low-level tractor beams, or by replicating objects that can actually be touched and held."

"I'm familiar enough with the process." He had felt in his own hands the fine-grained hide, the rows of tight stitches curving around a spheroid surface, an artifact from the ancient sport of baseball, perfectly re-created by a replicator component within a holosuite.

"What makes the CI technology so powerful—and so much more dangerous—is that it bypasses the sense organs entirely; it operates by inducing the desired current flow and synaptic discharges in the neurofibers of the user's brain. The resulting experience is much more commanding in the intensity of the illusion created; if undergone often enough, it can begin to override the user's perception of reality itself. This is a threat that's qualitatively different from the essentially benign effects of the regulation, unaltered holosuites. In addition, holosuites normally have built-in safeguards to prevent users from programming any experiences with extremely negative psychological consequences, such as deliberately injuring oneself, sadistic and self-reinforcing acts of violence against others, and the like. Even the holosuites that Quark operates on the Promenade, while admittedly being oriented toward erotic fantasy material, function within those safeguards. These other holosuites, the ones that Odo found have been tampered with—" Dax pointed to the bench. "These cognitive-induction modules essentially remove all such barriers. The consequences, as we've seen, can be severe."

Her voice had been calm and level, the words measured as those in a scientific lecture—which in effect it had been, albeit at a simplified level. Sisko knew that if necessary, Dax could have given him a complete technical breakdown of the CI technology and its malign influences on the humanoid nervous system. Anything other than that reflected her assessment of what he needed to know to begin making the decisions that would insure the station's survival. His own thought processes would have to match Dax's in cold rationality, to sort through this situation's elements and determine the one proper course of action.

"And are you quite sure," he said, "that there's a definite connection between these CI modules and the outbreak of murders on board DS9? It is possible after all, that these phenomena are merely coincidental. We could wind up wasting valuable time and resources by acting on this theory, when the underlying cause might be something entirely different."

Dax gave an acknowledging nod of her head. "You're quite right to be cautious, Benjamin. My investigation into the matter is still at a preliminary stage; a great deal will be determined by the correlation I find between the CI programming and the analysis of what I've been recording from the subject Ahrmant Wyoss. And of course, Odo is following up on a number of other leads."

"Very well. Keep me apprised—immediately—of any new developments." His gaze moved again across the sparkling and mute pieces laid out on the bench's surface. The coded words that they might spell out were still not legible. He turned away from them and strode toward the laboratory door.

CHAPTER
5

SHE CAUGHT HIM AS HE HEADED FOR OPS DECK. SISKO FELT HIS ARM snared; his stride was broken for only a moment as Major Kira matched speed with him.

"Commander—" She had gotten some rest and regained her usual sharp edge, since the last time he had seen her. "I've received some transmissions from our contacts on Bajor, updating the political situation. There've been some developments, just in the time that I've been back here at the station."

"Oh? And what are they?" It required a mental effort to bring his thoughts around to Bajor and its seemingly endless power struggles. DS9's murder epidemic had absorbed all his attention for the last shift.

"Unfortunately, it's all in line with what I've previously reported. The Severalty Front has made some significant advances; they've acquired a highly effective spokesman, a General Aur."

"I seem to have heard the name before." His brow furrowed in concentration. "Who is he?"

Kira shrugged. "A hero of the Bajoran resistance . . . that's where the military title comes from, at least. Since the Cardassian occupation ended, though, he's been a constant thorn in the side of the provisional government. Certain amount of charisma, but not much of an ideologue. My own assessment would be that he can shift his positions to whatever will bring him the most power. So he can be pretty dangerous."

"Major, I have yet to meet a Bajoran that I wouldn't consider dangerous." They had arrived at the entrance to Ops; Sisko turned and gave her a mollifying smile. "Yourself included, of course." He rubbed the corner of his brow, as if pushing back the concerns accumulating behind the bone. "Keep me posted; if anything happens with this General Aur, we'll make containing the effects a top priority."

He walked away from her, knowing full well that there was more that she had wanted to tell him, and more that needed to be taken care of. There was always more.

Odo was waiting for him in his private office. The door slid shut, and the security chief's gaze followed Sisko as he sat down behind the desk.

"How's the investigation going?"

"We've made considerable progress," said Odo. "I've been able to extract a record from each of the holosuites that had been tampered with, establishing all of the recent users—"

"I'll consider that as being off the record, of course." He had never officially disapproved of Odo's skating just the other side of DS9's regulations. Such procedures were necessary and excusable, as long as they were carried out with discretion.

"Of course." Odo gave a quick nod. "My initial suspicions were borne out: all of the murderers and Ahrmant Wyoss were frequent users of the altered holosuites. The pattern of usage for each individual shows an escalating trend ranging over a period of months, from a few scattered visits separated by intervals of several shifts at the beginning, to several visits per shift, lasting for hours at a time immediately preceding the violent episodes. At this time, I think it would be a justifiable assumption that there's a causal connection between the holosuites and what we've experienced on board the station."

"Looks that way. Let's go with that until we can prove otherwise. Anything else?"

"I believe Lieutenant Dax is continuing with her analysis of the modules that were found in the holosuites. She uploaded an initial report to me, concerning this so-called CI technology; I should be meeting with her later this shift or next. In the meantime, I have some leads to follow up on how the modules might have been smuggled aboard. If I can trace that down, we might be able to determine who's behind all this."

"Fine, Constable." Sisko reached out and switched on the computer panel; the first screenful of what he knew would be a dismayingly long procession came up on the screen. "Do it and get back to me." He looked up a few seconds later, when he realized that Odo was still sitting across the desk from him. "Is there something else?"

"Yes . . ." An odd hesitancy tinged Odo's voice. "There was something else I wanted to bring to your attention."

"Does it have to do with our epidemic?"

"Perhaps not; I can't be sure." Odo slowly shook his head. "It's a personal matter, I think. To do with you."

"Then I'm afraid I don't have time for it." He had a good idea what it might be; there was a continuous circuit of worry among the station's other officers about what his work pace was doing to his health. "Right now, I don't have a personal life."

"I believe it's important, Commander."

He sighed. "Everything's important. That's what I've

learned since I took on this post. Sometimes . . . I think I've lost the ability to tell what's important and what's not." Sisko glanced at the computer panel, a brief surge of tiredness blurring the words in his sight. "Whatever it is, I promise you my full attention about it—just as soon as I can. In the meantime, we both have jobs to do."

"Very well, Commander." Odo rose from the chair. "Perhaps I'll have more facts at my disposal, when we speak again."

Someone else slipped into the office as Odo left. He was aware of the other's presence without even looking up. "Yes, what is it?" He could hear the impatience in his own words.

"An explanation, sir, if not exactly an apology . . ."

His gaze swung up to Dr. Bashir's face. "Is either one necessary?"

"I just wanted to reiterate, Commander, that the objections I made to the ongoing investigation were . . . well, based on principle."

"I never doubted that."

Bashir appeared even more uncomfortable. "And I wanted to assure you there'd be no interference coming from me in that regard."

"Oh? Have your principles changed, Doctor?"

"No—" Bashir quickly shook his head. "Of course not. But let's just say that my sense of diplomacy has."

Sisko leaned back in his chair, regarding the young officer standing on the other side of the desk. "No interference, you say? That is, of course, an improvement. And what if I were to order you to assist Science Officer Dax in her work related to the investigation?"

Bashir managed a weak smile. "I think my principles could accommodate that as well, sir."

"Fine. Explanation, or whatever you wish to call it, accepted, Doctor." He swiveled his chair to face the computer panel. "Those are your orders, then. I imagine Dax might welcome the help."

He heard the door slide open, then shut again. The office's silence, now that he was alone, was almost soothing to him.

There were things he needed to tell the commander—things about the altered holosuites, and what he had found there—but they would have to wait. Other jobs had to be done first.

Odo leaned across the table. "Are you ready to talk to me now?"

Across from him, a thick-necked freight handler sat with a sullen expression, arms folded across sweat-darkened coveralls. The man's jowls bristled with coarse stubble. "I got nothin' to talk to you about."

Through the windows of the unused manifest office that Odo had taken over, he could watch the ponderous activities on the main pylon's cargo ramp. Cantilevered gantries swung over the bay of a Proximian freighter, the articulated crane arms lifting out the battered transport containers, each dwarfing the small humanoid figures below. From farther in the dock's recesses, sparks from plasma torches sizzled through the flooring's open grates, as meter-wide chain links were cut apart. Odo turned his gaze away from the familiar sights, and back to the individual he had collared for questioning.

"Let's not play these games with each other. You have information I require, and eventually you *will* tell it to me. Why waste your time and mine by pretending to be obtuse?"

The freight handler had eyes that looked like razor nicks drawn in unbaked dough. "Haven't a clue, what you're goin' at me for."

Odo had brought a small drawstring bag with him. He reached down beside him and set the bag on the table. From inside it he took the empty black casing for the CI module that

71

he and Chief of Operations O'Brien had pulled from the holosuite. "You know what this is, don't you?"

The other's eyes opened wide enough that watery blue pupils could be discerned. A few seconds ticked by before he managed to shake his head. "Never saw it before in my life."

The little hesitation told Odo that he had hit the target with his first try. If he hadn't got the response he wanted here, he had a short list of other miscreants to move on to.

"I don't appreciate being lied to, either." Odo set a fingertip on the gleaming black surface. "Given the record you have in my files, I might have hoped that you would have learned the value of honesty by now."

A new layer of sweat seeped into the folds of the man's neck. "Hey . . . I haven't done anything like that in a long time. I'm *clean—*"

"I'm the one who makes that determination." He pushed the casing a few centimeters closer to the freight handler, then drew it back, like a chess move he was considering. "Now, it would certainly be . . . *unethical* to plant items in an individual's file. But what I've found useful in the past is to not *remove* quite everything from a particular individual's file—an individual such as yourself—but to leave a few . . . *interesting* items in there. Little improprieties, shall we say? Simple matters, of just stepping over the line of DS9's regulations now and then—incidents that someone might not even be aware that I know about." Odo smiled. "It's remarkable how well such information can insure an individual's cooperation when needed."

The other's eyes narrowed again. "You're lying."

"Am I? Perhaps we should go down to the security office and find out. But I promise you—" Odo leaned across the table, his voice dropping a notch. "If I'm not lying, then you'll leave the security office in wrist restraints. And your next stop will be a Federation criminal court."

"All right, all right." The freight handler's face now looked as if it had been boiled in sweat. "Look, I don't even know what that thing is—and I don't wanna know, either. I didn't even *like* doing a job for that guy. Gave me the creeps."

"But you apparently didn't mind getting paid by that person. Because you did the job, after all. Though I'm still wondering how you managed to get these devices aboard the station. I've been keeping a close watch on what comes in from these loading docks."

An expression of smug self-satisfaction lifted a corner of the freight handler's mouth. "There's ways."

"If I had the time," said Odo, his voice level, "we'd talk about that a little more. But right now, all I require is a name. Who paid you to smuggle these into the station?"

"I dunno . . ." Smugness changed to fear. "It ain't worth it to me to squawk."

"Perhaps you should reconsider whether you're more afraid of this other party than you are of me. Whoever he is, he's not around, and there's no need for him to find out whatever you might tell me. Whereas I'm sitting right in front of you, and I can guarantee you some unpleasant consequences if you maintain your silence." Odo looked at his own hand as he raised and held it above the empty module casing. "All I need is a name."

Small yellowed teeth bit into the freight handler's lower lip. Then two syllables blurted out. "McHogue."

Odo drew a blank; he had no recollection of ever having heard the name before. But he carefully maintained his facade, to keep the other from realizing.

"I see. . . ." He nodded slowly. "McHogue, is it?" He picked up the casing and deposited it back in the drawstring bag. "Why don't you run along now and go about your business? Just as if you hadn't had this conversation with me. Just be sure to stay where I can find you."

With a look of relief, the freight handler scuttled out of the manifest office.

Odo sat still for a few moments longer, both to give the freight handler time to disappear, and to draw his own ruminations together.

A name unknown to him . . . that made it even more interesting. And, as was always the case with unknown elements, perhaps more dangerous.

He pushed the chair back from the table and stood up. Once outside the manifest office, he headed for the nearest turbolift.

The voice spoke inside his head. He had wanted to hear for himself; now he regretted that decision.

. . . it hurts does it but that's good it hurts and it bleeds I hurt and bleed good that's good. Red on blade—don't—it's too bright redbright hurtgood—I won't I promise I'm sorry—I'm sorry—red is here red and bright and hurt—I'm sorry bright my hand red and bright and you hurt—red and dark . . .

Chief Medical Officer Bashir pulled the headphones from his ears and handed the apparatus back to Jadzia Dax. "Well. That was . . . *interesting.* To say the least." He shook his head, as though the voice—murmuring, growling, even crying out beneath the weight of the drug—had left some tangible residue inside.

"I told you," said Dax. She stowed the rarely used headphones in one of the laboratory's equipment drawers. From the bench beside her, she picked up her data padd. "It's all been transcribed." She smiled. "You would have been much better off reading it instead."

She was right so often—in the calmly stated fashion all Trills had—that he had long ago ceased feeling any sparks of resentment on such occasions. Bashir took the data padd as she held it out to him. On its screen, the outpouring of words that he had just listened to now scrolled upward, line by line. Even in that reduced form, they were disturbing.

"How much of this do you have?" He tapped his finger against the data padd. "In terms of actual time, that is."

"Six point four hours." Answers like that always came from Dax with mathematical precision. "From my monitoring of the subject's vital indicators, I determined that some fatigue factors were beginning to be apparent. I thought it best to discontinue the drug flow and let him get some rest."

"Any sedation?" As much as Bashir had agreed to assist with Dax's investigation, the welfare of the subject was still a priority with him.

She shook her head. "I felt it was contraindicated, given the amount of pharmaceuticals already present in his bloodstream. Plus, the nonstop verbalization seemed to have had a significant cathartic effect on the subject; he had ceased struggling against the restraints as he had been doing before, and there was much less of the contorted facial grimacing he had previously displayed."

"All right. I'll check on him and make sure of his condition." Bashir raised the data padd again and studied the transcription of Ahrmant Wyoss's drug-induced rantings. The voice was still echoing inside his head.

. . . red and dark . . . bright it hurts . . . good . . .

With an effort, he forced the memory back into silence. "Have you already done an analysis on this material?"

Dax nodded. "I had the station's computer do a preliminary breakdown and cross-indexing of key phrases and imagery. As I suspected, there's quite a lot of underlying structure here; it's not just a chaotic profusion of fragments unrelated to each other. The concept formation is admittedly unpleasant, but it *is* consistent."

"So I see." His initial repulsion, triggered more by the violence than the words' overt graphic nature—a doctor was used to seeing blood—had abated enough that he could begin studying the transcription. "It's really as if the subject is describing the contents and experiences of another world.

There's parallels, of course, to our normal shared universe, but everything's skewed toward . . . I don't know . . ." He searched for a means of description. "A rage-filled hurtling into death. Or is that too baroque a construction?"

Dax looked sympathetic. "Actually, that's rather well put, Doctor. The toxic nature of these obsessions goes beyond anything else I've ever encountered. It's as if this other universe's inherent entropic nature is not a blind, unconscious process, but something actively malign. And intelligently so."

"More's the pity, at least for poor Wyoss and the others. There may or may not be a God in our universe, but they found a universe in which there certainly is. Just their bad luck that it turned out to be a murderous one." Bashir fell silent; these theological musings were something new for both himself and Jadzia, an indication of how deep the abyss was that they had each discerned beneath the subject's onslaught of words. He took a deep breath, as if physically drawing himself back from the edge that he had looked over. "What about the attack on the commander? Any clue what brought that about?"

She nodded. "That's a perfect example of how this delusional fantasy world seems to operate: it distorts an element of reality into something altogether different. It appears that Ahrmant Wyoss previously had a normal awareness of Benjamin Sisko as an authority figure, the tip of DS9's hierarchical pyramid, as it were. The process of the change in that conception can actually be traced in the transcript; it becomes a full-fledged obsession, a monomania centered around a vision of *Sisko* as the malign universe's controlling deity. In a sense, Wyoss's intended murder of the commander was a desperate attempt at autotherapy; he was trying to cure himself of the perceived evil that had taken over his psyche."

Bashir had enough psychiatric experience to recognize the

pattern: a spiral whose turns moved claustrophobically tighter and tighter, until the inevitable lashing-out. Without intervention, the result was always some form of death . . . either for the one undergoing the psychotic collapse, or for the target of his fixated attention.

"And you're sure that these so-called CI modules are the source of the psychosis?" He pointed to the rectangular black boxes arrayed on the workbench. "After all, even if Odo has established that Wyoss and the others were all frequent users of the altered holosuites, it's still remotely possible that it was only a coincidence. Or their attraction to the holosuites was a consequence, rather than a cause, of their mental aberrations. We could waste a lot of valuable time here, if the epidemic's triggering agent is actually something for which we should still be looking."

"A valid concern, Doctor, but at this point I estimate the chances of finding any other source as being well below operational significance." Dax turned the larger computer panel on the bench toward him. "I created a simulation of a functioning holosuite and then downloaded the additional programming from one of the modules into it. With the run time accelerated by a factor of ten, the culminating effects of the CI technology could be seen relatively quickly. Even the most benign holosuite programs are subsumed into a toxic psychological environment. And that effect is consistent, no matter what the initial programming might be; these modules have a defining orientation, what might be termed a constant gravitational pull toward that dark experiential universe. The one that Ahrmant Wyoss is in right now."

"The question is, how much damage has he suffered already? Computer, give me a visual scan on the subject Wyoss." He saw on the panel's screen an overhead view of the isolation chamber, with the unconscious figure still in restraints. To all appearances, the man now seemed peaceably asleep. "Vital indicators." Across the bottom of the screen, the lines tracing the subject's respiratory and cerebral functions appeared.

"I wish that were our only concern," said Dax. "But it's not. Odo informed me that there were others who were exposed to the altered holosuites. The effects upon them, and the consequences for the station, will need to be determined. What actions we take will depend upon—"

"There's something wrong here." Bashir tapped the screen with his fingertip. "This brain-wave trace—there's something funny about it."

Dax looked over his shoulder. "The monitors are set to sound an alarm if there's any crisis, such as a stroke."

"That's not it. This is something happening below the physiological threshold. Look at how smooth the wave's become; there's no jags or spikes to it, no irregularities at all. It's all just steady-state, like a sine wave with no modulation." He turned away from the panel. "Come on, we'd better take a hands-on look at him."

The isolation chamber was only a few meters away from the lab. Within seconds, Bashir was bending over the raised pallet, drawing back the subject's eyelids with his fingertips, as Dax watched.

"Pupil dilation seems normal. There's some level of cerebral activity going on, but . . ." Bashir glanced behind him. "Give him some more of the drug."

They both stood back and waited, the minutes freezing into silence.

Dax shook her head. "He should have started talking by now."

"I don't think he's going to." Bashir stepped forward; he brushed the hair back from the subject's sweating brow. "He's gone. Wherever he was, he's found his own way out."

* * *

Just as Quark finished pouring a drink and setting it with a flourish before one of his customers, *Deep Space Nine*'s chief of security stepped behind the bar and grabbed the Ferengi by the collar.

"Let's go." Odo had lifted his startled quarry off his feet. "We have a *lot* of talking to do." He began dragging Quark toward the end of the bar and the private booths beyond.

"Hey—" The customer pointed to the drink, a frothing blue concoction. "I haven't paid for this yet."

"It's on the house," growled Odo.

"No, it's not!" Quark's natural instincts overcame his panic. "I'll be right back—"

Odo slammed the Ferengi down in a booth and drew the security curtain. Quark shrank back as the security chief loomed over him from the other side of the table. "Now you can tell me everything you should have told me to begin with."

"What?" Confusion tightened Quark's voice to a squeak. "I don't know what you're talking about." He peered anxiously through the translucent curtain; the bar's patrons could be seen leaning toward each other and buzzing about this interesting event. "What are people going to *say,* your hauling me in here like this . . ."

"I did you a favor." Odo sat back in the booth, his unamused gaze pinning the Ferengi. "Anything less gentle would only have triggered the suspicions, among your less-than-savory companions, that you're always worrying about. This way, they'll merely think you've run afoul of the law—again—and thus incurred my wrath. I'm sure this will make you even more trustworthy in their eyes. Or as much as any of you ever trust one another."

"That's a fine way to speak to an honest businessman." Quark ignored Odo's snort of disgust, as he straightened his jacket, his wounded dignity reassembling itself. "I'd lodge a complaint about some of your patently biased remarks, if I thought it would do any good."

"You'll have a lot more to complain about, if you don't tell me what you know."

Quark sighed wearily. "About what?"

"An individual named McHogue."

A few seconds of silence went by. Odo detected a minute contraction of the dark pupils at the centers of Quark's eyes.

"Never heard of him," said Quark at last. He made a show of racking his memory, looking up at a corner of the booth, then back to Odo with an apologetic expression. "Sorry, the name doesn't ring a bell for me."

"Now, that *is* odd." Odo's voice was uncharacteristically gentle and thoughtful for a moment; then it turned to steel again. "Inasmuch as the Starfleet criminal-investigation files have records of your business dealings with this certain McHogue, going back fifteen years before your arrival here at DS9."

"Oh." Quark turned on his attempt at an ingratiating smile. "Oh, *that* McHogue. Well, my dear Odo . . ." He spread his hands apart. "I meet so *many* people in my line of work—as do *you*. We can't be expected to remember them all, can we?"

"So you only had some minor connection with this person?"

"Who knows?" Quark shrugged. "Perhaps we went in together on a Trilantine lottery ticket. Some small thing like that. It's all lost in the proverbial mists of time, I'm afraid." He slid toward the booth's exit. "Now, if you'll allow me to return to my customers . . ."

Odo reached over and hauled him back by his lapel. With his other hand he took out a data padd and with a press of his thumb brought up a screenful of information. "According to the files, you and this McHogue were equal partners in an Arcturan chartered corporation that was found to be selling worthless stock certificates to the natives of several nondeveloped planets—"

"Now, wait a minute. We *told* those people that there were risks involved in any financial investment—"

"So, stock fraud; charges were dropped upon seizure of the corporation's assets and a pledge by the principals not to return to the Arcturus system."

"As if I'd ever want to." Quark looked grumpy.

"Let's see, what else do we have . . ." Odo pulled up another screen on the data padd. "Quark and McHogue, joint ownership of a transit-station bar that was determined to be a front for various smuggling operations; a shared indictment on tech-running charges—now, that's interesting. I might want to look into that a little deeper, given the nature of the case I'm currently investigating. Those charges were quashed on a technicality. . . ."

"Why is it that when people like me are found innocent, people like you always say it's 'on a technicality'?"

Odo didn't look up from the data padd. "That's because, as we both know, there is the law . . . and then there are the lawyers. What else . . ." He slowly shook his head. "This is a *very* long list, Quark. Impressive in its own way. You've been a busy person over the years—but then Ferengi are noted for their industrious personalities, aren't they? I'm amazed that you were able to find a non-Ferengi partner who was able to keep up with all your energy." He laid the data padd down. "Is the point I wish to make sufficiently clear to you now? Let's just say that if we were to go into a courtroom, and you made this claim of barely knowing our mysterious McHogue, you'd quickly be found guilty of perjury."

Each detail from the files had hammered Quark farther down in his seat. "Give me a break," he pleaded. "All right, I knew the man—all right, all right, I did business with him, even—but all that was *years* ago."

"I assume that the two of you must have had some sort of falling-out. I'm not surprised; it would be difficult to imagine anyone who could stay hooked up with you for very long, Quark."

The Ferengi seized on the security chief's remark. "That's right," he said quickly. "A big, *big* falling-out. Why, we wouldn't have anything to do with each other now if our lives depended upon it."

"Is that so?" Odo mulled over the statement for a few seconds. "Then you certainly shouldn't have any reluctance about providing information against someone who's no longer your partner, but has actually become your competitor."

"What do you mean?"

"Don't waste my time, Quark. Let's just say there's a certain matter of the holosuites that you run here on the Promenade, and a number of holosuites elsewhere in the station that are not yours. That make your operation look hygienic by comparison."

"Oh." Quark's expression turned glum. "You know about those, huh?"

"You were the one who as much as complained to me about the 'unfair competition' they represented to your own enterprises."

"I did? Well, in that case—" Quark's face brightened. "Complaint withdrawn. I've decided that unrestricted free enterprise is, after all, the Ferengi way. Now, if you'll excuse me . . ." He started to scoot out again, but stopped when he saw Odo's hand coming for him.

"This is a little more serious than your business problems." Odo laid his hand flat on the table between them. "Two things you should consider: first, there's been an epidemic of murder aboard the station, and we've determined that it's related both to those altered holosuites and to your former partner McHogue."

Quark looked puzzled. "What's the second thing?"

"The second thing is that I've reached the end of my patience with you. Start talking."

"All right, all right." Quark took a deep breath. "There's somebody aboard the station and he's been walking around, claiming to be McHogue. He even came here to my bar and talked to me."

"What about?"

"His latest scheme. It was something to do with the holosuites; he wanted to use mine for whatever he had up his sleeve. Told me he'd cut me in on the profits. But I didn't even want to hear whatever it was he'd cooked up; I eighty-sixed him right out of the place. He gave me the creeps."

"Why?"

Quark leaned across the table. "Because he's *not* McHogue. I should know, right? I spent a lot of time with the real one. I don't know who this person is, but he's no former partner of mine."

Odo frowned. "But he does look like McHogue. Correct?"

"So? That sort of thing can always be faked." A thin smile lifted the corners of Quark's mouth. "You have to remember, my dear Odo, that Ferengi can see into other people's souls—well, a certain part of them, at least. It's what makes us so good at what we do. I looked into this pseudo-McHogue, and there was *nothing* that I recognized. There wasn't even anything that I wanted to *deal* with."

"That's an unusual display of morality on your part."

"I have my standards." Quark drew himself up, as if offended. "Of practicality, if nothing else. This imposter didn't fill me in on what his plans were for the holosuites—I cut him off before he could even *start* to tell me. And now it appears as if my assessment of this person—whoever he is—was right." Quark shook his head. "I mean, after all—a murder epidemic? Turning your patrons into killers—how can you build up any repeat business that way? Let alone what'll happen to your *other* customers."

For a moment, Odo was silent, trying to piece this new datum in with he had already discovered. "There was no visual ID of McHogue in the Starfleet files—"

"Isn't it amazing what can be accomplished with a little bribery?"

He ignored that. "Can you give a description of McHogue? Or this person claiming to be him?"

"Oh, I can do better than that." Quark reached into a pocket of his coat; on the tabletop he deposited a small, glimmering data disk. "As you're no doubt aware, I'm in the habit of recording everyone who comes into my establishment here—for security purposes."

"And the occasional blackmail."

"If people lead such messy lives that they wind up embarrassed to be seen patronizing a harmless entertainment facility, that's their problem. In this case, I think you'll appreciate the results of my precautions." Quark pushed the disk across the table. "I was debating with myself whether I should turn this over to you. Fortunately, my sense of responsibility, as one of DS9's leading citizens, seems to have prevailed."

"Fortunately," said Odo dryly. He picked the disk up between his thumb and forefinger and studied it.

"I think you'll find everything you need on there. So I'll just be . . . running along . . . if that's all right with you."

Deep in thought, Odo made no reply.

"I'm going now. Always a pleasure having a chat with you . . ."

Odo glanced over as the booth's security curtain fell back into place. Through it, he could see the Ferengi heading at high speed back to the security of his bar.

Alone in the booth, Odo fed the disk into his data padd. The only thing on it was a video clip some fifteen seconds long. The concealed lens near the entrance to Quark's establishment had caught the individual in question; he had actually stopped, looked up, and smiled, as though he had known the camera was there.

Odo didn't recognize the man. A lean, vulpine face and a relatively tall, wide-shouldered physique clad in somber black; the partnership with the diminutive Quark must have been a study in contrasts.

He froze the image on the data padd's screen, then magnified it, drawing in upon the right eye.

There had been one item of identification in the Starfleet files on McHogue. "Computer," he said aloud. "Call up and compare retinal patterns, onscreen subject and name index McHogue, security office working file area."

The screen divided, showing a circle of distinctive markings on either side. Even before the computer spoke, he knew.

"Confirm match between patterns," came the measured voice. "Onscreen subject identified as McHogue."

"Possibility of error?"

"Below estimation threshold. Not statistically significant."

Odo blanked the screen. Another interesting datum: Quark, with his needle-like Ferengi gaze, had looked into this individual's mercenary soul . . . and hadn't recognized him. His old business partner.

There was a lot to gnaw on here. He nodded slowly to himself; as disturbed as he was by the threat to his DS9, a certain pleasurable tension came with such a tangled knot to pick apart. And even more satisfaction to come, when all the strands would be laid out neatly before him.

But that was still in the future. Right now there was another job to take care of, a duty that he was ashamed that he had put off. Something that he should have already told Commander Sisko, no matter the pressure of time on both of them. He should have forced the commander to listen to him. . . .

All the while he had been digging information out of Quark,

it had still been at the back of his mind. Before anything else could happen, before he could concentrate his full attention on the epidemic of murder, this needed to be laid to rest.

Odo picked up the data padd and drew aside the security curtain. It would be only a matter of minutes before he was at the Ops deck and in Sisko's private office.

Now he was alone.

His chief of security had departed, after having caught him as he'd left Ops and coming back with him to his private living quarters. Sisko sat leaning forward on the couch, his forearms against his knees, hands knotted together; the surrounding lights had been dimmed to a soft glow. He sat and thought about what Odo had told him.

"Is it really that urgent?" Sisko felt a pang of remorse for having asked that. "I really need to get some rest."

"I think it is," Odo had replied. He had insisted—rightly so—on getting away from the crowded Ops deck, where the other crew members might inadvertently listen in.

So it had been here, in this little world, as much of a home and refuge as was possible to create inside DS9, that Odo had informed him of what he had discovered during his investigation.

"It's about your son Jake." Odo had been forthright, even blunt, in telling him. There had been no other way. "I've extracted the list of frequent users of the altered holosuites. And Jake is one of them."

His thought processes had seemed to take a step back, operating at a safe remove from the world. "Are you sure?"

Odo had nodded. "I had O'Brien check out the device he constructed for me, that reads out the access codes. The device is working perfectly; the data I've obtained with it is reliable."

"I see." He remembered glancing over his shoulder, toward the corridor that led to his son's bedroom; Jake was already asleep there. Despite all his pledges to himself, he had again missed having dinner or spending any other time with him. "How bad is it?"

"Your son's usage of the altered holosuites appears to still be in a preliminary stage; the pattern we've seen, of increasingly frequent use, has only just started to accelerate in his case. There's time . . ."

Time, mused Sisko. The memory of Odo's words faded away. There was always time; there had always been time enough. If he had remembered what was important.

Odo had said something to him about being sorry, and had left him to his thoughts. And his being alone.

If Jake's mother were still alive . . .

Inside his head, he closed a door firmly against the empty rooms that those words led to. He had spent enough late-shift hours in there already, and would spend more, he knew. It was unavoidable; she had been the only woman he had loved. But now he had to think just of their son.

He looked over to the side of the room. The wooden crate that Kira had brought from Bajor had been moved there; it sat mute in the shadows, still unopened. That was another person gone from him, whose advice he could have used. It seemed, in moments like this, that the function of time itself was to carry away, one by one, all those closest to him. . . .

Perhaps that had already started to happen to Jake.

A current of anger rose inside him, enough to force his fists clenched. Seconds passed before he sat back and used his comm badge to reach the security chief.

"Constable—were all of those CI modules removed from the holosuites in question?"

"Actually, they weren't, Commander." Odo's reply was clipped and professional. "We left one module on-line with a security monitor attached, in case we needed to investigate its effects in situ, as it were. As long as the sector is sealed off, I felt the chance of any further harm being done was minimal."

"Thank you." He broke the connection.

For a moment, Sisko stood outside Jake's bedroom, listening in the dark to his son's breathing. Then he turned away and headed for the living quarters' door.

As commander of the station, he had no problem in entering the restricted sector—with a simple computer override. The small light on the access panel told him that the last holosuite along the corridor was the one that had been left functional. He peeled away Odo's security seal and dropped it on the floor beside him. With a press of his finger, the door slid open and he stepped inside—

To a sunlit world. The doorway closed behind him, completing the holosuite's illusion. A warm summer wind moved across a field of yellow grasses; the barely perceptible scent of cool running water came from beyond the dense stand of trees some apparent distance farther on. He had been here before, with Jake; he had set the holosuite's programming for what he knew was one of his son's favorites. The path's loose earth and broken stalks—or the perfectly contrived sensation of them—moved beneath his steps, the sun overhead hot enough to bring beads of sweat onto his brow.

In the woods' darkness, he found the first wrong thing. The whitening bones of a cat, the dry fragments spread obscenely apart by coarse twine looped around the nearest tree trunks. The blood had long ago soaked into the leaf-covered ground, but there was still a gut-tightening sense of pain and death in the shade's motionless air. The cat's skull bared its teeth in a silent howl.

What Dax and Bashir had stated in their preliminary report was true. This was how the CI modules worked, taking the normal, benign holosuite programming and warping it into something different. There had been no reason to doubt his officers, but he had to see it for himself. He could only wonder how far it went, what he might find on the other side of the perceived horizon.

He walked on. Back into the sunlight, to the creek's edge. The water purled against the rocks, glinting achingly bright. When he shaded his eyes with his hand, he found more death. Less than a meter away, the body of a man sprawled facedown, fingertips clawing into the muddy bank.

Kneeling down, Sisko turned the body over. And found himself gazing at his own face, sightless eyes fixed upon the sun.

Somebody was watching him; he could feel it. He looked up and saw a man with arms folded across his chest, eyes dark as holes into the night on the other side of this world. A mocking smile twisted one side of his narrow face.

"Who are you?" Sisko let the corpse with his face slip from his grasp.

"Don't you know?" The figure's voice was a parody of gentleness. "I'm McHogue. I live here."

The rage he had felt before burst like a red flower in his vision, blinding him as he leaped forward, hands outstretched for the throat of the image—

Which vanished. His fingers scraped hard into the wet earth and rounded stones at the creek's edge.

He drew back onto his haunches. His hands slowly curled open; the illusion of water, mingled with his own blood, fell into the stream and was borne from his sight.

McHOGUE

CHAPTER
6

FROM AN ARCHED, OPEN WINDOW OF THE TEMPLE, SHE COULD see the runabout *Mekong*, which had brought her home once more. The rough stone, set into place centuries ago and ornamented with the carved tracery of a long-dead artisan, contrasted with the smoothly functional lines of the craft.

"We did not expect to see you again, so soon after your last visit." One of the acolytes stood beside Kira; they had both come to the tower to watch the first rays of morning disperse the flocks of birds that nested beneath the compound's tiled eaves. The last of the fluttering specks were even now disappearing into the vastness of the golden sky. "Was there something else of the Kai's that we forgot to give you, that you wanted?"

"No—" Kira shook her head and smiled sadly at the acolyte. "I'm afraid the only thing any of us want of Kai Opaka is for her to be with us again."

"You speak truly. For her to have answered the call of the Prophets . . . did we not know that it would happen someday? Such being the nature of time, for even the wisest among us. And yet we find ourselves weeping like children, at the fulfillment of the inevitable." The acolyte gazed across the dew-wet fields surrounding the temple. "And as always with unguided children, we are in danger of wandering off and becoming lost."

The acolyte's words touched a nerve of apprehension in Kira. "What do you mean? The faith . . . our people's faith . . . it can't be lost."

"Perhaps not." The acolyte kept her hands tucked inside the heavy sleeves of her robes. "At least not while it remains in the heart of one such as yourself. A fire that can light worlds is contained in a single spark. But as for the people of Bajor . . ." She fell silent for a moment. "These are difficult times."

"We've been through some pretty tough times already. The Cardassians—"

"Ah, but those times were a forge. The oppressors could never have destroyed us, but their efforts to do so made something harder and more resilient of us, like a sword blade hammered upon an anvil. You yourself, child, were born of that process. All that was taken from you—your home, your family, all that would have been a comfort in your most lightless hours—all that was given back to you in a different form. So that you could serve Bajor and its people."

If that's true . . . She had heard that simple teaching before, from the Kai herself. Not just redemption through suffering, but apotheosis: a transformation into another order of being, carbon to diamond. But if it was true, if all she'd lost had been restored to her, she had no way of explaining the emptiness she felt inside herself. Except by admitting the possibility of failure, unworthiness; the blade forged in the purifying fire had broken at the first blow, the diamond had shattered like false glass.

She had told no one, not even Kai Opaka, of the doubts that came to her in sleepless nights, along with the bad dreams and memories. The commander and all her fellow officers aboard *Deep Space Nine*—none of them had ever suspected. Or would ever, as long as she could keep her perfect mask and armor in place.

"Now," continued the acolyte, "the people of Bajor face trials that are as dangerous as those that came before, but are of greater subtlety. When the Cardassians ruled us, we knew who our enemies were, and we knew by what sacrifices our freedom would be achieved. But now that we have that freedom in our hands . . ." The acolyte watched the last straggling bird dart toward the east. "We find our bitterest enemies in those of our own blood, those for whom such a little while ago we would have given our own lives."

"It's harder now. To know what to do." Kira laid her fingertips against the rough stone sill. "We *all* wanted the Cardassians gone, or in their graves. Even the Kai, I think, could envision them being . . . *translated,* so to speak, to another plane of existence. But with the Cardassians gone at last, we have to face the fact that we don't all want the same things for Bajor."

"Is that not what you have learned, Kira? That one may be a Bajoran, a sharer of the same blood and past, and still disagree—even disagree violently—with another Bajoran?" The acolyte smiled gently. "And if that be so, and if among those who disagree some may be right and some may be wrong about what should be done—then it raises the possibility that it is *you* who are in error."

Kira laughed, short and mirthlessly. "As if I hadn't thought about *that* already. Everything I do—everything any one of us does—we could all be messing things up in a big way."

"The cynical among us might say that that is why, in retrospect, our oppression seems such a state of grace. When one is a victim, there's no doubt that one is in the right."

"I don't know. . . ." Kira shook her head, fighting off a familiar weariness. "Maybe we should ask the Cardassians to come back—that would solve all these new problems, at least. Then we could just go on suffering and struggling in glorious martyrdom. We did it for so long, is it any wonder we never learned how to be good at anything else?"

"Now you're the cynic," chided the acolyte. "It ill-suits you. What shall we do if you are lost to us in that way, when you are Bajor's link to the worlds beyond our sky?"

"They don't even know I'm here. I didn't tell anyone at *Deep Space Nine* where I was going, I didn't submit a flight plan before I left; I just went. And came here."

The acolyte nodded. "We knew that your return must have come of your own initiative. The station notifies us beforehand of any official visit." The acolyte turned to study her. "What we don't know is your purpose in coming this time."

"I'm not even sure I know myself." The sun's edge had risen over the horizon, enough to bring a smokelike mist up from the damp fields. "There's some other, completely unrelated crisis going on aboard the station; right now, Commander Sisko's attention is completely taken up by that. And frankly, if he were burnt out on dealing with every little twist and turn in Bajoran politics, I wouldn't blame him. He must feel sometimes like a nursemaid to a whole planetful of squalling brats, every one of them trying to climb into his lap."

"So you decided to take care of this latest problem all by yourself."

"I suppose." Kira shrugged. "This business with the Severalty Front—it's too important to let it slide, and then just hope that we can pick up the pieces later. There might not *be* a later, if Aur and the other Front leaders get their way. At least not as far as Bajoran involvement with the Federation is concerned."

The acolyte raised an eyebrow. "And you feel that, by yourself, you can change all that?"

"There was one person who kept it from happening before."

"Yes—but you're not Kai Opaka."

Kira sighed. "Don't think I'm not painfully aware of *that*. I don't have her saintly patience, for one thing—I'm afraid that if I start talking with some of these people, and they don't immediately see things my way, I'm going to be sorely tempted to just clop them over their heads."

A smile from the acolyte: "I don't think that would accomplish what you desire. Though perhaps if you persist in this endeavor, you will learn much; I doubt if even the Kai was born with all the virtues she possessed before she answered the call of the Prophets."

"The problem is," said Kira glumly, "I don't think I was born with even the *ability* to learn patience." She stepped back from the arched window. The morning birds had long since vanished, and the shadows stretching from the horizon had crept back into themselves. As much as the temple's quiet had restored a measure of strength to her soul, she knew that the time to leave had come. There were people in Bajor's capital whom she needed to see, words to be spoken, and—with any luck—negotiations to be made.

"Perhaps not." The acolyte turned toward the worn steps that led back to the temple's central courtyard. "But you have something that will help, despite your failings."

"What's that?" She followed the other woman down the twisting stone.

"You have our hopes. And the blessing of that one who is no longer with us."

"And why do you think the general would be interested in seeing you?"

The man behind the wooden desk was one of those, she knew, who had never had power in his life—until now. A little taste of it had turned him into a petty bureaucratic tyrant; he had the power to make life difficult for others, to say yes or no to anyone who had business with the truly powerful ones above him. That savoring of that much authority had intoxicated him; the pleasurable effect could be seen in his glittering eyes.

Kira didn't have time to waste with him. "I think that if you'll let General Aur know I'm here, he will in fact be *greatly* interested in seeing me. I am, after all, second-in-command of the *Deep Space Nine* station and Bajor's main liaison with the Federation's Starfleet."

"Ah." The young man did not appear impressed; he barely concealed a sneer. "The *famous* Major Kira. A true luminary —of the *past* regime. I take it that your appearance here is as part of an official mission to the Severalty Front?"

The building to which she had come was no more than a hundred meters away from the council chambers of the Bajoran provisional government; it had once held the offices of one of the Cardassians' puppet organizations, a sham workers' committee that did little more than give rubber-stamp approval to whatever murderous conditions the occupiers dictated. The oppressive atmosphere that had filled the corridors, equal parts toadying obsequiousness and seething hatred for the hands that held the other ends of the leashes, had been replaced by a bustling energy. The confidence in the faces Kira saw around her was only a few degrees away from blind fanaticism.

"No—" She shook her head. "I came here of my own initiative. I represent no Federation interests. Except, of course, the friendship and goodwill they've shown toward the Bajoran people."

"Indeed." The sneer froze sourly in place. "How *kind* of the Federation to have our welfare lodged so firmly in its heart. And of course history bears out how much we can depend upon the charitable feelings of offworlders."

Kira felt her temper boiling up inside her; with an effort, she held it in check, not wanting to give the officious little twit in front of her the satisfaction of seeing that his needling remarks had hit their target. Plus, as much as she could anticipate the momentary pleasure of wrapping her hands around his neck and plucking him from the chair like pulling a sun melon from its vine, she recognized that the action wouldn't be likely to accomplish what she wanted in the long run.

Patience, she told herself. *Emulate those wiser than you.* It sounded good in theory, but putting it into practice was proving difficult.

"Look," she said, leaning forward to plant her hands on the desktop. "I know that General Aur is a busy man; I can assure you that my own schedule is not exactly filled with leisure time. You're doing your job, and that's fine. I'm sure you get a lot of loose cannons rolling in here and you're supposed to filter them all out. But let's face it: I'm one of the senior officers aboard the DS9 station, and I report directly to Commander Benjamin Sisko regarding Bajoran affairs. The path of communication with Starfleet and the Federation goes through me. One way or another, either now or later, I'm the person that General Aur is going to have to deal with." She heard her voice growing steelier and decided to go with it. "If it's later, he and I will first have an interesting little discussion about how somebody sitting way down the line prevented me from seeing him. If you think General Aur will be happy when I tell him that, then carry on as you have been. If not . . ." She straightened up. "Do I make myself clear?"

The malice remained in the other's expression, though the self-congratulating amusement had withered away. After a few seconds of silence, the man turned to the ancient hard-wired computer terminal on the desk and typed in a few commands. "The general's not in the building at the moment."

"When is he expected to arrive?"

Hand to chin, the man contemplated the screen. "He has a staff briefing at noon. . . ."

"Fine." Kira pulled the terminal around so she could see for herself. "Notify the others that the briefing has been rescheduled for a half hour later. I'll be meeting with the general at noon." She pushed the screen back toward him. "There, that wasn't so hard, now was it?"

As she turned away and strode toward the exit of the Severalty Front's headquarters, she could feel the man's gaze like twin daggers between her shoulder blades.

"Nice work, Kira." A familiar voice sounded beside her. "That pompous little ass has been asking for it for a long time."

She stopped in her tracks, amazed. It had been years since she had last heard the person's slyly edged words.

"Malen—" She couldn't help smiling at him. "I thought you were dead."

"You know what they say about rumors and gross exaggerations." Malen Aldris pushed her forward by the elbow. "May I suggest we keep walking? Before our conversation attracts any undue notice."

Outside, they found an alleyway tavern dark enough for concealment. Something resinous and lethal was served to them in cracked porcelain cups; Malen sipped at his while she scraped her tongue across her front teeth to get rid of the taste. It was on occasions such as this that she appreciated the standards of Quark's establishment back aboard DS9.

"You're looking well, Kira." Malen leaned across the wobbling table to peer at her in the dim light. "You must be getting something to eat on a regular basis these days. In the old days, you were always such a starved little rat."

"Thanks." Her old comrade in the resistance looked older and grayer than she remembered him, his thinning hair reduced to a few snow-white wisps straggling behind his ears.

"The last time I saw you, some distinctly unfriendly people were dragging you away to be shot—"

"Oh, that." He waved a dismissive hand. "You know, I can't even remember anymore which side it was that wanted me dead, the Cardassians or the Bajorans. Maybe it was a joint effort on their parts."

"So you can imagine how surprised I am to see you again."

"By now," said Malen, smiling, "you should never be surprised."

She knew it was unlikely that Malen Aldris would ever be listed as one of the heroes of the Bajoran resistance; that designation was usually reserved for those like General Aur, who had no hesitations about bringing about the deaths of others, and little apparent regard for their own lives. Malen valued his intact skin too highly, and was too squeamish about violence, to earn any medals. Not that he would have wanted them; any recognition would have interfered with the clandestine nature of his affairs. During the Cardassian occupation, Malen had specialized in ferreting out warehouse managers, distribution supervisors, military logisticians, anyone who was involved in shifting Bajor's increasingly meager food production from one spot to another, and cajoling, bribing, or otherwise inducing them to look the other way while a precious trickle of supplies was diverted to the resistance fighters. As much skin-and-bones as she had been during that time, she and the comrades beside her would have been actual whitening skeletons without Malen's efforts. The brain inside the overly prominent dome of his skull had been skilled at juggling figures, delivery dates, inventory databases —essentially making two sacks of meal appear where only one existed. Unfortunately for that brain and the hunched, fidgeting body attached to it, such activities involved close, even friendly-seeming contact with a large number of Cardassians, a state that was subject to being interpreted as collaboration with the enemy by less well informed members of the resistance. Kira wondered how fast he'd had to talk to escape the firing line.

She also had to wonder what he had been doing at the headquarters of the Severalty Front.

"Were you trying as well to get in to see General Aur?" She was willing to assume that he had some scheme of his own in motion.

"Why should I have to try? I see Aur practically every day, whether I want to or not." Malen sat back in the rickety chair. "I'm the head economics adviser for the Severalty Front's shadow cabinet."

"Oh." She hadn't expected an answer like that. "You're working for them."

"Of course I am—the Front's where the action is right now. And I'm at a pretty high level, Kira; when the Front comes to power, I'm in line to run the entire Bajoran treasury."

"I see. Not *if,* but *when,* is it?"

Malen shrugged. "Would I be hooked up with them if that weren't the case? Let's face it, Aur's got all the trump cards. The provisional government is falling apart; if they last out the year, it'll be a miracle. And where there's a vacuum, something is bound to rush in and fill it. That's what Aur and the Severalty Front are ready for."

Kira nodded slowly. "You know, there is something else that I'm surprised at. You always used to think everything through so carefully, Malen. Have you considered that there won't be much of a Bajoran treasury for you to run, after your new government breaks off all contact with the Federation? You'll be lucky if you have two minim coins left to rub together."

"Given your position with Starfleet, Kira, I could hardly have expected you to be jumping up and down with joy at the prospect of the Severalty Front setting its program into effect. But you needn't be worried about *me;* let's just say that I've got a good deal more inside information than you do, at least about Bajor's economic potential. The Federation might be a bit discomfited when it finds out what Aur and his advisers have up their sleeves. The new Minister of Trade . . ." Malen picked up his cup and took a hefty swallow.

She peered sharply at him. "Minister of Trade? Who's that going to be?"

"Hmm . . . this stuff's stronger than I remember it being." He gazed into the empty cup. "Has the unfortunate consequence of loosening tongues, doesn't it?" He waggled a finger at her. "You'll have to pump somebody else for secrets, I'm afraid. Didn't care for yours?" Malen reached across and took her cup, draining it before setting it back down in front of her. He pushed back his chair. "Kira, I'm really sorry we wound up on opposite sides on this one—but I suppose it couldn't be avoided. Good seeing you."

"Same here." She watched as he walked, a bit unsteadily, toward the door and the bright daylight beyond it. Only when she looked before herself, eyes readjusting to the tavern's gloom, did she notice the tiny scrap of paper stuck to the side of the cup.

Carefully, so that no one would notice, she peeled the slip back with one fingernail.

WE'RE BEING WATCHED AND LISTENED TO. Below those words were a hastily scrawled address, one that she recognized as being in one of the city's more disreputable quarters, and the notation 7 P.M. Looking around the tavern's dimly lit interior, she saw two disheveled men hunched over their drinks, their sidelong gazes still directed toward the doorway.

Unobtrusively, she rolled the paper into a tiny ball and slipped it into her uniform pocket. Getting up from the table, she knew that the time was already close to noon and her appointment with General Aur.

* * *

She was out of breath by the time she reached the top of the last flight of steps. The building was close enough to the edge of the city to have sustained damage during one of the resistance's skirmishes against the Cardassians; a chill night wind billowed through the tattered canvas that had been nailed over a missing section of wall. Shards of broken stone mingled with the years' accumulated dust.

That does it, thought Kira as she waited for her pulse to slow back down. *No more taking the turbolift everywhere I go aboard the station—at least until I'm back in shape.*

"There was a time when you could have sprinted all the way up here." Malen had read her thoughts; he peered at her from around the edge of a door cobbled together from scavenged wood planks. Yellow light fluttered from the lamp he held in his hand.

"That's what desk jobs will do for you." Kira took a deep breath and straightened up.

"Come on, get inside." He drew back into the dark behind the door.

She looked around as Malen set the lamp down on a low table. "A little shabby for the future head of the Bajoran treasury."

"I've done business out of worse places—you should know that." He glanced over his shoulder at her. "How did your meeting with Aur go?"

A shrug. "As I'd come to expect it would. I came ready to talk sense to these people, and no one is having any of it. Aur and the others may or may not have something special up their sleeves, but they're certainly acting as if they do."

"They've got a lot of reason for being self-confident." Malen fussed with the lamp, to keep the flame from extinguishing in the oil below. "The Severalty Front can rightfully say that history—plus a lot of other things—is on its side."

"You sound like a true believer."

"Me?" He shook his head. "I've gotten to the age where I can justify being interested solely in my own welfare. I've already done enough for Bajor, remember? Though I suppose for someone like you, there's no such thing as enough."

She ignored the last comment. "If all that were true, Malen, you wouldn't be talking to me now. Not in a dirty little hiding hole like this."

"Let's just say I like to be prepared for any eventuality. Such as the remote chance that the Severalty Front *won't* pull off all that it's planning."

"A remote chance that'll be brought a little closer by what you're going to tell me now."

He said nothing, but smiled thinly over his shoulder at her before turning back to make a final adjustment to the lamp.

The yellow radiance grew a fraction brighter, enough to send their shadows wavering over the ash-smeared walls. Kira watched as he paced across the narrow chamber. "It's this Minister of Trade—the one that Aur's going to install in office once the Front takes power. All their plans hinge on that one individual." Malen appeared to grow more agitated as he walked, rubbing a bony fist into the palm of his other hand. "These are things that can scarcely be credited. If they didn't need me to keep the books, I doubt if I would have been told anything at all." He stopped in front of the door and turned toward her. "The new Minister of Trade—"

There weren't any more words. But instead, a rose that blossomed from his chest—it looked like that to Kira, though she already knew what it really was, and had dived toward the corner of the room to get out of the line of fire. Crouching there, she watched as the last consciousness faded from Malen's eyes, one hand trembling as though in wonderment against the jagged splinters of his breastbone. A corpse, that looked like a bundle of rags with an empty face attached, crumpled to the floor.

A figure that Kira had last seen sitting behind a desk at the Severalty Front's headquarters stepped over the body and into the room. The functionary who had tried to keep her from seeing General Aur held an archaic particle weapon poised in his hand. Kira had used identical sidearms when she had fought in the resistance; the familiar, sharp explosion of its thrust charge still echoed in her ears.

"Don't move." The functionary turned the muzzle of the gun toward her. He glanced behind himself at Malen's corpse, then brought the resulting thin smile around in her direction. "Surely you're not surprised—didn't he say that everything the two of you did was being watched? And knowing that, to try and set up this little rendezvous . . ." He shrugged. "Very foolish. Or perhaps your old comrade had grown tired and had developed a bit of a death wish. And this way it could happen the way he thought it should have a long time ago."

"Spare me the philosophizing." She could feel the muscles coiling inside her limbs as her brain raced, calculating some way around the weapon's small, lethal black hole. "Thoughtful murderers disgust me."

"Indeed. I hadn't expected such tender sensibilities from one of your reputation, Major. But I assure you that this man's death comes about with genuine regret on my part. Malen's skills would have been very useful for the purposes of the Front's coming government. I should know; I was the one who compiled our dossier on his . . . *interesting* financial activities during the Cardassian occupation."

"I see." Kira carefully gauged the distance between herself and the weapon. "You're obviously not the doorkeeper flunky I took you to be." If she could keep him talking, there was always a chance of distracting him, breaking the concentration that kept the weapon unwaveringly pointed toward her.

"No—and I'm neither inexperienced or foolish enough for you to have a chance of succeeding at what you're so obviously thinking about." The functionary's smile vanished. "You forget how widespread the resistance was, across the face of Bajor; there were elements—groups, organizations, even individuals such as myself—of which you would have had absolutely no awareness. Just as now you have no real idea of the Severalty Front's intentions."

"They must not be too admirable, if you didn't want Malen telling me what they are."

The functionary hazarded a glance at the corpse, his gaze immediately flicking back to Kira before she could move. "Unfortunately, for all his potential worth to the Front, there had been some questions all along about the depth of his loyalties—a logical consequence, given the nature of his rather shifty reputation. Believe me, Major, if it hadn't been for my own intervention on his behalf, he would have been dead long before now." The functionary shrugged, causing the muzzle of the weapon to tilt slightly, then settle into aim again. "But I guess I was guilty of mere sentimentality. I was reluctant to believe that all members of the resistance's old guard, such as Malen and yourself, should be eliminated out of hand—or at least not until it could be proven that they couldn't be brought around to our way of seeing things." He gestured with the weapon. "Please stand up, Major. You must be uncomfortable."

Now she was able to look straight into the functionary's eyes. "If you're planning the same fate for me, you might want to remember my technical status as a liaison to Starfleet. It's unlikely that you'd be able to conceal my death for very long—or eventually being held responsible for it. And Starfleet does not regard the elimination of its personnel lightly."

"I admire your self-possession in what many others would consider to be an intimidating situation." The thin smile returned to his face. "But how Starfleet feels about the brushing aside of, shall we say, impediments to the course of Bajoran progress is not something that concerns me. Your Commander Sisko and all the rest of Starfleet are at the end of a leash held by the Federation. Only the utterly naive are ignorant of the fact that both murder and the toleration of murder are often required in the interests of diplomacy."

Kira's gaze grew harder and narrower. "I'm beginning to think you got these annoying little lectures from someone else. This all sounds like General Aur to me."

"Whatever. It's true, no matter whose words they might be."

"Aur better hope he's got one hell of a trump card stashed away." Kira's muscles tensed, ready to feint down and to one side, then knock away the functionary's weapon hand with a forearm blow. "If he's going to take on the whole Federation . . ."

"At this point, it doesn't really matter." The functionary lowered the weapon, its muzzle pointing harmlessly to the floor. "Perhaps later. Fortunately for yourself, you present no threat to the plans of the Severalty Front. Even if Malen had been able to tell you what he knew, what he had found out—that wouldn't have changed anything. Because it's too late now." He stowed the weapon in a pouch slung from his uniform's belt. "You're free to go." He stepped back and gestured toward the doorway. "As, in fact, you always were."

She heard the explosions then. In the distance, trembling the night air. But close enough that she could hear the shouting voices mingled with them, somewhere at the city's heart . . .

The old building's stairwell echoed with her running. She came to a halt in the street outside, looking up at the fiery lights slicing open the sky.

Already, the distant shouts had begun to change, to cries of jubilant triumph. She had heard that sound before, when the

108

gears of this world had turned and meshed with each other, when one rule of power had changed and another had begun. *A coup*, she thought. What else could it be?

"We decided not to wait." The functionary stood right behind her. Without turning around, Kira was able to detect the smile in his voice. "And . . . we didn't have to."

CHAPTER
7

HE KNEW THAT THE DOCTOR WOULD ERR ON THE SIDE OF KINDNESS. If he let him; that was why Commander Sisko ordered the station's chief medical officer to tell the truth, no matter what pain and guilt was involved.

"It actually looks pretty good," said Bashir. The two men stood in one of the infirmary's small consulting rooms; on the wall-mounted computer screen was a dense section of the results he had been reviewing when Sisko had entered. "I ran a complete battery of tests on Jake; everything from real-time neural pathway charting and catecholamine receptor indices, to old-fashioned Rorschach inkblots and draw-a-picture sequences. Given the resources we have on board DS9, there aren't any further diagnostic procedures I can administer to him."

Sisko nodded slowly. "And what did you find?" He could hear how grim his own voice sounded, as though the words themselves were laden with the weight that had formed around his heart.

"Commander, I found a healthy young boy." Bashir gazed level into his superior officer's eyes. "Physically and mentally. There's no sign of either the synaptic degeneration or obsessive thought-patterning that we saw with Ahrmant Wyoss and the others. The only indication of negative functioning on your son's part is the apparent frequency increase in use of the altered holosuites—and we only know about that because of the data that Odo was able to extract from the holosuites themselves."

"But, as you say, your diagnostic techniques here *are* limited." He didn't want to give himself hopes that could be cruelly shattered. "There may be more sophisticated tests that would reveal things that you weren't able to detect."

Bashir spread his hands apart. "There's always that possibility, Commander. At one of the sector medical facilities, Jake could be scanned right down to the subatomic level, if anyone thought that it would yield results of any significance. But to undertake such a course is a decision that you'd have to make on your own. You have to weigh the diminishingly small chance of finding something wrong—anything at all—with the risk of producing an iatrogenic condition from the testing procedures. There *are* diagnostic techniques beyond what I've done here, but they can be very long and arduous—and they'd involve sending Jake away from the station. And away from his primary source of emotional support—that's you, Commander. In the absence of any discernible harm that Jake may have suffered from his exposure to these cortical-induction modules, I believe that the greatest therapeutic value would be gained from his staying in contact with his father."

Discernible harm . . . The overly precise words, the technical language into which the chief medical officer so readily lapsed, echo inside Sisko's head. He closed his eyes, trying to sort out the jumble of thoughts he'd carried into this room, that the doctor's advice had failed to disperse. It was so hard to know what to do . . . what would be the best, or only, thing he could decide upon and carry through. The dark meditations that came over him at the end of shifts welled up now—he couldn't stop them—and, with the slow, aching grief that had become so familiar, reminded him how essentially alone he was. Even here, in this brightly lit room, surrounded by the corridors and chambers of *Deep Space Nine*, filled with living intelligences, human and nonhuman alike. Without Jake's mother, his wife, the woman he had loved . . . For a moment, a dizzying near-hallucination swept across him, that the voice and presence of the man standing beside him had vanished into emptiness and silence. That they had all vanished, every voice and gaze; leaving him in the station's hollow shell, enclosed in cold, unfeeling metal and the uninhabited reaches of the stars beyond. Alone in truth, as he'd often felt himself to be.

He drew in a deep breath, as though willing Dr. Bashir back into existence. And the rest: he could sense them again, all the lives aboard the station, moving through the corridors and walkways like the blood of a larger organism. That life, and the smaller ones—DS9's life—those were his responsibility. As long as there were so many depending upon him, he could resist the temptations to which he might otherwise have yielded.

Against all that, however, could be weighed a single small life. His own son.

The doctor hadn't mentioned a third possibility, one that allowed Jake to leave DS9 and go to any Starfleet medical facility that could perform further tests upon him and still remain in contact with his father. . . .

As simple as that, Sisko knew. He would just have to go with the boy. Turn over his command of the station, abandon these duties for the sake of another one—who would blame him if he did that? There were others—weren't there?—who could administer DS9 as well as he could; perhaps better. But Jake only had one father. One parent.

"Commander—" Bashir laid a hand upon Sisko's shoulder. "I know what you're thinking."

He turned his brooding face toward the doctor. "Do you really?"

"If you thought it best to leave the station, to do whatever you thought was necessary for your son's welfare, I'd be the last to advise you not to. But consider this, Commander: *Deep Space Nine* is Jake's home. As much as it is yours now. He's been taken away from so many places, he's lost so many things and people in his short life—do you think it's wise to do that to him once again?"

A brief spark of anger flared inside Sisko. *What do you know about loss, Doctor?*—someone so young and inexperienced in the realities of life. He supposed that was something that had been taught to Bashir in medical school: that omniscient, caring tone, words read off a page from some grief-counseling textbook. . . .

He fought the anger down, letting his hands uncurl from fists, his pulse slowing. In another few seconds, he realized, he might have ripped the doctor's head off—verbally, at least. And pointlessly so; everything Bashir said had been well intentioned. And, even more chastening, it was all very likely true. But still . . .

"You've forgotten something, Doctor." Sisko could hear his own voice as though it were coming from someone else, a creature temporarily bereft of emotions. "I've seen evidence of my son's condition, that doesn't show up in all your scannings and tests. In that holosuite . . . I saw my own death. I saw my murdered corpse lying on the ground."

"An illusion, Commander."

"Oh?" Anger flared again inside him. "An illusion that

couldn't exist at all, unless it reflected something true. Something in Jake. That was *his* world in which I was walking around, Doctor. The CI module found something inside my son, some part of him that wanted his father dead . . . and it granted him that wish."

He fell silent, pulse swelling up at the corners of his brow. He had spoken, put into words that which had been inscribed on his heart since the moment he had seen his own emptied eyes gazing back up at him. And beyond, to the harsh sun that lit a small, endless world, turning every leaf's shadow to a knife's edge.

"Commander . . ." The other's voice pried at the door of his thoughts. "When you were a child . . . when you were Jake's age . . . did you ever wish your own father dead? Even just in a little flash of anger?"

He turned a fierce glare toward Bashir. A deep breath before speaking allowed him to regain a measure of self-control. "Many times, Doctor. Every child does."

"Exactly. And what kept you from ever trying to actually kill your father?"

"I thought better of it," Sisko said dryly. "For most of the time I was a child, my father was considerably bigger than I was."

"Any other reason?"

"Only that I knew—once I got over being stupid and angry—that I loved him very much."

"Just as most children do, Commander. They conquer the murderers inside themselves—as you and I, as we all did." Bashir pointed toward the computer screen, as if the numbers and graphs it displayed might have resolved into a human face. "Just as your own son Jake has—in this world. The real one. But what you saw in the holosuite, Commander, wasn't done by Jake. The illusory murder was committed by something that once might have been a part of Jake, but is no longer. The CI module appears to work that way: it finds the weakest part of someone's soul, for lack of a more scientific term, removes it and isolates it, nourishes it in the absence of all the rest of what a thinking and feeling person can be. It takes that small killer that's inside all of us, and lets it run wild. But you'd be making a terrible mistake if you thought you had seen something that is inside Jake." Bashir's voice lowered in pitch. "Consider this, Commander: I did a memory probe upon your son, and I found no trace of him having done anything to cause your perceived death inside the holosuite. Jake doesn't remember that because *he* didn't do it. That other thing, that McHogue took from inside your son's mind, that McHogue changed into something that was no longer your son—*that* was your murderer."

He made no reply to the younger man's words; for a moment, he was incapable of any. The weight upon his own soul eased a fraction, as if he had found a way to get his shoulders beneath it.

"Very well, Julian." He managed a faint smile. "In medical matters at least, I yield to your greater expertise." *And more than that,* he thought. The doctor's lecture had been a humbling experience. "I suppose that right now, there's a lot I need to talk to Jake about."

With his hands clasped at the small of his back, Bashir gazed up at the room's ceiling. "About some things, Commander. But not everything; not what you found in there, inside the holosuite. You've had a glimpse into your son's heart—or at least a small part of it. If *your* father had seen inside you—when you had been, as you said, stupid and angry—would you really have wanted him to talk to you about it?" Bashir slowly shook his head. "There are some things that are worth feeling ashamed about. That's another thing we all learn."

He knew that Bashir was right. And that was the hardest

thing of all to learn, to even admit to himself. That there were matters about which he could do nothing. Except wait and trust.

"What I need to think about, then," said Sisko, "is what Jake would want me to do. About us leaving DS9."

Bashir nodded. "Of course, whatever your son's wishes might be—that is, if he tells you he wants to stay here at DS9—then you can be assured that I'll maintain a close monitoring of him. If any symptoms manifest themselves, if there's any sign that he may have been harmed by his exposure to the CI modules' effects, we can reevaluate our course of action then."

"All right." He nodded. "I'd better go speak to him."

"He's waiting for you." Bashir pointed to the corridor. "In the examining room."

His son looked up at him as the door drew open. "Hello, Jake." Sisko stepped into the small room, their privacy sealed by the exclusion of everything outside. "It's been rather too long, hasn't it?"

Jake studied him warily. "I thought you'd be angry."

"Not at you." He sat down beside his son. *Only at myself* . . .

Somewhere beyond, the affairs of the station and the surrounding worlds clamored for his attention. He ignored them as he talked with Jake.

As they spoke, a part of him stood aside and watched. Studying the boy, to see if there was anything a father could detect, that all of Bashir's instruments and batteries of tests had been unable to.

And then, between one word and the next, he realized he didn't have to worry. Not about this, at least. Jake had been scared, and was still frightened and confused by the things he had experienced inside the altered holosuites . . . but he hadn't been damaged by them. Not in that intangible part of him that those wiser than doctors called the soul. Sisko felt as if an invisible stone had been lifted from his heart, breath rushing in to fill his starved lungs.

"Let's go home." He stood up, wanting to squeeze his son tight against his chest, but knowing that all he could really do was wrap his arm around the boy's shoulders.

As they walked through the station toward their living quarters, they passed by the entrance to the Promenade. Through it, Jake caught sight of one of Quark's holosuites, still presumably safe and uninfected by the CI modules. "I don't want to go in there again." He looked up at his father. "Ever."

"That's all right; you don't have to." Sisko steered his son toward the turbolift. "But not even for a game of baseball?"

Jake's face clouded, brow creased with deliberation. "I'll have to think about that."

He waited, controlling his impatience as best he could. Odo knew that if the commander was busy with family matters, there was no one to blame but himself; after all, he had been the one who had notified Sisko about his son's use of the altered holosuites. The commander's situation was one that Odo both deplored and envied, keeping both those reactions tightly contained inside. The lack of family—indeed, the lack of any creature in the known universe similar to himself— meant that he could devote his full, undivided attention to the security of *Deep Space Nine;* that same lack left a hollow space at his core, like an airless bubble in his natural liquid state.

His watch on the door of the commander's living quarters had lasted for over an hour now. Odo stood with his back against the corridor wall, trying to make himself look as inconspicuous as possible to anyone who might pass by. It would have been easy enough to achieve effective invisibility, transforming himself into a transparent membrane on one of the curved panels, the way he had when he'd been tailing Ahrmant Wyoss—but he knew that when the commander emerged from his conference with his son, Sisko would likely stride toward the nearest turbolift at top speed, heading back to the crises left hanging on the Ops deck. Odo didn't want to miss his chance at grabbing a share of the commander's attention before anyone else could have a shot at him.

He pulled himself to full alertness as he heard the initial hiss of the door sliding open. Just as he had anticipated, Sisko bulled out in the hurried manner, not looking to either side, that had come to characterize him in the last several high-pressured shifts.

"Commander—" Odo hurried to match his pace with the commander's. "I take it that your son is all right. Dr. Bashir indicated as much to me; I hope you won't consider that a breach of confidence on his part. It is, after all, a matter that touches upon the station's security."

"Jake appears to be fine." Sisko glanced round at him. "But I appreciate your concern."

"There are some other things, however, that should be brought to your attention. Some more recent developments."

"Such as, Constable?"

They had reached the turbolift door; Odo turned to face the commander. "We've found more holosuites; virtually all of the new units have been altered with the illicit CI modules. Our Chief O'Brien has determined that the modifications were performed within the last two shifts. It seems as if whoever's behind this operation—perhaps our mysterious McHogue—was somehow able to bring a large quantity of the modules on board in a way that can't be traced through the pylons' loading docks."

"I see." Sisko nodded as he mulled over the data. "And I suppose there's still no indication of how this McHogue himself might have gotten into DS9? Or if he's still here?"

"You mean physically, rather than as an apparition in one of the altered holosuites?" Odo had been informed by the commander about the spectral figure he'd encountered when he'd gone into his son's hallucinatory world. "At this point, there's no way of determining that. With the manpower available to me, it would take weeks to conduct an exhaustive search of the station—the structure is riddled with hiding places. And if we didn't find this McHogue person, we still couldn't be sure whether he's aboard or not; he could evade detection by simply moving from place to place ahead of the search teams."

"In other words, it's up to our mysterious visitor as to whether he shows himself to us or not."

"I'm afraid so, Commander. Surveillance has been increased in the Promenade and in all the sectors where the CI modules have been found in the holosuites, on the off chance that McHogue might return to those areas. Other than that, there's not much we can do."

The turbolift opened beside them. "That will have to suffice for now." Sisko stepped into the transportation device. "Let me know if anything further develops."

"There's something else I need to discuss with you—"

Sisko's hand stopped a few centimeters away from the turbolift's controls. "What's that?"

He hesitated for only a moment. "Technically, this is something beyond my sphere of authority, Commander. Nevertheless, I feel it's my duty to inform you. Major Kira's whereabouts are unknown; as I believe you were previously notified, she left in one of the station's runabouts, without filing a flight plan."

"So where is she?"

"At the moment, she's in transit, returning from Bajor; her estimated time of arrival is within the next hour or so—"

The commander's shoulders lifted in a shrug. "I expect Major Kira had her reasons. She's made similar trips before."

"This may be a little different," said Odo. "While you were occupied with these concerns regarding your son, Ops received an official subspace communication from the Bajoran

119

capital. There's been a successful *coup d'état* against the provisional government. The Severalty Front led by General Aur has taken complete control of the planet."

Sisko's eyes widened. "You must be joking, Constable."

"I'm not known for humor; the communiqué and the further details that have come in are waiting for you at Ops."

"The way things were going, I suppose this was inevitable." Sisko gave a weary sigh. "We'll just have to deal with it, then. At least until the Bajoran people toss this lot out."

"That may not happen for a while, Commander. I've been in touch with my own informants on Bajor; it seems that the new government has every sign of enjoying wide popular support. But that's not what I wanted to tell you about. My informants were also able to fill me in on Major Kira's activities while she was planetside. It seems that she had private meetings with various members of the Severalty Front, including General Aur, immediately before the coup."

"Indeed." The commander's expression grew hard. "Are you making an accusation against Major Kira?"

"Of course not." Odo returned the other's level gaze. "I'm merely providing information which I believe you should have. It's up to you to determine what it means."

"Meeting with members of the Severalty Front could mean anything. Or perhaps nothing."

Odo gave a single nod. "As I said, Commander: it's your determination to make."

"Very well." Sisko reached again for the turbolift controls. "You acted properly by informing me of this matter. I assume that, for the time being, the report of Kira's activities remains confidential?"

"Absolutely."

"Carry on with your other investigations, Constable." Sisko pressed a button and the turbolift chamber slid from sight.

That was unpleasant, thought Odo. Relaying information

about a fellow officer, especially a . . . respected one. Still, as Sisko had pointed out, it could all mean anything, or nothing.

He turned and walked away from the turbolift doors, heading back to the security office on the Promenade.

They were all waiting for him. He knew that; there were so many things at Ops, every crucial matter that required his decision, for him to say yes or no to. He had to set policy, and deal with the complex, interwoven net of communiqués and demands from the Federation and all the non-aligned worlds. While the station's enemies, those who would destroy DS9 and terminate its mission, circled around, searching for an undefended spot—some weakness that he had overlooked, that *he* was responsible for—that they could seize upon like earthly prey in the jaws of wolves . . .

The interior of Commander Sisko's head seemed sometimes to echo with the tumult of all the calls upon his time and attention. As the turbolift moved through the station, he closed his eyes, gathering his strength. The weight upon his shoulders had been great enough already—and now this information about Major Kira's activities on the surface of Bajor had come to light. In the DS9 chain of command, she was second only to himself; as much of the burden of administration as could be shifted from him, she had taken up. There had been enough occasions when she had demonstrated her abilities and ongoing loyalty to *Deep Space Nine;* yet at the same time, Sisko knew that inside herself, Kira maintained a deeper loyalty to Bajor, to the people of her own blood. As a fighter in the resistance against the Cardassian occupation, she had risked her life more than once; she would have given it with little regret if she had thought it necessary. The basis of her loyalty to DS9 was that she felt Bajor's interests would be best served by the eventual success of the station's mission here, that through it Bajor could be raised to the status of a full, participating member of the Federation.

That was Bajor's future, that Kira was helping to bring into reality . . .

Sisko's thoughts raced unimpeded, as though in synch with the turbolift's rushing course through the station. Only a few seconds had passed, and already his brooding had reached an inevitable point, one that he faced reluctantly.

What if Kira had changed her mind, reevaluated what she thought Bajor's future should be? Not the Federation, but something else, something that General Aur and the rest of the Severalty Front were busy conjuring up. Then her divided loyalties, to Bajor and to DS9's mission, would no longer line up quite so neatly. And if that was the case, there would be no question which would take precedence in Kira's mind and heart. There wouldn't even be two loyalties to choose between, but just one, to her homeworld and its people. And what Kira had now seen as their future.

The turbolift came to a halt, its destination reached. Eyes still closed, Sisko rubbed the ache at the corner of his brow. Kira hadn't even arrived back at the station yet; he'd have to sort this all out with her soon enough. In the meantime, though, even with that and the other problems stacking up, there was something else he needed to take care of first. Some unfinished business, between himself and someone who had slipped out of his hands like the shadows cast by another world's warming sun . . .

He stepped from the turbolift, not into the Ops deck, but into one of the station's shabbier and more dimly lit corridors. Nothing had changed since the last time he had been here.

A crackle of energy lit up the passageway, a coruscating energy field blocking his progress. The voice of the station's central computer sounded from above him. "Access to this area is restricted, by orders of Security Chief Odo. Please vacate the area."

"Computer, this is Commander Sisko." From habit, he

gave the rest of his identification code, though he knew the voice pattern recorded in the data banks would be sufficient. "I'm countermanding the restriction protocols; allow temporary access for myself and no other individual at this time."

"Access granted." The energy glow, like the St. Elmo's fire that ancient sailors had encountered, blinked off and then sparked back into existence behind Sisko as he walked farther into the corridor.

The door of the holosuite, the one that had been left with the CI module still in place, slid open at his touch upon the control panel. The dim corridor, and all of DS9 beyond it, vanished as he stepped inside. Once more, the sun of an eternal summer day leaked through the fingers of the hand with which he shielded his eyes. His irises adjusted, allowing him to see the individual yellow stalks wavering in the soft wind, the field rolling to the horizon's stand of trees.

His brow was dotted with sweat when he reached the cooling shade. Beneath the interlaced branches, the small white bones were still scattered where he had kicked apart the dead cat—the hallucination of a dead cat, he had to remind himself. The sensory impression of an actual physical environment was stronger here than in any other holosuite he'd experienced. *It's inside my head*—the disquieting awareness of the cortical-induction process, the illicit technology reaching through the barrier of his skull and manipulating the brain's neurotransmitters, grew sharper. He knew that his senses weren't lying to him, tricking him into mistaking the artificial construct for reality; it was the other way around now, the gray matter dictating to his eyes and ears and skin what they perceived.

And more than that. He turned slowly, scanning across the visual field. A regulation holosuite, untouched by the CI technology, was a dead thing, even when populated by the ghosts of famous ballplayers; a replicated Louisville Slugger remained inanimate wood in one's hands. Here, in this illusory place, a malign intelligence could be detected inside each broken twig on the ground. Through the shifting screen of leaves, Sisko could feel the sun watching him with an unblinking gaze.

Inside . . .

Everything here, the bright daylight, the breeze that smelled of dust and pollen, the sounds of water rippling nearby—it had all been inside Jake's head, too. As well as the small white bones and the broken things that leaked red into the dirt, and the face that could almost be seen from the corners of one's eyes, smiling as it regarded the world it had made in its image. The thought of that made the blood simmer a few degrees hotter in Sisko's veins.

"Yeah? And what're you going to do about it?"

From the direction of the creek, beyond the trees' edge, came a voice he recognized.

He wished he hadn't.

Ducking beneath the lowest-hanging branches, the glade's green fringe, Sisko stepped into the sunshine again, the reflections off the narrow path of water brilliant as heated coins. He winced as the light stabbed at his eyes.

He could just make out the figure sitting on the broad, flat rock, knees hugged to the thin chest. A boy, gazing at the creek's tumbling motion with a sullen intensity.

Sisko felt his heart stumble in his chest as the boy turned and looked at him. The face, as had been the voice, was Jake's.

"What're *you* looking at?"

But different—the slitted eyes held a burning malice that he had never seen in his son's eyes, could never imagine seeing there.

He stood a few meters away from the image. "Who are you?"

"Don't you know?" A smile twisted one side of its face. "I'm your son Jake."

"No, you're not." He had to struggle against the impulse to stride forward and knock the smirk away with a sweeping backhand. "You're nothing. A hallucination. A fiber in my brain being tugged at. That's all."

"Oh, you want to discuss metaphysics, do you?" Another voice, deeper and harder, entwined around the words. "Or is it neurophysiology? It doesn't matter. In that other world—" The squatting figure pointed toward the horizon. "Your percept system detects a certain pattern of light and shadow, sounds at your ear, even molecules of sweat upon the atmosphere . . . and you immediately say *Hello, Jake, my darling boy, true offspring of my loins.* Don't you?" The image's head tilted, studying him from another angle. "The same processes happen here, sensory throughput and pattern recognition, all adding up to the same thing—and you reject it." The voice became that of a young boy again. "You're breaking my heart, Dad. I feel like an orphan."

A wave of nausea rose inside Sisko, his body and mind fighting to reconcile the gap between what was perceived and what was known to be real. "This is a waste of time," he said angrily. "I came here to speak to McHogue. But you . . . you're just an illusion."

"Ah." Jake's image nodded. "Who was it who said that reality is that which, when you stop believing in it, it still exists? Look at this." The image kneeled and leaned over the water; one hand darted down, inhumanly fast, striking below the creek's surface. Something silvery bright wriggled in the image's fist as it turned back toward Sisko.

He knew what was going to happen, what he would be shown. The awareness of this world's malign intelligence grew closer around him, as though the sun's gaze had darkened in a cloudless sky.

"Come on, watch—"

Sisko closed his eyes; he could still do that. He had caught just a glimpse of the fish struggling in the image's grip, the round eyes staring, the mouth open and gasping as the fingers had tightened.

"You're no fun."

The image of the boy stood up on the rock; Sisko watched as the mess in its hand was thrown into the water, snared by the current and sluiced away. The image wiped its palm on its tattered jeans. "Just like your stupid kid. I mean, just like *me.*"

He made no reply; there was no point.

"All right, all right, I'm going." The image shot another murderous glance at Sisko. "Sheesh." Balancing from one small stone to another, the image crossed the water and plunged into the tall, dry grasses on the other side. A notch-eared cat left off its stakeout of a field mouse's burrow and darted away, a ripple through the stalks marking its passage.

"You didn't want to see that . . . but you did. Whether you believed in it or not. The bit with the fish, I mean."

Sisko looked over his shoulder and saw McHogue then, the narrow face still touched by its mocking smile. He stood at the edge of the holosuite's glade, his black garb almost of a piece with the trees' darkening shade.

"I'll assume," said Sisko dryly, "that you're real. In some way, at least."

"That's good of you." McHogue's expression grew even more amused. "It would certainly expedite matters if you did. I'd hate to think that you believed you were standing here all alone, talking to yourself."

"Was that something you cooked up to scare me?" He pointed to the boy's image, now almost at the limit of his sight. A wavering row of parted grasses traced a path leading to a distant wooden barn. "Something to rattle me a bit?"

"Why would I want to do that?" McHogue stepped forward. "Really, Commander Sisko, we should be friends. Or let's just say that it would be in your best interests if we were. We have a great many interests in common. The ongoing welfare of *Deep Space Nine,* for instance."

"You should be concerned about that." Sisko studied the figure standing before him. The other man looked as real, as flesh-and-blood, as himself—though here, he knew, that proved nothing. "I could pull the plug on you in ten seconds. If I had to—or even if I just wanted to—I could jettison every holosuite aboard DS9 out one of the airlocks. You'd be the one talking to himself . . . *if* you existed at all."

McHogue nodded in approval. "That's a good attitude to maintain, Commander. True friendship is really only possible between equals, don't you think? A certain measure of reciprocity is needed. If you feel you have your hand on my throat, and I have mine on yours . . ." He shrugged. "Well, if we can't be friends, then at least we can *respect* each other." The smile grew wider. "Though actually, getting rid of the holosuites wouldn't affect me much, or my plans. It's far too late for that. Surely you don't believe that this is the only place I exist?" He gestured toward the sky and the surrounding fields. "It's comfortable enough, and it serves my purposes— or at least some of them—but I have to admit I find it a bit dull. But then I have a standard of comparison; I've traveled quite a bit in my career—I'm sure by now you've had a look at the various files on me. Whereas the boy you just met, that rather interesting variation on your own son Jake—I'm pretty sure he doesn't exist anywhere else. He was born here, so to speak. Or at least I think so."

"Why aren't you certain?" Sisko regarded the other with deep suspicion. "This world is yours. You created it."

"My dear commander—it's not as simple as that." McHogue slowly shook his head. "The cortical-induction modules represent a very powerful technology. I know more about it than any living creature, and I've only begun to explore its possibilities. My experiences outside this realm have suited me for a life as an entrepreneur, a businessman such as our mutual acquaintance Quark—though I believe the scope of my ambitions always somewhat outstripped his. Consequently, I have no training as a scientist; I deal only with what can be accomplished with something . . . profitably, that is. I can only speculate about *how* some of these things work. That boy . . . he really is your son Jake, you know; or at least part of him. The CI technology isn't just a one-way street; it observes and learns from everyone that comes into it. It creates what you might call *echoes* of the various users of the modified holosuites. The characteristic patterns of identity are preserved—the essences, if you will—and, in time, they acquire a certain life of their own. They become . . . different. But still with an inner truth about them; they reveal *interesting* qualities about their original sources." McHogue shrugged, his smile becoming that of an indulgent parent. "There's even an echo of me here, as a boy just about your own son's age. He's quite a rascal."

"I bet he is," Sisko replied grimly. He looked across the expanse of yellow grasses, then back to McHogue. "So you've already started to populate your little self-contained world. That should make it very pleasant for you—or at least not as lonely. Inasmuch as I'm going to make sure that not just my son—my real son—but no one, absolutely no one else, will be coming in here to join you in your twisted little games. If what you wanted was to be lord and master of your own pocket universe, then congratulations; you've achieved that. I hope it makes you happy." The last words were spoken with a vehemence that made his hands clench into fists at his side.

A fragment of McHogue's smile remained, but his eyes had turned steely. "As I told you, Commander, I consider myself to be a man of rather large ambitions. Now, *you* may be satisfied—perhaps even fulfilled—to be the great, high-and-mighty emperor of a rusting steel ball floating in the vacuum, with all your Starfleet minions carefully arrayed around you.

You *enjoy* having millions of petty decisions to make, don't you?—it eats up so much of your time that you might otherwise spend thinking about things you don't want to. Remembering things. The problem is that you find ruling a little world so much to your liking, you tend to assume that's what everybody wants. But that's not the case with me. I didn't come here to turn myself into the tin god of a private universe. These fantasies—" McHogue gestured again, with a wide flourish of his arm; his voice rose. "I have no use for them, except . . ." He stopped, then made a small parodic bow toward Sisko. "Except as a means of achieving my ambitions in *your* world, Commander. And all the ones beyond it."

"We've already seen some of your 'ambitions.'" Sisko allowed the contempt he felt to register in his own voice. "The murderers you unleashed on DS9—are there echoes of them here as well? I'm sure they must make delightful company for you."

McHogue dismissed the last remark with a wave of his hand. "Oh, they're here, all right . . . somewhere or other. Not in this bright summer that you and your son have always enjoyed so much. But someplace darker, someplace a little more suited to their limited temperaments." He feigned an expression of concern. "I hope you didn't take all that *personally.* Your 'epidemic,' as I believe you've been calling it—these kinds of tiny mishaps always happen with a start-up operation like this. I admit that we seem to have got things rolling with a few . . . less than desirable individuals— unstable types, really—but what can you do?" He gave an elaborate shrug. "Actually, Commander, I'm somewhat disheartened by the triviality of your complaints. If all you ever had to gripe about were a few people trying to kill you every now and then, you'd be a lucky man." The unpleasant smile showed again on McHogue's face. "Believe me, there are far worse things."

"Indeed." Sisko's expression remained unamused. "And what might those be?"

"If we're friends, Commander, then you won't ever have to find out. But unfortunately, I'm afraid you will." McHogue glanced up at the sun. "Time's a-wastin'—not that you'd know it in a place like this. This perpetual noon you programmed does have its disadvantages."

"There's still plenty of time for you to tell me about these great plans of yours."

"You'll find out soon enough. But right now, I must be on my way." McHogue held up his hand and rolled the fingers one by one into his palm. "Good talking to you—we'll do it again, I promise. But now I have to pull the plug on *you.*"

The smiling figure disappeared; a moment later, so did the trees that had been behind him.

Sisko turned, watching the yellow grass fade away, the creek dwindling to a mist. The distant hills became steel walls studded with the holosuite's optic transmitters.

The sun went last of all.

CHAPTER
8

"I WOULD'VE THOUGHT YOU'D BEEN PUT ON *MAJOR* RESTRICTIONS. For screwing up like that. Didn't your father get mad and stuff?"

Jake shook his head in reply to the Ferengi youth's question. "No, he was pretty cool about it." There were things he hadn't talked to Nog about—things he didn't *want* to talk about. On the outside, the part that other people could see, he let on that the trouble he'd gotten into, all that stuff with the holosuites and what happened there, it was all no big thing. But on the inside, he still felt kind of sick and dizzy; he had to be careful not to think about those things too much. It was easier, a lot less scary, to just hang out with Nog, here in the solid and real world of the station.

Right now, as Nog walked alongside Jake, his eyes had widened in disbelief. "My uncle would have flipped out, if it'd been me. Nobody would've even seen his vapor trail, he would've come down on me so fast."

Nog was virtually the same age as him, so they had a lot of the same problems—most of them dealing with the adults in their lives and the positions they held aboard *Deep Space Nine.* What with his own father being the station's commander, and Nog's uncle Quark being the undisputed number-one wheeler-dealer on the Promenade, they were both connected to a couple of DS9's leading lights. There was even some debate—and a series of arguments of varying ferocity between him and Nog, that had finally simmered down to an agreement not to talk about it anymore—as to whether his dad or Nog's uncle possessed the greater status. Benjamin Sisko wore a Starfleet uniform, while Quark was a private entrepreneur, something that Ferengi would just naturally think a lot more of.

"It's not such a big deal. They all make a lot of noise; that's what they're *supposed* to do." Jake shrugged. "What could your uncle have done to you, anyway?"

"You'd be surprised." Nog gazed down glumly at the corridor's flooring. "I don't know. Maybe put a leg shackle on me and chained me behind the bar; I'd be washing out glasses and mugs for the rest of my *life.*"

"Don't worry." From his shoulder, Jake lifted the baseball bat he carried. "I would've come and busted you out."

"Yeah, thanks. You'd be a big help, all right." Nog raised his head, looking a small measure more cheerful. "But then again, I didn't screw up, so it's okay. You know, I think it was different with your dad, because he always let you use the holosuites—the regular ones, that is. He'd even go in there with you, and everything. But they've been off-limits to me from the beginning. My uncle always said the holosuites were just for the suckers—the customers, I mean."

"You haven't missed anything. Not really." The outfielder's mitt had slipped down the length of the bat and now rested against his shoulder. With the mitt that close to his face, Jake could smell the sharp mingling of leather and sweat it gave off. He didn't know whether the mitt was genuine, something that had come all the way from Earth itself, or an exact re-creation, something that one of the holosuites' replicators had cooked up. In one way it didn't matter, and in another way it did.

He had left the bat and the mitt at school, the one that Mrs. O'Brien ran for all the kids aboard the station. Instead of restricting him to living quarters, Jake's father had made a specific point—an order, really—about him going back there this shift, despite all the stuff that had happened in those creepy holosuites. The bat, with the mitt slung around it, had stood propped up in a corner of the schoolroom for several shifts—Jake couldn't remember how long it had been. That showed how wrapped up he'd gotten in that other world, hanging out with that strange boy with the knife and the cruel smile. He was real glad that was over. Having his father find out about it hadn't been the most pleasant thing in the world, and he had his suspicions about who had snitched on him— on DS9, the discovering and revealing of secrets was pretty much Odo's job. But in his heart, he was grateful for that; he might not have been able to end it, to stop going in there, by himself. And then who knew what might have happened to him, if it had gone on any longer? Dr. Bashir hadn't run all those tests on him just to keep in practice.

"Some people really go for it," mused Nog. "The holosuites and all that. My uncle says he's got some real regular customers. And your dad—he uses one every now and then."

"Yeah, he's got a bunch of old ballplayers programmed into one at Quark's bar. He likes talking to 'em. But they all seem to, like, *spit* a lot. You know? I guess that's authentic and all, but it's really weird."

They had reached the end of the corridor, to where it opened out to a view above the Promenade. Jake leaned against the rail, looking down at the milling crowd.

"The way I see it," said Jake, "is that it's more important for them. For old guys like my dad, I mean." He had given a lot of thought to the matter, and was still working it out inside his head. "Because it's like going back home for them. They didn't grow up in places like this." Jake gestured at the enclosing metal walls and ceilings of the station. "My dad remembers all that stuff, trees and grass and everything. But I don't." He fell silent for a moment, thinking about the first time he had gone with his father inside one of the holosuites —he couldn't remember how old he was then; it hadn't been here aboard DS9—and the difference he'd been able to discern, even at that age, between the way his father had looked around at the re-created summery world and how strange it had seemed to him. Or maybe not strange, or at least not any more so than the zillion other places he'd already seen, real worlds and Starfleet vessels and Federation outposts that he had stuffed inside his own personal memory bank. Could he help it if a holosuite's simulation of Earth didn't punch his buttons the same way it did for his father? Though he'd been smart and had kept his mouth shut about it, except for saying how great it was—he knew how much it all meant to his dad. He wouldn't have wanted to hurt his feelings.

"You're probably right." Nog stood beside him at the rail. "Though from what Uncle Quark told me, a lot of his customers go into his holosuites just to . . . you know . . . have sex. Then again, when you look at some of his customers, you gotta figure that's the only way they *could.*"

Jake knew that his friend had inherited a wide streak of mercantile cynicism from his Ferengi genetics; the family traits were bound to show up sooner or later.

"There'd be some things about it I'd miss, though. If there weren't any holosuites." He turned his back to the Promenade view and weighed the wooden bat in both his hands. "Playing all that baseball—that was kinda fun." He hadn't yet decided whether it was worth going back in just for the sake of a game.

"Why do you need a holosuite to do that?"

"Come on." He looked at Nog in exasperation. "You need a lot of room to play baseball. That's the main thing." He used the bat to point to the closest bolted panels and girders. "We're just a little cramped for open space here, remember?"

"Not in the loading docks, out by the pylons—they're huge. They bring those freight containers big as whole ships in there."

"Oh, sure—and they'd be happy to let me set up a baseball diamond right in the middle of the cranes and all that other heavy action." Jake rolled his eyes upward. "I thought you Ferengi were supposed to be so smart."

"Yeah, well, you're the son of the station's commander, aren't you?" Nog poked him in the arm. "Why not pull a little rank?"

Jake slowly shook his head. "You're not even as smart as I thought you were a moment ago. Believe me, it just doesn't work that way around here. Not with my dad, at least."

"So? Then we'll just have to deal with conditions as we find them—as my uncle would say. What's there to the game, anyway, except hitting the ball and running around the bases? We could do that much right here." Nog looked over the area surrounding them. "How many bases did you say there were?"

"Four. First, second, third and home plate. That's why it's called a diamond."

"Maybe we better make it a triangle, then; kind of a long skinny one." Nog pointed down the length of the corridor. "Okay, right there between those service panels on either side—we'll make that home." He turned, tracing an imaginary line with his fingertip. "That girder is first base, and the vent grid's second. How's that sound?"

"Maybe you're not so dumb, after all." The notion had never even occurred to Jake. If you couldn't squeeze a diamond in, and you couldn't change the space, then change the diamond. Simple. As he thought about it, he remembered his father telling him about other games, street games, that were like baseball—hitting and running—but not exactly;

you didn't even need a bat for them, just a sawn-off broom handle. That's what you were supposed to do: use whatever you had. He nodded as he looked around the improvised field. "Yeah, that might be all right. . . ."

They worked out a few quick rules. No pitcher—it would have been difficult to manage, anyway, with just the two of them—and hits off the corridor's walls weren't fouls, but bank shots.

Nog backed up toward the area's guardrail. For a moment, as Jake rubbed his thumb across the baseball's stitches, the sick and dizzy feeling surged over him again, the same one he got when he didn't stop himself from thinking about the holosuite and some of the things inside it. The metal bulkheads and stanchions of DS9 wavered in his sight, as if they were somehow unreal. He had to squeeze his eyes shut to hold everything in place.

"Hey, come on!" Nog's shout seemed to come from somewhere else, another world. "What're you waiting for?"

He gripped the ball tighter. It was real, he knew; he'd told himself that before. Not like the things in the holosuite. Everything there had always been slightly . . . off. Like they were out of focus, even when they were sharp in his sight and solid in his hand; even when he had been scared of them. Things in the holosuite were always trying to *be* real. They came out of nowhere and read your mind, and then tried to become the things they found in there. But they never got it exactly right. He knew that now. He could tell the difference. Real stuff—the whole real universe—waited for you to deal with it, on its own terms.

Jake opened his eyes. The station's metal bulkheads looked solid and hard once more. "Okay," he said. "Comin' at ya." He tossed the ball up, then got both hands on the bat and swung.

He connected harder than he had intended—the feel of the bat in his grip had pumped adrenaline into his system. With a sharp crack, the ball flew the length of the corridor. For a moment, Jake traced the arcing course—it leveled off a centimeter shy of brushing the ceiling—then dropped his gaze to watch Nog backpedaling, hands awkwardly raised above his head to try making the catch. Jake's smile changed to an expression of alarm when he saw how far away Nog had gotten.

"Nog! Watch out—"

His shouted warning was too late. Nog hit the guardrail with the small of his back, just as the ball grazed past his outstretched fingertips. He was too far off balance to stop himself from toppling over.

Jake ran to the spot where his friend had disappeared. Panting for breath, he looked over and saw the Ferengi youth, eyes immense in panic, clutching the bottom edge of the walkway with one straining set of fingertips. Below him, the Promenade's visitors continued about their business and pleasures; none of them had looked up and noticed.

"Grab my hand!" Jake braced himself and reached over. As soon as he had circled his own fingers around Nog's wrist, he tugged and let himself fall backward. That was enough to bring Nog landing heavily on top of him.

"What happened to the ball?" Nog raised his head and looked around. "Does that count as an out?"

Standing at the rail, the two boys saw what had happened. The ball's velocity had wedged it into a narrow crevice between two of the structural beams above the Promenade— but only for a moment; as they watched, the ball dropped free. It struck an angled girder below with enough force to send it caroming toward the side of the Promenade, and into the doorway of Quark's drinking establishment.

They both held their breaths. The sound of glass breaking was appropriately spectacular, as the ball skittered crazily along the bar, toppling some of the patrons backward on the stools.

"No," said Nog in admiration. "That's definitely a home run."

A moment later, Quark appeared in the doorway, teeth clenched in fury, gaze darting around the Promenade for the perpetrators of the outrage. The ball was clutched in one white-knuckled, trembling hand.

"We better split." Jake scooped up the bat and ran, with Nog at his heels.

They slowed to a walk when they were well away from their impromptu playing field. "You know, I don't think my uncle's going to let us have that ball back."

"That's all right. We can get another." Jake hoisted the bat back onto his shoulder. He nodded thoughtfully. "This was a good idea . . . but it's definitely going to take some more work."

"Access granted."

She stepped through the spot where the energy beam had crackled and sparked. It snapped back into place behind her, with a surge that lit up the distant corners of the passageway.

Dr. Bashir was waiting for her on the other side; the security system had dictated that they had to separately identify themselves and gain entry to the restricted area. "Are you ready for this?" He held up a small datacard between his thumb and forefinger.

Dax nodded. "I think we can go ahead with this stage of the investigation, Julian." As always, she was aware of the fine line she had to tread with him, to maintain a cordial working atmosphere while not encouraging his persistent romantic fantasies about her.

The lights on the altered holosuite's control panel blinked into life as Bashir restored the unit's power. The entrances to the other holosuites lining the corridor remained dark rectangles, cut off from both the station's energizing grid and any humanoid contact. Until everything about the epidemic of murder had been explained—and rectified—caution dictated a complete shutdown of all the holosuites that had been tampered with, even after the suspect CI modules had been removed; Chief of Operations O'Brien would have to determine whether a lingering toxic effect had been created in the holosuites' original circuits.

She watched as Bashir opened a small access slot on the control panel. A part of her—a part that was not quite as coldly rational as the rest—felt the slightest chill touch of apprehension. The doctor's quick, precise labors with the small tools he had brought reminded her of ancient video recordings she had once seen, of the timers to high-explosive bombs being dismantled. *One wrong move and it goes off in your face—that's not likely to happen,* chided a familiar voice inside her. The voice, one that had become as much hers as the one with which she spoke aloud, didn't use words to make its meaning clear. It didn't have to; the thoughts of the centuries-old symbiont inside her abdomen ran in virtual parallel to those of the cerebral matter, less than three decades old, inside her skull. She had been one with the symbiont for so much of her body's life that it had become impossible to make any distinction between where its existence left off and hers began. But there were infrequent moments such as this, when a minute twitch upon the nervous system, a release of hormones into the bloodstream, reminded her that the physical form had a life, even a mind. of its own.

Her attention was brought back by Julian's voice.

"What I'm doing," he said, bending low to peer into the access slot, "is wiring in the programming that we were able to download out of the other holosuites that Ahrmant Wyoss used." He poked a logic probe into the maze of circuits, drew it out, and read the LEDs on the handle. "He started out with one of the standard programs, a generic urban simulation, but it seems to have been extensively modified by the influence of the CI modules. We'll know better what's in the program when we get it up and running."

"Wouldn't it have been easier to run a model simulation through the computer?" *And safer,* that same part of her thought without speaking aloud.

Bashir shook his head. "There's some kind of interlock routine that's been interlaced with the program—O'Brien tried to break it out but he had to give up eventually. Apparently, the only way to get into it is by activating it with one of the CI modules." He made a few final adjustments. "There, that should do it." He glanced round at her. "All set?"

"Of course."

"Here goes, then." The holosuite's door slid open.

They stepped through and into darkness. As the door shut behind them, sealing away the corridor and completing the illusory world surrounding them, Dax quelled the twinge of physiological panic that accelerated her pulse for a few beats. She had spent so many hours poring over the transcripts of Wyoss's drug-induced ravings that she had a reasonable idea of what to expect. But the impact of the reality—or artificiality, she corrected herself—was still oppressive.

In the perceived distance around her and Bashir, a sulfur-tinged night fog clung to damp, crudely surfaced streets. The mists threaded between looming buildings of dirt-stained brick; empty windows gaped down upon them like the hollow eyes of idiot spectators. Ragged curtains fluttered listlessly across the glass teeth left in the broken frames. The blue radiance from the overhead streetlights barely penetrated the gloom, serving more to make the hallucinated night a tangible sensation upon the skin.

"Well. This *is* cheerful," said Bashir. He turned, studying the claustrophobic vista. "Sort of an exercise in negative mood induction, don't you think? It's got that—what did they use to call it?—that *film-noir* look to it."

She caught the reference to the ancient art form, the cinema of the late twentieth century having been a limited sensory-input predecessor to the holosuites themselves. "If by that you mean overtly depressing, I'd have to agree."

"It has a certain bleak charm, I guess. Though if I had known this was what was going on inside Ahrmant Wyoss's head, I would have argued for pharmaceutical intervention."

Dax took a step forward; a sudden wave of dizziness swept across her, nearly toppling her from her feet. She felt Bashir catch her by one arm and around the shoulder.

"Are you all right?" He peered in concern at her. "What's wrong?"

"I don't know—" She felt weak, as though Bashir's grasp was all that kept her standing upright. She pressed one hand to her brow. "I seem to be experiencing some kind of processing lag." Around her, as she raised her head, she saw not the illusory city, but the actual walls of the holosuite chamber itself, the hexagonal grid of percept transmitters and low-level tractor-beam apertures. Beneath her feet, she perceived bare metal rather than the rough surface of hallucinated asphalt and stone. "All of a sudden, I'm not picking up the sensory effects. Wait a minute. . . ." Dax held out her hand. The walls faded a bit, enough to be overlaid with ghost images of the programmed buildings. "Something's off—the effects are erratic. . . ."

Bashir glanced over his shoulder. "It seems to be working all right for me. Unusually solid for a holosuite, in fact." He turned back to her, studying her eyes. "It must have something to do with the cortical-induction module—I can't think of any other explanation." He nodded. "That must be it. Plus your being a Trill—the CI technology works directly on the user's neurosystem, instead of just feeding in stimuli through the sense organs the way unaltered holosuites do. The problem must be that in your case, there's *two* neurosystems operating in tandem, the humanoid one and the symbiont's. The two systems are obviously different enough that they're not experiencing the CI module's effects at exactly the same rate—you're like a subspace receiver catching two transmissions at the same time and scrambling them together."

If the disorientation had been less severe, she would have arrived at the same theory. "I believe you're correct." In her vision, the holosuite walls and the illusory buildings went through a blurring fluctuation. She swayed, holding on to Bashir's arm even more tightly. "Severe loss of . . . equilibrium . . . sense of balance is well below operational thresholds . . ."

"I'll have to take you out of here—"

"No." Dax shook her head, sending her visual field even farther askew. "We came in here for a reason—there's things we need to find out. I think there's a way I can take care of this."

"How?"

"Under normal conditions, a Trill cannot separate the parts of its joint consciousness—once the fusion has taken place, the symbiont and host are as one, even though there is some occasional bilateral functioning."

Bashir nodded. "Just as there is with the left and right hemispheres of the human brain."

"Exactly. But here," said Dax, "because of the interference effect of the CI modules—it appears that the two neurosystems inside me are not functioning at equal strength; the synchronization between them has been thrown off." She closed her eyes, holding her fingertips to the side of her brow. "I can feel it. It's as if the field created by the CI modules is dividing me into two separate creatures again. . . ."

"That does it." Bashir's tone was emphatic. "I'm taking you out of here."

"No—" She grabbed his forearm. "Don't you see? We can use this. Instead of fighting the interference effect, I can yield to it. That way, instead of struggling to resynchronize the two neurosystems, one can simply take precedence over the other and operate as a de facto separate entity."

"I don't know. . . ." Bashir looked doubtful. "This sounds somewhat risky."

"It would only be for while we're here in the holosuite. As soon as we're out again, the two neurosystems would align together once more." Dax closed her eyes again, attempting to minimize the chaotic sensory stimuli that assaulted her. "I *know* it can be done. And there isn't any other way."

"Well . . . if you say so; Trill physiology isn't one of my specialties. But I'm telling you—if I even suspect something's gone wrong, I'm carrying you back out the door." He peered more closely at her. "So which part of you is going to go away for a while?"

"In this situation, it's probably better if the symbiont withdraws; the humanoid consciousness retains better control of the host body's motor functions. . . ." Her awareness had already turned inward, toward that world contained by her skin, a world populated by both one creature and two. The symbiont's thoughts had echoed the words she had spoken to Bashir; the decision had already been made, the process set into motion. Dax willed herself to let go, to allow the interference effect to work upon her. . . .

There was no pain or drama to the separation; just a growing sense of *aloneness,* a loss greater than the merely human ever realized, endurable only because she knew it would be temporary. . . .

There was perhaps one aboard the station who had ever felt the same. The friendship between the symbiont Dax and Commander Sisko went back many years, to the humanoid host before her. Somewhere in all that accumulation of memory was an hour when Sisko had spoken of the grief he carried within, the death of his wife. As if he had lost something that was as much a part of him as his breath and heartbeat. He had loved her that much.

The withdrawal was complete; she could feel the symbiont's separate mind at the edge of her own consciousness, a touch that was even closer than Bashir's supporting arm.

She opened her eyes. In the holosuite's simulated distance, she could see the oppressive night folding around the seemingly solid buildings. A fragment of another time, a crumpled newspaper, tumbled in the draft moving through the low mist. Julian had been correct: it was easily the most convincing holosuite environment she had ever experienced.

"I'm all right now." The nausea and disorientation had receded. She gently removed Bashir's hand from her arm and stepped away from the grasp by which he had held her up. In the dim radiance from the nearest streetlamp, she could see her shadow wavering across the pitted asphalt surface and broken concrete edge of the curb. "We should proceed with the investigation."

They walked together down the street, their mingled shadows falling in and out of the empty doorways. They were looking for something human—or reasonably so.

Commander Sisko had uploaded a hurried memo to them, giving a few details about what he had called "echoes" in the altered holosuites. He hadn't made it clear what he had been doing inside, whether he had been working his own personal investigation, following a hunch . . . it didn't matter. What was important was that his information had given them another lead to trace down, just when they had apparently exhausted all the possibilities of their previously collected data.

If the users of the altered holosuites had left behind electronic echoes of their personalities, they might yield clues to the CI modules' operations—and their source. At a dead end in the research lab, Dax and Bashir had redirected their attention to the infectious vector of the epidemic.

"There's something here; I can feel it." Bashir stopped and looked around. One dismal street had led to another, as if the holosuite were an endlessly repeating field of urban decay. "Definitely a presence."

Dax had to agree with him. An almost subliminal thread, sounds that were just barely at the edge of perception, had led them on a winding course between the crumbling buildings. She held up her hand, signaling him to be silent as she tilted her head to concentrate. Whatever she heard, she would have to interpret it on her own, without the aid of her silently watching other half.

"Over there." She pointed down a dark alley branching off the street. In some ways, it had been easier to pinpoint the sound; as much as she had been diminished from being temporarily separated from her symbiont, there had also been a sharpening, a cleansing, of her perceptions, as though the sensory data were coming undiluted through one less filter. "It sounds like breathing."

The alley ended blind against a dank wall; it reached several stories above her and Bashir, as though the altered holosuite had labored to produce the ultimate symbol of futility, the death and abandonment of every human endeavor. Close to where they stood was a row of battered metal canisters, obviously a re-creation of the artifacts of a primitive waste-removal system; they smelled like rotting food and airborne disease.

Bashir laid a hand against the alley wall, then drew it back, looking in revulsion at the wet residue on his fingertips. "This couldn't be something from Ahrmant Wyoss's own past." He wiped his hand off on his uniform trousers. "From his personnel files, we know that he didn't grow up on any planet as undeveloped as this. My guess is that he indulged in a preference for these ancient films and then, bit by bit, the contents of his subconscious were altered to match up. The literal truth of his past became less important than what he believed, on some deep level, to be its essence. At one time, it was a common enough psychotherapeutic fallacy that subjects could get trapped in."

"But if what Commander Sisko told us is correct, there should be some version of Wyoss himself still here, his echo." The sound of breathing was closer now. Away from the feeble glow of the streetlights, Dax's eyes had adjusted to the alley's darkness. She could see no break or doorway set into the walls on either side, until she looked down and saw a grime-clouded casement window at the level of the pavement. Kneeling down, she wiped a layer of dirt away with her palm. "Look—" She gestured for Bashir to stoop down beside her. "This must be it."

A primitive light-emitting device, a glass sphere with a flickering electric current inside, dangled from a bare wire, illuminating a basement room. If anything, the aura of decay and stilled cycles of time was even more palpable on the other side of the glass pane. Wooden shelves along one of the cellar walls sagged under the weight of what Dax took to be food-preserving containers, some of the jars broken, others oozing their contents through the seals of their metal lids. An assortment of worn-out brooms and mops, which looked like bones and straggly hair of emaciated corpses, filled one corner of the space; cardboard boxes collapsing with their burdens of forgotten and incomprehensible objects lined the other walls.

And in the center, beneath the light's yellow glare, was a single cot of tattered canvas. With the figure of a boy upon it, his face buried in his arms.

"That's him," came the whisper at Dax's ear. Bashir nodded toward the child visible through the smeared window. "That's Wyoss."

She knew it was true; there was no need to see the boy's

features. At her back, it felt as though the holosuite's dark limits had closed tighter around them, the cellar room being the dead center of this small world. The innermost circle of a private hell.

Beneath the boy's ragged shirt—he looked to be about nine or ten years old—his shoulder blades moved with each inhalation. Dax realized now that it hadn't been his breathing that she had heard and that had led them to this spot; it had been a muffled sobbing, a sound both heartbroken and exhausted, one that might have been going on forever, in the hopeless way in which a bleak eternity is confronted.

"There's somebody coming—" Beside her, Bashir pointed to a shadow that had appeared on the wooden steps leading from the floor above.

The boy lifted his tear-wet face from the cot and looked up at the figure that had entered the cellar space. An adult, face cast in shade by the light dangling just a few inches over his head. Dax could see that, even though the boy didn't move from the cot, didn't try to escape, his torso still cringed back from the apparition. The figure held something in his hands, cradling it like a beloved thing; an object long and slender, rigid where its grip was laced with leather straps, tapering to a flexible curve, point studded with a bright spark of metal. As Dax watched, the figure raised the whiplike instrument; the boy rolled away from its approach, drawing his knees toward his chest and guarding his face between his bare forearms and trembling fists. She saw then that his shirt was not ragged but torn, as was the bleeding flesh beneath.

"It's not real," said Bashir as she turned away. "You have to remember that. It's all illusion. Even the boy—that's just an echo, a little bit of data caught in a loop in the circuits. . . ."

She didn't care. Perhaps if the symbiont had been part of her consciousness at this moment, instead of merely observing all that happened at the edge of her mind, that would have provided enough ballast for her to have maintained a clinical detachment. But right now she didn't want to see what she knew was going to happen. It was bad enough that she could still hear it, the high, singing note of the lash as it cut through the air, the sharp impact upon the skin, the gasping sound that was half a cry, half the fearful stifling of that cry.

With her eyes closed, Dax could see the figure more clearly, dissecting the glimpse she'd had of him. Not his face, but what he wore: an exact simulation of Benjamin Sisko's uniform as a Starfleet commander, complete to the small insignia upon the collar.

There was at last—mercifully—silence; she looked at the casement window and saw that the cellar was empty now. She didn't know, and didn't want to ask Bashir what had happened; perhaps the adult figure had led the weeping boy up the stairs, or all the echoes and images had simply vanished, their time-locked rituals expiated for a while. Though something had been left behind: on the cot, like a sleeping snake, lay the instrument the figure had carried in its hands.

"Let's go, Julian." A different nausea had settled at the base of her throat. "I think we've seen enough."

"Wait a minute." He searched the ground, finally prying up a loose stone from the wet pavement. With it, he broke out the window glass, carefully brushing loose the shards from around the edges. The opening was just big enough for him to slide through and land on his feet inside the cellar.

"What're you doing?"

"I think . . . we just have a piece of interesting evidence here." When he climbed back out, he had the lash coiled in one hand.

Neither of them spoke, even after they had exited the holosuite chamber and stepped out into the corridor beyond; not until they had returned to the brightly lit research lab.

Bashir laid the instrument out on one of the benches. It had persisted after its removal from the holosuite, indicating that it was a replicated material object and not just an illusion created by the interaction of the holosuite's low-level tractor beams.

"What did you bring that out for?" Dax looked at the object with a residue of distaste. She felt whole again; the symbiont's neurosystem had resumed its normal functioning, operating in parallel with that of the humanoid host body. As though waking from a partial slumber, her augmented mind had begun processing and sorting through all that it had perceived.

"I thought so," murmured Bashir. He traced the object's length with a fingertip before turning toward her. "You noticed, didn't you, how the altered holosuite was a jumble of stimuli from several different sources—"

"I saw that there was some apparition seemingly dressed as Commander Sisko, if that's what you mean."

Bashir nodded. "That certainly explains the murderous fixation Wyoss had formed upon the commander. Wyoss had apparently been caught in a cycle of endlessly repeating some trauma suffered while he was a child; the CI module wired into the holosuite translated that into an environment where Sisko assumed the role of that malignant authority figure. Poor Wyoss had been trying to break out of that toxic world in the only way he could figure out."

"We had already hypothesized that, Julian."

"True; it's the other elements of the hallucinated world that are important. Obviously, the CI module has its own internal programming that it uses to warp the user's perceptions along certain specific patterns. It has to *fill in* certain bits and pieces to make everything work out. So there's always something left behind—that's something I learned from O'Brien, when he told me how he'd shown to Odo that someone had been tampering with those holosuites." He picked up the object from the bench; it lay heavily across his upturned palms. "Take this, for instance—it's actually a more clever apparatus than it initially appears. Technically, it's known as a limited

trauma-induction device; the metal tip has miniature repul
sion flanges that can be programmed to a maximum epider
mal penetration depth. Very useful for achieving the mos
pain with the least life-threatening damage to the individual.

Dax studied the object in Bashir's hands. "How do yo
know about all this?"

"During my internship, I pulled a brief tour of duty in
rehab clinic for Starfleet personnel who had been prisoners c
war." His fist closed around the instrument's knotted handl
"This . . . *thing* is only used in one system. It has a primitiv
effectiveness that makes it of particular appeal to th
Cardassians." Bashir tossed it back onto the bench. "Now w
know where the CI modules came from."

CHAPTER
9

SHE WENT TO THE COMMANDER'S OFFICE ON OPS, STRAIGHT FROM docking the *Mekong*. As soon as she entered and the door closed behind her, she could discern that this meeting was not going to go well. The expression on the commander's face was as ominous as banks of storm clouds gathering at the horizon.

"Have a seat, Major." Sisko pointed to the chair in front of his desk. "There's a lot we need to talk about."

"I expect so." Kira sat down, feeling the bone-weariness from the journey seep through her body. After everything that had happened this last time on Bajor, she would have been even more grateful to have gone to her quarters and dropped onto the bed for several hours' sleep. But now the situation had gone from imminent crisis to actual emergency; there never seemed to be time for mere physical—and mental— recuperation.

"We've already been apprised of the latest developments with the Bajoran government." Sisko leaned back in his own chair, forming a cage out of his fingertips. "Or perhaps I should say the *late* Bajoran government. It now looks as if we'll be dealing with the Severalty Front on a much more formal basis than we had anticipated would be the case."

She nodded. "You're right about that, Commander. I'll be preparing a full report on the *coup d'état*—"

"That won't be necessary, Major. I've instructed Odo to put me in touch with his primary intelligence sources on Bajor." The commander's voice was stiffly formal. "All pertinent data will be routed through an analysis team that I've assembled here aboard the station. As of now, and until further notice, you're relieved of your liaison duties."

"What?" Kira stared at him in disbelief. "Are you joking? There's no one aboard DS9 with the kind of expertise I have in Bajoran political affairs—"

Sisko's expression remained grim. "That may well be, Major. But there aren't other personnel with the same suspicions attached to them, either."

"Suspicions?" She couldn't believe what she was hearing; her incredulity cut through the fatigue she had felt only a moment before. "With all due respect, Commander, what the hell is *that* supposed to mean?"

"Rest assured that I'm handling this entirely on an informal basis, Major. Nothing's gone on your record—yet."

"Oh? I presume that's because, whatever 'suspicions' you might have, nothing's been proven." There was no preventing the sarcasm from sharpening her words. "Yet."

He gave a single nod of his head. "That is in fact the case. And I'm certainly committed to the principle of accepting your innocence until such time as any degree of guilt might be established. But at the same time, I can't allow the possibility of disloyalty to the mission of *Deep Space Nine* to adversely affect our operations at this critical time—"

Kira gripped the arms of the chair, to keep herself from rising up like a barely contained explosion. "Are you making an accusation against me, Commander?"

"As I said, not at this moment." Sisko carefully kept his voice level. "I don't have the time right now to decide upon an interpretation of your recent actions. It may well be that you are responsible for nothing more than some severe lapses in judgment. That would be bad enough, but it would also be a great deal more excusable."

She held her silence for a moment, restraining the outburst of anger that swelled at the base of her throat. "What exact actions are you referring to?"

"You piloted a runabout to the surface of Bajor without filing a flight plan or making notification to me or any other DS9 officer—"

"Is that all? Commander . . ." Kira shook her head in disbelief. "I *am* second-in-command here—or at least I was. I believe I'm not only within my right, but within my *duties,* to take such courses of action as I might deem necessary, without an overly strict observance of regulations. I recall you describing some of these rules as petty formalities."

"That's not all, Major. While in the Bajoran capital, you were observed meeting with key members of the Severalty Front. Including General Aur. Almost immediately thereafter, the first stages of the coup were launched by the Front."

"And you think *I* had something to do with that?"

Sisko's expression remained unchanged. "Quite frankly, I don't think so—that's why I'm not making any formal charges against you or initiating any official investigative procedure. No one would be happier than I, or less surprised, to find out that you were not part of any conspiracy against the long-standing Bajoran provisional government. But at this point, I can't take the risk of being wrong on that count. Given what we know about the Severalty Front's stated policies and intentions, I have to be prepared for the worst-case scenario regarding our mission here. My duty is to represent the interests of the Federation; if things go as badly for us as General Aur and the others in the Front apparently desire them to, and Starfleet's administration of DS9 is terminated, there will undoubtedly be a high-level review board convened to investigate the matter. All the officers that served here will be placed under oath, and the station's log and all other records will be turned over. I've dealt with these boards before and I can assure you that they're very thorough."

"I have nothing to hide from them."

"Good. Because one of the first things they'd inquire about would be this journey of yours to Bajor just before the coup took place. And then they'd look into whatever actions I took once it had come to my attention. If it were to come out that I left you on full duty—and didn't begin an immediate investigation of my own—then the interpretation of that sequence of events would be severe."

"I see." Kira could still feel the anger simmering inside her. "So who exactly are you protecting? Yourself?"

"There would be a lot better ways to accomplish that, if it were all I was interested in, Major. I could have you restricted to your living quarters until after an internal investigation had taken place; in fact, if I wanted to play this situation entirely by the book, I could have Odo place you under arrest and lock you up in one of the security office's holding cells."

"You certainly could do that, Commander. And then I'd know how I'm to be repaid for all the loyalty I've demonstrated, and all the efforts I've made on behalf of DS9's mission." She rubbed a tightly clenched fist against the arm of the chair. "And all those like General Aur, who always maintained that non-Bajorans couldn't be trusted—then I would have to rethink my attitude toward them."

"Major, I *am* taking your record here into account. That's why I'm giving you a break. As I said, I'm handling this informally for the time being—and that's not going to be easy." Sisko tapped a finger against his computer panel, indicating the lines of text glowing on the screen. "I've also received an account of the murder of a Bajoran citizen named

Malen Aldris—who was in fact one of Odo's network of intelligence contacts on Bajor. There are indications that his death was a politically motivated assassination—and that you, Major, had been in contact with him as well."

"I could tell you all about Malen's death," said Kira dryly. "Since I was there when it happened."

"Indeed?" One of Sisko's eyebrows raised. "Then that will give you something to do while you're relieved of normal duties. You'll need to prepare a full report on the incident that resulted in the death of this individual and deliver it to Odo. I'll review it at such a time as I can document that your statements had no bearing on my decisions regarding the current Bajoran political situation." With his fingertip, he blanked the computer screen. "That's all we have to discuss right now, Major. You're dismissed."

She didn't move from the chair. "Commander, I really was on Bajor for a good reason. I was there working for the interests of DS9 and the Federation."

"I know that." Sisko's voice modulated softer. "Off the record, of course. But you've also demonstrated to me enough times in the past that you have a great deal of impatience regarding red tape and formalities—you're always trying to cut a straight line to the core of these matters. And that works sometimes. But this is one occasion when you should have stuck to official channels for whatever you hoped to accomplish. This mess is going to take a considerable amount of cleaning up."

She had no answer for that. Because she knew it was true. There had been instances when Sisko's actions as the station's commander had seemed so overly cautious and deliberate to her that she had barely been able to contain her frustration. Only to wind up acknowledging later that his years of experience had given him a degree of hard-won wisdom that far outstripped her own instincts.

It had never become any easier for her to admit, though.

Silently, she pushed herself up from the chair, turned, and headed for the office's door.

One of the lab benches was converted to a conference table by the simple expedient of moving several tall stools over to it. The researchers into the station's epidemic of murder sat and waited for the last needed person to arrive.

"I'm sorry I'm late, people." The lab's door slid shut behind Commander Sisko. "I know your time is valuable—now more than ever." He took his place at the head of the bench. "Shall we begin?"

Dax spoke for herself and Dr. Bashir, detailing what they had discovered on their expedition into the altered holosuite's hallucinatory world. When Bashir laid the whiplike instrument on the bench, Odo reached across from the other side and picked it up, examining it minutely.

"Their analysis of this object's origin is undoubtedly correct, Commander." Odo turned toward Sisko. "When this station was under Cardassian control, I was provided with just such a device for use on possibly recalcitrant prisoners. I destroyed it and told Gul Dukat, the Cardassian then in charge, that I had my own methods for maintaining order. To the best of my knowledge, there were never any more of these introduced to DS9—until now."

"I've scanned it," said Dax, "and I found the telltale atomic structure of a replicator-manufactured object. A review of Ahrmant Wyoss's records shows no period at which he might have been exposed to such a device in reality; the few times that he was incarcerated for minor offenses were all in various Federation jurisdictions. Obviously, the only experience he could have had of such a device would have been inside the altered holosuites. Short of doing an exhaustive deconstruction of the CI modules' programming—and that might take months—I believe we have as solid evidence as we're likely to get regarding the Cardassians' involvement in their origin."

The implement had been passed to Sisko. He studied it for a moment before nodding. "I quite concur. If nothing else, bringing the CI modules on board the station would be consistent with the Cardassians' previous attempts to regain control over the wormhole to the Gamma Quadrant; anything that would disrupt our mission here would be to their advantage."

"But how were the CI modules brought aboard?" Bashir pointed to the only other object on the bench, the black casing for one of the units that had been removed from the holosuites. "That's the big question. Security has been so tight on the pylons that nothing could get through without being detected."

"I'm afraid that we may be encountering some deficiencies in our perimeter maintenance." Odo's voice indicated a brooding tension. "That this might turn out to be the case is something that has been on my mind for some time now—since Starfleet took over the administration of DS9, as a matter of fact. There are large sectors of both the station's interior and exterior that we've simply sealed off as having been sabotaged too extensively by the departing Cardassians to be of any practical use. It's not inconceivable that the vandalism on the part of the Cardassians was not the relatively simple destruction that we had initially thought it to be, but actually a cover for various entry and exit points—trapdoors, if you will—that could remain undetected until such time as the Cardassians would need them." Odo shrugged. "A crew member working on the hull of a ship docked at one of the pylons, a small craft passing by and releasing a packet with a magnetic honing device attached . . . there could be any number of ways that something might be placed outside the station and later retrieved from one of the sealed-off interior zones. But only the Cardassians, or someone working for them, would know how to go about it."

"There's one other element which points to our old

friends." Sisko looked around the faces assembled along the bench. "A Cardassian vessel commanded by Gul Dukat himself has reentered our navigational sector; it's not a warship, but a top-level diplomatic emissary. Before I left Ops, I received word that Dukat had already extended official recognition of the new Bajoran government on behalf of the Cardassian ruling council." Sisko allowed himself a wry smile. "I find it difficult to believe that the Gul just happened to be in the neighborhood when the Severalty Front's *coup d'état* took place. Or that the coup could have taken place at a worse time for us here aboard the station, with our resources and attention distracted by the murder epidemic."

A look of doubt crossed Dax's face. "What you're suggesting, Benjamin, is collusion between the new Bajoran government and their bitterest enemies. General Aur and the other leaders of the Severalty Front all risked their lives fighting in the resistance against the Cardassians. What could possibly induce them to join in a conspiracy with the only force in the galaxy they despise more than the Federation?"

"I don't know . . . but I have a feeling we're going to find out." He tossed the lash back into the center of the bench. "There's only a few general possibilities, and none of them are very savory. Gul Dukat may have managed to dupe some of the elements of the Front—I know from past experience that he can be quite convincing, even dazzlingly so, when there's something he wants to achieve. The Cardassians did not rule and exploit Bajor for such an extended period of time by force alone. If there's been some kind of arrangement worked out between Dukat and the Front's leaders, they simply may not be aware of its consequences. Or—and it's not a possibility I can lightly dismiss, either—some elements of the Severalty Front may actually be traitors to the cause of Bajoran independence. The Cardassians didn't stay in control of the planet for so long without collaboration on the part of at least some of the Bajorans. If some of those individuals have managed to keep what they did during the occupation a secret, they could have maintained their pro-Cardassian sympathies while establishing themselves in the Front—and now they're actually part of the new government."

"But, Benjamin—we might not be able to determine if that's the situation until after it's too late."

Across the bench from Dax, Odo turned toward the commander. "She's right. Gul Dukat is obviously behind everything that's happened so far. If we do nothing but wait and react to whatever his next step might be, we could find ourselves all being thrown out of this station. I know Dukat as well; he didn't enjoy having to turn DS9 over to Starfleet. He'd do anything to get it back in his control."

"People . . . please." Sisko held up his hand. "You're not telling me anything I haven't already thought about. What we all need to start working on—and immediately—is what our own course of action should be."

Bashir spoke up. "It would be a real help if we brought into the loop our best source for analyzing what's going on with the Bajorans. And that's Major Kira—she knows the individuals in the Severalty Front better than any of us could hope to."

"At this time, Doctor, that's not possible. I've briefed Odo on my recent decisions about Major Kira; you can get the details from him. Until such time as the major is brought back onto full duty, we'll just have to do the best we can without her." Sisko pushed the stool back from the bench and stood up. "Right now, I have to call this meeting to a conclusion. I would suggest that if any of you have ideas regarding the present situation, you should get them to me as soon as possible—we have even less time than you may previously have thought. As I was heading down here on the turbolift, I was notified by Ops that a Bajoran vessel is due to arrive at the station within the hour. It's an official visit, our first from the new government. Apparently, General Aur himself and the new Bajoran Minister of Trade wish to speak to me."

The lab door slid open as Sisko pressed the control panel. He turned in the corridor outside and looked back at his senior officers.

"I don't expect it to be a cordial visit."

"They're already waiting for you, sir." One of the younger Ops staff walked Sisko toward the door of his office. "I thought it best to show them in, rather than have them standing around out here."

"Good thinking." He felt a twinge of resentment, imagining the way in which General Aur might have looked around the station's command center, like a new landlord inspecting his property. "Continue to carry out normal operations. If I require anything, I'll let you know."

The door slid shut behind him. Sisko saw two figures in the office, one seated in front of the desk, back toward him, and the other standing and gazing out at the expanse of stars visible through the curved viewports.

General Aur, hands clasped behind his back, turned toward Sisko. Sisko recognized the leader of the Severalty Front, and now the new Bajoran government, from the briefing files he had scanned on the computer panel. The rigors of the struggle against the Cardassian occupation had bowed the man's back and silvered the sparse hair on his skull; the prison-camp years had creviced the face well beyond his actual years. But now that lined face broke into a smile.

"I've looked forward to making your acquaintance, Commander Sisko." The Bajoran gave a formal nod. The expression that could be read in his eyes was one of deeply rooted self-assurance. "We have a lot to talk about."

Sisko managed to return a fraction of the smile. "Well, General, at least we're starting with something we agree on."

"The new government of Bajor has sent someone else who

will be critical to our discussions." Aur gestured toward the chair before the desk. "This is our new Minister of Trade."

The chair swiveled around to show the black-clad figure in it. The man stood up and grasped Sisko's hand, giving it a firm shake.

"Actually," said McHogue with an even broader smile, "we've already met. Haven't we, Commander?"

CHAPTER
10

FOR A MOMENT, HE FELT DIZZY; HE HAD TO CLOSE HIS EYES AND SHUT
out the images that assaulted him, to keep from falling.

"That's a normal reaction, Commander." The voice
seemed to come from far away, as though the interior o
Sisko's office needed a subspace link to cross from one bulk
head to another. "I've encountered it before. I'm not of
fended by it."

A measure of Sisko's balance returned, though he had to
concentrate to maintain it. He opened his eyes and saw again
McHogue's face before him, with the same mocking half
smile that he had last seen in the holosuite's illusory world.

"Are you all right?" That was General Aur's voice, coming
from somewhere beside him. "Perhaps we should call for one
of your crew, to help you."

"No, no; I'm . . . I'm fine." He waved off Aur's assisting
hand. "I just need to sit down, that's all. The hours I've been
keeping seem to be catching up with me." The excuse
sounded weak, he knew, no matter how forceful he set his
voice.

Behind his desk, he put his hands flat against its surface, as though it were still necessary to steady himself. The inner-ear disturbance that had rocked him for a few seconds had now faded away; a different imbalance, subtler and at the same time more profound, afflicted him.

The smooth expanse of the desktop felt somehow unreal beneath his palms. As though he could push only a little harder, and his fingertips would sink through, his forearms lapped by an opaque mist, only marginally real-seeming in his sight.

He turned away from his visitors and looked across the office. The bulkheads seemed to be painted backdrops that the brush of a hand could have billowed away from the flimsy struts and framing behind. Through the viewports, the galaxy's stars were nothing more than idiot points of light, fed by fiber-optic microfilaments into a sheet of black plastic. A trick, mere stagecraft, and not very well done at that; couldn't Aur see it as well? It was enough to bring a hollow laugh into Sisko's throat—the Bajoran leader had traveled all this way, and found *Deep Space Nine* to be nothing more than a dusty closet, a storeroom where discarded scenery flats were kept until they might be needed again.

"It's just a simple matter of perceptual misalignment." The mordant figure of McHogue leaned back in the opposite chair and watched him. "A slippage of the reality field you carry around inside your head—as I said, I've seen it before. It's one of those things that, in my line of work, I've learned to be careful about. An occupational hazard, as it were. Not that *I* suffer from it anymore, but if the people with whom I need to deal are having a hard time telling what's real and what's not, I've found that it tends to erode that measure of *trust* that's so vital for interpersonal negotiations."

"I expect you're right about that." Sisko couldn't tell if the other man was joking or unctuously sincere. It didn't matter, at least until he knew for sure that there even was someone actually sitting in the chair.

McHogue turned toward the viewports. "General, I know we're pressed for time, but would you indulge me while I have a little chat with the commander? I feel it would be best for all parties concerned."

"By all means." General Aur made an expansive gesture with one hand, then resumed his satisfied contemplation of the stars, only occasionally glancing over his shoulder at the other men in the office.

"I know what's going on inside your mind right now." McHogue leaned forward, his voice dropping to a soothing confidentiality. "I really have come to be something of an expert on these matters. The exposure you had to the cortical-induction modules and their effects—there's a definite persistence factor associated with them that you don't encounter with your regulation, unmodified holosuites. It has to do with the intensity of the hallucination produced by the CI technology—after all, it works upon the actual neurofibers inside one's skull, rather than on input buffered by passage through the peripheral sense organs. Even ordinary reality—this stuff that's supposedly around us right now—is just something that you see and hear and taste." A sweep of McHogue's hand took in the surrounding office, the station and universe beyond. "So in that regard, the CI technology's reality is more real than this one. Or so it seems—it's no wonder that parts of your brain have gotten a little confused."

Sisko made no reply. The sensation of everything around him being essentially false had abated. He rubbed a finger against the desktop's surface. That seemed real enough—at least for the time being.

"What most people in this kind of situation worry about," continued McHogue, "is whether they might be caught up in some sort of self-perpetuating hallucination, a completely enfolding loop of artificially generated realities."

"The thought had crossed my mind." Sisko kept his voice level, as though he were talking about nothing more ominous than the bills of lading on the main pylon. "For all I know, I'm not sitting in my private office at all. Perhaps I'm still in the holosuite with you and all the rest of the CI module's effects inside my brain, and I've been fooled into thinking that the experience is over."

"A common fear, Commander, but a fallacious one." McHogue shook his head. "That's one of the oldest philosophical chestnuts about the holosuite technology in general —it goes back a long way. You can relax; in actual practice, rather than mere theory, it's simply impossible. An infinite regress of that nature, hallucinations inside hallucinations, is rather like trying to multiply by zero in ordinary mathematics. Think about it, Commander: to achieve an infinitely self-perpetuating hallucination would require a time-dilation effect equal to infinity itself. Yet the holosuite that you stepped into can, of necessity, be no more than a subset of infinity. There are real-world limits to what you can pull off along those lines; to even attempt it immediately raises the holosuite's drain upon its outside power sources on an exponential level. The whole thing 'grounds out,' as it were, and you're immediately dumped back out into reality. *This* reality, Commander."

"I suppose I'll have to accept your reasoning. . . ."

"You don't have a lot of alternatives." McHogue leaned back from the desk. "If you're having trouble believing that all this is really happening—that you're sitting in your office and having this meeting with us—it's going to make our discussions very difficult. The little spiel I just gave you doesn't come simply from kindheartedness on my part, Commander—I dislike negotiating with someone who doubts my existence, even as I'm sitting face-to-face with them."

"Very well." The black-clad figure's smug delivery had a restorative effect on Sisko; his growing irritation at the lecture had burned away the last residual doubts. When he had first encountered McHogue, in the holosuite's perpetual summer landscape, the desire to get his hands around the man's throat had been irresistible. A vestige of that impulse flared up inside him now. *That would be one way,* he thought grimly, *of finding out what's real.* He pushed the notion away; as of now, he had to treat this person as an official representative of the Bajoran government. "How's this: I'll just deal with what I see right now, and I'll reserve my judgment until later as to whether it's real or not."

He turned toward the other person in the room, before McHogue could reply. "General Aur—if you'd care to join us, perhaps we could get down to business."

The general took the other chair in front of the desk. "I trust you'll give our Minister of Trade your full cooperation, Commander." He indicated McHogue with a brief nod. "One of our new government's first acts was to make an official exemption to the requirement that all top-level ministers be Bajoran natives. Mr. McHogue brings some unique qualifications to the position, that we felt made him the perfect choice."

"I can well imagine."

"So in the future, I expect all your dealings with our government will be through him. He has our complete trust and authority. I came along on this trip just to assure you of that."

"Really?" Sisko reached over and turned the screen of his computer panel toward Aur. "I could show you some very interesting things about your new minister. Little details of his past career—"

"We know all about that, Commander." The general patted McHogue's arm. "Let's just say he has a *colorful* background."

"That's putting it mildly." Sisko ignored the Minister of Trade's smile. "There's about a dozen recent murders here aboard *Deep Space Nine* that can be linked to some involvement on his part."

Aur shrugged. "Regrettable, but . . . perhaps necessary. For the future of Bajor. I'm just sorry they happened on your watch, Commander."

The last comment was enough of a needle to penetrate Sisko's facade of politeness. He turned toward McHogue. "So what exactly are we going to talk about, then?"

McHogue's smile vanished. "I've made a better offer to the Bajoran government. Better than the one that was made by you and the Federation. Let's face it: Bajor may not have much, but it has one thing that's of incredible value. And the Federation's offered the Bajorans not much more than zero for it.

"The wormhole, of course." McHogue pointed to the viewports. "It's a shame that it's not visible all the time, rather than just when a ship passes through it. If it were, you might be a little more mindful of why you're here."

"I know very well why I'm here." Sisko let his voice grate even more harshly. "And why Starfleet is here."

"Oh, yes; of course." McHogue glanced over at General Aur, raised his eyebrows, then came back to Sisko. "Are you going to give us that old song-and-dance about developing Bajor into a major locus for interstellar commerce and research?"

"It's hardly a song-and-dance. The wormhole is the doorway to the entire Gamma Quadrant—"

"Exactly. And that's why the Federation has kept you and your crew here to sit on it. Doesn't it seem a little odd to you that it's already been established that the wormhole is Bajoran property, yet somehow Bajor doesn't control access to it?"

"That objection has been heard here before." He could feel his spine stiffening. "And as I made clear to representatives of the previous government, Bajor is simply not ready to take over the administration of this station. When that time comes—"

General Aur interrupted angrily. "The previous government was composed of traitors and spineless compromisers. That's why the Bajoran people rose up and got rid of them. The so-called representatives you met with before were slaves to the colonial mentality that served the interests of the Cardassians for so long—and now the Federation would like to exploit us the same way." He gripped the arms of the chair, thrusting his scarred face forward. "You're not dealing with those people anymore, Commander; you're dealing with true Bajorans now."

"Gentlemen, gentlemen; let's take it down a level, why don't we?" McHogue smiled and spread his hands apart. "There's no need to get overly upset about these things. It's been my experience over the years that all politics, when you boil them down, are essentially business matters. And business is always something that's best conducted with a certain measure of . . . cold-bloodedness." The smile grew broader. "And then we can all shake hands and be friends afterward."

"That's not likely to happen." Sisko returned his gaze to General Aur. "What is this 'better offer' that this person has made to you?"

McHogue answered. "It's the opportunity for Bajor to become something besides a glorified rest stop and maintenance center for the Federation. This talk of 'developing' Bajor is a giant scam, and you know it. The Federation gets control of the wormhole, and with it the access to the Gamma Quadrant, and the Bajorans get to wait on tables and maneuver fuel cells into position on the vessels passing through— we're talking your basic unskilled labor, Commander. Service jobs. If you were a businessman such as myself, I'd expect you to be more familiar with the principle that the real money in any enterprise comes from holding an equity position in it—*real* equity, and not just this nominal ownership that the Federation will allow to Bajor. Without *real* control over this station and the wormhole, there's never going to be a time when Bajor gets anything other than the thinnest sliver of the pie."

Sisko shook his head. "General Aur, if this is the line—the sales pitch—that has been used on you, all I can say is that he's completely misrepresented the intent of the Federation here."

Aur regarded the commander coldly. "Our Minister of Trade has stated some very convincing arguments."

"But they're totally absurd!" exploded Sisko.

"Is that so?" McHogue's dark eyes fastened onto the figure opposite him. "Then maybe you can explain a few things about your ongoing research activities here. For the sake of argument, let's just say that the Bajorans should be satisfied with the slice of the pie you're offering them; that their share of the revenues from the exploitation of the wormhole will be much bigger than what I've told them will be the case. Isn't it true, Commander, that you've already established that the stable wormhole that's been discovered here is not a naturally occurring phenomenon, but an artificially created one?"

Sisko couldn't detect what McHogue was driving at; he nodded slowly. "That appears to be the case; we've assumed that the intelligent creatures we've encountered inside the wormhole did in fact create it—"

"And isn't it also true that a large proportion of the Federation's research efforts scheduled to take place here at DS9 will be devoted to finding out just how the stable wormhole was created?"

"But . . . of course—"

McHogue sat back with a smug expression, as though he had just won a debating point. "You say 'of course' so easily, Commander. You don't even try to conceal the fact that this research regarding the wormhole is so obviously for the benefit of the Federation, and *against* the interests of the world whose property it supposedly is. The wormhole is Bajor's one remaining possession of value; its *scarcity,* its uniqueness, is what makes it valuable—and the Federation would like nothing more than to find out how to make a billion more wormholes! Right now, the Bajorans own the only practical route to the Gamma Quadrant; the Federation's scientists could discover tomorrow the secret to creating a stable wormhole, and the value of Bajor's asset would be reduced to approximately zero."

"Well, Commander Sisko?" The general peered sharply at him. "What's your answer to that?"

In frustration, he struck the desktop with his fist. "You have to understand—the results of finding out the wormhole's secrets would be enormous. The benefits for every world in the Federation would be almost incalculable."

"Ah." McHogue smiled. "But Bajor isn't part of the Federation. Is it?"

"Not yet—but—"

"Nor will it ever be." General Aur broke into the discussion. "Not if we have any say in the matter. Even if the Federation's offer to us was legitimate—and I've seen no evidence that the Federation has our interests at heart any more than did the Cardassians—why should we accept it? Why should we become one among many, spreading the wealth that will come from the exploitation of the wormhole among worlds and peoples with whom we have nothing in common? It's far better—from *our* viewpoint, at least—to keep Bajor's riches for the sake of Bajorans."

"But there are things of value that you would get from membership in the Federation. The technology alone—"

"If there's anything we want from the Federation," said General Aur, "then we'll *buy* it from you. Because we'll be able to do that."

"And just what do you think you'll sell, for Bajor to have that kind of capital?" If the general wanted to discuss hard economic realities, then Sisko was ready for him. "There's a built-in limit to how much you can charge for access to the wormhole and passage to and from the Gamma Quadrant. A great deal, perhaps even a majority, of the traffic will be speculative in nature, voyages of exploration to see what's exactly out there and whether any profitable use can be made of it. That kind of investigation doesn't pay off for a long time. By turning your back on the Federation's assistance, you'd be condemning the people of Bajor to decades, perhaps centuries, of continuing poverty. After their having freed themselves from the Cardassians and having a taste of the possibilities that were just beginning to open for them, do you really think your own followers will have much enthusiasm for going down a path like that?"

"The Bajoran people are used to sacrifice, Commander." Aur folded his arms across his chest. "If such hardships were required for the greater glory of Bajor, they would see the wisdom of it."

"Fortunately for all concerned," said McHogue, "there aren't going to be any hardships. I'm not in the business of giving people a rougher time than they've already had. I'm here to make life *better* for everyone." His smile showed again, even more radiant. "You as well, Commander Sisko. From the little bits of time we've been able to spend together, I have to admit that I've developed a certain . . . *interest* in some of your more personal concerns. I'd like to help you with those."

"I've seen the results of your 'help.'" Sisko felt his own glare tightening his face. "Let's just keep this discussion limited to Bajoran affairs."

"As you wish." McHogue's smile faded. "You want to talk cash flow? Fine. Because I've got news for you. The planet

171

Bajor isn't going to be flat broke anymore, the way that the Federation has kept it. Bajor has something even more valuable than the wormhole to sell. Something that everyone else in the galaxy will be happy to spend their money on, starting right now."

"And what might that be?"

"*License,* Commander. Pure, unadultered license. The permission to do whatever one wants, and a place to do it in—as long as the bill can be paid." With one hand, McHogue made a sweeping gesture, matching the salesman's fervor rising in his voice. "We have here an unprecedented opportunity to re-create the long-neglected—but *essential*—aspect of the great frontier communities of the past. This is tradition, Commander; history—and humanoid nature—is on our side. We're talking unhindered personal anarchy here; isn't that what everybody wants? It's just that it's usually hard to pull off, I admit. But Bajor is in a unique situation for making this a viable commercial proposition. I wouldn't be here, otherwise."

Sisko gave a deep sigh. *"This* is what you've sold the new Bajoran government on?" He glanced over at Aur. "I'm surprised, General. But also a little disappointed. You've been dealing with a con man, a scam artist. This is one of the oldest money-for-nothing schemes in the galaxy. Megacasinos, pleasure emporia, worlds given over to satisfying every possible vice and indulgence—they all sound like a good idea at the beginning. But then they inevitably collapse, and the operators are left with nothing but a planetful of broken Dabo tables and empty brothels. When the cash registers stop ringing, and every other possible revenue source has been allowed to fall into ruin, it's not a pretty sight."

"You know, I expected exactly this kind of reaction from someone in your position." McHogue shook his head slowly. "After all, you do represent not just the Federation's interests, but also its rather, shall we say, *antiquated* morals. And in my experience, there's nothing that Starfleet officers like better than putting on their little uniforms and zipping around the galaxy to look down their noses at what other people do for a living."

"In your case, that's not difficult."

"Oh—" McHogue made a show of wincing. "Careful, Commander; remember, you're talking to a minister of the Bajoran government. But then again, if you want to dispense with all the diplomatic niceties, I can handle that." He leaned across the desk, jabbing a finger toward Sisko. "The Bajorans are not quite the fools that you and all the rest of the Federation take them to be. They didn't go for the economic development plan I presented them because they were suckers for a fast line. I gave them hard facts and figures, about just what kind of money they can expect to generate."

"The numbers add up," said General Aur. "That's why we put Mr. McHogue in charge of the Trade Ministry."

"Did he also tell you what the Federation's reaction to your business enterprise was most likely to be, and the effect that would have on your profits?"

"Fortunately, Commander, you're bound by Starfleet's own Prime Directive. You're forbidden to meddle with the internal affairs of a non-Federation world."

Sisko nodded. "That's true, of course. Bajor and any other world is free to go to hell in whatever particular handbasket it chooses. But if you believe that the Federation has no other courses of action available to it, then you're sadly mistaken. There's quite a bit that we can do to minimize the negative effects of such an enterprise as you're contemplating. The Federation can place an embargo on such a rogue world, effectively sealing it off from commerce with all other Federation members. That greatly diminishes the chances of economic success for anyone taking that route of total, unhindered personal anarchy. So much so that all the worlds that have tried it in the past eventually saw the light, and wound up abandoning that course, so as to reap the benefits of achieving full Federation membership."

"Ah, yes, the embargo tactic." A sneer formed on McHogue's face. "If the Federation doesn't get what it wants, it has other ways of bullying others into line. It's really too bad that that tactic has been successful so many times in the past. Too bad for you, Commander—because it's created a blind spot for you about the situation here. The Federation's embargoes have worked before because those worlds you employed them against had nothing else going for them except the behavior the Federation was so offended by; they had no other way of insuring that customers would come to their door for what they had to sell. But things are different here: *Bajor has the wormhole.* The Federation can't cut Bajor off, no matter how offensive or negative it might find our economic activities to be, without cutting itself off from the wormhole and the access to the Gamma Quadrant. And if the Federation should be so foolish as to be willing to pay that price, there are plenty of other political forces in the galaxy who are less prudish and more pragmatic than that. And they'd be happy to fill the vacuum created by the Federation's withdrawal and take advantage of the opportunities here. The Cardassians are still kicking themselves for giving up Bajor just before the wormhole was discovered. A Federation embargo would be perfect for letting them get back into the game as a significant force."

Sisko turned toward the general. "And is that how you see it? After spending your whole life fighting against the Cardassians, you'd be willing to let them back into Bajoran affairs?"

"If it was on our terms, then yes." Aur's hardened gaze shot back at Sisko. "In a minute. I don't think you appreciate how desperate conditions are on Bajor. We're a broken, starving people, Commander; we have little left to us besides our hunger. If we have to climb back into bed with the devil to feed ourselves—to feed our children—then it's going to happen, no matter what. I'm just trying to create a situation where *we* call the shots, and not Gul Dukat. Or you and the Federation."

"Do you really think your fellow Bajorans have a moral sense as flexible as yours, General? What happens to your new government when the people you lead find out that you've been making deals with their sworn enemies, the exploiters who raped their world in the first place? I imagine that their reaction will be disgust, and then a wrath that you won't be able to survive."

A thin smile formed on Aur's face. "Your estimation of my people is very flattering, Commander. But you speak of a finely principled disdain, and that's an expensive indulgence —and one that the Bajoran people cannot afford any longer. If Bajor should wind up wealthy from the indulging of other peoples' vices—and the Cardassians made it possible—I don't think anyone's going to complain too loudly." He leaned back in his chair. "Read your history books, Commander. Or just look around at your fellow Starfleet officers —you'll see that yesterday's enemy is often today's friend." The smile widened. "Why shouldn't Bajorans be as wise— and flexible—as you are?"

With evident pleasure, McHogue had listened to Aur's speech. "You see, Commander, I didn't have to make any sales pitch to the new Bajoran government; they're perfectly capable of seeing the advantages to a straightforward proposition—one that pays off now, rather than at some remote pie-in-the-sky time in the future. If then. So your big talk about an embargo doesn't scare us much. Quite frankly, I don't think the Federation would even have the nerve to try it.

There's so many reasons why the various members of the Federation would want to continue dealing with Bajor—mainly to get access to the wormhole—that any embargo would be widely disregarded by them. As the general has pointed out, history can be very instructive; it shows that if you've got something people want, they'll find a way to do business with you. That's why black markets were invented. The Federation would find itself in the rather embarrassing position of turning a blind eye to violations of the embargo, or trying to enforce it with various sanctions against its own members. Do you think the Federation would really want to risk a split in its ranks? Though of course, there's always the military option; Starfleet could ring Bajor with battle cruisers, to try and prevent anyone coming in from outside. Would *you* like to be the one in charge of that operation, Commander?—especially when it would inevitably lead to a full-scale confrontation with the Cardassians. And Gul Dukat would love to have an opportunity to represent the Cardassians to the galaxy as the heroic defenders of the Bajorans' right to self-determination against the meddling Federation. Whatever the Cardassians didn't win in battle, they'd more than make up for on the field of public opinion. In some ways, that's a pity—I'm really afraid you'd come out looking like the villain of the story."

It was difficult to come up with a reply; the smugness apparent on McHogue's face, as he had delivered his spiel, had thrown a flaring spark upon the tinder of Sisko's anger. A few moments of glaring silence passed before he spoke. "If you've managed to convince the Bajorans that they could trust their interests to the Cardassians, then you're an even better salesman than I had previously thought."

Aur's voice was mild by comparison. "Diplomacy, Commander, is the art of arranging as many things as possible beforehand—and then pretending to be surprised afterward, when things just happen to work out the way you want. Let's just say that the Severalty Front has been in touch with Gul Dukat for some time now—long before we were ready to take over the government. Agreements have been made, of which you have absolutely no awareness." Aur smiled. "It might almost be fair to say that we've all become business partners now."

"And we can't wait to get started, can we, General?" With his hands clasped behind his head, McHogue tilted his chair back. "This is the deal of the millennium, Commander. Everything I've done up until now looks pretty small next to it. On top of everything else, we've got an arrow in our quiver that *nobody* has ever had before—and that's the cortical-induction modules. Well, nobody's had the CI technology since the Federation yanked it out of the holosuites' original design and banned it."

"It was banned for good reason," snapped Sisko.

"Yes, right; whatever. Just more Federation prudishness, as far as I'm concerned."

"Gentlemen—I think we've talked long enough." A degree of McHogue's smugness had transferred to General Aur's face. "Commander Sisko, I just wanted to be sure that you had been made fully aware of the new Bajoran government's intentions. I don't imagine that we can expect much cooperation from you, but I'd also like to hope that there will be no futile attempts at interference. These matters have gone far beyond the point where you could do anything to change them. It's a wise man who knows when he's been presented with a *fait accompli."* He turned to McHogue. "We should be getting back to Bajor. There are other arrangements that need to be taken care of."

"I'll join you at the ship in a few minutes. I wanted a little time alone with the commander."

When the door had slid shut again and the two of them were

alone in the office, McHogue gazed up at the ceiling before speaking. "You know, the general is exactly the kind of business partner I like to have. Very forthright; he believes everything should be out in the open."

Sisko studied through narrowed eyes the figure remaining before him. "It's obvious to me that your preferred business partner is one that you've managed to keep in the dark about your actual intentions. I can't imagine that someone such as Aur would go along with your plans, if he was aware of the true nature of the CI modules and what they can do."

"Perhaps." McHogue shrugged. "But at this point, you'd have little chance of informing him about that. Why should he trust anything a Starfleet officer would tell him?"

"Because—unlike yourself—I'd tell him the truth."

"Commander . . . you're flattering yourself, if you think you know the truth. All of it, that is. When the Federation banned the CI technology, they hadn't even yet determined the limits of its potential—if they could see what I've done to make it even more powerful, they'd really go out of their minds. Just like our customers are going to. People from all over the galaxy are going to flock to Bajor, not just to experience CI-generated hallucinations, but to actually live them—in *this* reality. The holosuites on Bajor will be the ultimate advertisement for what we're actually going to be selling. Experiences that our customers will be able to get nowhere else."

"Even if those experiences lead to the destruction— physical or psychological—of the person involved?" Revulsion swelled in Sisko's gut.

"*Caveat emptor,* Commander." McHogue shrugged. "We can't hold everybody's hand, and prevent them all from having a good time. We just want to make sure that they buy that good time—maybe the ultimate good time—from us. And that's what we're ready to do." His smile turned into a teeth-revealing grin. "Whatever happens, I can promise you that it's going to involve a major drain on credit accounts all across the galaxy."

Sisko contemptuously regarded the figure. "You're certainly open about revealing your intentions. To me, at least."

"Perhaps . . . but then again, I do like to keep a few cards close to my chest. Force of habit, really; the beauty of this setup is that there isn't anything you, or all the rest of Starfleet and the Federation, can do about it. That's why I have no objection to Starfleet retaining control of DS9—though of course, I'd just as soon not provoke the Federation into any rash attempt at interfering with my plans. It's just good business practice to leave your opponent with at least *something*." McHogue nodded slowly, mulling another thought over. "Actually, I'd like to think that I'm doing the same for you. You personally, that is. Giving you an opportunity that you might not have had otherwise." The self-amused malice had faded from his voice. "Maybe you'd feel better about all this if you just looked at it the right way."

"Oh?" Sisko felt like bodily throwing the man out of the office, but restrained himself as before. "And how's that?"

"I think we'd both agree that a successful salesman—or con man, if you'd rather—is always something of a psychologist as well. I have to know what you want before I can provide you with it. And I know a great deal about you; I've made it my business to. The way I see your problem, Commander, it's that you want two different things. Part of you wants to run your little empire here aboard *Deep Space Nine* . . . and part of you might just want to quit and go home to Earth to raise your son." McHogue tilted his head and smiled. "Am I getting close? It'd be hard for anyone to choose between two desires —two *duties*—like that; the choice would have to be made by someone else. And that's what a debacle such as losing the Federation's control over Bajor and the wormhole would be good for; the only possible outcome after that would be for you to be transferred to a safe desk job back on Earth. And maybe that's what you really want."

He said nothing. He couldn't; the words had been like a finger tapping against a secret chamber of his heart.

"Look on the bright side, Commander." McHogue pushed himself up from the chair and took a few steps away from the desk, then stopped and turned back around. "You can start packing your bags now."

The door slid open and he was gone, leaving Sisko in the office's enfolding silence.

He woke, not even knowing what time it was. The data padd on which he had been entering his homework assignment dropped onto the bedroom floor as he sat up. Listening, he could tell that someone else was in the living quarters.

Jake looked around the room's door and down the short corridor. He could see his father sitting on one of the couches in the main area, gazing ahead of himself as though deep in thought. One of his father's hands rested on the wooden crate that had been brought back by Major Kira from Bajor. The crate hadn't been opened yet, but Jake knew what was in it; his father had told him that it was all stuff that had belonged to the Kai Opaka. She had been his father's friend, and was missed by him now that she was gone. There had been things that his father had discussed with the Kai, that he didn't talk to anyone else about. Not so much important things— important in the big sense—but things that were inside him. It was no wonder that he missed her.

Barefoot, Jake walked out to the main area and sat down on the edge of the couch. His father looked tired, eyes closed, head slumped forward as though pulled by some invisible weight.

"Dad—"

Sometimes his father came back here to their living quarters and kept on working on stuff that he should have left back at his office on the Ops deck. Sometimes Jake could almost see it all stirring around inside his father's head, as though he could look right through his father's skull.

The heavy-lidded eyes opened and glanced over at Jake. His father hadn't been asleep.

"Dad, maybe you should go to bed." If he didn't take care of him, who would? "It's late."

"Is it?" His father's voice was a murmur. The outstretched hand brushed across the surface of the crate. "I suppose you're right. . . ."

He watched as his father drew a deep breath, shoulders lifting and then falling. His father spotted something on the floor beside the couch, reached down, and picked up the baseball bat that Jake had left propped in one of the room's corners. He studied it for a moment, the polished wood lying across his broad palms.

"Jake . . ." His father didn't look up at him. "Have you ever thought what it would be like . . . to go home?"

That puzzled him. "What do you mean? We *are* home."

His father smiled sadly and shook his head. "No, I meant your real home. I meant going back to Earth." His gaze lifted to Jake's. "Would you like that?"

The question made him feel uncomfortable. "I don't know. . . ." He couldn't be sure what his father was really asking. "I guess it'd be okay."

"Just okay?"

Jake shrugged. "If that's what *you* wanted. But I'd miss being here."

His father peered more closely into Jake's eyes. "You'd miss the station?"

"Well . . . sure." He was trying to think of some way of explaining it. "You know how we'd always go into one of the holosuites together, and there'd be all that grass and trees and stuff, and the blue sky?"

Slowly, his father nodded.

"I always went in there with you," said Jake, "because it was what you wanted. Because that's your home. Earth and everything." He glanced around the dimly lit living quarters. In his mind's eye, he could see all the richly intricate spaces and corridors beyond. A little world. A big world. He looked back at his father. "This is my home."

His father was silent for a long time. Then he nodded. "It's my home too, son. Now it is." He set the baseball bat down on the table in front of the couch, then tapped the comm badge on his uniform. "Computer, give me Ops."

The voice of one of the Ops deck staff responded. "Yes, Commander?"

"Notify all senior officers that I wish to see them in my office in four . . . no, make that six hours. Top priority— we've got a lot of strategy to work out."

Jake's father stood up. "Come on—" He reached a hand down. "We better get all the rest we can. Might be the last chance for a while."

MOAGITTY

CHAPTER
11

HE LOOKED AT THE SPHEROID OBJECT, UNABLE TO RECALL EXACTLY what it was. It seemed to be made of some kind of treated organic matter—most likely the skin of an animal—and stitched together with what appeared to be crude surgical sutures.

"Just what is that?" Odo pointed to the sphere in Quark's hand.

On the other side of the bar, Quark had been contemplating the object as well, but not with any visible mystification. Rather a brooding sullenness, the focus of his attention deep in that part of his Ferengi brain that calculated both revenge and profits. His ridged thumb rubbed across the stitches like an unhealed wound.

"This?" Quark drew himself back to real time. "I believe it's what is known as a *baseball*. Used in a certain primitive athletic endeavor. Though I'm not quite sure what you're supposed to do with it." He held the ball up on the tips of his fingers. "Maybe throw it at someone." He ventured an experimental tap with it against his own skull. "Doesn't seem

185

very efficient. Now the other thing that's used in the game, what they call the *bat*—a nice big heavy stick—I can see the point of that." He nodded in satisfaction. "Maybe I should get one."

"Really?" Odo peered at the Ferengi. "I would never have imagined you being interested in these so-called sports. Though I approve—it might burn up some of the energy you devote to less savory pursuits."

"There's nothing unsavory about making money. Actually—" Quark scowled. "It's everything else I can't stand. That's why I thought it might be handy to have a baseball bat around; I could use it to clear out some of my so-called customers who think I'm running a social parlor and not a drinking establishment."

"Spoken like the genteel host I've always known you to be." Odo looked across the tables and booths filling the space; as at any moment of a shift, the place was well stocked with patrons, all of them downing Quark's synthale and more elaborate concoctions at a steady rate. Any faster, and Quark would have had the problem of them keeling over backward in their chairs. Odo brought his stern gaze back around to the Ferengi. "However, I don't advise you to add assault and battery to your menu here. That's still against regulations."

"Merely a joke, my dear Odo." The ball was left on top of the bar as Quark spread his palms in a mollifying gesture. "You should try to maintain your sense of humor—the way I have to. No one saw me getting all upset when this thing came bouncing in here." His expression clouded. "Not very upset, at any rate. Considering the damages . . ." His voice had sank to a mutter.

"Damages? You didn't report anything like that to the security office."

"Oh, sure—just as if that would do any good. *Nobody* on this station cares about the problems of the poor, beleaguered businessman."

"I think I've heard this line from you before—"

It didn't matter; Quark was on a roll. "Just look at this!" He stooped down and pulled a box from behind the bar, setting it down with a jingling thump in front of Odo. "There must be at least a dozen broken glasses here, a bottle of imported *arrak* that was nearly full when it got hit by this stupid baseball . . ." Quark poked a finger through the shards of glass; the sharp odor of spilled alcohol wafted up. "Not to mention that I wound up paying the cleaning bills for the two Klingons who were sitting right here when it happened."

"That was decent of you."

"They were going to pull my head off. As if it were *my* fault!" Quark's expression grew even gloomier. "Though how anyone's supposed to tell the difference between a Klingon who's had his laundry done and one who hasn't, is beyond me." Like a suddenly released spring, he leaned past Odo and shouted. "Come on, you campers, drink up! I've got bills to pay!"

Odo pushed him back with a gently restraining hand. "You're not doing yourself any favors by badgering your patrons."

"Why not?" Quark looked sincerely puzzled. "They're a captive audience. Where else are they going to go?"

Across the establishment, faces had turned toward the bar and the irate figure behind it; then shoulders had been shrugged and conversations resumed.

"Perhaps you could regain your equanimity while sitting in one of the security office's holding cells." Odo drew his hand back from the Ferengi's chest.

"On what charge?"

"Disturbing the peace. Your premises are, after all, part of this station and thus under my authority as well."

"Hmph." Quark straightened the lapels of his jacket. "Just the sort of reaction I expected from an alleged public servant. For this I pay my lease and license fees." He stowed the box of glass fragments under the bar. "I don't suppose the problems of a relatively honest man trying to make a living around here will be very high on the agenda of this big meeting you're having with Commander Sisko."

"What do you know about that?"

Quark looked smug as he stood back up. "Oh, one hears things." He rolled the baseball around with one finger. "Talk travels fast, you know."

"Especially when one pays to have it come this way." It was a constant annoyance to Odo, that a Ferengi innkeeper would have an information source on the station's Ops deck.

"Well . . ." Quark shrugged. "Nobody would tell me these things otherwise."

Odo turned away, watching the flow of traffic on the Promenade. "I think you can rest assured that we won't be dealing with your petty concerns."

"Just talking about McHogue, huh?"

He glanced back at the Ferengi. "Why would we discuss him?"

"Come on. What else is there? Everybody knows he's been made the new Bajoran Minister of Trade. Quite an interesting development."

Odo kept his voice casual. "What else do people know?"

"You mean, what else do *I* know. I'd be more inclined to tell you, if your attitude was a little more helpful and a lot less hostile." Quark picked up the baseball and contemplated it in his hand. "My old partner actually found time to come by here and have a chat with me." His brows creased for a moment. "If it really was McHogue; I'm still not sure . . ."

"I'm sure enough." Odo leaned in close to Quark's face. "Tell me what McHogue wanted with you, and we'll discuss the price of the information afterward."

"Normally, I don't do business except cash up front—" Quark emitted a panicked squeak as Odo reached for his collar. With his back against the bar's racks of bottles, he smiled with nervous ingratiation. "But in this case, I'll make an exception. McHogue made me a job offer. That's all."

Odo eyed him suspiciously. "What sort of job offer?"

"He wanted me to manage the concessions for alcohol and, ah, *stronger* intoxicants in the new city that's going to be built on Bajor. Where all the casinos and pleasure emporia are going to be located. McHogue said he wanted someone with my kind of experience in charge; he'd observed how I run my place here aboard DS9, and he thought I could do as good a job down there, on a much larger scale. Naturally, I had to agree with him."

"So you're taking this job of his?" Odo had mixed feelings about the prospect. As much as he despised the Ferengi, he had also gotten him to the point of being a semireliable informant.

"Of course not." Quark indignantly drew himself up. "I've worked a long time to establish myself as my own boss. I take a great deal of personal pride in my humble enterprise, thank you. As far as I'm concerned, I'd rather empty my customers' pockets my own way and be able to sleep at night than get rich working for someone else. Or some *thing.*" Quark shook his head in puzzlement. "You know, he *says* he's my old business partner McHogue . . ."

"A whole new city . . ." Odo mulled over the new information. That kind of operation would require a significant amount of capital—more than the Bajorans would be able to provide. Which indicated that the Cardassians' involvement in McHogue's schemes extended beyond their connection to the CI modules. "Interesting."

"That's what I thought."

Odo pushed himself away from the bar. "Perhaps Commander Sisko and the others at the meeting will have something to add to it—"

"Hey, wait a minute—you owe me one now!"

He raised an eyebrow as he regarded the Ferengi. "Really? I

thought that perhaps you had merely decided to perform your duty as one of DS9's good citizens."

"Come on," pleaded Quark. "Fair's fair."

"That's an extraordinary thing for you to say. All right, then." Odo turned back toward the bar. "What is it?"

"This." Quark held up the baseball. "I want to know who slung this dangerous projectile into my peaceful establishment."

"Surely you already have a good idea who's responsible."

"Yes, but I want *proof.*" Quark did his best to look self-righteous. "Unlike some people here, I don't go around making baseless accusations."

"Very well. I'll see what I can do." Odo reached for the ball.

"Uh-uh." The Ferengi drew the stitched spheroid back against his chest. "I'll hang on to the evidence, if you don't mind."

"As you wish. But, as I believe is commonly said in your circles—don't hold your breath." Odo turned and headed for the door.

He looked around at the faces assembled in the office. As they had been before, and not too long ago, either—despite all their efforts, the situation in which they found themselves had gotten worse rather than better.

"There's one thing in our favor," said Commander Sisko. "Our attention is no longer divided. The political crisis on Bajor has dovetailed with our investigation into the murder epidemic here aboard the station. The same individuals were responsible for both." He managed to produce a thin smile. "Now all we have to do is find a single solution, rather than two different ones."

"For what it's worth, Commander—" Chief of Operations O'Brien shifted in the chair at one end of the semicircle. "We wouldn't have had to worry about the problem with the murders any longer. Once we had their source pinpointed to the altered holosuites and their effects, it was mainly a technical problem after that. Wasn't too hard to design a retrofit circuit that could be installed in-line on all the station's holosuites; the circuit can identify any form of the CI technology and immediately reject it. Sort of like an immune system identifying a contagion factor and immediately eliminating it. Plus there's an autodestruct function built in; anybody tries to pull the retrofit circuit, there'll be a power surge that'll blow out every filament and microdevice in the suite. That alone would set off an alarm right here in Ops." O'Brien sounded justifiably proud of his handiwork. "I've got my engineering crew building and installing the retrofits as fast as they can. The question is, do you want us to shut down the one holosuite that we left the CI module running in, and fix it up as well?"

"I think we should leave that one as is, for the time being." Sisko glanced toward the security chief. "Constable, is that holosuite still under security lockdown?"

Odo nodded. "Per your orders."

"Maintain that status on it. Now that McHogue's used DS9 as a cage full of guinea pigs, and he's presumably satisfied that the CI technology works to his satisfaction, he'll be shifting all his activities to Bajor. As long as we have that one altered holosuite, though, we still have a window into how his mind works—there might still be something of value to be gotten from that."

"McHogue's plans for Bajor seem to be already in motion." Odo glanced at a few notes on his data padd. "Before I arrived at this meeting, I had a discussion with Quark down on the Promenade. It seems that there's going to be an entire new city built on the planet, just for McHogue's operations."

"Hm." Sisko swiveled his chair toward Odo. "Your analysis, Constable?"

"I would venture that there's a high degree of probability for this particular datum. Not so much due to the source from which I received it, but simply because it would be the most advantageous setup for McHogue. There's really no city on the planet's surface, other than the capital, that would be large enough for the enterprise that McHogue is apparently contemplating. And using the capital would have too many political drawbacks for General Aur and the rest of the new government. There are large segments of the Bajoran population with deeply rooted puritanical tendencies; they might be willing to endure this newfound wealth coming from an enterprise that would otherwise offend them, but not if it was taking place right in front of their eyes. If any of the religious factions pulled out of the Severalty Front's coalition, it could topple the government."

Sisko nodded as he followed the security chief's argument. Odo was doing as good a job as possible, filling the gap created by Kira's absence from the meeting. If she had been here—and brought back onto full duty—he would have had that much more of an insight into the Bajoran situation.

"Very well," said Sisko. "We'll have to operate as if it's true, then. Any further analysis?"

"The kind of resources necessary would indicate a greater degree of Cardassian involvement than we had previously assumed."

"With Gul Dukat in our navigational sector, that's almost a given." He swiveled toward Dax and Bashir, sitting immediately across from him. "Do you have any more data from your work on the CI modules?"

"Everything we've discovered so far, Benjamin, just confirms our initial theories about the cortical-induction technology." Dax pointed to the computer panel on the desktop. "I uploaded a full report on our latest findings."

"We were able to break down the CI modules' programming to its initial level," added Bashir. "Most of what we saw with Wyoss and the other subjects were the terminal stages of the process. Essentially, all the sequences have an extremely low addiction threshold, followed by a steeply ramped burn-through cycle. It's a classic pharmacological analogue, similar to inserting permanent stimulus molecules in the brain's opiate-receptor sites—except that the CI technology uses the neurosystem's own catecholamines, so the process is even more efficient. It would be virtually impossible to develop a pharmacological antagonist system to block it. And past a certain level, the chances of a successful therapeutic response would be minimal. Once they're introduced to the CI technology's effects, a high percentage of McHogue's customers would wind up the same way Ahrmant Wyoss did."

"It doesn't make sense." Sisko frowned and set his fist upon the desk. "McHogue is supposedly more familiar with the CI technology than anyone—or at least he claims to be. He knows that the fantasies evoked in the altered holosuites are deliberately addictive—and unsatisfying. The cortical induction actually brings to the surface—or it even creates—desires that have to be acted upon. This isn't just business on his part: he's creating an environment that goes far beyond just draining his customers of their money. He's made the CI modules' effects even stronger than they were originally designed to be—to the point of lethality. Even as greedy an operator as our own Quark knows better: a successful business enterprise doesn't kill off its customers. It keeps them coming back for more—indefinitely." He clenched his fist tighter. "There must be something else that McHogue is trying to achieve. . . ."

Odo shrugged. "Undoubtedly, there were some hazards in his research on the CI technology. The echo that you described encountering in the altered holosuite may be indication of his present mental state. Quite frankly, the possibility exists that McHogue may be insane."

"No—" Sisko shook his head. "That's not enough to

explain what's going on. Even if it were true, it doesn't account for the Cardassians' involvement. It's not likely that Gul Dukat is insane as well. Or at least not in the same way."

"Given the data we have, Benjamin, there are no other theories available to us." Dax glanced at the station's officers on either side of her. "The only option for us at this point is further investigation."

"Of what? You've taken everything down to the end of its various blind alleys." Inside himself, Sisko could feel the frustration knotting his gut. "McHogue's plans are already under way—we don't have time to just wait for information to fall into our laps."

"I'd like to make a suggestion, Commander." Odo leaned stiffly forward. "I believe you've been informed that a Cardassian diplomatic vessel has approached the outskirts of our sector, and that Gul Dukat himself is aboard—"

"Of course." Sisko gave a quick nod. "Dukat was apparently empowered by the Cardassian council to give immediate recognition to General Aur's new government after the coup."

"Precisely. Gul Dukat is obviously the point man for whatever the Cardassians' intentions are for Bajor; thus, he is also McHogue's co-conspirator. I have long experience with Gul Dukat; under his administration of DS9, I served in the same position as I do now. So I can state with some authority that I know how his mind works. I don't have the same familiarity with McHogue, except as a criminal type that I've encountered many times before. Dukat is preternaturally suspicious of everyone, including his own allies and fellow Cardassians—that's a fundamental trait of their species. I would expect McHogue to be of the same psychological makeup. Their distrust of each other is the exact type of situation that we may be able to derive some advantage from—or at least some further information."

"Isn't there some old police adage, Constable, about thieves falling out with each other?"

"That's more literary than forensic, Commander, but it's true nevertheless."

"The problem would be to find someone else, in whom Gul Dukat has at least a small measure of trust."

"We can provide that easily enough." Odo laid a hand on his own chest. "That person is myself. Gul Dukat trusts me—because he underestimates me. He has the typical Cardassian arrogance that results in his assuming that all other sentient creatures are inferior to him. If anyone shows servility to him—as I had to, in order to survive under the Cardassians—he naturally regards that as his due."

"Servile?" Beside him, O'Brien raised an eyebrow. "You?"

"Let us just say that my shapeshifting ability is not the only means of disguise that I possess. It would have done me little good to reveal my true feelings to Dukat and the other Cardassians, if by doing so I wound up being jettisoned from one of the station's airlocks. As Dukat's chief of security, I had regular contact with Bajoran freedom fighters that were brought here for interrogation—and execution. So I was able to keep track of the Bajoran resistance movement. That enabled me to keep my mouth shut and bide my time."

Sisko regarded him. "And you're sure that Gul Dukat never doubted your loyalty to him?"

"Quite sure, Commander. As I said before, I know how his mind works."

"Very well, Constable—a runabout will be prepared for your immediate use. I'll have the Ops communication staff contact the Cardassian emissary vessel and tell them that you'll be arriving shortly."

Dax spoke up. "On what pretext, Benjamin?"

"Routine inspection. We'll say that with the change in the Bajoran government, we're concerned that certain parties might try to take advantage of the confusion to smuggle in Federation-prohibited contraband."

"They'll refuse inspection—Dukat's vessel is under diplomatic immunity."

"By that time, Odo will already be aboard." Sisko swiveled toward his security chief. "I'll leave it to you as to how you go about seeing your old friend Dukat." He pushed his chair back from the desk. "Dismissed, everyone. If there are any further developments, report them to me at once."

Odo was the last to reach the office door. Sisko called to him.

"Constable—"

"Yes?" Odo stopped and glanced over his shoulder.

"Be careful. I'd hate for you to find out that Dukat isn't as much of a fool as you thought he was."

It was easy. Miraculously so—Gul Dukat sent for him.

"Ah—there you are, Odo." The Cardassian turned around from the viewports in his private quarters. What passed for a polite smile appeared on his harshly angled face. "It's been so long. Hasn't it?"

Not long enough, a voice spoke inside Odo's head. He was well versed in not letting any trace of his thoughts become apparent. "It's a pleasure to see you again, sir." The guards who had escorted him now stepped back.

"Leave us." Dukat dismissed the guards with a snap of his hand. "We have a great many things to discuss."

Behind him, Odo heard the door retract, a sharper metal-on-metal sound than its equivalent aboard the DS9 station. It closed again, and he knew he was alone with the Gul.

"I hope my crew was at least reasonably courteous to you." Dukat sat down behind the angled projection that served as a desk. "If not, perhaps you'll excuse them. The younger officers aren't aware of the many services you once performed in our behalf. They naturally assume that anyone who works for Starfleet is their enemy. They're trained that way."

Odo stood with his hands clasped behind his back. "I'd like to think, sir, that I have no enemies."

"Oh?" The smile on Gul Dukat's face grew to a scale-edged slit. "What an . . . *enlightened* view to take."

He made no reply. For a moment, the rush of memories overwhelmed his thoughts, the past evoked by being in Dukat's presence. That, and the sounds, both overt and subliminal, of the Cardassian vessel. As he had been led through the corridors, the clipped, barking tones of the Cardassian tongue had reminded him of the time when his daily orders had been delivered in those guttural words.

"Sit down, Odo." The Gul gestured toward a chair. "May I offer you a refreshment of some sort?"

"You know me better than that, sir." He sat stiffly, an extra tension locking his spine. "I require nothing."

"Yes, of course." Dukat poured himself a measure from the squat flagon on the desk. He swirled and studied the glass's viscous contents. "I do know you, don't I? Well enough to realize that you're a fraud and a liar. Your whole visit here is a sham. Isn't it?"

He was taken aback by the lash of the Gul's words. "I . . . I don't know what you mean. . . ."

"Please, Odo. Don't try my patience. Did you really think I'd be taken in by this pathetic charade? I know that you're perfectly aware of interstellar protocol. You should be; the rules governing contact between sovereign entities was one of the matters you handled for me when I governed the *Deep Space Nine* station. Perhaps you thought I'd ascribe this error to memory lapse on your part?" Dukat took a sip from the small glass. "Asking to perform an inspection on a diplomatic vessel . . ." He shook his head in disgust. "Really, Odo. That's such an obvious breach of etiquette . . . so obvious that it makes me wonder. I have to consider the possibility that it was a deliberate mistake. And that you were just trying to devise some way of coming here and talking to me." After the next sip, the thin smile showed again. "Talking . . . just like old times."

The only option was to go with Gul Dukat's theory. "Perhaps . . . you're right, sir." Odo bowed his head a carefully judged fraction of an inch. "I'm glad to know that you still remember my service to you." He lifted his gaze to Dukat's watching eyes.

"Of course, Odo, I always knew that you were more than just loyal. Or, let us say, that your loyalty came from more than the personal relationship between us. Loyalty can came from intelligence as well, the ability to evaluate the situation one is in, and alter one's actions thereby. Loyalty can be a very fluid thing, can't it? Rather like yourself, it can change its shape and appearance, adapt to the necessities that intelligence presents to it. And I always knew, Odo, that you were an intelligent creature."

He could feel the Cardassian's gaze measuring him, evaluating and rendering a judgment behind the carapaced brow. That brought back memories as well, of the day-to-day tension that had colored his life before Starfleet had taken over DS9. Cardassians demanded loyalty, but rarely extended any in return; all other beings were expendable, their employment terminated in the most efficient means possible. Which meant that there weren't a lot of ex-employees of the Cardassians still alive in the galaxy.

Odo had conquered his fear, by the simple expedient of ceasing to care whether he lived or died. He was, after all, alone among the beings of the inhabited worlds; who was there who would grieve over his passing? If his manner became cold and unfeeling, his fluid nature made rigid and unbending, then that was the burden of the armor he had created to hide behind. And in which he carried the fear, conquered but not eradicated, reduced to a small chamber that he might have been able to conceal in one hand, if it had had any concrete substance at all.

And which had seemed to dwindle and disappear, when his home, the confines of the station, had become a different world, one without Gul Dukat.

The little chamber was still there inside him; Odo felt it open and a bitter tincture seep out. *I always knew that you were an intelligent creature*—he could hear Gul Dukat's voice again, sly and invasive, like the point of a knife searching for weak points in armor made suddenly fragile. *Loyalty comes from intelligence . . . the ability to evaluate the situation one is in . . .*

What if that other world was about to end? The one that had swept through *Deep Space Nine* like the warming spring that those born on real planets had sometimes told him about. And now Gul Dukat's winter, endless and harsh, would return.

And alter one's actions thereby.

"You seem to have become very quiet, Odo." Dukat's voice pried at him. "I wonder what you're thinking."

Loyalty can be a very fluid thing. Can't it?

He brought himself back from his grim meditations. "Just reminiscing, sir." Carefully, as though handling a toxic substance, Odo sealed the small chamber inside himself. Carefully, so that Gul Dukat had no perception of what was happening. Sealed—and crushed within his fist.

Gul Dukat nodded, as though deeply satisfied. "Come here. I'd like to show you something."

The Cardassian's computer screen was a translucent panel set into the desktop, on which monochromatic red symbols and images floated up like fragments submerged in dark water. Dukat worked his way through the levels of data, one fingertip sliding across the strip of control sensors at the side. The system's interface was familiar enough to Odo—the security office aboard DS9 had had a similar one before the Starfleet equipment had been installed.

"Take a look at this." Dukat leaned back from the desk.

Standing beside the Cardassian's chair, Odo studied the panel. The lines and symbols seemed to represent an architectural design, but of nothing that he recognized. "What is it?"

"This is the overall layout for the new city we're going to erect on the surface of Bajor. McHogue City—I'm afraid our partner in this venture is not subtle about displaying his ego. Though he's already had to accept that the name has become shortened to 'Moagitty.' That has sort of a raffish sound to it, don't you think?"

Odo made no reply. He reached past Dukat and touched the control sensors for the computer. The Cardassian made no move to stop him as he paged through level after level, the data appearing in more detail with each screenful. He absorbed and committed to memory as much as he could—location coordinates, elevations and plans, power-source specifications—without making any discrimination as to possible usefulness. That could all be sorted out when he returned to DS9 and made a full report to Commander Sisko and the other officers.

The last screen of data was an artist's rendering, done in the spare, thin-lined style that the Cardassians preferred, of what the new city would look like as one approached the main traffic entrance from the attached landing area. It looked like nothing that had ever been set down on the planet before, an assemblage of inorganic shapes and aggressive spires. The immense buildings lacked the rounded grace of what Odo had seen of the Bajorans' native architecture.

There was one other telling detail in the sketch: none of the buildings were shown as having windows or any other means of connecting to the outside world. They were sealed environments, a self-contained world turned in upon itself.

"It's going to be quite a thing," said Dukat proudly. His

finger tapped upon the panel. "And it won't be long before it actually exists—the first cargo vessels bearing the construction modules are already approaching the Bajoran system. The buildings will go up in a matter of days." He smiled at Odo. "Rather like a military operation—you know how efficient we Cardassians can be when it comes to that sort of thing. Up and running, primed for all the races of the galaxy to come and . . . *enjoy* themselves. Moagitty will be very big—and important." Dukat's gaze sharpened as he studied Odo's reactions. "Much bigger than, say, *Deep Space Nine.*"

Odo stood back from the computer panel. "I imagine it will be."

"I hope you appreciate the confidence I have in you, Odo; some of my fellow officers might feel it was bit indiscreet of me to reveal so much sensitive information to someone who is, after all, in the pay of the Federation." Dukat smiled. "But then, as I was saying before . . . you and I know each other better than that. Don't we?"

"Of course." Odo regarded the other for a moment. "I also know that you undoubtedly have your reasons for showing me these things."

Dukat gave a single nod. "Your perceptions are accurate, as usual. Something as big as this will require very competent individuals running it. Frankly, a continuing operation such as Moagitty is somewhat beyond the expertise of most Cardassians—we don't often deal with what might be termed the industries of entertainment and hospitality. And the nature of this enterprise is going to create some rather unique problems. Any time you deal with people's deepest desires and fantasies, there are going to be problems. Security problems, Odo. Am I making myself clear to you, Odo?"

He nodded. "You want me to work for you again. As chief of security for this Moagitty."

"Exactly." Gul Dukat's smile became both more sinister and ingratiating. "I know that our partner McHogue is already approaching others with whom he is familiar, and making similar offers regarding different aspects of the operation. We want the best—you should be flattered I thought of you."

"I would regard such a position of trust as an honor, sir."

Dukat peered more closely at him. "That's not really an acceptance of my offer, is it?"

He made no reply.

"I understand, Odo. As I said before, you're an intelligent creature—and you have your own interests to look after. You're wise to be cautious—much of the success of this venture will depend upon our partners, General Aur and the others in the new Bajoran government. And as you know, I've never been given to placing my trust in Bajorans. They're a treacherous lot."

"Then why trust any of them now?"

"A good question." Dukat smiled. "But I don't think 'trust' is exactly the right word for my relationship with Aur. He undoubtedly derives some satisfaction from the notion of Cardassians working for the benefit of Bajor—it's a kind of revenge for him. He wants it so badly that he's willing to set aside any caution that he might otherwise have felt. But that's his problem, not mine."

Odo mulled over the other's words. "Are your plans other than what you've told General Aur?"

"Actually, no. This is one of those rare occurrences where deception is not called for. It's not *me* that Aur should worry about. Let's just say that he may have greatly overestimated his fellow Bajorans' willingness to engage in commerce with us. I know the collective Bajoran soul better than Aur does—and why shouldn't that be the case? I was their master for a good many years, and even I wouldn't say that I was a gentle master. The Bajoran people may not be as ready to forgive and forget as Aur would like to believe."

"But then—" Odo peered more closely at the Gul. "You're

isking a great deal by having any involvement at all in this
cheme that McHogue has concocted."

"Not at all." Dukat's expression showed the pleasure he felt
n his own cleverness. "This is a situation in which I cannot
uffer any losses. Perhaps—at least in this particular
nstance—I am wrong and General Aur is right. Very well;
hen I and my fellow Cardassians reap all the benefits of the
rrangement that has been set in place. *And* we are in an even
etter position to derive even more advantages, in ways that
ur wouldn't have anticipated. But if Aur is wrong, and the
ajoran people aren't ready to do business with us . . ."
)ukat's unpleasant smile appeared again. "There are other
ajorans besides Aur and his followers who have—shall we
ay?—expressed an interest in coming to an agreement with
1e. If Aur's government were to collapse, swept away by the
utrage of the Bajorans, that would allow these others—who
re just as reasonable but more discreet—to come to power.
nd then certain other of my plans might come into fruition.
ut—that's all in the future." Dukat gestured at the computer
anel. "Right now, the city of Moagitty doesn't even exist yet.
Ve'll have to wait and see what happens with it. It could very
ell turn out to be . . . quite wonderful. Don't you agree?"

Slowly, Odo nodded. "The potential is indeed great."

"Perhaps then, we should just agree to keep this discussion
n hold for a little while longer. You don't have to give me an
nswer now." Dukat regarded him in a silence for a moment.

"I'll give your offer my deepest consideration."

"I'm sure you will." Dukat walked Odo to the door, then
opped and turned toward him. "Though there is something
se that might influence your decision. As security chief for
1e city of Moagitty, you would naturally have complete
ccess to the CI technology we'll be employing—and there's
1ore to that than you're presently aware of. It can be a very
owerful tool, Odo—not just something for indulging one's
ildest fantasies." Dukat reached up and placed a single

fingertip against Odo's brow. "There's things locked inside here. Things you might never discover any other way." He smiled and drew his finger back. "Another world. The past, perhaps."

The door opened, and Odo stepped through. He glanced over his shoulder.

"It was good to see you again, Odo." Dukat pressed the control panel. "Remember what I told you." The door slid shut, and Odo let the Cardassian guards lead him back to the docking port.

CHAPTER
12

THERE WAS NEWS FROM HOME—HER REAL HOME, THE WORLD SHE had been born on—but it didn't cheer her up.

Kira ordered another drink but didn't touch it, any more than she had the last couple that Quark had brought to her table. A sip, just enough to detect the sharp tang of the alcohol, making sure that the Ferengi wasn't taking the opportunity to cheat her—then she would push the slender glass away so she could better concentrate on the data padd in front of her.

"You seem to be in a wretched mood." Quark stood back with the empty tray. "You're usually so ... bright and cheery."

She turned her head and gazed balefully at the other's pointy-toothed smile. Buying drinks that she didn't consume was a cheap enough rent to pay for the space she took up in Quark's establishment. She had been slowly going crazy sitting for shift after shift in her living quarters, by herself; nothing in her personality, she knew, was suited for quiet introspection. The stimulus of the Promenade's hustle and buzz did more to soothe her nerves than anything else could. At the same time, the last thing she wanted to do was get even slightly inebriated in a public place; she could sense—or imagine—the eyes of those surreptitiously watching her, the whispers that her absence from Commander Sisko's top-level war councils had triggered.

"Then again," said Quark thoughtfully, "nobody around here has ever actually described you as being a bundle of laughs."

"Sorry to bring the festive mood down." Kira took a sip of the drink he'd brought her, as if to demonstrate a cooperative spirit. "But I've got a lot on my mind."

"No, no; that's quite all right." It was Quark's turn to look dejected. "I'm grateful for any business at all. Look around you." With the tray tucked under one arm, a sweeping gesture of his other hand took in the entire premises. "My receipts are *way* down. This has been the worst spell since I first opened up this place."

Kira looked where he pointed and saw a third of the tables and booths empty; a single drinker, a hulking Denebian, stood at the bar and nursed a synthale. Quark's establishment was hardly a morgue—yet—but it was distinctly more subdued and less crowded than she had ever seen it before. When she had come in, she hadn't perceived the situation; she had thought that the relatively gloomy atmosphere was something she had brought with her, like some kind of mildly depressing radiation.

"What's the problem? Has everybody heard all your jokes?"

"I don't have anything to joke about, Major." Quark gave a deep sigh. "The problem is . . . competition." He spoke the last word with the heartfelt loathing of the true capitalist. "Just about the time you think you have a good thing going—serving the community, mind you—then somebody else comes along to horn in on the action."

"There's another bar on DS9?" *Maybe I should go there,* thought Kira. This place was beginning to feel a little glum, even to her.

"Of course not. Everybody on the Promenade knows that I'd cut them off at the knees if they tried. No, I'm talking about down on Bajor. My old partner McHogue and that fancy-shmancy new pleasure city that he's got the Cardassians putting up for him."

Kira held up the data padd. "That's just what I've been looking at. Quite a deal, huh?"

"'Quite a deal,' my back incisors." Quark's glare became even more murderous. "A naked grab at establishing a monopoly, is what I call it—and worse yet, it's not *my* monopoly! They're taking the bread out of my mouth. . . ." He lapsed into muttering obscure curses, the meaning of which was still apparent.

She couldn't resist needling him further. "I thought Ferengi were in favor of the free-market system."

"Well, sure—but there are limits! This," he sputtered, pointing to the images on the data padd, "this is beyond the bounds of decency! McHogue has whole buildings full of holosuites, all of them wired up with those CI modules of his—you've *seen* what those do to people."

"I'm proud of you, Quark." She wasn't joking now. "You've developed an actual moral sense."

"I know. . . ." Like a deflating balloon, he sank into the table's empty chair. "I must be getting old." Morosely, he propped the side of his face against one hand. "Outclassed . . . left behind in the dust . . . ready for the scrap heap." Self-pity radiated from him. "Maybe I should just climb aboard one of their shuttles and go down there myself. McHogue can put me in one of his holosuites and take me back to the days when I was young and rapacious."

"They're running shuttles down to this place? This Moagitty, or whatever it's called?"

"Of course. That's where all my customers have gone—or they soon will be."

"I knew the first sections were already up and running, but still . . ." Kira slowly shook her head in disbelief. "I'm amazed Commander Sisko would give them permission to arrange travel right from the station."

"He didn't. McHogue's set up a docking substation within transporter range—they'll beam aboard anyone who asks, and then send them on down to Bajor on one of their own shuttles. What's Sisko going to do about it? He can't refuse people permission to leave the station, if they want to go."

"I suppose not. . . ." She mulled over the Ferengi's information. It presented certain possibilities. Since she had been taken off duty by Sisko, there had been no way that she could requisition one of the station's runabouts—she had been stuck here on DS9. But if McHogue was going to be this obliging . . .

She picked up the data padd from the table and pushed back her own chair. "Don't worry," she told Quark. "I'm sure you've still got what it takes."

"Thanks, Major." Quark busied himself, setting her drink onto his tray and wiping off the table. "It's good to know that one's efforts don't go unappreciated in this universe."

An unpleasantly familiar face was there to greet her.

"Ah, Major Kira." The functionary she had first met at the Severalty Front's headquarters now gave a small bow toward her. "Our last time together was not nearly as cordial as I would have wished it."

The last time she had seen this person, he had been standing over Malen's body, with the weapon that had killed her old friend still in his hand. And the functionary had been smiling in the same humorless, mocking way.

"That was probably my fault," said Kira. "I react poorly to murder."

"Now, that's interesting—so do I." The functionary nodded thoughtfully. "It's fortunate for me that I've only had to deal in, shall we say, political necessities." He gestured toward the other end of the corridor. "Would you care to follow me?"

The other passengers that had come down on the shuttle—a dozen or so, most of whom she recognized from DS9—had been herded in another direction. The ornately engraved doors, several meters high and depicting McHogue as a cordial demigod with arms spread in welcome, had closed and sealed off the landing area. The murmur of the others' voices faded in the distance.

"So I take it that you're my official escort?" Kira glanced at the figure walking beside her. "I'm flattered that you think I deserve the special treatment."

"Oh, we're aware of your having been taken off full duty. Your Commander Sisko seems a bit given to groundless suspicions." The functionary made a dismissive gesture. "That will pass, and you'll be in his good graces once more. For whatever that's worth. And besides—" He turned the malicious smile toward her again. "You're a celebrity in your own right. It's a basic operating principle of an operation such as this, that you have to separate the VIPs from the more . . . *common* elements."

"How did you know I was going to pay you a visit?"

"Major Kira . . . please. If you hadn't, then we would have had to invite you." He stopped at another door, smaller and without decoration. "This way."

From the corridor, they stepped out onto a curved balustrade, its horizontal arc encompassing an area larger than the Promenade aboard DS9 by several orders of magnitude. At the guardrail, Kira could look down upon a milling crowd of the galaxy's sentient species. They were too far distant to make out as individuals, but they gave off en masse the same aura of mingled excitement and greed that had repelled her before—if anything it was even stronger here than on the Promenade.

"This is just the annex off the transportation area." The functionary pointed to the bays along the sides of the vast enclosed space; the crowd eddied around and through them like water swirling in a rock-lined stream. "We have centuries of recorded experience to draw upon, going all the way back to Earth itself, on how to design our operations for maximum profit generation. There really is a science to this sort of thing—the psychology of extracting wealth, as it were. You might remember that ancient political maxim about taxation being the art of plucking the most feathers from a domesticated fowl while causing the least amount of squawking. Here, we'd like to think we've transcended that state: we prefer the goose to pull off all his feathers himself and happily present them to us on a plate."

Kira brought her gaze up from the gaming floor. "You wouldn't be making a very successful pitch to tourists with that approach."

"On the contrary, Major. With all due respect, an observation like that only indicates how naive you are in these matters. That's one of the remarkable aspects of the business of satisfying people's innermost desires: the cynicism is on both sides of the equation. What all these people wish for, along with everything else, is a sinister glamour, the thrill of finding co-conspirators in the engineering of their self-destruction. They want to lose themselves in an abyss of vice and corruption; it amuses them to think of themselves as fated and damned, rushing to a personal apocalypse. How could the Federation, with its essentially hygienic, problem-solving approach to reality, ever satisfy drives like that? Starfleet is like a torchbearer, bringing enlightenment to every corner of the galaxy—how noble of it. But that light must inevitably create shadows of its own, and those shadows have to go somewhere. Better they should come here to Moagitty, where Bajorans can garner the proceeds."

She studied the figure beside her while he delivered his dark sermon. A leaping fervor, like fire coursing across the branches of drought-withered trees, shone in the functionary's eyes. She could barely recognize him as a creature born of the same blood that flowed in her veins. *This is what it's come to,* she thought, her own voice masking the other's flow of words. *This is what McHogue, and all the outsiders before him, have brought to our world.* First the Cardassians, then the Federation, and now every intelligent species in the galaxy, swarming to Moagitty like insects to an overripe fruit rotting on the ground; the outside universe had impinged upon Bajor, and things could never be the same again. The Bajorans wouldn't be the same; they were already in the process of becoming different to each other. Their suffering had made them one, but that had ended. Wealth and power would split them apart, each a stranger to what had been a brother or sister. She had seen this functionary coolly slay her old comrade Malen, with no more reluctance than the assassination of a Cardassian during the resistance might have evoked. Perhaps less; the functionary—and how many more like him?—was now closer in nature to McHogue and the Cardassians than to other Bajorans. They had evolved somehow, in a way that she could never have anticipated; they had become the very creatures that the resistance had fought to cast out from Bajor.

Her meditations took her to a dead place inside herself. *Maybe this is the reason that Kai Opaka left us*—a thought even bleaker than the steps that led to it. Perhaps the Kai hadn't answered the call of the Prophets at all; perhaps she had been cast out in her turn by the Prophets, those who could see what the future of Bajor would be like. A future that had no place for one such as the Kai.

"Why did you come here?"

For a moment, Kira suffered an auditory hallucination; it had sounded to her as if it had been the Kai's gentle voice that had spoken. Her breath came back into her lungs, and she realized that the words had come only from the functionary who had guided her to this inferno of excited laughter.

"Or why do you *think* you came here?" The functionary smiled as he peered more closely at her.

"I . . . I don't know. . . ." Kira shook her head, as if that might dispel the dream that had folded around her. She wondered where she would be if she did wake up—in her quarters aboard DS9, or on the bare ground of her homeworld? She could remember a time when she had slept under the night sky of Bajor, surrounded by the forms of her fellow resistance fighters, their weapons at their sides; they had all expected to die in the morning's action, a raid on a Cardassian armaments dump. Half their number had wound up exactly as feared; but in the night before, she had felt at peace, beyond hope or desire. . . .

The functionary's voice seemed to speak right at her ear, soothing her heavy eyelids closed. "I can tell you why. The same reason you came the last time, before the *coup d' état* by the Severalty Front. You have this vision of yourself, don't you, Major? The avenging angel, the fiery sword, the one-woman hit squad. The people around you, your fellow officers up on *Deep Space Nine,* they think that you're always so irascible and impatient, that you go charging off on your own because you don't feel anyone can keep up; you have to do everything all by yourself. When really it's quite different: you don't *want* anyone else to help you. You *want* to do it all by yourself. What did you think you were going to do this time?" The voice became slyly mocking. "Find some switch to throw that would overload the power generators and blow all of Moagitty to atoms? One big cataclysm, with you at the center of it—I'm sure that would have made you very happy. Or perhaps something less flamboyant but just as satisfying—you could have leapt and with your bare hand torn out my throat."

Her eyes flew open. She saw before her, not the functionary, but the image of McHogue turned to flesh. The transformation had been accomplished as easily and swiftly as discarding a mask—the narrow face that she had seen photos of now smiled at her.

"You shouldn't act so surprised, Major." The black-clad figure was an optical vacuum, holding her attention with no chance of her breaking away. "You've entered my territory—this is the city that bears my name, is it not? You should be flattered that I'm giving you such special treatment."

It almost seemed as if she had stepped from the shuttle that had brought her here into one of the CI-modified holosuites. Anything could happen.

"Major, I regret that we seem to be on opposing sides; that's unfortunate. This—" McHogue gestured toward the vast open space before them. "It's all going to be much bigger than what you see; this is just the beginning. That's why General Aur and so many others—so many of your former comrades, Kira—that's why they joined me in this great enterprise. Because they could see the possibilities. I'd find it very convenient if one of your capabilities took part as well. There'd be a place for you."

"Spare me the recruiting pitch." The shock of the transformation had passed, though it was still a mystery how it had been done. "I've got a better idea of just what your program entails."

"No, you don't. You don't have the slightest idea." McHogue's smile turned cold. "If you did, you'd realize that you might not have a choice about joining or not. Come on—" He turned and started walking farther along the balustrade. "There are some other things I'd like you to see."

Away from the murmur of the gaming floor, a balcony

framed by raw girders and nets of dangling electrical cables opened to a view of the hills surrounding the new city. The landscape had been scraped bare by the towering construction equipment arrayed along the horizon. Cranes taller than any of the capital's minarets dangled pre-formed panels and modular units toward the waiting plasma torches. The scale of the partly finished buildings was beyond anything Kira had seen before. DS9 itself could have been settled between the massive walls like an egg in a steel and cementene nest.

"I suppose I should be impressed," said Kira. "Your friends the Cardassians certainly have a taste for epic architecture. But then, I already knew that they like to build monuments to themselves."

"Gul Dukat has been very useful . . . and discreet." McHogue leaned his hands against the balcony's rail. "He's been quite agreeable to the proposition that the Cardassians should not just be silent, but invisible partners in this enterprise. They've suffered serious public relations problems before; they're not universally well liked. It's better for all concerned that the Cardassians should stay in the background. We wouldn't want anything to keep potential guests away."

"Or their money."

The look in McHogue's eyes grew distant as he gazed across the empire being assembled before him. "You don't understand yet, do you, Major? It's not that simple." He pushed himself away from the rail. "I'm not done giving you the tour yet."

Another corridor, high-ceilinged, with soft, dreamy light the color of a perfect dawn; McHogue indicated the doors extending in a curve whose end couldn't be seen. "Look familiar?"

"Holosuites." Kira shrugged. "Should I be surprised? There's obviously a limit to how much you can mess with people's minds in reality."

214

"Bravely spoken, for one who's not quite sure who she's talking to." McHogue regarded the holosuites with a proprietary satisfaction. "But of course, you're right about that. Everything else—the Dabo tables, the ordinary brothels and simpler pleasures of life—that's all pretty much a loss leader to attract a wider range of customers. Though I think that once word spreads across the galaxy about the rather more outré delights that can be sampled here, all of that other stuff could be largely dispensed with."

The vision she'd had before, when the person with her had still been in the guise of the government functionary, came once again into her head. A vision of a darkness that could swallow whole worlds and everybody on them, Bajor included.

She thrust the vision away, unwilling to admit that it could be true.

"Do you really think intelligent creatures are going to fall for this?" She gazed at McHogue, willing the contempt she felt to strike him like one of the fists she held at her side. "Once people find out that there's nothing but death and madness at the end, you'll be walking around your precious Moagitty by yourself."

"I'm hardly worried about that. You speak from ignorance, Major; what you know about the possibilities here is nothing, no more than the small unpleasantness you encountered back on DS9." McHogue nodded thoughtfully. "Perhaps you should have a little talk with someone more experienced. Someone you might trust . . ."

He pressed the control at the side of one of the holosuites; the door slid open. Inside, a figure knelt at the center of the chamber. The head was bent so far forward that Kira couldn't see the face.

"Go ahead," said McHogue, smiling. "It wasn't that long ago that you and this person talked with each other."

Slowly, Kira stepped into the holosuite. Around her, the

grid of sensory projectors formed a dead cage. The kneeling figure didn't move as she approached. Only when Kira stood immediately before—a face radiant with belief looked up at her, and she recognized the acolyte from the capital's temple.

The acolyte's gaze pierced Kira and focused on a vision far beyond the physical limits of the holosuite. Kira reached down and touched the side of the acolyte's face.

"I saw her," murmured the acolyte.

"Who did you see?" But she already knew what the answer would be.

The acolyte's voice was a whisper of reverence, as though a revelation greater than the world's limits had been witnessed.

"The Kai . . ."

She knew that McHogue stood somewhere behind them. Stood at the door, watching. And smiling.

In her living quarters, she lay on her bed and gazed up at the ceiling. For a long while, she had seen faces there, conjured from recent memory; a face rapt and transcendent, focused upon an unseen image, and another, that rendered judgment upon everything before it with a twist of one corner of its mouth.

On the shuttle back to the station, Kira had picked apart the events of this brief journey. A few hours spent in another world, McHogue's world. The sky no longer guarded a Bajor that she could recognize. All had changed, or was about to.

Change—the word brought a flare of resentment inside her skull. Nearly an entire shift had passed since she'd returned to the station, and the memory of the cheap magic trick by which McHogue had appeared in front of her was still irritating to think about. It meant nothing—or so she wanted to believe. A distracting of her attention, an opportunity seized when she had closed her eyes, McHogue stepping into the place of the functionary that had been standing there. DS9 had a shapeshifter aboard that was certainly more impressive —you could *watch* Odo change from one thing to another.

She clasped her hands behind her head, her eyes narrowing as she gazed harder at the ceiling. What ticked her off, she decided, was not the efficacy of McHogue's full-body sleight of hand, but the fact that he had attempted it at all. There was a commingling in the man's character of inflated boasting that verged on mysticism and a child's glitter-eyed cruelty. It infuriated her to think of one who had befriended her, such as the temple's acolyte, lost in thrall to such a mind and its creations.

Another emotion stirred inside her, that she had tried to extinguish but had failed. *What if it's true?* A simple question, but one whose answer meant everything. The whispered fervor in the acolyte's words, the vision that could be seen in the window of her eyes . . .

A fake, as fraudulent as all the rest of it. Not on the acolyte's part, but McHogue's. He had devoted his life to trickery, for the sake of putting his hand into other people's pockets, just as the acolyte and the others carrying forth the temple's work had devoted themselves to seeing the truth.

And illusion had won, had proved itself to be the more powerful force.

An interesting philosophical problem, one that Kira could have imagined herself discussing in another life with the Kai. If lies were so mighty, at what point did they become omnipotent? When would the Great Liar McHogue declare himself to be the truth? And if he did so, would he be wrong . . .

Kira pressed her hand over her eyes, as though trying to shove down the voices that had risen clamoring inside her head. *Sisko should never have taken me off full duty,* she thought. The inaction, the inability to get her hands on the controls, a weapon, anything with which she could have put

217

up a struggle, had left an empty space inside, that torments of useless reasoning had rushed to fill. It was why she had known there had never been any place for her inside the temples of her world's faith, among those who contemplated eternity through the quieting of their souls. What those of her fellow Bajorans possessed could never be hers, as much as she envied them; the constant restlessness that she had been born with, and that had been sharpened by the years of fighting in the resistance, made it impossible.

The storm inside had already been building when the shuttle had left the surface of the planet. Through one of the small craft's viewports, she had been able to look back and see clouds just as furious swirling in Bajor's upper atmosphere, as though a season of hurricanes had begun to prematurely gather its force. That was what the world behind her brow had felt like, as though it were a mirror of Bajor itself.

She sat up on the edge of the bed, feeling the muscles tensing across her shoulders and down into her arms. Her fingertips dug into the thin mattress.

You want to do it all by yourself—McHogue's words were a bitter echo among her thoughts. *The fiery angel, the avenging sword . . .*

"I can't stay in here any longer." That was her own voice. And a bad sign, speaking to herself, with no one else around to hear. Much more of this—of nothing—and she knew she wouldn't be far from going crazy. She fastened the collar of her uniform, stood up, and hit the control panel for the door.

She had no taste for company, which precluded going down to the Promenade and listening to Quark moan about his financial troubles. From what she had observed of his competitor's booming business in Moagitty, the bar's tables and booths would be even more deserted, the Ferengi's mournful expression setting deeper into his face. It was hard to imagine how a sight like that could do anything to lift her mood.

The station's corridors were empty and silent except for the echoes of her footsteps. She paid no attention to where her wanderings took her. Only when a crackle of energy barred her path—then she was abruptly brought back from her brooding thoughts to present time.

"Entry to this sector is restricted." The voice of the station's computer spoke above her. "Per orders of Security Chief Odo."

Kira looked down the corridor before her. She saw the row of holosuite entrances with their small control panels darkened and inactive, except for one halfway down. It came as no surprise that her seemingly random course had brought her here. Beneath the storm inside her head, there was another part that wordlessly pursued its own intentions.

"This is Major Kira Nerys," she spoke aloud. She waited a moment for the computer to match up her voice patterns with the ID files in its data banks. There was no telling what would happen next, but it was worth a shot.

"Access granted." The low-level sizzle from the barrier emitters at either side of the corridor died away. "Proceed."

Of course, she thought. As Commander Sisko had told her, her being relieved from duty had all been handled informally. As a consequence, no change in her administrative status had been logged into the station's computer. Inside DS9, she could come and go as she wished, just as before.

She stood in front of the holosuite, her hand a few centimeters away from touching its control panel. McHogue's mocking words were as loud now as if he were there with her, speaking them into her ear.

You speak from ignorance . . . what you know is nothing . . .

The acolyte had found out. Something had brought her there, to that small enclosed space in the heart of Moagitty, a chamber whose walls could fall away, to reveal—

What? There had been no answer to that question then,

when Kira had bent down to look into the acolyte's face, to try and decipher the few cryptic words that had been spoken. Something about the Kai Opaka; the acolyte had seen her.

The acolyte had seen nothing; a trick, a fraud, another of McHogue's endless displays of illusion. Lies that killed, darkness that extinguished light. Kira knew that, could believe nothing else . . . yet the acolyte had believed otherwise. That was what Kira had seen in the acolyte's face: the sureness of complete devotion, the grace and peace that might have been bestowed by the Kai's hand being laid upon the upturned brow.

She couldn't figure it out. The acolyte was trained, as were all the servants of their faith, to tell the difference between the true and the false; thus they served all who carried even the smallest fragments of the Bajoran religion in their hearts. If such a one could be fooled by McHogue, then his lies *were* indistinguishable from the truth.

And that would mean the truth could be found inside the liar's holosuites . . .

"There's only one way to find out." Kira spoke aloud this time, to be comforted by the sound of her own voice in the empty corridor's silence. It didn't help much; her heart was still beating faster as she laid her fingertips against the holosuite's control panel.

The door slid open and she stepped inside. A noise as soft as her breath signaled the door's closing, sealing her into the holosuite's limitless world.

She half-expected to find McHogue waiting there, to welcome her into his domain. Instead, silence deeper and more profound than that of the corridor beyond folded around her; she listened intently, but heard nothing more than her own exhalation and the movement of blood within her veins.

The darkness yielded as she stepped forward; she could feel the soles of her boots treading upon dirt and loose gravel. That was an illusion, she knew as well; the holosuite's low-level tractor beams fed their tactile sensations to her nerve endings. But more than that; any time she had been in a holosuite before, she had found the artificial world more entertaining than convincing. She'd always had to short-circuit the last measure of disbelief inside herself, a process that had never seemed worthwhile to her; the whole experience, as far as she had been concerned, was for those who found it easy to let go of the reality outside the chamber. Now that wasn't a problem for her; the problem was in forcing herself to remember that there was another, presumably larger reality outside this world in which she had found herself. She knew that was the effects of the cortical-induction technology; she had read the reports that Dax and Bashir had uploaded from their research lab. An uncanny feeling plagued her now, that McHogue's hand had somehow reached into her skull and was manipulating each cell and fiber.

Looking upward, Kira saw a field of stars, familiar ones; she could trace the constellations visible from Bajor's northern hemisphere. *He took those out of my head,* she thought, *and put them up there.* It was a personal touch that chilled her more than the night air surrounding her.

Another light flicked before her; she could smell the wood fire's smoke, hear the crackle of the small branches that had been placed upon it. The confines of memory closed around her; she knew where she was. She looked behind herself and saw strands of barbed wire, laced with deadlier electrified lines; the glow of the fire made the points of metal look like sparks permanently etched into the blackness.

This was home.

Another home, a smaller world, the first one that she had ever known. Something else that McHogue and the CI module had reached in and taken out of her head—the refugee camp in which she had grown up. There were no memories before this.

A group of Bajorans, emaciated limbs visible through their

rags, huddled near the fire. Their faces were hollow-eyed, with no thoughts perceptible behind, just the bare consciousness of misery. A child with bones sharp enough to poke through the parchment skin crouched next to her mother, as much to give comfort as to receive it. Words that someone else had spoken now passed again through Kira's head—

. . . *starved little rat* . . .

—and were gone. None of the people seemed to be aware of her presence, standing at the limit of the fire's glow. She felt like a ghost, come back to spy upon the living, the ones who would never die inside her. The hungering girl-child would always be there, locked inside a place she could see at any time, but never touch.

A sound of something whistling through air, and striking flesh with bone beneath, came from the distance. The only reaction from those around the fire was a squeezing shut of their eyes and an instinctive hunching of the shoulders, as though the blow had landed upon their backs. The sound came again, accompanied this time by a cry of pain.

Kira watched as the child looked up at her mother, then silently drew away, into the wavering shadows cast by the fire. The child looked at her elders for a moment longer, then stepped silently toward the dark shapes of the camp's barracks. Kira followed, her boots making no impact on the ground.

She knew what the child would find. What she herself had found, in a night that had begun so long ago and still hadn't ended. A group of Cardassian guards had a gray-haired Bajoran elder spread-eagled against the side of one of the wooden buildings, the knots of the leather strips cutting off the circulation to the man's feet and hands. His back had been flayed raw, the metal-tipped lash set to maximum penetration. A Cardassian officer watched with a bored expression; all the questions had been asked, the gasped and screamed answers noted. Less than a meter away, another Bajoran knelt, greedily wolfing the ration scraps that had been his reward for betraying the escape plot. A smile passed among the guards as they saw their officer leisurely extract the hand weapon from his uniform's holster and level it toward the informant's head. The man looked up and gaped, his mouth falling open to reveal the dry crumbs upon his tongue.

The child, hiding around the barracks' corner, saw everything. Kira knew the lesson that was being written on her heart.

You want to do everything yourself . . . you can't trust anyone . . .

The officer pressed the weapon's trigger stud.

Go it alone. That's the best way . . .

A line of flame leapt to the informant's brow, as simply as if the officer had laid his finger there. At the centers of the watching child's eyes were two sparks of the same fiery color.

Kira's hand moved to her side; she found not the regulation phaser, but the armament that had become her favorite during the battles of the resistance, a heavy-duty assemblage of metal and power with a barrel that extended almost to her knee. Somehow it seemed light as the air itself as she raised it and locked her arm straight.

They saw her then, the ghost become living and visible. The Cardassians turned away from their victims, the one crumpled upon the ground and the other still bleeding where he stood fastened to the wall.

A greater fire leapt, as though her heart had broken open and poured out its contents, a rushing wave that slammed against the Cardassians' amazed faces. The weapon's force caught both guards together, lifting them from the red-mottled ground and casting them broken upon the dark field beyond. With exquisite, pleasurable slowness, she turned the flame toward the officer, illuminating him, a new and purified thing that yielded its own puny weapon from a suddenly outflung hand.

Kira gathered her breath into herself, a heated joy that filled her lungs. She closed her eyes, knowing that the child had seen as well, the child had already seen this in her sullen dreams. *She* had seen this.

The air turned into fire. She could feel the weight of the armament in her hand, as though it were an extension of her arm, a burning vein running straight from it to a point between her breasts. She knew the watching child was gone, no longer separate from her; the child saw everything from behind her eyes. She opened them and saw the refugee camp spiraling below her, the ragged buildings pushed away by the fiery column at their center.

Another voice spoke inside her head. *Whatever you want . . . I can give it to you . . .*

She didn't care where the power came from. In this world, there were no lies or truths. A murderous rage swept through her body, granting its own incendiary grace.

In the night sky of memory and dream, Kira rose higher; she could gaze upon all the Cardassian occupation forces, their disbelieving faces turned toward the new sun that had bloomed in the darkness. There was no weapon in her hand now, but she no longer needed one; a sweep of her arm sent an angel's holy fire toward the horizon, a rain of death at her intoxicated command. The surface of this world would be scoured clean . . .

"Kira!"

Who had spoken her name? She turned in air, face contorted with anger. Her burning hand struck toward a visage that she could barely discern.

Something grabbed her around the shoulders. Darkness enveloped her and she fell, striking an angle of hard metal a second later.

She opened her eyes and saw Commander Sisko standing above her, the bare and empty walls of the holosuite chamber behind him.

Against her shoulder, she turned her face, feeling a child's sobbing well up and burst inside her. The tears were a child's tears, not of shame, but of incalculable loss.

CHAPTER
13

"You were lucky the commander found you in there." She looked over the diagnostic results on her data padd. Some of the brain-scan numbers were a little out of line, but returning to normal.

"Tell me about it." Lying on the examination table, Major Kira gazed up at the infirmary's ceiling. "Or better yet, don't."

"I'm not joking." Dax set the data padd aside. "It could have been much worse. From what we've been able to tell, the strength of the CI-modified holosuite's effect has actually increased—and on an exponential basis. Even an exposure of limited duration, a few hours or so, could have the same impact that we saw in the subjects who had spent a cumulative total of several weeks under its influence."

"How long was I in there?"

"Believe it or not, seven point five minutes, from the time the door closed to when Sisko hit the shutoff control."

Kira rubbed the corner of her brow. "It seemed like hours. Especially . . . toward the end . . ."

226

"That's the time-dilation effect. There had been some indications of it before, but never to this degree. That's why we had O'Brien wire an alarm into the unit; as soon as it went off at Ops, the commander was on his way there." Dax began putting back the rest of the instruments she had used. Properly speaking, it should have been Bashir's job to run a post-stress check on Kira, but he had collapsed, near exhaustion from the hours he had already spent in the research lab. She would check her results with him when he had gotten at least a couple more hours' sleep. "It might be of some value if you told me exactly what you experienced while you were in the holosuite." Dax glanced over her shoulder at the major. "Is it anything you would feel free to talk about?"

"Nice of you to ask." Kira had sat up, leaning forward with her hands against the edge of the table. "Sure, why not? I can't see how I can embarrass myself any more than I already have."

She listened to the major's description, categorizing the hallucinated perceptions and actions as classic revenge fantasies, with delusions of grandeur. Though there was an interesting philosophical question posed, one that Dax would have to think about later, when there was more time. Just whose delusions had they been? Kira's, McHogue's . . . or those of a starving child in a Bajoran refugee camp that no longer even existed?

"Lock me up and medicate me," said Kira, throwing her head back to gaze at the ceiling again. "I'll go quietly."

Dax smiled. "I don't think that will be necessary. Just don't do it again."

"That'd be against medical advice, I suppose."

"It's against *my* advice, at least. And—as you might imagine—against Commander Sisko's specific orders. He asked me to tell you that."

Kira groaned softly. "Just my luck that he was at Ops when I tripped the alarm. I seem to have this memory flash of him looking like he was going to pull my head off with his bare hands."

She had long experience with knowing how intimidating Benjamin could look when he was angry. The fact that Major Kira could even talk about it indicated how much ego strength she carried around with her.

"I'm sure it was directed more toward McHogue than it was toward you. If there were anything that he wanted to do with his bare hands, it would be to dismantle that holosuite until it was particularly small pieces of scrap. *Then* he'd commence doing the same to McHogue."

"Maybe I could help him." Kira refastened the collar of her uniform, where the tip of one of the instruments had read out her vital signs. "Maybe I could do anything at all around here."

"'They also serve, who stand and wait . . .'"

"What?" Kira stared at her.

Dax closed the instrument cabinet. "Just something I've heard Benjamin say; a quote, some Earth source that he didn't identify to me. Though actually, if you study the ethnography of enough cultures across the galaxy, a similar sentiment or variation thereof is quite frequently encountered."

"I suppose you're right; I can remember hearing something pretty similar from Kai Opaka." Kira stood up from the examining table. "Well, right now I'm not going to put up any argument about it. I'm beat; what sounds good to me is going back to my quarters and collapsing for a shift or two. That session in the holosuite—seven minutes or whatever it was—really took it out of me."

"That's the depletion of the brain's catecholamines; very similar to the aftereffects of certain chemical use. There's no sign of permanent damage, but it will take a little while for the neurotransmitters to reach their proper levels again." Dax hit the control panel beside the door, opening it for Kira. "However, you are correct about the proper course of treatment: sleep, and plenty of it. I don't think we need Dr. Bashir to write you a prescription for that."

After Kira had left, Dax tapped her comm badge and was connected to Sisko's office at Ops.

"Well? How is she?" The commander's voice was level and controlled, but Dax could detect the tone of concern in it.

"She's fine, Benjamin; or as well as can be expected. The time spent in the altered holosuite didn't have as much of an impact as her being relieved of full duty has had."

"Is that a psychological assessment of her condition? I didn't think you'd take it upon yourself to run any tests along those lines—"

"I didn't need to," replied Dax. "And it's not a psychological assessment; it's a personal observation. I don't have to have known Kira for as long as I've known you to have insight into her character. Her actions of late have been irresponsible and erratic; most of that is a direct result of the informal administrative action you took against her. Her personality structure is almost entirely based upon the status she had here as a liaison to the Bajoran government and a Starfleet officer. General Aur and the Severalty Front took the first part of that away from her—and then you removed the rest. Frankly, Benjamin, whatever has happened is as much your responsibility as hers."

There was silence for a few seconds; she could picture her old friend alone in his office, his face heavy with brooding.

"I'm aware of that," came Sisko's voice. "It's just something that I'm afraid I haven't been able to turn a great deal of my attention to. What do you advise?"

"Restore Kira to full duty. As soon as possible."

"There's a problem. I relieved her of duty for good reason. The security of this station and its ability to carry out its mission has to be my overriding concern. As long as there's any doubt about Kira's loyalty to those ends, then I have to take the appropriate measures."

Dax had already anticipated that response from him—and was ready for it. "Think about it, Benjamin. It's been established conclusively that the Cardassians are involved in the current situation on Bajor—Gul Dukat practically boasts about his hand-in-glove relationship with the new government's Minister of Trade. And at the same time, this experience that Kira just had in the altered holosuite proves that she would be psychologically incapable of any dealings with the Cardassians. The kind of rage that she has built up inside her would be impossible to overcome. That she's been able to channel that anger into constructive modes of behavior is largely a tribute to her strength of character—and something that we're fortunate to have working in our behalf."

"Your point is well taken, Dax." Sisko's voice turned thoughtful. "Very well taken, actually. All right, I'll take the responsibility for this one. Immediate notification will be made to Major Kira that she's been restored to full duty."

"I'd like to make a further suggestion, Benjamin."

"What's that?"

"Delay notification for at least two shifts. She needs the rest."

That advice was accepted as well. After Benjamin had broken the comm link, Dax closed her eyes, trying to let her own fatigue seep out of her body. Rest was something she could have used, too. In addition to the research she had been doing with Bashir, the prying apart of the altered holosuites' secrets, there was the burden of the other, the bits and pieces of data that she had kept to herself so far. Those secrets weighed far more heavily upon her.

Things so small, and so far away . . . *I should tell him,* thought Dax. Her old friend would take the load, the responsibility that belonged to DS9's commander, upon his shoulders; she had no doubt of that. But how could she let him do that, when there was already so much pressing upon him?

Surely there was a breaking point, even for one as strong as Benjamin.

She rubbed her eyes with her fingertips. The readouts from the station's remote sensors moved in shadow inside her skull, small ghosts, their significance—if any—not yet determined. Perhaps the scraps of information meant nothing, just random perturbations in the universe's workings, dust upon unseen and unknowable gears. . . .

Dax drew in her breath, opening her eyes to the lab's familiar surroundings. For now, until the data added up to something definite—or nothing—she knew she'd have to go on carrying this secret inside herself.

The glare of the plasma torch had lit the space a lurid white-yellow, the color of a star's core. When the torch was switched off, quiet replaced the sizzling of metal being welded fast to other metal.

Odo had been able to watch the process without any protective gear, simply by forming a reflective shield over his eyes, letting only a fraction of the intense light through to the optic receptors behind.

"There, that's done." O'Brien lifted up his own work shield, revealing his face bathed in sweat. The air in the cramped angle of bare girders and wiring conduits had grown hot and stale, unrelieved by any flow of ventilation. He laid the torch down and straightened up, rubbing the small of his back. "That should be the last of them."

"At least of the ones that our freight handler told us about." He looked past the chief of operations to the thick steel panel that had been sealed in place, blocking off one of the surreptitious entry points to the station. It had been easier to work on them from inside rather than sending a protected crew out onto DS9's surface.

"If any more turn up, we'll plug 'em." O'Brien had to keep

his head ducked to avoid banging it on the network of heavy pipes above. "I don't think that's going to be the case, though; the new structural analysis program I ran on the computer indicated that there aren't any other spots anyone could get, not without setting off a full-scale perimeter-integrity alert. We nailed down places that McHogue and the Cardassians didn't even know about." He started breaking down the torch and stowing it in its case. "Too bad it's all rather like securing the barn door after the horses have not only bolted, but they're in the next county already."

The analysis by O'Brien touched a sore spot inside Odo. It still rankled him that his beloved *Deep Space Nine*—his home, his world—had been violated by a creature as loathsome as McHogue. He could well believe that this was what a family man such as the commander felt, upon hearing that his son had been exposed to this person's machinations; it was hard to remain quite rational about the subject. The more that he and O'Brien had investigated the holes in the station's physical security and filled them in, the more his simmering anger had approached an internal boiling point. He could easily have laid down his commission as DS9's security chief for the sake of five minutes as a private citizen, alone in a locked room with McHogue; he would have guaranteed that only one of them would have walked back out in one piece.

"Calm down, man." O'Brien had caught sight of the anger stewing behind Odo's ordinarily blank visage. "You'll blow a gasket if you don't. Or maybe you'll just swell up and burst like a big bubble, or whatever else it is an apoplectic shapeshifter might do. We'd have to sweep up little pieces of you with a wet-dry vacuum cleaner."

"Very amusing." Odo's scowl remained frozen in place. "I fail to see how you can remain so lighthearted about all this. What McHogue was doing, waltzing in and out with his CI modules, it's . . . it's *offensive.*"

"Lighthearted I'm not." O'Brien had finished packing up

his gear. "Those clowns could have blown an atmospheric seal and we would all have wound up exploding from the drop to zero pressure. No, what it is, is that essentially you're a cop and I'm a glorified engineer; you have an idea of perfection and I'm trained to deal with the reality that nothing *ever* works exactly the way it's supposed to—God knows that's the truth around this place. Life is a kludge, Odo, otherwise I'd be out of a job." He hoisted his tool case. "Come on, I'll buy you a drink."

Given his nature, he didn't require liquid sustenance; nevertheless, for the sake of working sociability, he let O'Brien order two synthales and have them set down on the table between them by Quark. The Ferengi said nothing, but returned to the bar in wordless gloom.

"Cheers." O'Brien hoisted his mug as Quark gave a polite nod. The chief of operations wiped his mouth and looked around. "Saints, what's happened to this place? It's bare enough to use for a loading dock up on the main pylon."

Odo glanced at the empty tables and booths. "I'm afraid our host is suffering the effects of a severe drop in his business—hence the lugubrious expression. Those bent on pleasure seem to find more to their liking in Moagitty, on the surface of Bajor."

The explanation prompted an amazed head shake from O'Brien. "You'd hardly believe seeing people turned into murderers would make for successful advertising."

"On the contrary. In this case, the expectations of a 'cop,' as you put it, are more in line with reality. I'm not surprised that the jaded and bored, in search of new and exotic stimuli, would be attracted to an enterprise that virtually guarantees the ultimate in self-destruction."

"There's a cheerful thought." O'Brien had already knocked back half of his synthale.

"You should take a look at the transit logs. Now that McHogue has his operation completely up and running, the traffic passing through this sector and going straight on to Bajor has gone from virtually zero to the point where it's causing some serious navigational difficulties. The weather that the planet is undergoing is only compounding the problem of offworld vessels stacking up outside the atmosphere. Though in the long run, there's no amount of hurricanes that will keep McHogue's would-be customers from reaching their destination."

"Bit of divine retribution there." The last of the synthale went down O'Brien's throat; he thumped the empty mug down upon the table. "McHogue must have played hooky the day they talked about Sodom and Gomorrah at school."

"I'm unfamiliar with those worlds."

"Everybody is, these days." The drink appeared to have loosened O'Brien's tongue. "Though maybe McHogue knows more than we do about these things. How does the old song go? 'What's so horrible about a hurricane, compared to somebody who wants his fun?'"

Odo gazed at the chief of operations in bewilderment. "I have no idea what you're talking about."

"Never mind. Just showing off my erudition, quoting a little Bertolt Brecht at you. Early twentieth century—you wouldn't be familiar with him." O'Brien pushed his chair back and stood up. "As always . . . it's been fun. But I think my wife's waiting for me." He turned and headed for the door.

Odo was left as the sole customer. He gazed at the one full and one empty mug before him. Beyond the limits of Quark's establishment, the Promenade was deathly quiet. His job as chief of security had become much easier over the last few shifts—so much so that he was finding it increasingly difficult to keep himself occupied. Rearranging his old files and purging out-of-date ones had taken only a few hours. There had been no need for him to accompany O'Brien on his rounds of blocking the surreptitious entrance points to the station, but doing so had been better than nothing.

He could afford to be nostalgic about the murder epidemic. Now those seemed to him like glory days, a last great flowering of tension and activity. *Perhaps I should have taken Gul Dukat up on his job offer*—it was a thought that he used to torment himself with, rather than giving it any serious consideration. Since coming back from his visit to the Cardassian diplomatic vessel, the feeling had grown in him that there was going to be plenty of action in Moagitty.

A shadow fell across the table. Odo looked up and saw a familiar face, one that he hadn't seen in several shifts.

"Mind if I join you?" Major Kira managed a weary smile. She glanced over her shoulder. "Though it doesn't look like you would've come here if you were looking for company."

"By all means, Major." He pointed to the chair opposite him. "You're more than welcome." He peered more closely at her. In the dim lighting that Quark favored for his establishment—more out of cheapness than any desire for atmosphere—Odo had almost been unable to recognize his fellow officer. He watched her sit down. "Though if you'll allow me to say so, perhaps you would be better served by making an appointment to see Dr. Bashir. You don't look well."

"Thanks for the concern." Kira rubbed the side of her face with one hand. "I'm just tired, that's all. I've already been told on good authority that I should just go back to my quarters and get some sleep."

"Why don't you?" Odo felt genuine alarm as he gazed at her drawn face; the major looked the way he felt when he was due for his periodic reversion to a liquid state.

Kira shrugged, her shoulders lifting as if a massive weight had been laid upon them. "I tried, but my eyes kept popping open. There just seems to be too much whirling around inside my head. I got tired of looking at the ceiling, so I came down here."

He wondered how much she knew about the current state of

affairs on the surface of Bajor. The last time he had checked with the weather-monitoring staff on the Ops deck, the storm winds had increased in force, lashing at the jagged, irregular shapes of Moagitty. Perhaps the clouds that roiled above the planet had their counterpart inside Kira's skull.

"As it happens, I do seem to have some spare time for conversation." He felt enough sympathy for her that he was willing to make an effort at distraction. "More than enough, actually."

"That's life among the unemployed. At least you have enough sense to stay out of trouble."

"Ah, yes—" Odo nodded. "I heard about your unfortunate visit to the altered holosuite. You'll forgive, I hope, my asking you a few questions about that. It's for professional reasons, not just idle curiosity."

"I'm too tired to care. Ask away."

"What did you . . ." He hesitated for a moment. "What did you see in there, Major?"

She told him, her words coming slowly at first, then in a rush that belied her state of exhaustion, as she described the sensation of mounting into an illusory sky, her physical being translated into a pillar of fire.

"But somehow . . . that wasn't the most disturbing part." Kira shook her head in wonderment. Her gaze moved away from Odo, as though she were seeing again the world inside the holosuite. "It was all the things before that. The things that the skinny little child in there saw—that *I* saw. Those were true things, things that really happened. I remember seeing them . . . a long time ago." She closed her eyes and spoke without opening them. "But I had forgotten all about them; I made myself forget. So it would be as if they hadn't happened at all." She brought her gaze back to Odo. "That's what I wanted. To forget all of that . . . to forget everything. But I couldn't—not forever. Because . . . the past was in there. And . . ." With a single fingertip, she touched the side of her head. "And in here."

Odo made no reply. His own thoughts formed an invisible wall around him, through which he could barely see the person on the other side of the table.

"At any rate," said Kira, "that was the worst part."

"The past . . ." Odo's voice was hardly more than a whisper.

"Pardon?"

"That's what *he* said. . . ." He pulled himself back. "I'm sorry. It's . . . it's not important."

The major let out her pent-up breath. "All of a sudden . . . I could just lie down right here and go to sleep." She gave a quick snap of her head, to keep herself awake. "It just came over me. . . ." She managed a wan smile at Odo. "Maybe it does some good to talk about these things."

He nodded. "Perhaps it does."

"If you'll excuse me . . ." Kira stood up, leaning against the table for balance. "Now I *am* ready to take everybody's advice. If anybody needs me, I'll be in my quarters—for a long while."

Odo watched her cross the empty Promenade and head toward the nearest turbolift.

Another voice sounded in his head. A voice that smiled and promised things. He didn't have to close his eyes to see Gul Dukat's face, the Cardassian's gaze weighing and measuring what it beheld in turn. Everything that Dukat said had been perfectly calculated to evoke a response, if not at that time, then later, a seed planted that would be harvested when ripe. . . .

It didn't help to know that. There had never been a time when he hadn't been aware of Gul Dukat's manipulative skill, the ability to look right into another creature's soul and discern what was the one thing most desired. In that regard,

Dukat and McHogue were spiritual brothers, two of a kind; they both fastened upon the innermost weakness of their prey and turned it to their own use.

Odo knew all of Dukat's machinations, yet still couldn't keep himself from wondering about the things that the Cardassian had said to him . . . and what Major Kira had inadvertently added to confirm those things.

The past is in there.

A world of ashes remained, after the flames had died, dispersed across the cold stars. When she had been here before, the fire had given her wings, carrying her like a mounting storm above the petty things that crept and cowered on the surface of another Bajor. Her murderous glance, a shining weapon of pure intent, had struck down those who had offended her. Which was all; fire, at last, made no discrimination between the weak and the strong, the victim and the boot upon his throat. And that left ashes for her to weep over as they sifted through her trembling fingers.

I didn't want to come back here—Kira looked up from where she knelt on the black field. *Ever again.* Several meters away from her—it was hard to judge distances; points beyond her reach came closer, then retreated as though carried by the waves of a slow ocean—the barracks of the refugee camp were in ruins, the wooden roofs and walls splintered by a giant fist. Beyond them, the barbed wire and dead electrical cables sagged toward the cindered ground.

It was enough—more than enough—that she'd had to remember these things. But to return to this place, that had once been safely locked away inside her head . . . that was beyond endurance.

Someone was watching her; she felt the pressure of the other's gaze. "Who's there?"

Kira saw the figure then, a shadowed silhouette at the limit of the vision, where the night became solid. She knew it wasn't McHogue or anything from the distant past, the past of the watching child, gone now.

She could almost recognize him, her mouth speaking his name, when she felt the handful of ashes in her grip change to something else. Looking down, she saw a fold of white cloth held tight in her fist, cloth that spilled around her waist and legs. She raised her eyes to see the ashen world falling away from her, as though the night ocean's tide were drawing back to its unfathomable depths. . . .

Her eyes were already open when she woke, sitting up in bed. Around her, the familiar spaces of her living quarters opened into one another. Her mouth was dry from the ragged breathing that was just beginning to slow inside her lungs.

Kira swung her legs out from under the thin covers and shook her sleep-mired head. The digits of the chronometer beside the bed showed that only a hour had passed since she had lain down. *Great,* she thought disgustedly. *Bad dreams are all I need right now.* She still felt exhausted.

Something about the dream nagged at her, kept her from laying her head back upon the pillow. Despite her weariness, she concentrated on bringing the pieces into focus. Not fire, but ashes this time; that came easily to her. The standard revenge fantasy that had been Dax's interpretation had apparently metamorphosed into . . . what? Grief, perhaps. For that child who had watched and seen all, and had been changed herself into something different.

There had been something else; Kira's brow creased as she tried to see it. In the shadows . . . that was it. A figure that she had just been about to recognize, call out his name. Someone . . . who didn't belong there.

She saw his face clearly then, as though a comm line had broken through visual static. She heard his voice as well, slowly and wonderingly repeating what she herself had told to him.

From the end of the bed, Kira grabbed her discarded

clothes. She was still fastening the collar of her uniform as she went through the doorway and into the corridor beyond, her steps running for the turbolift.

He leaned over the shoulder of the crew member sitting at the meteorological console. The screen cast its shifting light across both their faces. "How does it look down there?"

The ensign glanced at the station's commander standing beside him, then shook his head. "Not good, sir. This is the worst global weather pattern anyone's ever seen on Bajor. We've accessed the databases left over from the Cardassian occupation, and all available records preceding that, and we can't come up with any comparable situation."

"What specific disturbances are you picking up?"

A finger pointed to a curve of dark, irregular shapes on the screen. "There's a parade of hurricanes across the major oceans that's virtually unbroken. And worse, when they move onshore, they don't seem to be dissipating; they just pile on top of each other. There's a churning effect with wind velocities steadily mounting; a lot of the coastal territories have already been flooded by the increased tidal action." The ensign tapped a button and the display drew back, showing the round outline of the planet. "Upper atmosphere's a mess as well. The tracking satellites from which we receive the data are reporting high-level funicular activity, with zero success at predicting where the edges of the shear currents will be. All traffic on or off the planet has been suspended for the time being; any vessel attempting to go through that soup would stand a good chance of getting torn apart or slammed into the ground."

Sisko straightened up, regarding the screen with his arms folded across his chest. "If we needed to implement any evacuation procedures, could we get a vessel close enough to use a transporter beam?"

"That's possible, but it wouldn't do any good, sir. The

electromagnetic fields radiating from the system's sun have gone haywire as well. Under these flux conditions, we wouldn't be able to lock on a beam long enough to effect any transfer."

He turned to one of the other crew members. "Do we still have communications with Bajor?"

"Negative, Commander. All subspace comm links with the planet have been interrupted due to the field disturbance; we're not having much luck getting through on any other band. We've been able to pick up some garbled transmissions, just enough to indicate that most of the population has hunkered down for the duration. There's bound to be pretty extensive reports of physical damage and casualties afterward. If there is an afterward, sir."

"How about from . . . the new city?" Sisko couldn't bring himself to pronounce the name *Moagitty*.

"Negative, sir. Indications are that all structures have been completely sealed off. Like everyone else down there, they seem to be riding it out as best they can."

He had to wonder if any of McHogue's customers would even be aware of what was happening outside. So locked in their own worlds, pursuing in the CI-modified holosuites whatever pleasures they had traveled across the galaxy to find. Pleasures—and more. And all sealed within the walls of McHogue's centripetal universe, a pocket cosmos with no need for anything beyond. When the storms had passed, the walls might still be as unblemished and perfect as a crystalline egg.

"Very well; keep monitoring the situation. Let me know if anything changes." He turned away, just in time to observe the turbolift sliding open. A figure darted from it, looked around, then rushed up to him.

"Commander Sisko—" Kira's words came just as fast. "I have to talk to you—immediately—"

He pulled her away from the other crew members. "What

are you doing here, Major?" His surprise was based on an assumption that she would still be resting in her quarters.

"I know I'm relieved of my duties, but that doesn't matter now. This is important. I think someone else has gone into the altered holosuite—"

"That's not possible. The alarm hasn't sounded."

"Who besides yourself has authorization to take the alarm circuit off-line?"

He had to consider for only a fraction of a second. "No one. No one but the chief of security—"

"That's who it is." Kira's face set grim. "Odo's gone in there."

They found him sprawled facedown on the floor of the holosuite chamber. Before even heading for the corridor with Kira, Sisko had had O'Brien cut off all power to the sector. The emergency shutdown circuits built into the holosuite had triggered the retracting of the door; the beam from the portable light in Sisko's hand had swept across the area, immediately catching the unconscious form at the center.

He handed the light to Kira and knelt down, turning Odo onto his back, then lifting him to a sitting position. "Constable—" Sisko drew a hand across Odo's face; the eyelids fluttered for a moment, then blinked and held open. "Are you all right?"

Odo's gaze looked past the commander for a few seconds, as if still focused on some vision conjured by the holosuite's hidden workings. Then he nodded slowly. "I'm . . . I'm quite satisfactory. Thank you. . . ." His voice sounded hollow and distant.

"What happened?" Sisko helped him to his feet. Beside them, Kira watched, her face marked with worry. "What did you see in here, Constable?"

The look that Odo shot the commander was one of undiluted fury; he pushed the commander's arm away. "Nothing—" His voice softened as he regained control of himself. "I saw . . . nothing."

Sisko studied him for a moment longer. He decided against making any further inquiry, at least for the time being. "Perhaps you should go down to the infirmary, and have Dr. Bashir check you out—"

"That won't be necessary, Commander." Odo's voice resumed its normally brusque tone. "I know more about my own physiology than any doctor does. I can tell that I've sustained no injury." He gave a short nod to both Sisko and Kira. "I'm sorry for any anxiety I may have caused you. This was an ill-advised experiment on my part. However, there seem to have been no consequences stemming from it, either good or bad."

"Be that as it may," replied Sisko. "There are not going to be any further opportunities for such research—on anyone's part." He hit his comm badge and was put through to O'Brien. "Chief, I want the CI module pulled from this holosuite. Immediately."

"Gladly, sir."

He broke the connection and looked back to the others in the chamber. "I regret not having ordered that sooner. At this point, I don't think there's any further value to be derived from keeping a trap like this up and running."

"As you wish, Commander. I'll have the security barriers taken down as soon as O'Brien has finished with the unit." Odo stepped toward the holosuite's door. "If you'll excuse me—I have . . . work to do."

When Odo had departed, Sisko turned toward Kira. "Perhaps when you have time, Major, you could give me some details about how you knew Odo was here. But right now, I'm equally concerned about you. Dax informed me that you were close to total exhaustion."

"Believe me, Commander, I feel that way. You don't have to give any orders—I'm heading back to my bed right now."

Once he had seen the major to the door of her quarters, he decided against immediately returning to Ops. It would take only a few minutes for him to go and check on his son Jake.

The interior of his own living quarters was dark. He needed no light to walk through the familiar spaces. Outside Jake's bedroom, he pushed open the door and looked in. Jake's computer panel had been left on; even with the screen blanked, it gave enough dim radiance for Sisko to see by. Jake had fallen asleep, still dressed. His baseball bat and glove were propped up in the corner near the bed. Sisko drew back, pulling the door shut.

The temptation to fall down on his own bed and try to catch a little rest was almost overwhelming. He was about to contact Ops and tell them that he would return in an hour or so, when he sensed that someone else was there with him, out in the quarters' main area.

"Who's there?" he called out, but no reply came.

Cautiously, he walked back down the short corridor. His eyes had adjusted to the point where he could make out the shapes of the furnishings . . . and the figure sitting on the sofa.

Silver metal and pinpoint gems flashed like the stars visible through the viewport, as the waiting person turned her face toward him. He recognized the Bajoran ear ornament, even before his thoughts could comprehend the rest.

"Benjamin . . ." Kai Opaka smiled at him. "Did you not think I would be here with you? At such a time as this?"

JADZIA

CHAPTER
14

IN THAT OTHER WORLD, WHERE HE WALKED AMONG MEMORY AND dreaming . . . even there, he had never thought of her coming to him in this way. To this place, a tiny section of *Deep Space Nine,* where its metal skeleton had been partially hidden beneath the touches of human life—he had always thought of the Kai only on her own world, in the temple's sheltered peace.

"Sit beside me, Benjamin." Kai Opaka gestured toward the vacant side of the couch. "We have much to talk about. And there is so little time—at least for you, at this moment."

Then I can't be dreaming, thought Sisko. That explanation for what he saw had already occurred to him: that he had fallen asleep, exhausted from overwork and all the concerns that had swarmed over him in the last few shifts, and was even now lying with his eyes closed on the couch or his own bed. But if what the Kai said was true—and why, in this world, would it not be?—then he knew it was no dream. In dreams, there was always plenty of time, or no time at all, merely eternity.

She smiled, having perceived the course of his thoughts. "You trouble yourself over matters of no consequence, Benjamin. What wisdom is there in dividing one life from another, of saying that one happens while you are sleeping and the other when you are awake, and that one is greater or lesser than its opposite? Better you should hold it to be all one life—your life, Benjamin—and one experience of it."

The fatigue seemed to drain from his shoulders as he sat down beside her. Or what he perceived of her—this close, Sisko was able to discern another element of the truth. "But you're not really here." He couldn't keep a note of disappointment out of his voice. He reached and touched her arm, or where he saw her arm to be; his hand disappeared through the folds of her robe. "You see that, too, don't you?"

"Of course I do," chided the Kai. "Has it been so long since we've talked, that you would think I had become old and foolish? I still have eyes with which to see, and a way of knowing what is seen. Perhaps it is you that appears as a ghost to me."

A more worrying thought struck him. "Kai . . . are you dead? In the way that I would know?" He looked more closely at her image. "Is that how you've come to be here?"

"In the way that you would know . . ." She shook her head. "That moment is not yet arrived, Benjamin. My physical being is quite well, thank you. Though there is part of it—here—" She touched a few inches below the base of her throat. "A part that still grieves at having been cast so far from Bajor. That is a small death that I suffer with each dawning of light upon the place I have chosen for my labors—my answering of the Prophets' call. It hurts a great deal to be separated from the world and the people that I served for so long. But as long as that pain is there, then I know that my body and spirit are not yet set apart from each other. Someday, the empty husk will be brought back to Bajor, for its silent rest . . . but not yet."

"Then you're still there . . . out there on that moon in the Gamma Quadrant."

The Kai raised her hands, palms upward. "I'm here with you, Benjamin. Or enough of me is; this part that your eyes have enough wisdom to see, though your touch still doubts. What does distance matter? You step through the wormhole as though it were a door from one chamber to another, and light-years of *distance* are vanished in the blink of an eye. Did you believe the Gamma Quadrant, and all the stars and worlds it contains, to be an illusion?"

"But the wormhole is *real.*" Sisko knew why he was trying to argue her away. It had been crushing enough to discover that the Kai wasn't physically aboard the station; if he were to accept even the least part of his perceptions as true, and then wake from a dream or brief mental lapse to find himself alone . . . that would be too much to bear. "And a vessel that goes through the wormhole," he persisted, "is real. In every world."

"Benjamin . . ." The voice of Kai Opaka's image turned even gentler. "Is it not too late, for you to worry about what is real and what is not? Even as you and I speak with each other—however we do so—that which you were so sure was an illusion, a world of illusion held within a small chamber, that false world seeks to destroy the world of the real. Destroy it, and take its place. What would be real and what would be illusion, then? All the distinctions you have so carefully made between one world and the other would have been for nothing."

"Very well." Sisko clasped his hands together before him. "I've seen enough apparitions inside the holosuites—and outside them—that turned out to be real in a way that I wasn't ready for. You, at least . . ." He smiled ruefully. "You had the courtesy to ask me to sit down." From over his shoulder, he glanced toward the living quarters' short corridor. "Perhaps I should try to speak more softly; I wouldn't want to wake my son."

"Don't worry, Benjamin." The image laid its hand on Sisko's forearm, though nothing could be felt. "He'd know he was dreaming."

He closed his eyes for a moment. "Why did you come here? Surely it wasn't just to show me that things could be real and not real at the same time."

"I came to warn you, Benjamin. Is that not what a ghost—even a ghost of the still living—should do? There are such expectations within you; it would be a pity for them to become disappointments."

That much was true; in some ways, he would have been surprised if it had been otherwise. Since the first time he had met the Kai, he had been aware of having entered a universe where things happened with the logic of dreams.

"Of what could you possibly warn me?" He studied the Kai's image beside him. "That I don't already know about?"

"You know of many things—more than when we made our acquaintance with each other, so long ago. Yet there are still aspects of your own being that remain beyond your grasp. You will need to find those things—find the truth, Benjamin—if you are to walk through the storms that have already broken."

"Storms? Do you mean what's happening on the surface of Bajor?"

The Kai nodded. "There—and elsewhere. In the worlds of falsehood and of truth. The storms have unleashed their fury, and what you have been able to see so far is but the least of that wrath. The very rocks and air of Bajor are suffering the consequences of the unholy alliances to which General Aur has bound my people . . . but there is worse to come."

He had never heard the Kai, in all the time before she had traveled through the wormhole, speak in such a manner. Her soft voice had changed into another, that of a prophet bearing fire and its scathing redemption. The gaze of the image pierced him like a weapon that brooked no resistance to the message inscribed on its shining blade.

"In the new city, the abomination that has been built upon the soil of Bajor—"

"In Moagitty," said Sisko. "That's what it has been named."

Anger moved across the Kai's face. "It has another name, an ancient one, that cannot be spoken. Just as the evil it represents is an ancient one—did you really think, Benjamin, that such things have not been encountered before, although in different guise? Though the dark gift of time, the shadowed mirror of the possibilities that your kind has brought to Bajor, is to make this manifestation of that evil stronger than it has ever been. Perhaps that is what the more foolish of your blood would call progress—that dizzying rush to potentiate and enlarge that which was already dreadful enough before."

Her words chilled him, as though an icy cloth had been drawn across the skin of his shoulders and arms. He remembered the first time he had encountered McHogue, in the bright summer world of the altered holosuite, a landscape that had once been no more than his son's daydreaming and had become a nightmare of red-soaked earth beneath the trembling leaves. Even then, he had sensed the dark radiation emanating from the smiling figure, as though from an inverse sun, a shadow that swallowed warmth and life. McHogue's dark eyes, optical black holes, had also shown in the face of the boy, the child who had knelt on the stream-washed rock, glittering knife in his grasp. And with the same smile, that looked inside whatever stood before it and found a silent brother there. A sleeping twin, that could be woken and coaxed into an annihilating life of its own. That was what had struck a blow to Sisko's heart, deeper than any blade could have reached: when he had come upon the holosuite's echo of his son Jake and had seen those dark, dead eyes looking back at him, judging and condemning . . .

"I'm sorry," he said aloud. "Perhaps you'd be right, if you believed that it would have been better if all the universe beyond had never touched Bajor. Better for your people, and for everyone else. But it's too late for that. I'd only want you to remember that some of us at least meant well. We still do."

"There is no need for any apology. How could Bajor have kept the universe outside its walls, when it is a part of that same universe? Be assured, Benjamin, that this too was foreordained. There is yet a great blessing, for the people of my blood and all others, that the conjunction of the great and the small will bring about. But at this moment, Bajor's fate and the fate of all the worlds beyond is threatened. That which is at stake is past all your present imagining; that is the burden you carry, Benjamin, and the destiny you must bring to light."

Slowly, as though that world had been placed back upon his shoulders, Sisko nodded. "What must I do, Kai Opaka?"

She raised her hand, palm outward, a few inches from his brow. "Know first, that what you have perceived of storms upon the surface of Bajor is only the external manifestation of this evil's consequences. The storms, the lashing of the soil by wind and furious rain, is but the planet's own cry of pain at its violation. I heard that outcry, at a place far from here—how could I not, when Bajor and I are part of one another? I heard, but did not understand how such a wound could have been inflicted. Not until my meditations brought me here again, to gaze upon that world of suffering—then I saw, and knew. This being you call McHogue—he is an ancient enemy, one who wears this man's face as a mask, the better to deceive those who see only with their eyes and not with their hearts."

The Kai's words brought back a memory, something Sisko had almost forgotten. Of what had been reported to him, of Quark's odd perception of one who by all appearances should have been recognized as his old business partner. It was somewhat humbling to realize that the Ferengi had had more insight into the truth than anyone else could have realized.

"There's another storm, isn't there?" Sisko looked deep into the eyes of the image. "That we can't see yet."

"Soon enough, and you shall. I know what had happened here aboard your station, the epidemic of murder that moved through these corridors. That was madness enough, but what is happening now in the place called Moagitty far transcends it. The storms that scourge the walls outside will seem but the mere echo of the firestorm that has been unleashed inside. If the barriers were to crack and break apart beneath that fury, the rains would not be enough to wash away the rivers of blood that have already begun to flow."

"This was my fear," said Sisko. "That McHogue would reach some kind of critical mass with his CI modules and the holosuites he'd built with them. If he unleashed as much chaos as he did here aboard DS9 with just a few altered holosuites, the possibility of an exponentially greater reaction would come into play, once he had an unlimited field of action. Now he has all of Moagitty, and everyone who has come to it."

"If only the consequences were limited to this new city and those foolish ones who have let themselves be locked inside it by their desires. But the results of that intermingling of evil and folly reach through all of Bajor—and beyond." The Kai's voice had grown stern, becoming that of a prophet foretelling the wrack of nations; now her words softened again, to those of a teacher. "The people of Bajor carry a great spiritual burden, one that has been rendered even purer and more sanctified through their suffering. Their faith—my faith, Benjamin—is a light unto other worlds, even to those who bear the darkness within their hearts. Have you not heard me speak before, as each Kai through the centuries before me has spoken, of that aspect of the universe which is not material in nature, a reality that is comprehensible only through the stilling of desire?"

Sisko nodded slowly. "Of course I have. That teaching is found on many worlds, in one form or another. The learned ones say that to achieve wisdom, consciousness itself must be changed, molded to take on the eternal, unchanging nature of the universe itself."

"Then you must realize that what McHogue has brought to Bajor is the complete opposite of that teaching. Through his powers—the powers of illusion and the material world, which are the same—desires are increased and made stronger, to the point of complete and utter insatiability. Hungers are created that are greater than the universe which contains them; there is nothing in reality which can fill that void. How can this not have a reciprocal effect on the world in which it happens? The material and nonmaterial aspects of the universe are inter-twined and cannot be separated; the wound inflicted on one part is suffered by the other as well. And that is exactly what is happening upon Bajor now; the storms that lash its surface are proof of that. The physical part of the universe encom-passed by Bajor is itself taking on the darkest aspects of unenlightened consciousness."

"What will happen? If that process goes unchecked?"

The image of Kai Opaka seemed to waver for a moment, as if doubt had interfered with the apparition. "That is beyond even my understanding. The eternal is in danger of becoming a thing based in time, transitory and then finally instantane-ous. Time and space are one; you know that, Benjamin. If time ceases, then so must space. All of the Bajoran system, including this end of what you call the wormhole, would no longer be."

"And what of us? What would happen to the station?"

"I do not know." The image shook its head. "The station is of a nature foreign to the world it serves; it represents the inward flowing of all that lies beyond in the universe. And yet at the same time, it has become linked to and has begun to share aspects of Bajor; the worlds have mingled together. If one should die, the other might yet live—it is not for me to say. But surely it would be a crippled existence, torn from all memory and purpose, in a place far from what had been here. Nonexistence would be thought of as a better fate."

He fell silent, mulling over the Kai's words. The matters of which she spoke were at the limit of his own comprehension; it was hard to know how much credence to give to the image's mystical pronouncements. Even before the Kai had answered the call of the Prophets, it had been clear to Sisko that she observed and moved in a sphere other than the one which he inhabited. As a Starfleet commander, he had to deal with the reality that was perceived in common by all of the galaxy's sentient beings; a reality whose dimensions, however vast, could still be measured and agreed upon.

And yet, at the same time . . . there were things he had seen, that belonged to that other universe, the one from which Kai Opaka spoke. When he had first been inside the wormhole, and time as he had known it had ceased, replaced by something fluid and malleable, a dimension where his consciousness and that of the wormhole's mysterious inhabitants had merged and expanded through all the worlds of memory and possibility—he had not emerged from that experience as the same human being he had been before. Some part of him, he knew, was no longer human . . . or at least not bound by the usual definitions of that state.

Perhaps that was the reason the Kai had come to him now, or had even been able to. The apparition Sisko perceived of her was something that existed outside of space and time; the mortal part of the Kai's existence was still located on the other side of the galaxy, past the wormhole's distance-annihilating transition to the Gamma Quadrant. Another part, the eternal one, could somehow hold Bajor within its palms, as one might cup a precious handful of water. The human shell of Commander Benjamin Sisko stood mute before these mysteries; the seed within, that had been planted in the wormhole's timelessness, could encompass the smaller world of *Deep Space Nine.*

"Benjamin . . ." The Kai's voice broke into his thoughts. "In your world, your existence, there is still time. But little of it. You must decide upon what it is that you will do."

He gazed before himself, at his fingers knotted into a doubled fist. "But I don't know," he murmured. He turned toward her. "What do you—"

His words fell into silence, as he saw that he was alone. Where Kai Opaka's image had been, now empty space; nothing of the apparition remained behind. At the side of the couch stood the wooden crate that Kira had brought back from Bajor, still sealed tight, its dead remnants of the Kai locked in darkness.

They listened . . . and were appalled. Somewhere inside himself, Dr. Bashir analyzed his reaction, with a cold-bloodedness that insulated him from shock, and put the label to it. For lack of a better word, he knew; *appalled* was suitable for mere disasters and horrors within human scope. The report that Ops had relayed down to the research lab went far beyond that.

"Do you require a repeat of that transmission?" The comm technician on Ops managed to keep his own voice controlled and professional, though Bashir detected a slight waver undercutting the words. It would have been impossible for the tech to not have had a similar gut-level response.

"That won't be necessary," said Dax. From where she sat next to Bashir, she reached over to the computer panel. "Thank you." With a touch of her finger, she blanked the screen and its last frozen video frame.

He was relieved at that; even with the lack of squeamishness that his medical training had given him, he had been able to glance only from the corner of his eye at the sight of the blood-drenched interior of Moagitty's main casino area. The madness of which he had caught the barest glimpse, in Ahrmant Wyoss's drugged mutterings, had seemingly found a new and more powerful incarnation, one that walked through the corridors of the distant pleasure city and wrote its name in letters that ran from the ceiling to the crowded floor.

"We knew this was coming . . ." Dax's voice had retreated to a soft murmur. "Didn't we?" She looked beside her at Bashir. "It's what we were afraid of all along. And now it's come to pass."

His silence and hers closed over them, as though the lab had been sealed against the vacuum surrounding the cold stars.

What they had viewed together on the computer panel's screen had been only a few minutes long . . . but that had been enough. The comm technician had signaled them that a fragmentary transmission had been received from the surface of Bajor; the exact source was the new city of Moagitty. Even with the reconstructive enhancement techniques run on the transmission by the station's central computer, what remained of the signal's audio component was little more than roiling static. But the visual portion was more than enough to indicate what had happened in Moagitty—or what might still be happening, if there were any inhabitants left alive.

Murder, thought the doctor. But even that word implied some function of humanoid intelligence, a comprehension of an action and its consequences, even if that was the psychopathic desire for the shedding of another creature's blood. What the images received from Moagitty showed was something beyond that, a force of nature implacable as the hurricanes buffeting the walls from outside. It was as if the storm had broken through and brought with it not the cleansing fury of wind-driven rain, but a red torrent that washed battered corpses against the gaming tables and other abandoned instruments of pleasure. A war zone contained within the domed spaces of the city—or its aftermath, when the force whose enemy was all life had strode onward.

"There may be still someone alive there." Bashir pointed to the blank screen where the images had been. "Whoever sent the transmission . . ."

Dax shook her head. "It's possible, but this doesn't constitute any real evidence. The transmission may have been recorded and then beamed here by the city's autonomic security system. It would be a standard design protocol for such an alarm message to include as much detail as possible on whatever situation might be encountered by an outside rescue operation. As it is, there was so much data lost coming through the electromagnetic fields surrounding the planet that the time stamp encoded on the sub-band frequency is missing. If the transmission *had* been assembled by a living person, it may have been recorded hours, even days ago, and set on a repeater uplink until DS9 received it; by this time, the person responsible may be as dead as the others that we saw."

"True, but . . ." He tried to find a rebuttal to her argument; the thought of so much loss of life was beyond his ability to bear. "But we don't know," Bashir said slowly, "how much of Moagitty's interior the alarm transmission would show if we had received it intact. There may be sectors of the city that at least some of the people were able to seal off, to protect themselves from whatever this . . . this process is that's started."

The Trill science officer considered his words. "There's always that chance—but I would hesitate to raise our hopes on that basis. From what we've been able to ascertain of the CI modules' effects, any psychotraumatic behavior would have erupted on a nearly simultaneous basis throughout the city; it wouldn't have spread from area to area, like a traceable vector of contagion. The likelihood of anyone being able to take defensive measures against such a rapid and widespread outbreak of violence would be infinitesimally small."

Bashir had found one thread to cling to; he wasn't about to let it go, however the odds weighed against it being correct. "I can't operate on that assumption, even if it is the most logical. As a doctor, that is; I have to base my actions on the possibility, no matter how remote, that some fraction of the city's population will be found still alive, when the storms finally pass and the station will be able to launch a rescue sortie. And if that's the case, then those survivors will require medical attention. The DS9 infirmary will be the first place to which they'll be brought; I need to have our facilities ready for an undetermined number of casualties, anywhere from one to hundreds of them."

He slid off the stool that he had dragged over to the lab bench, and began gathering together his data padd and the hard-copy working notes that had accumulated over the last several shifts. The weight of Dax's gaze was palpable against his shoulders.

"Am I to assume that your assistance in this research will no longer be available?"

With the stack in his hands, Bashir glanced back at her. "I'm sorry," he said. "But at this point, I believe we've already found out all we need to know. We could go on forever, tearing apart that one CI module and running computer simulations of its programming, and every time we did that we'd find out a little more—and what good would it do? We'd essentially be right back where we started from."

Listening to his own voice, its rush of words, he knew that he was unloading his sense of frustration upon Dax—a frustration that he was aware she felt as well, that Commander Sisko and everyone aboard the station felt by now. All that had been their hope to accomplish, the mission of *Deep Space Nine,* was being annihilated in front of their eyes. The fragmentary transmission from Bajor hadn't been the sounding of an alarm, but a death knell, a mute obituary sealing others' lives and their own hopes. The development of Bajor, after its ransacking at the hands of the Cardassians, was to have been a triumph of Federation policy against the type of consuming greed that left only wreckage and bare-scraped, valueless stone behind; this world would have someday joined with others as an equal. . . .

Or perhaps more; he was not so much of a rational materialist to be unaware of the ennobling grace that sometimes resulted from such suffering as the Bajorans had endured. There had been a few occasions when Commander Sisko had broken his silence about such matters, commenting briefly and somewhat mysteriously about the unique spirituality shared between this world and the absent Kai Opaka. The commander hadn't achieved his rank by an indulgence in softheaded mysticism; yet Bashir knew that something inside Sisko had been changed, made different from ordinary humanity, by what he had encountered both on Bajor's surface and inside the wormhole. The doctor had had his own experience along those lines, just enough of a meeting between himself and the wormhole's extratemporal inhabitants so that he would know better than to doubt the existence of the universe beyond the one he normally saw. Perhaps that knowledge was what Bajor would have brought in turn to the Federation, a means of passage even greater than the wormhole's access to the Gamma Quadrant. A passage to something within each sentient creature, that would never have yielded to a scalpel or the finest optic probe; a passage to the soul.

And that was what was being murdered upon the surface of Bajor; all those possibilities beyond present understanding. What would become of a world that had suffered such a wound? A wound to Bajor's soul, the consequence of its bartering away the grace it had once possessed. Bashir and everyone else aboard DS9 could only wait and watch, listening for the silence that would mean all the storms were over. And they could go down and unseal the oddly peaceful city, and find whatever was left inside . . .

"I understand." Dax's voice entered the desert to which his thoughts had led him. He glanced at her and saw the same bleak realization apparent inside her. "It wasn't that long ago that we started this investigation; I really believed then that we would find some kind of answer, some way of preventing this from happening." She touched his arm. "Julian . . . I still think it's possible. If we just keep trying . . ."

He shook his head. "It's a little late for that now." The lab door slid open, and he carried his things out into the corridor.

At the infirmary, he dropped the data padd and the other items onto his own desk—it had been a number of shifts since he'd last seen it. He propped his hands against its edge, working out the fatigue that had accumulated across his shoulders.

You should get busy, he told himself, head lowered. He opened his eyes and looked across the unoccupied beds. There was no way of telling how soon he'd need to be ready. He pushed himself away from the desk and straightened up.

Walking through the dimly lit area, Bashir came to the last door. The one that led to the infirmary's attached morgue. It at least had one occupant.

He went in and stood looking down at the face of Ahrmant Wyoss. At peace, as though asleep . . .

"That was smart of you," said Bashir. There was as much pity as irony in his soft words. "You beat the rush."

She slept. And dreamed: again in air, in the night sky of her home planet. But not wrapped in fire this time; Kira felt only a cold emptiness in that place where her heart had been torn by a scouring wrath.

As though on a bed of stars, she turned, opening her eyes to look down upon the world below her. A cry of anguish caught in her throat, almost breaking through the silent chambers of her sleep.

Below her was ashes. And whitening bones. As though the contents of her stricken heart had covered the bared mountains and dry seabeds of Bajor. No living thing remained; all had been transformed to the denizens of this new, harsh landscape. The dead creatures of a dead world.

"No . . ." Kira tasted ashes upon her tongue. Her eyes squeezed shut. A single tear emerged and fell. It glistened diamondlike against the other cold sparks of light.

She saw it fall and strike the scorched, lifeless ground of Bajor, as though the tear had been a last, futile drop of rain.

She saw, as the night's sharp wind filled her clenched fists. She saw, but did not, could not, waken.

CHAPTER
15

SHE KNEW MORE THAN HE DID. PERHAPS THAT WAS WHY SHE HAD made no more than a token protest when he had wanted to leave. As much as he had been her partner in the research up to this point, there were now things to be done—decisions to be made, actions to be taken—that would be easier without him.

Carefully, Dax set the rectangle of the glossy-black casing to one side of the lab bench. The innards of the CI module formed a glittering assemblage before her, the microcircuits like a maze rendered too fine for the humanoid eye to follow. There were mysteries locked inside the tiny components and networks of fibers that trembled at the touch of her breath, as she bent her face lower to study them. Some of the mysteries had been revealed, opened by the patient force of her investigation; others still waited, beckoning her to enter their domain. . . .

And the mysteries outside the CI modules, outside the boundaries of the station, entwined into the fabric of the universe; those had come closer, the pattern of data from the remote sensors growing clearer. The questions that were posed by the bits and pieces of information were more discernible, even if they still lacked answers. The connection between what was happening on the surface of Bajor and the web of seemingly random anomalies that had slowly formed both through and beneath space itself was real now, if still invisible. To others, but not to her. Bashir and the others would have been able to see it as well, if she hadn't made the decision to keep the growing data file a secret.

It would be a secret no longer. After Bashir had left, she had recorded another message, in addition to the research logs already in the computer's data banks. A private message, addressed to the only other person on board DS9 who would understand—not just what she had done, but why. She had tagged the message for a delayed delivery to the recipient; a delay of no more than an hour, but still enough to make her actions and their consequences irrevocable.

That message had been the last thing she'd needed to take care of. Now, sparks of light glowed along the circuits as Dax switched on the power supply that she and Bashir had rigged up for the CI module. Now that the last of the altered holosuites had been shut down on Sisko's orders, this device was the last functioning piece of the CI technology aboard the station. Like a caged animal, its tearing claws pulled to render it even less capable of harm—if Dax loosened the grip of her rational thought processes upon her imagination, she could almost feel the sense of sleeping danger contained by the object. But not entirely asleep; with the power activated, it seemed as if one of the glinting points was the corner of an eye, twitching open just enough to watch her, waiting for its chance to spring.

Stop that, commanded the wordless voice of the centuries-old symbiont inside her. The younger half of her shared consciousness could sense the other's stern but patient tolerance of humanoid folly. Right now, the symbiont—with its accumulated wisdom, its perspective that reached beyond the births and deaths of its host bodies—served as an anchor against the running wild of her fears and dark fantasies. She was safe that way . . . yet at the same time, the humanoid part felt a twinge of resentment. It was easy enough for the symbiont to take a lofty, enlightened attitude; it hadn't walked around in the nightmare world that had been created in the altered holosuite for Ahrmant Wyoss. The CI modules' interference effect had divided her into two, and only one of those two had gone into that other world. The symbiont had had no knowledge of what she had seen and felt, the claustrophobic streets and decaying buildings, until their separate minds had been merged again into a single consciousness, and the symbiont had been able to examine the new memories presented to it.

The voice moved within her once more, bringing emotion into synch with wisdom. It was *her* voice that told her to go on with her work, with the tasks that she had made her own.

"Computer," she spoke aloud. "Initiate simulation sequence." Dax drew her hand back from the CI module.

"Sequence initiated and holding at input stasis level." As the computer's level voice responded to her order, a cluster of the module's filaments glowed brighter.

Inside the CI module, Dax knew, a little world had been created; one that was infinitesimally small, not even existing in the dimensions of physical space. Yet one that was still real enough, in the fluid and shifting definitions of reality that she had come to embrace since beginning this investigation. The CI module's internal programming had been, at her command, set into motion; through the linked microcircuits, a loop held steady. And waiting.

"Increase power to operational level." She stood back from the device, her arms folded before her. "Break stasis and begin external effects relay."

"Warning—" The voice of the station's computer held no emotion. "Order as given will result in possible neurosystemic perception of simulated reality, as programmed within the subject device. You are advised to set field limits before proceeding."

Dax had heard the cautionary statement before; she had been the one who had entered it into the computer's data banks. She didn't need to be reminded, but if anyone else had come into the lab in her absence—such as Julian—and activated the CI module, the unanticipated results could have been dire.

"Set radiated field at one meter from center axis of subject module." She stood just within the sphere she had described. "Terminate field effect at maximum abruptness; no distance-algorithm taper to field strength."

"Settings established. External effects relay commenced."

She closed her eyes, placing herself in darkness as the CI module's reality expanded from a mathematical point of nothingness to a circumference that held her within. She could feel the reordering of the synapses inside her skull, the microscopic tug upon the delicate fibers of the nerve and brain cells. Like the pull of a magnet upon iron filings, the simplest possible demonstration of the touch of the unseen upon the visible—the image had struck her before, of how the CI technology worked. But an inexact simile: the magnet, whatever its powers, was an inanimate thing, without thought or volition. Whenever she had felt the CI module's effects, a disquieting certainty had risen within her, of a malign intelligence unfolding to embrace her own.

From the computer's last statement, Dax had silently counted off three seconds. From previous experience, she knew that was long enough. She opened her eyes, and found herself in another darkness. A world of it; one that she had seen before, that she had walked through, with Dr. Bashir at her side. She kept herself still, not even turning her head; the slightest motion could trigger the crippling nausea she had felt the first time she had been here, the result of the processing lag between the humanoid neurosystem and that of the symbiont within her. Looking straight ahead of herself, she saw the blind windows and ashen walls of Ahrmant Wyoss's hallucinated world, the bleak urban landscape that had been his personal hell.

The illusion was not total; dimly, through the shapes of the deserted buildings and the cluttered horizon beyond, the outlines of the research lab aboard DS9 could be seen, like a brighter video image leaking through the dark one masking it. Without the aid of a holosuite's sensory transmitters and low-level tractor beams operating on her perceptions, the hallucinated world depended entirely on the effects of the CI module for its transitory existence. But those effects had become stronger: less of the research lab could be seen this time than when she had last performed this experiment. The rudimentary intelligence contained within the module had become more adept at manipulating her neurosystem; its function was to continuously learn how to draw any particular subject farther and farther into the world it created.

Dax took a single step backward; for a moment, the vision of the empty city blurred sickeningly, her digestive tract clenching in protest against the dizzying assault. The sensation passed, like the dying of a sudden stormwind; she could see around her nothing but the familiar confines of the research lab and its equipment. On the bench in front of her lay the exposed CI module, its empty black casing pushed aside; the filaments winding among the miniaturized components still glowed as brightly as before.

She had stepped out of the limited range of the module's effects; at this distance, and with the sudden drop-off she had programmed into its operation, the CI technology couldn't reach inside her skull. All of that other world, Ahrmant Wyoss's interwoven fantasies of pain and abandonment, were contained by an invisible sphere, just within reach of her outstretched hand.

"Append research notes," she spoke aloud. "The cortical-induction field appears to have increased effective strength since my previous experience with it; gain in perceptual validity is an estimated twenty-five percent." She paused for a few seconds. "I attribute the additional CI strength to the ongoing aftereffects of repeated exposure to the module's operations, specifically upon my own humanoid neuro-system. As I anticipated, there's been an unconscious learned response on the part of the field-receptive neurotransmitters; interpretation of the CI effects is at an increasingly high level, resulting in apparent perception of the programmed reality simulation without concurrent sensory stimuli from a holosuite. End notes, computer." As the data was being logged into her memory-bank file area, Dax continued to regard the activated CI module, mulling over her previous findings.

The things that she hadn't told her research partner, that she hadn't wanted Bashir to know, at least not yet; those bits of information struck to the heart of the CI technology's mysteries. That the technology represented a two-way pas-sage, she and Julian had already determined; the phenome-non of the black-cased modules reading a subject's innermost desires and then feeding them back, in a spiraling loop of murderous obsessions, had appeared to be the most signifi-cant alteration to the holosuites' functioning. But just within the last shift, she had traced down another, equally important element.

All of the CI modules were connected on a subspace communication link. The bandwidth was narrow enough to have eluded her first attempts at detection; she'd had to perform a manually directed frequency sweep to find it just below the station's own transmission range. The modules from the deactivated holosuites had been taken off-line, but there was a sufficient data stream from the one on the lab bench for her to analyze. From a central locus on Bajor's surface, a network united the CI modules in all of the holosuites in Moagitty; whatever took place in one holosuite was instantly communicated to the others and factored into their joint programming. The altered holosuites were not creating a multiplicity of different perceptual worlds, based upon the input of their various users, but instead were drawing those users into facets of a single, master-programmed alternate reality. That all-encompassing halluci-nation had an essentially centripetal, or inward-directed, nature, Dax had discovered; the minor variations between the users' perceptions were eliminated over time, and at an exponentially accelerating rate, resulting in a single world shared among them. The world that McHogue had created for them.

The microcircuits of the CI module on the lab bench glowed with the mute life that coursed through them. Dax thought—not for the first time—of how the module itself was a like a microcosm of the city that had been built almost overnight upon the planet; every component in its appointed place, all designed to serve one function, and merely awaiting the energy and desire needed to bring all to its culminating moment. Moagitty, McHogue's city; his world . . . and his will, on Bajor as it was in the holosuite.

None of what McHogue had brought into being aboard DS9, the epidemic of murder and the artificially generated madness that had erupted in the narrow corridors, had been his true intent; Dax and the other officers had determined that McHogue had used the station for his testing ground, a dry run to calibrate the CI modules' effects. He had said as much himself, in his face-to-face confrontation with Commander Sisko; Bajor and the establishing of Moagitty had been his goal from the beginning.

And beyond that? wondered Dax. The question remained

unanswered; given the overweening megalomania that McHogue had displayed so far, she found it hard to believe that a pocket empire—even one named so grandiosely after himself—could be the limit of his ambitions. As Julian had pointed out to her during their investigative shifts in the lab, McHogue showed all the classic signs of a criminal mentality, a true sociopath; by comparison, DS9's own Quark was no more than a sharp Ferengi businessman, content to keep a good thing going.

For someone like McHogue, every achieved goal became a stepping-stone toward ever wilder and more far-reaching schemes. The reality principle was lacking in him; that had been Julian's thumbnail psychiatric diagnosis. McHogue possessed no ability to moderate his appetites, his spiraling egotism, based upon the limits of ordinary creatures. The CI technology and the altered holosuites had been as much a trap for him as any he could have set for his unwitting victims; the perfect hallucinatory worlds he had been able to create with the black-cased modules served to validate a delusional state that was already out of control, like throwing an incendiary liquid upon a raging fire. He had made himself a god in a private universe, one bound by the walls of Moagitty.

And that privacy, Dax had reasoned, was the motive for McHogue's abandoning DS9 and moving on to his purpose-built city on the surface of Bajor. His megalomania dictated a world built from scratch, one that partook of not even the least contamination from a reality beyond his control. In every mirror, he wished to see his own face; in every girder and extrusion-molded stretch of wall, he would demand the shaping of his own hand, the outpouring of his prodigal mind. *Like walking around inside his head,* thought Dax; that was what the patrons who were now locked inside Moagitty would have found. That had been her own perception of her journey through the altered holosuite's illusory world: the ultimate solipsism, one so vast that it could subsume all that entered into it, make them as much a part of the contents of McHogue's head as the curved bone that formed his skull.

"Thus, Moagitty itself," said Dax aloud. In the limited spaces of the research lab, without Bashir or anyone else listening, her voice sounded remote, almost disembodied. The time had come, she knew, with the careful working of her thoughts, that she would have to speak and let the station's computer record what she had discovered about McHogue and his world—and what she had determined her course of action to be. She didn't want to leave her working notes in disarray; there might not be a chance to straighten them out later. Not for her, at any rate . . .

"His own little world." She held out her hand, fingers just touching the invisible field of the CI module's radiation. "His own universe." Not here, aboard *Deep Space Nine,* but in his own self-willed, hermetically sealed environment, where nothing not of his own creation could intrude. And where, as in that ancient Earth story, *The Masque of the Red Death,* he could pull the great doors shut and let the grim revels begin, free of any interference from the outside.

"But you forgot one thing," murmured Dax. A back door to that world, that private universe, a door left open aboard the station; she could almost imagine it against her fingertips, waiting to be pushed wide enough for her to enter once again. All she would have to do would be to take a single step forward—and she would be there. Walking inside McHogue's head, the night and stars at the horizon of his skull.

He had forgotten about the one CI module left operable aboard DS9; operable, and connected to all the others by the subspace link they shared. So that made one world among them, the world that McHogue had created. Dax had wondered if, in his furious rush toward the fulfillment of his desires, that apotheosis named Moagitty, all that had preceded the city's rising upon Bajor had been heedlessly discarded behind him . . . or if McHogue had remembered, but had thought he'd succeeded in making the crossing of this threshold too frightening to contemplate.

For she was frightened; Dax had to admit that to herself. The memory of what she had seen before in that world haunted her. With every step taken in that dark vision had come the sure knowledge that more lay beyond its surface, things darker yet and wrapped around a heart concealing even greater violence. The apparition of Ahrmant Wyoss as a battered and abandoned child had been essentially saddening in effect; the weeping figure at the foot of those basement stairs had been no more than one of the holosuite's electronic echoes, and perhaps even less than that. An echo of an echo, the last fading vestige of that fragment of the hallucinatory world that had once been Wyoss's mind and soul. When Wyoss died in the world outside the altered holosuite, there was no one left to bear him from memory into eternity; McHogue, the god of the new world, had other business to take care of. Always rushing forward toward his own glorious destiny, leaving the broken corpses behind . . .

Rushing toward that bright doorway, the one that Dax had seen the last few times she had gone alone into the CI module's field, her humanoid neurosystem separated by the interference effect from the anchor of the symbiont. At first a spark, just at the horizon of that dark world; enough to cause her to suspect what it might be. And then, a discernible opening, from the oppressive, smothering night to a furious illumination. She could hear the voices and shrieking laughter from beyond. And this last time, from which she had just now stepped back, into the safety of the research lab and the enclosing station—the doorway had been bright enough, light spilling out to cast knife-edge shadows around her, so that she had been able to tell for certain where it led.

"To Moagitty." The fear that arose in the humanoid part of her kept the voice a whisper, throat tightened to just her breath. She could speak the name of the opening's destination, the luminous break in the artificial world generated by the CI module on the lab bench. It led straight to the interior of McHogue's city, into the shared hallucination that had grown so large as to consume the reality that held it. Into McHogue's world . . .

She had already decided what she was going to do. There wasn't time to consult with Benjamin. No time—plus there was the chance that as commander of the station, he would forbid any such action as she was contemplating. Dax could easily picture him telling her that the risk to her life and sanity was too great; they would have to find another way to forestall the catastrophe that was already reaching toward them.

Before coming to the lab, she had studied the latest reports at Ops's meteorological-observations desk. All the other crew members' attention had been focused on the storms battering the surface of Bajor; only she had noted the other numbers, the ionic discharge factors surrounding the upper atmosphere, the indices of positron emissions rippling through the fabric of space itself. The numbers were just a few degrees off normal readings, but she could see the direction in which they were heading. An exponential acceleration; soon enough they would hit the steep part of their slope, and that would be when *Deep Space Nine* would feel the first shock waves. The disturbances whose epicenter lay within the walls of Moagitty would have reached this far, like an ocean-bound tidal wave, one that gathered strength as it rolled outward. At that point, McHogue's private universe would have attained its own critical mass; there might be no way to stop the implosive subsuming of the outer reality into the voracious black hole he had created. Beyond that, Dax could not visualize; nothing in her symbiont's centuries of experience had prepared her for such an eventuality.

Or for what she had to do now.

"Computer—begin recording; append to research notes file."

It took her only a few minutes to bring everything up to date. That much was her duty as well; now, if for some reason she was unable to return to the lab—to DS9 and this world outside the CI module's field—someone, perhaps Julian, might be able to come along afterward and complete her work.

"End record."

Another voice, yet still her own, spoke inside her. *Are you ready?*

There was no need to answer aloud. Her symbiont knew the thoughts they shared, as easily as her left and right hands could bear a common weight cupped between them.

The decision had already been made, each part, the humanoid and the symbiont, aware of the needed actions—and the consequences thereof. One hand would have to carry the burden, and the other close tight . . . and wait. That was the lesson Dax had learned from the first time she had gone into the altered holosuite's illusory world; a Trill's shared consciousness had to be divided, the CI module itself forcing the symbiont's mind from the intermingled contact with the humanoid's, for the hallucination to take hold and become real.

Dax stepped forward, into the range of the CI module's field. The research lab disappeared from around her; she felt the skin of her arms grow chilled as a night wind brushed across her.

For a moment there was silence, and then a greater silence, heart-aching, inside her; she knew that the symbiont had already been torn from what had been their shared consciousness. Somewhere immeasurably far from her, part of her self had become an observer at her mind's perimeter.

She gazed around at the empty, darkness-shrouded shapes that filled the world into which she had entered. McHogue's world. Then she began walking, toward the bright doorway of the horizon.

The first impact hit as he entered Ops. A silent shuddering rolled through the station's frame, strong enough to jar him back against the open doorway. As the tremor subsided and he regained his balance, Bashir could see the Ops crew scrambling to their emergency positions; the deck's readouts erupted with a surge of data and sector alarms.

"Where's Dax?" Commander Sisko, leaning over the central control panel, turned quickly toward him. "We're going to need her up here—immediately."

"I don't know; the last time I saw her was in the research lab." Through the soles of his boots, Bashir could feel another low-level pulse moving through the station. "I came straight here from my quarters when the general alert went out. What's going on?"

Sisko nodded toward the perimeter-scan readouts. "We've got some spatial field disturbances coming our way; major ones. Their point of emanation seems to be Bajor. Severity seems to be increasing as well; I've already sent O'Brien on an all-levels sweep, to secure as many stress points as possible before the next one hits."

The readout was only roughly decipherable to Bashir. He looked back to the commander. "Is this something we'll be able to ride out?"

"Hard to tell. Dax has much more experience with interpreting these phenomena. She can tell us if the acceleration curve is close to its peak or whether it has further to go yet—"

"Commander, we've been able to get no response from Dax." Odo came up beside them. "There's been no answer to the direct comm request we've sent to her."

"That first jolt may have caused some damage inside the lab; you'd better get down there, Constable." Sisko looked toward Bashir. "You, too, Doctor; she might be injured. Get her patched up and back here to Ops, as soon as possible." He turned away, clasping his hands behind his back as he studied the spread of readouts on the overhead panels.

If she's alive—Bashir couldn't stop himself from thinking the worst, as the turbolift swept him and the security chief toward the lab.

Odo glanced from the corner of his eye at Bashir. "I'm confident we have nothing to worry about, Doctor. It's been my observation over the years that Trills are remarkably resilient, especially to sudden blows or falls. They do, after all, have two functioning neurosystems within their bodies."

Another rumbling surge hit the station, knocking Bashir against the side of the turbolift. The lights of the small space flickered and dimmed; beyond them, he could hear the structure of DS9 creak and groan, the frame members straining against their connectors, like an ancient sailing ship heeling beneath a storm-force gale. *That was a bad one,* he thought, feeling then a trace of embarrassment at how simple and stupid the words had sounded inside his own head. Of course it had been bad; for the mass of DS9 to have registered any shock at all was an indication of the storm fury radiating out of Bajor. A storm without wind, without any atmosphere at all in the vacuum surrounding the station; it was as if the fabric of space itself, the network of invisible connections between atoms and stars, was being crumpled like a rag into a fist. This little bubble of light and sentience floating in the Bajoran asteroid belt could be snuffed out between one tightening fold and the next.

The turbolift's interior brightened; with a hissing noise, it resumed its course, a twisting path through DS9 that had always reminded him of med-school diagrams of peristaltic motion. That didn't seem amusing now; if the turbolift's advance sensors had detected sufficient torsion damage to the transit shaft, it might have shut itself down, trapping them midway until a rescue crew reached them. If one ever did.

"Thanks—" He let Odo pull him by the forearm, steadying him again on his feet. "Maybe I should worry more about us than her."

When they reached the lab, they found it empty. Or apparently so—Bashir thought he could sense Dax's presence, or some intangible remainder of it. He and Odo stood next to the bench, looking around the area.

"She should be here," said Bashir. His level of concern had gone up another notch. "Where else could she—"

"Watch out!" Odo's voice was a sharp command, simultaneous with his hand grabbing and pulling him back away from the bench.

He saw it then, below eye level; he had almost set his hand on it as he'd stepped forward, searching for Dax. The disassembled CI module, its black casing set to one side, had been powered up; he could tell that much from the luminous sparks moving through its microcircuits. At the same time, he caught the scent of charred wiring insulation and burnt-out components. Even as he looked at the module's exposed innards, another piece of it failed, bursting into a white-centered flare, then darkening just as quickly to a twisted black lump the size of his thumbnail.

"Careful," admonished Odo, as Bashir reached to touch the module. He could feel its heat against his fingertips; he drew his hand back and picked up one of the probe tools that had been left scattered on the bench.

A cautious insertion of the tool's point unleashed a fury of sparks; he shielded his eyes and leaned away, to keep his brows from being singed. When he dropped his protective forearm, he could see that the module was dead, its circuits reduced to black cobwebs, already crumbling to ash.

"What happened to it?" Odo regarded the object's remains with his usual deep distrust.

"Hard to tell . . ." He poked a few more times into the blistered circuits. "I think even O'Brien would have a hard time running a post-mortem analysis on it now. My guess would be that a self-destruct program was triggered somehow; damage this thorough is pretty hard to explain any other way. It'd have to be deliberate."

"Perhaps our friend McHogue decided that he didn't want people prying into his secrets anymore." Odo looked away from the device, toward the unlit recesses of the lab. Another low-level vibration passed through the station, strong enough to rattle a case of glass chemical vials mounted on the wall; Bashir steadied himself against the edge of the bench. "We don't have time to concern ourselves about it now. We still need to find Dax."

A quick search through the rest of the lab yielded no sign of her; Odo returned to the bench area and contacted the Ops deck. "We're not having much success down here; has any other indication of Dax's whereabouts been found?"

Sisko's voice answered him. "Negative, Constable. We've been attempting to run a trace on her comm badge, but we're not getting anything." A barely controlled frustration ran beneath the words. "If something had happened and her badge had been destroyed, the comm desk would have picked up a interrupt signal. Otherwise, the only possible explanation is that Dax has somehow managed to exit or been taken from the station. But there hasn't even been a runabout leaving the docking pads in the last two shifts—"

"Transporter activity?"

"None, Constable. It's as if she's disappeared right out of our midst. . . ."

Bashir tuned out the others' voices, leaving them behind himself as he peered at the computer panel's screen. He was fully aware of Dax's thoroughness; if her mysterious absence was somehow related to her work on cracking the CI module's secrets—and the charred state of the device indicated as much to him—then she would have left a record on the file directory they had shared between them.

He found the most recent additions, date-stamped only a couple of hours ago. Leaning closer to the screen, he quickly scanned across the words into which Dax's voice had been transcribed. He could almost hear her calm, dispassionate tone, the careful dissection of event and evidence. . . .

Another voice spoke, the echo of what he had heard spoken by Commander Sisko less than a minute ago.

As if she's disappeared . . .

Bashir slowly shook his head, already beginning to realize the truth of what had happened to her. Of what she had set out to do.

"Commander—" He straightened his arms against the bench's edge, pushing himself back from the computer panel. "Are we presently capable of getting any signals to and from Bajor?"

"We've managed to establish a comm link. It's weak and erratic, but we can get through. Why do you ask?"

He rubbed his forehead, as though the ball of his thumb could erase from his eyes the words—Dax's words—that had shown on the computer screen. "I suggest, Commander, that you redirect the tracer you have out for Dax and her comm badge. If you use as narrow a beam as possible and increase the range, there's a good chance you'll find her. Down there, on Bajor. In the city of Moagitty, to be precise."

There was no need to wait however many minutes it would take for Sisko to get back to him, to confirm what the narrowed and pinpointed tracer had found. He reached out and switched off the computer panel.

"What's all this about?" He heard Odo speak from behind him.

"We'd better get back to Ops—I'll explain there." Bashir shook his head. His gaze moved from the blank computer screen to the burnt-out remains of the CI module. "He came out here and got her," he murmured. "Just like that . . . McHogue did . . ."

"What are you talking about?"

He didn't turn around. He knew, from deep inside himself, what had happened, though he couldn't be sure how it had. How that other world had become even more real than the coolly rational Dax could ever have anticipated. Real enough to step into, as her research notes had indicated was her plan . . .

And too real to step back from.

CHAPTER
16

A DELAYED MEMORANDUM HAD BEEN ROUTED TO HIM; SISKO FOUND the notifier tag on the screen of his computer when he stepped back in from Ops deck. It was from Dax; she had marked it both URGENT and CONFIDENTIAL.

The memo's tag continued to flash red on the computer panel. "Proceed with memorandum delivery." He leaned back in his chair, awaiting the answer to one more mystery.

No visual display accompanied the message. Dax's voice came from the computer's speaker module. Sisko frowned, hearing an odd note of tension running beneath the science officer's words.

"Benjamin—I'm routing this information to you personally, as you can best determine what use should be made of it. Given the speculative nature of what I'm about to tell you, I'm naturally hesitant to place it in the computer's research files for Dr. Bashir and the others. I may be in error concerning these matters—and I certainly hope I am—so until proof is at hand, one way or the other, I'll leave it to your decision as to whether anyone else should be brought in on this."

The recorded voice fell silent, as though Dax had taken a moment to collect and order her thoughts. Sisko swiveled his chair, bringing himself closer to the computer panel, the blank screen within reach of his fingertips.

"To state it very briefly," continued Dax's memo, "the situation regarding McHogue and his plans may be much worse than we had previously thought. It may, in fact, be worse than we can imagine. Up until this time, the research that Dr. Bashir and I have done on the nature of the CI technology has supported the conclusion that its negative effects are essentially limited, despite McHogue's rather grandiose claims. That is, the damage caused by the altered holosuites is upon their unfortunate users, manifested in severe psychological deterioration and consequent externalizing of violent and self-destructive impulses. Most of the effort that Dr. Bashir and I have expended has been directed toward determining possible preventative and therapeutic methodologies that could be used to reverse the harm that would be brought by McHogue's continuing deployment of the CI modules; naturally, other officers such as yourself and Security Chief Odo have sought means of containing the outwardly manifested criminal and political damage stemming from the inner, personal devastation. All of this is, of course, well known to you.

"However, Benjamin, I'm afraid that our responses to McHogue's operations have been misdirected. Some of McHogue's statements that were interpreted by us as symptomatic of megalomania, perhaps as a result of a psychopathological condition due to his own exposure to the effects of the CI modules, may in fact have a basis in reality."

Dax's words, released from the computer's data banks, prodded Sisko's memory. He had given a full report on his conversations with McHogue to the other officers, for whatever use it might have been in their investigations. The diagnosis of megalomania had largely been one of his own making;

how much of that, he wondered now, had been cold, rational analysis on his part, and how much a deep visceral loathing of the entity that had sat smiling across from him, speaking of mad things?

The memorandum continued. "Concurrent to my joint research effort with Dr. Bashir, I gathered and analyzed on my own certain data that I felt it best to keep confidential at that time." On the surface, Dax's voice might have been describing an accumulation of dry, inconsequential statistics. "Even before the present atmospheric storms on Bajor and the ongoing spatial disturbances in our sector, there were indications of a deeper underlying phenomenon taking place. Dating from the time at which it may be assumed that McHogue first placed the CI modules into operation, there is a growing body of evidence—navigational instrument deviations, subspace sensor readings, and the like—that a fundamental cosmological shift is taking place, with the city of Moagitty functioning as its epicenter. I didn't want to believe this, Benjamin, but the data allow for no other conclusion. *Moagitty has become a black hole, but one unlike any we've ever encountered before.* It is not an object of such colossal mass that light cannot escape its gravitational pull; instead, it appears to be creating a warpage of dimensional relationships *beneath* the universe in which we exist. An analogy, Benjamin: it's as if the cosmos that we normally perceive were reduced to a map spread out and fastened upon a table. Now that table—the subspace dimensions that maintain our universe—is being destroyed. Somehow, the operations of McHogue's CI modules are drawing subspace in upon itself and collapsing it, just as a gravitational black hole does with light radiation. That is what is causing the planetary storms and the spatial disturbances; the tension between the imploding table and the map above it is reaching catastrophic proportions. At the moment, that disturbance is limited to the sector surrounding DS9; however, the sensor readings that

I've been following already indicate a widening of the destructive phenomena. There's no reason to believe that the subspatial collapse will not spread beneath all *possible* space. This would be a cataclysm beyond our imaginings, Benjamin; an eclipsing of the galaxies themselves."

The words ceased for a moment, as if that which could be neither imagined or spoken had claimed her voice. In the silent office, Sisko heard his own shallow breath mingling with a whisper that could not be heard but only felt, the motion of the stars wheeling in their ancient courses. A hand had been laid upon both his heart and the nearest star, halting each between one fragment of time and the next. If there was to be a next one . . .

"I'm unsure as to the causal relationship between the operation of the CI modules and the subspatial collapse." The murmur of Dax's voice had resumed. "Further investigation would be required to establish the exact mechanism involved. Suffice it to say—that amount of time isn't available to us now. The consequences of McHogue's operations upon the surface of Bajor have reached a critical point. That's why I'm forwarding this memorandum to you, Benjamin. I don't think it will be long before you'll be aware of what I've set out to do. I just wanted you to know—and to understand—that I had my reasons."

Again, silence; a few seconds ticked by, before Sisko turned his head and saw the words END OF MEMORANDUM set in place on the screen before him.

He tapped his comm badge. "Commander Sisko to Dr. Bashir. Any sign of Dax?"

"Negative, sir. I'm afraid that—" Bashir broke off his reply. "Odo and I are heading toward Ops. There's a lot we need to talk about."

"Very well," snapped Sisko. "Make it quick."

Another series of bone-jarring impacts rattled through the

station before Bashir and Odo arrived. The office door slid shut behind them.

"All right, then—" Sisko leaned back in his chair and placed his fingertips against each other, as though the cage they formed would be enough to contain the worry and anger that had grown so large inside him. "I want to hear exactly what you found, and I want to hear it now." There hadn't been time to waste before; that it might already be too late for him to do anything was the chief goad to his self-lacerating fury.

On the opposite side of the desk, Dr. Bashir slumped down into one of the other seats, without being prompted to; he looked drawn with fatigue and an even more visible anxiety. Behind him, the station's security chief remained standing.

"It seems that Dax, as is her usual practice, left detailed notes about what she had discovered, and what she was planning on doing—"

"I'll tell him," interrupted Bashir. He pushed himself upright in the chair, making the effort to bring his emotions under control. "I was Dax's research partner on this investigation, so I think I have a slightly better idea of what's happened to her."

Odo raised an eyebrow, then nodded. "As you please, Doctor." He took a step backward and folded his arms across his chest.

"Dax figured out a way—or so she apparently believed—of entering the hallucinatory environment created by an activated CI module, and then going *beyond* that to an alternate reality that's hidden behind the sensory perceptions that are evoked in the subject neurosystem—" Bashir looked up at the office's ceiling, drawing in a breath between rigidly clamped teeth before returning his gaze to the commander. "This is all somewhat difficult to explain. . . ."

"You seem to be doing an adequate job of it," said Sisko

dryly. "I'd like to remind you that I *have* managed to keep abreast of your and Dax's research efforts, at least until these latest developments."

"Well, yes . . . of course. I didn't mean—"

"And if there were time, I'd be able to tell *you* a few things about Dax's research." He studied the chief medical officer through his arched fingers. "I take it that the notes you found, regarding the plans Dax had made, were based upon your previous discoveries regarding the CI modules' interference effect? I'm already aware that Dax previously used the effect to achieve a temporary separation of her symbiont and humanoid neurosystems."

"Precisely, Commander. She had gone back to what had been observed the first time that she had experienced the CI module's effects, when we went into the altered holosuite together. The processing lag between the humanoid cortex and that of her symbiont was immediately apparent, manifesting itself as a severe nausea and disorientation. Basically, it's a failure of the CI technology to coordinate its inductive force upon a shared consciousness; McHogue apparently didn't have Trills in mind when he programmed his holosuite modifications."

"I recall from the report you filed that Dax found a way around that problem."

Bashir nodded. "By using the CI modules' interference effect for her own purposes, Dax was able to separate the components of her dual consciousness—and that was what enabled her to enter into the CI module's illusory sense-world, and for her to move and operate within its field."

"Perhaps it would have been better if Dax hadn't come up with that little maneuver." Odo spoke up. "Or if at least she had refrained from using it again."

The doctor had glanced over his shoulder at Odo, then turned back toward Sisko. "I'm sure that Dax felt she had come up with an entirely rational course of action, given the rather unusual circumstances in which we've found ourselves." A defensive tone entered Bashir's voice. "A thorough review of her last research notes—"

Sisko turned a hand outward to interrupt. "Dr. Bashir, I've known Dax a great deal longer than you have, in both Jadzia's host body and his previous one. You don't need to convince me that Dax had perfectly sound reasons for whatever's been done. At this point, however, no one has explained to me exactly what that is."

"Yes, of course—" Bashir pressed his hands against the arms of the chair. "As I was saying: Dax found a way to separate the symbiont's consciousness from that of the humanoid host body, *and* she had recent experience of doing just that, from our research into the CI module's effects. What she had done before, though, was to merely have the symbiont's consciousness removed from the merged state, so that the humanoid consciousness could experience the effect of the CI technology upon its neurosystem unimpeded by any processing lag. What Dax had done then was to establish a temporary state of dominance by one component of her shared consciousness over the other; the symbiont essentially became, for the duration of our time inside the altered holosuite, passive and without sensory input or awareness of the humanoid host's perceptions and actions." Bashir leaned forward, his voice edging up. "What Dax has done now, according to the notes she left behind, is to attempt achieving a *parallel* consciousness, with each half of her conjoined mind operating simultaneously and equally."

"Can that be done?"

Bashir shrugged. "I can't say—it certainly goes beyond the limits of my knowledge about Trill neurophysiology. No conjoined Trill would have tried to do such a thing before now, because there had never been a situation where such a state was called for. There would have been no advantage achieved, inasmuch as a Trill's shared consciousness invariably has a synergistic nature, resulting in an effective intelligence greater than the sum of its parts. For Dax to sacrifice that synergism, and all the strengths it gives her, only points up the unique nature of what she's undertaken."

"And that is?" Sisko leaned back in his chair. Only the pressure of his fingertips against each other betrayed the impatience he felt.

"As I understand it from her notes, Commander, what Dax has attempted is to use the CI modules' interference effect to split her joined consciousness in such a way that one component—the symbiont half—goes under the influence of the CI module and experiences its effects; for all practical purposes, the symbiont's neurosystem would perceive the hallucinatory environment that McHogue has created. The other part of Dax's consciousness, the humanoid host that is Jadzia, would not be a passive observer of the symbiont's percepxions and actions. Do you see what I'm getting at? *Dax found a way to go beyond the hallucinated world.* One neurosystem undergoes the CI technology's effects, and thereby *both* components of the Trill consciousness achieve entry into McHogue's private universe—but once there, the other neurosystem uses the interference effect to force a division from its partner, so that it can perceive the actual raw data stream being put out by the CI module. It's as if you were watching images on your computer panel, and you then shifted focus to the actual screen itself instead. Or even beyond that: it would be like studying the screen with a high-powered microscope, so that you could actually see each individual pixel that makes up the digitized image. That's what Dax set out to do, only on a much greater scale, with the CI technology's entire sensory bandwidth."

"But if she could do that . . ." Sisko nodded slowly. "I think I'm beginning to see."

"What everyone who has gone into one of the altered holosuites has discovered—including yourself, Commander

—is that McHogue himself is the basic substratum of that illusory world. All of us have agreed that the experience is like stepping inside his head. Even when he doesn't make an appearance, when you're not directly aware of him—he's still there." Bashir hunched his shoulders, as though from an involuntary reaction to his own memory of the altered holosuite. "He's made himself into the omnipresent deity of that universe; that's what makes it so essentially claustrophobic in there, no matter how far off the horizon might seem to be. Every brick, every leaf on a tree is McHogue; there's no getting away from him in there. Except for the way Dax had discovered."

"A shift in focus . . . like standing to one side of the data stream . . ."

"Exactly, Commander. Once the symbiont's neurosystem had locked onto the CI module's effects and gotten Dax into that hallucinatory world, she planned on separating her humanoid consciousness away from what the symbiont perceived—and thus go *behind* the hallucination. And directly into McHogue's consciousness."

"I can imagine," said Sisko, "the actual reason why Dax didn't consult me about taking this course of action. It wasn't a matter of time running out. It was that she felt I would never authorize such a risky undertaking."

From behind Bashir's chair, Odo regarded the commander. "And would you have?"

"I don't know. . . ." He wondered for a moment. Something had gone terribly wrong with Dax's plan; but without the virtue of that hindsight, it was impossible to tell what he would have allowed his old friend to do. Sisko drew himself back to the situation at hand. "It's not important," he said, shaking his head. "Right now, all we can be sure of is that somehow Dax has wound up not just mentally, or perceptually or however you want to put it, but *physically* in McHogue's world. She's down there in Moagitty at this moment." His hands drew apart and became fists. "How could it have happened? How did McHogue *do* it?"

"We seem to have underestimated our adversary's powers." Odo stepped closer to the desk, turning his gaze from Sisko to Bashir, then back again. "That's been our mistake from the beginning. We assumed that the essential transformations caused by McHogue were from the real—this universe around us—to the unreal, the universe that he had created. We were never prepared for the unreal to become real."

Bashir chewed at one of his knuckles. "That's unfortunately true. And Dax, who of all of us should have been able to see what was happening, made that same mistake. She had left herself an escape hatch, in case anything went wrong: the CI module's effects were a function of her physical proximity to it. All she had to do was take a step backward from the lab bench where the module was situated, and she would have been out of reach of the field generated by the CI technology —rather like stepping from one world to another. The symbiont would have been able to assume sufficient motor control of the host body, to do that much. But something else happened, that Dax hadn't foreseen."

The words Odo had spoken now stirred in the commander's memory. "The unreal . . . becoming real . . ."

Biting his lip, Bashir nodded. "That seems to have been the case here. Somehow, the powers that McHogue has gained through the CI technology have achieved reality in *this* universe. Once Dax had stepped into his hallucinatory world, McHogue was able to reach into the station, as though with a transporter beam, and remove Dax's actual physical being to Moagitty. We have the tracer signal locked on Dax's comm badge to confirm it."

"What shall we do, Commander?" Odo's voice reached again into Sisko's brooding thoughts. "We need to make a decision. . . ."

He didn't reply. Without asking for any more information

from Bashir, any more data from the research notes that Dax had left behind, he knew what she had been attempting to do with her risky course of action. To go beyond the CI module's illusory reality, into the one beyond it . . . into McHogue's head, the dark labyrinth of his mind, stripped of all sensory artifice, the bright-lit summer world and the empty twilight city alike. Impossible to guess what Dax would find there. But what she hoped to find, Sisko knew, was the solution, the cure to the insanity that had engulfed both *Deep Space Nine* and Bajor.

A line from an ancient folktale, one that had been read to him when he had been a child on Earth, echoed inside him. *To go I know not where . . . to fetch I know not what . . .*

That had been the mission that Dax had given herself. He had it easier; he already knew where he was going, and what he would bring back.

"Gentlemen—" Sisko roused himself from his silence, as though emerging from the darkness that had sealed over him. He looked at the faces of the two officers before him. "I *have* made my decision. I'm going after her."

Do you see it?

"No . . ." She shook her head. "Not yet . . ."

You have to open your eyes, chided the wordless voice of the symbiont, from that place both deep inside her and extending through the tips of her fingers. *You'll have to open them sometime.*

The symbiont had already told her not to worry, that it would be all right; that there was nothing to be afraid of. She had come here, to this false world, as a single entity, one conjoined mind. The decision, the plan, had been made by Dax with no division between one part of her consciousness and the other. To carry out that plan would require the ending of that state—for a time, a small death, such as the one she'd suffered when she had gone into the altered holosuite.

"It's you I worry about." Dax spoke aloud, though she knew she didn't need to for the symbiont to hear her. When she had first experienced the CI technology's effects, she'd had no personal knowledge of their soul-destroying evil; what she knew had come from her observations of its victims, such as poor Ahrmant Wyoss.

You needn't.

That had been part of her inner deliberations as well: which half of her joined consciousness should stay locked upon the illusory environment generated by the CI module, and which half should go on to whatever lay beyond that false world. The symbiont was over three centuries old; it had seen and experienced things that its current humanoid host only knew of through their shared memories. So much accumulated wisdom gave the symbiont a defensive armor against the toxic illusions; its soul, for lack of a more scientific term, had developed beyond the mortal concepts of desire and fear that McHogue preyed upon.

The nature of the symbiont made the decision simple enough, if no less intimidating for the humanoid part of Dax. The CI module's world was at least a known evil, one that had become familiar to her through the time in the altered holosuite and the computer simulations she and Bashir had been able to run with its programming. What lay beyond that was the unknown—though from what she and the others aboard DS9 had already discovered about McHogue, she knew better than to expect it to be anything pleasant.

Child, even in this world, time is passing. The symbiont had already withdrawn partway from the joined consciousness, enough that it could enter into an unspoken dialogue with its young partner. *Time that is not yours to waste.*

"I know. . . ." Jadzia's voice sounded lost to her, as though the world into which she stepped was so wide, the horizon so distant, that no echo could return to her ear. The cold wind she could feel touching her arms carried the words away.

She opened her eyes.

The world she had seen once before—McHogue's world, Ahrmant Wyoss's world; the world that held a weeping boy in a dark cellar, and was held in turn by each tear and drop of his blood—stretched on all sides of her. The dark, empty city, the crumbling walls, the bricks wet as if an inanimate fever were sweating from them; shadows that bled into one another, that would not flee even if a guttering flame were held against them . . .

And this was where she would be divided in two, the CI modules' interference effect forcing her humanoid neurosystem apart from that of the symbiont inside her. As though she were about to leave part of herself behind—the symbiont would be alone as well, waiting for its humanoid half to return.

"And what if I don't come back?" She couldn't stop herself from saying it. There was always that possibility, and no way of knowing what world lay beyond this one.

Then I'll go on waiting, came the symbiont's reply. *But I won't leave you behind.*

That was as much comfort as she could expect. And as much as she needed. She drew in a deep breath of the hallucinated world's night-heavy air.

Go on . . .

Already, the symbiont's wordless voice was farther away; she had to strain to hear it. The interference was already beginning to set in. The gap between the symbiont's neurosystem and the single one with which she had been born was widening, a space measurable both in microns and centuries. *Don't worry about me; I'll be fine.*

She smiled at the small joke, the way the symbiont said goodbye as if she were running an errand to another part of the station.

"What'll you do while I'm gone?" That was her joke in return.

Its reply was just faintly discernible to her; the image of a pair of shoulders shrugging formed in her thoughts. *Maybe I'll take a nap.*

The visualized incongruity was even more humorous; she found it hard to imagine what the symbiont's shoulders would be like, if it were to have any.

Go on now . . .

A whisper; all the efforts at alleviating her fears were over. Jadzia let the connection between herself and the symbiont come to an end, a thread drawn down to its final atoms and then broken. She was alone.

And in darkness.

The chill breeze she had felt against her skin had disappeared, along with even the faintest light that had seeped around the night world's buildings. All sensory processing of the CI module's effects had been taken over by the symbiont's neurosystem. Leaving her cortex, the humanoid part of what had been their shared consciousness, to pass beyond the CI data stream.

A voice spoke inside her again, but this time it was her own. *Go I know not where . . .*

She could feel it happening. She had moved through two worlds now, as though her steps could carry her across one universe after another. The real world, and that which would take its place. If it could, if she could not find a way to stop it.

There was no time here, so Jadzia could not tell how long the process took. The work of an instant, or centuries—she had counted upon the innate hunger of the senses, their constant searching desire for stimuli, their inability to tolerate a perfect lightless, silent vacuum.

A spark moved at the center of her vision, then twisted into a spiral, swelling and multiplying in fractal-like patterns, consuming darkness. Transforming it into raw color, then shade and form.

The infinitely small and busy machinery, the creating of

another reality, surged to the peripheries of her sight, then were gone. She saw a high-ceilinged, white corridor in front of her.

And someone waiting. Who smiled.

"How good of you to drop in," said McHogue. "I've been expecting you."

"It's impossible. There's no way it can be done."

Sisko turned a hard gaze toward his chief medical officer. "I didn't ask for your estimate of a rescue mission's chances of success. But since you've seen fit to speak up on the matter, I'll allow you to elaborate."

"There's not much to say." Seated before the desk, Bashir spread his hands apart. "The only operational CI module we had available to us, the one that we were working with in the research lab, has self-destructed; the damage to the components is so thorough that even O'Brien wouldn't be able to patch it back together. Without that, we have no entry to the artificial world that McHogue's created—a world that he's somehow been able to bring even further into reality."

"I had no intention of going after Dax by placing myself under the CI effects again." Sisko reached over and activated the computer panel on his desk. "It seems obvious now that whatever reality McHogue created with the altered holosuites has now become overlaid with his personal domain of Moagitty—why else would we have been able to trace Dax's comm badge to the surface of Bajor?" He made a few taps at the panel's keyboard, then leaned back to study the information that had appeared. "I'm surprised the solution doesn't seem more obvious to you, Doctor. I'm going down to Bajor myself, to find Dax and fetch her back here." He pressed his own comm badge. "Sisko to Ops; have a runabout prepared for immediate departure."

Standing beside Bashir, Odo slowly shook his head. "While acknowledge the gravity of the circumstances that prompt your decision, Commander, I feel compelled to express my reservations regarding it. There's been a temporary decrease in the severity of the spatial disturbances emanating from the planet, but all indications from the monitoring crew is that the next wave to hit the station will be considerably stronger —and we have no ability to determine when that will be; it could be anywhere from seconds to hours from now. The impact of the shock waves has been sufficient to cause extensive structural damage to DS9; a runabout caught in that kind of flux field could be crushed like an egg."

Sisko turned away from the computer panel. "Your concerns are well founded, Constable. That's why I'll be going alone on this mission. If anything happens to me, the full complement of the station's officers will be needed here to handle the situation as it develops further."

"I agree with Odo," said Bashir. "It's far too dangerous; even if you get past the spatial disturbances, the atmospheric storms above Bajor will make any kind of landing almost impossible. What would be the point of throwing away the life of the station's commanding officer? If anyone is to go down there, it should be me—I'm the one with firsthand knowledge of Dax's research into the CI technology's effects."

"Perhaps so, Doctor." Sisko kept his voice level as he replied. "But you don't have any experience at piloting a runabout under hazardous conditions. I do. The disturbances that have been hitting the station generally have a leading edge that can be punched through with maximum thrust, then a zone of gravitational rarefaction that requires a three-point visual scan to reestablish the instrument bearings—that's a little trickier than what I believe you're capable of handling at this point. As for when I reach Bajor . . ." He shrugged. "Every hurricane has an eye, where the air is relatively still. It's just a matter of threading the needle."

"I think," said Odo, "that even you will find this mission to be more difficult than you've made it sound."

Sisko managed a thin smile. "It must be a good thing then, that nothing that's happened lately has drawn upon my store of good luck."

To his own ear, nothing sounded in his voice but a calm confidence; he had long ago mastered the commanding officer's necessary skill of betraying no hesitation or doubt. To that end, he would forgo even returning to his quarters for a moment and seeing Jake before setting out on the mission. It was impossible to remove his son entirely from his thoughts; he would have to admit no other possibility—lying to himself, if need be—than that he would see Jake again, upon his own coming back from Bajor and whatever he found there.

He pushed back his chair and stood up. "We can continue this discussion when I return with Dax. Right now, I believe I have a runabout waiting for me."

Only two things were alive in this world. Herself and McHogue . . . and she couldn't be sure about him. Perhaps he had already transcended that state, and become something vast and impersonal as the galaxies that wheeled in the night sky. The points of stars glittered in the blackness at the center of his eyes.

"Yes, of course," said the smiling figure before Dax. "You're absolutely right to have such doubts." McHogue's image turned slightly away from her, an upraised hand gesturing toward the bare horizon. "It is rather an intimidating landscape, I admit . . . but not without a certain, shall we say, *bleak* attractiveness of its own. And one in which the seemingly animate—such as ourselves, my dear Jadzia—stand out all the more prominently."

That in a world of his making, he could step among her unvoiced thoughts, and pick each one up and examine it like a shell upon an empty beach, didn't frighten her. She had expected as much.

"It's not a matter of doubt," said Dax aloud. "In the

absence of confirmable data, I'm more than willing to take an agnostic position on the nature of your existence."

What had laid a chill hand upon her heart, tightened the breath in her throat, was the visual content of this world; what McHogue had chosen to present as such to his visitor. Surely it would have been within his powers, if he had wanted, to unroll an infinite tapestry of the green, unending summer that had once flourished inside the station's holosuites, the world that Benjamin had told her about.

"Oh, certainly," came McHogue's comment. "But that would have been so *boring*, wouldn't it? We've seen all that. Time for something new . . . and *stark*."

She would have closed her eyes, if she had thought it would do any good; if it would have blotted out what had already been burned into the optical processors of her mind.

A world of corpses.

Bones whitening beneath a glaring sun, a fiery scalpel that cut away the last of the deracinated flesh upon the fingerlike spread of ribs and rounded skull. The walls of the city of Moagitty had been breached—it looked like centuries ago, judging from the crumbling edges and rusted metal girders— and strewn across a baked-hard soil. No green shoot could break through the planet's armor; the withered branches of the trees were skeletal hands clawing at the sky. No wind stirred; with the life of Bajor at an end, the breath of its air had been stilled.

The city of Moagitty, in that other universe she had left so far behind, had been built upon the level plains close to the capital city, so that its corridors and chambers could expand to accommodate all the patrons that would flock to it from across the galaxies. Or that had come here; that time might have been centuries ago, to judge from the silence that had enfolded the planet. Since then, the low places had been raised high, as though the bones of the rocks beneath the dead soil had broken through, sharp-edged as knives. She could see down the barren slopes, to the valleys of skulls, the empty gaze of each once-sentient species mounded upon its neighbor.

"A tribute to the pertinacity of the inveterate gambler, wouldn't you say?" McHogue's smile displayed the pleasure he took in his own macabre humor. "They came and wagered away all the money in their pockets, then they pawned the clothes in the manner so traditional in these places—but I did all my predecessors one better. I let these poor losers pawn the flesh off their bones."

Dax turned away from the view that stretched beneath the cliff's edge. "I find it difficult to believe that any of these met such a fate at your Dabo tables."

"Right you are! How very perceptive—I really should have expected no less of you. But then again, you've devoted so much time and effort to the study of my little . . . eccentricities. Rather a self-taught McHogue-ologist, aren't you? I'm flattered; I'm not joking when I say that."

She felt revulsion growing in her throat. "It wasn't anything," she said with a cold fury, "that I did for pleasure."

"Oh yes, of course." McHogue nodded in a show of sympathy. "I understand—rather more than you do, as a matter of fact. You set out upon the journey that eventually brought you to these stony shores, all with the intent of somehow finding a way to defeat me. Well? Did you?" The mocking smile returned. "What've you got in your pockets?"

"Nothing . . ." Dax slowly shook her head. "I have nothing. . . ."

"And now you're wondering if you should have come here at all. What a shame. Well, I won't hold that against you. As you can imagine, I'm feeling pretty good about myself lately. *You* might not think so, but things have really worked out well. Just the way I planned, as a matter of fact."

She peered more closely at his image. "The way you planned . . . or the way the Cardassians did?"

"The Cardassians?" McHogue gave a snort of disgust. "Those clowns. Gul Dukat and that whole flock of lizards . . . I played them all like a cheap harmonica. Though perhaps they got what they wanted; I wouldn't begrudge it to them, just because I had a different agenda. Access to the stable wormhole—that was the limit of the Cardassians' ambitions. That's because they have small minds, like all mortal creatures. Even your other half, Dax, the symbiont you left behind in the world between this and the one from which you started. A few centuries of experience is not really very much. Not nearly enough, not to begin thinking big with."

There was no need, Dax knew, for her to speak.

"How big? That's a very good question." McHogue turned toward the still landscape that lay on all sides of Moagitty's shattered walls. "Let's just say that at a certain point, the idea of limitations ceases to have any validity." He glanced over his shoulder at her. "And it's not all selfishness on my part, either, you know. I've always been a magnanimous individual. It's been my curse, I suppose; I was born to be the host of the universe. Everybody welcome. We never close." He shook his head in self-amusement. "Even here. We're not really alone, despite the way things look to you now. The dead are not dead . . . not in the way you would ordinarily believe."

She couldn't stop the words in her mouth. "I wouldn't have expected such mysticism from you."

"It's hardly mysticism, Jadzia. Though there is a certain poetry to the matter. For these—" He gestured toward the tangled skeletal remains. "—the storms of mortality have passed. All those well-known ills that flesh is heir to . . . that's all over for them. Just as well, really. Now they've found safe harbor . . . in me." The star-points at the center of

McHogue's eyes shifted, brightening to needle glints. "In my world, Dax. In my mind."

The fields of bones might have spoken for her. "I can see what that world is like."

"No, you can't. Even as far as you've come, Jadzia, from one world and through another, you're still just standing at the doorway of this world. These others, those whose remains you think you see—they're the lucky ones. They're inside, where it's safe and warm, and the sharp breezes no longer cut their skin. All who came to me through the altered holosuites and the CI modules—they're all here." McHogue smiled and tapped the side of his head with a fingertip. "All still alive, forever, in their own way. My way, that is. Even poor old Wyoss—I know that you still feel sorry for him, tormented child that he was. Poor little murderer. You see, I freed him from all that pain. I *understand* him, Jadzia, him and all the others so desperate to be free of the terrors of existences, their lives and deaths all muddled together. Wyoss is part of me now. They all are."

She said nothing.

"Ah, here it comes." McHogue nodded in recognition. "The stuff of melodrama, the standard line addressed to big thinkers, by those who can't quite ramp up to their scale. *You're mad, McHogue. Crazy as a bedbug.* I'm well aware that's what you're thinking. But then, that's what you believed before you came here, isn't it? The usual tawdry therapeutic line: you're so wise, so sane, and you thought you could inject that sanity like some sort of mental vaccine into the madness I've created. What were you going to do, Jadzia, put me on the couch and have me talk about my unhappy childhood? What you still don't realize is that your notions of what is sane and what isn't no longer apply here. You yourself found out that all the CI modules were linked together on their own subspace frequency; now you know where that network led. Right here,

Jadzia; to me. And as every little fantasy was created and made real—as *I* made them real—then bit by bit, this world, this universe, became real."

Now she found her voice. "That's what defines insanity—for you, at least. You've convinced yourself that your fantasy has form, a substance, a physical existence."

"Oh? And you in your wisdom think it doesn't? Then prove it, Jadzia." McHogue's smile turned feral, his eyes narrowing to slits. "I know all about the plans you made—I can see it inside your head—and all about your escape route. It's really quite clever of you. All you have to do is take a single step backward, in that world you left behind you, and you'll be beyond the CI module's effect." He shrugged, in an elaborate show of disdain. "Then do so. Leave. You might as well—there's nothing you can accomplish here, anyway."

A knot of fear seized inside her gut, blanking out the rational control she had maintained. Instinctively, she stepped back, as the lord of this world had commanded—

And in that other place, in the research lab aboard *Deep Space Nine*—

There was no one.

"You see?" McHogue reached out and grabbed her wrist, squeezing it tight. "I told you so. The unreal *has* become the real."

CHAPTER
17

IN HER DREAMING, SHE TURNED FROM THE LIFELESS, BLACKENED ground drifting below her. Kira turned, and saw a streak of fire cut the night sky in two. From so far away . . . a spark brighter than the stars.

She wondered what it was. It was already gone, the dream wrapping itself tighter around her. She opened her hand as she slept; somewhere, she could almost feel her fingers brushing across the bed. But here, in her dreaming, there were only ashes trickling from the hollow of her palm. . . .

He wiped the blood from his brow.

Leaning forward, Sisko could see a blot of red that fallen upon the controls of the *Ganges*. He drew in a deep breath, the ache across his shoulder muscles beginning to ease.

At the midpoint between DS9 and Bajor, the shock wave of the spatial disturbances had hit again, the edge pulsing through the runabout's coordinates like an invisible tsunami; he had traced its approach on the craft's instruments and had braced himself as best he could. He still hadn't been prepared for the whipcrack blow, the gravitational inversion that had seemed to cycle from zero mass to a small sun's densest core in less than a second. Where the station's structural members had groaned *a basso* from the storm's force, the lighter frame of the *Ganges* had screeched in treble, as though the pulse engines were about to be torn from its heart.

While he had been struggling to regain control, a corner of the pilot seat's restraining harness had broken loose; the plastoid housing of the astrogation monitor above the forward viewport was now dented and cracked, the impression roughly corresponding to his bloodied temple. He'd had to claw a hold onto the instrument panel with his one free hand, knowing that the density trough between the shock waves would tumble him helplessly into the rear sections of the runabout if his grasp were to be torn free. The flow from his torn skin—he'd had no way of determining if the bone beneath had been fractured—had spun in a red mist before his dizzied eyes, then had spattered against the front of his uniform as he had punched in additional thrust. Only when the *Ganges* had broken through to less turbulent space did Sisko have a moment to press a forearm against his brow, trying to stanch the bleeding with his sleeve.

I shouldn't have bragged to Bashir, about how good I am at this. It had been the sort of remark that was listened to by the universe's deities, if Sisko had believed in such, who then promptly set about one's comeuppance.

There had been enough time, a few minutes between the pulses of the spatial disturbances, for him to fumble open the first-aid kit with one hand, while keeping the other on the runabout's controls. A sterile bandage pressed onto his brow had kept the trickle of blood from getting into his eyes.

The first impact had been the worst. After that, his combat piloting skills had risen from whatever chamber of memory in which they had been buried, and instincts faster than his thought processes had taken over the craft's operations. The instruments arrayed before him only served to confirm what his sharpened senses could feel coming: the prickle of a low-level ionic discharge across his arms signaling the approach of another shock wave, a hollowness in his gut foretelling the depth of the gravitational trough behind the pulse. His hands had darted from thrust advance to navigational vectors with a sureness born of long experience.

At the edge of Bajor's atmosphere, the *Ganges* was beyond communication range with DS9; the spatial disturbances he had managed to put behind him now effectively overwhelmed the small craft's subspace gear. There was no one with whom to consult, not a voice whose opinion he could ask, when Sisko looked below and saw the dark clouds part, as though in welcome. It didn't matter; he knew, at this point, he wouldn't have taken any words of help. All that he needed, prophecies and blessings, had been given to him a long time before.

I should have expected this as well. . . .

This close, to Bajor and the city of Moagitty, and to McHogue himself . . . the path had been smoothed for him. The storm clouds had parted, rolling back like the curtain before an old-fashioned theatrical performance.

Before he had exited from the station's launchpad, he had loaded into the runabout's onboard computer the building plans that Odo had brought back from the meeting with Gul Dukat. The entire physical layout of Moagitty could be scrolled onto the screen before him. But Sisko saw now that there was no need for the information.

As he let the *Ganges* descend through the stilled air, he could see below, brilliant in the rain-washed daylight, the broken walls and towers of the city McHogue had built. Its great central chamber was exposed to sight, the crenellated roof torn and scattered by the hurricane winds.

He's expecting me, thought Sisko. All had been made ready for his arrival. There was even space enough to land, within the white ruins.

Looking up, through the viewport's top edge, Sisko saw the clouds coming together again, sealing the rift that had been opened for him. As though he had been locked into this world, beyond even the vision of the sun.

His hand reached out to the control panel, finding and activating the braking thrusters. Even as he guided the runabout's slow descent, he sensed the watching gaze being raised toward him . . .

The gaze of one who smiled.

A shadow fell across them.

"You see?" McHogue's delight was evident as he turned his face toward the sky. "I think it's *admirable,*" he said fiercely, "that your old friend would come all this way for your sake. Especially when I know how terrified he is, deep inside."

Jadzia looked at the dark-clothed figure with contempt and loathing. "I very much doubt that Benjamin Sisko has any fear of you."

"Ah, well . . ." McHogue shrugged. "You've been acquainted with him so much longer than I have. Or at least that other part of you has, that part you didn't bring along with you when you came to pay me a visit here. But you forget that I've had some experience of our mutual friend that's a little different from yours. A little more . . . internal. There's nothing like walking around with somebody inside their deepest nightmares, to give you that sense of really getting to know him."

"But that's all you would know of him. Or anyone."

"Touché, Jadzia. That's a point well taken; I'd be the first to admit that my view of my fellow sentient creatures might be a bit on the jaundiced side. Though I'm glad to see that the argumentative tendency is still active in you." McHogue's expression turned glum as he gazed across the landscape of bones, like intricate snow sloping down from the peak on which he stood with Dax. "My one substantial regret about this glorious enterprise upon which I have embarked is that it's all been too easy. People just fold and toss in their hands, without putting up a fight. It all makes me rather nostalgic for those pleasant, innocent days when I was defrauding people in partnership with that rascal Quark. There were times when I had a knife put to my throat over a gold-pressed latinum chip no bigger than your fingernail. That *was* fun. Oh, well . . ." He slowly shook his head. "Can't be helped. I suppose it's what comes with selling a product that everybody wants. Immortality inside me, an expanded form of existence, the satiation of every perverted desire—you know, if I had it to do all over again, I might have made the deal slightly less attractive to the customers. So my salesmanship skills wouldn't have gotten so rusty."

The image's self-aggrandizing rhetoric nauseated Jadzia. It was as much to blank out McHogue's voice, as from any hope of rescue, that she focused her attention on the runabout that had appeared in the sky overhead. She recognized it as one of DS9's; her own expectations told her that Sisko was piloting it.

"Well done!" McHogue registered genuine approval as the runabout touched down and came to a halt in what had been Moagitty's grand concourse; there had been just space enough along the rows of decapitated pillars for the craft to glide to its landing. "Such professionalism—but then, we really couldn't have expected much less, would we?" He glanced round at her.

Jadzia made no reply; the relief she felt at Sisko's appearance in the runabout's hatch was like a rush of oxygen into her lungs.

"My dear commander; it's always such a pleasure to see you." McHogue made a small bow toward him. "And especially on such a reciprocal basis. Not that I mind always coming to your place. It's just the thought that counts, I suppose."

Sisko had sprinted the few meters from the runabout's landing point. He grasped Jadzia by the arm. "Are you all right?"

She nodded. "I'll be fine . . . soon as I'm away from here. And I'm reconjoined with my symbiont. You know, don't you, about—"

"Bashir found the last research notes you logged into the station's computer. That, plus the message you sent me, was enough to fill us in on your plans." Sisko nodded toward the runabout. "The CI field has apparently coalesced here; once we're out of actual physical proximity to its locus, the effects upon you should be reversible—just as if you had been able to step backward from the module aboard the station. Then you'll be able to merge your neurosystem's processes with those of Dax again."

"Maybe; maybe not." Arms folded across his chest, McHogue had listened to the words between Sisko and Jadzia. "They calculate poorly, who don't take me into account—at least around here, that is." He shook his head in disbelief. "What, you think you can just drop in, refuse my hospitality and take off whenever you feel like it? Really, Commander Sisko, I had thought Starfleet officers had more of an education in diplomatic etiquette than that. After all, there is an official relationship between us—I still *am* the Bajoran Minister of Trade."

"I hardly think your status applies any longer." Jadzia glared angrily at him. "Not when you've managed to turn the whole planet into a charnel house—"

A look of confusion crossed Sisko's face. "What are you talking about?"

"You'll have to forgive her, Commander." McHogue's smile became tolerant and knowing. "My fault, really. When you entered Bajor's atmosphere, your approach path was above the capital, so no doubt you saw the population there in relatively good health, all things considered; perhaps just a little battered from this spate of bad weather we've been having. Of course, there's no need to thank me for this brief respite I arranged just for your arrival—as I've always maintained, I am by nature a hospitable entity. Even more so, now that I've come into my own, as it were. Be that as it may, Commander; you're really only standing on the doorstep of my world." He gestured toward Jadzia. "Your colleague, however, has been inside and enjoying my company for some time now—though ordinary notions of time are not strictly applicable here. Let's just say that she's come to see the situation in its more fully developed state. When the weak and fallible flesh has been discarded, so that all who came here can assume the immortality they sought."

"He's insane, Benjamin." A trace of what Jadzia had learned from her symbiont emerged inside, enabling her to speak with clinical dispassion of the image standing before them. "There's no difference now between him and this world he's created. I had thought that I could come here and somehow change things; I believed that the rational nature of the universe outside—its original nature, before this madness began—I thought that could be brought to this place, like light into darkness. I was wrong." She grasped Sisko's arm, drawing him away from McHogue. "He's stronger than that; the infection from the CI modules has grown even more powerful than before. We should return to the station immediately; perhaps there is still some way we can find to limit the damage to the surrounding universe."

She saw the effect her words had upon her friend. Silent, Benjamin looked up at the sky. Or what had been, in this world, a simulation of Bajor's sky; now jagged lines of force could be seen writhing in it, shadow and fire intermingled, as though reality had become no more than a sheet of paper being crumpled in a gigantic fist.

McHogue's smile had faded with each of her words; the image's dark gaze took in both Sisko and Jadzia. "Now I *am* annoyed." The voice was a humorless, grating sound. "After all I've done for both of you—taken you in, shown you things you would never have imagined. I was even willing to let our little differences be forgotten, to welcome you here and make you part of all I've accomplished. You should have considered that a measure of my respect for you. And was any of that respect returned to me?" From the depths of his brooding, McHogue regarded them. "Fine; that's what I get for being nice to the marks. Well, no more of *that.*" He straightened his arm, index finger pointing to the center of Sisko's chest. "You want to leave here? All right, I'll make it easy for you. But you might be surprised about what you find when you get home."

Jadzia saw the blow coming, the hand curling into a fist. She tried to pull Benjamin out of its path, but was too late.

As close as she had been, she was still unable to discern exactly what happened. Which had been real, and which illusion. The fist or its target; they seemed to pass, one into the other, illusions overlapped and mingled—

But only one of them remained afterward.

McHogue dropped his fist and let the fingers slowly uncurl. "There—"

Dazed, she looked down at her own empty hands.

"That's what he wanted." McHogue nodded in grim satisfaction. "Let's see how he likes it."

He walked in a place where he had walked before.

One footstep came after another, unconscious and automatic; he could have been asleep, if his eyes had not followed the angle of the corridor, the metal grids and doorway indicating—to the watching part of his mind—where he was.

This is the station. Sisko's thoughts moved slowly inside his head, one word matching each pace. *I'm back . . . back aboard Deep Space Nine.*

He must have been asleep, and dreaming; that was the only explanation that appeared in the silent chambers of his skull

He had been someplace else, he knew—but where? Dax had been there as well . . . but not Dax; not all of her. Just the part of her named Jadzia. His old friend Dax had been . . . in a whole other world. How could that be?

And there had been another face, just for a moment, a vision that had appeared and then had been gone before he could catch it. And words that were just about to be spoken . . . He shook his head, knowing that those were lost as well.

That was the problem with dreams, mused Sisko as he walked along the endless station corridor. Dreams showed you things, but didn't explain them. Very much like the vision of Kai Opaka that he'd had, so long ago. Prophecies and blessings; he smiled to himself, remembering. Things that the Kai had warned him about; things that would happen and for which he would have to be ready. The unreal becoming the real . . .

McHogue.

The single name was enough. For him to wake from the last remnants of his dreaming. He stopped his walking, turning to look about himself. Now he could remember where he had been.

The last thing Sisko could recall, from his standing in the middle of the ruins of Moagitty, had been McHogue's glaring hatred and the fist aimed at his own chest. Jadzia had tried to pull him away; he remembered her tug at his arm. And then . . . nothing.

Until he had found himself here, back aboard DS9.

Or not DS9; that was a possibility he had to consider. He had stepped again into McHogue's world, not by walking into an altered holosuite this time, but by making the arduous journey through the spatial disturbances to Bajor. The result was the same; any dealings with McHogue wound up being on McHogue's terms. McHogue got to choose the playing field; in baseball terms, Sisko thought grimly, he had a permanent home advantage.

There had been a time, the meeting when General Aur and his new Minister of Trade had come to the station, when McHogue had made the assertion that an infinite regress, artificial realities nested within a spiral of hallucinations, was impossible, both in theory and practice. Even now, he had no reason to doubt the claim. McHogue was too much of an egotist to create more than one world to be in at a time; the CI technology's self-appointed deity would be unlikely to divide himself up.

Sisko started walking again. If he could reach the Ops deck, perhaps he would be able to determine the exact nature of the world into which he'd been thrust. There might be people there, the other crew members; anyone with a voice and face that wasn't McHogue's. He hastened his steps, heading from the empty sector to the regions where there would be life and sound. . . .

He came to the Promenade.

But silence greeted him. Even there, at the station's heart, where greed and appetite and the manifold lusts of sentient creatures had tumbled together in their own perpetual, noisy storm . . .

He felt the silence before he saw the rest, the other indices of death. Strewn across the Promenade's open walkways were blackened shapes that had once been living creatures, the human and nonhuman population of DS9, connected now to each other like a string of black hieroglyphs, sentences whose meanings were beyond the scope of mortal reading. Charred figures lay facedown and anonymous in the doorways of what had been the Promenade's business establishments; in Quark's bar, the tables and stools had been knocked aside by whatever fiery hand had left the last patrons curled around their own ashes.

Sisko stood at the edge of the grim display, his senses at war with a mind that refused to believe its perceptions.

This is what Jadzia saw. His thoughts struggled to connect the pieces spread out before him. *What she saw down there, in the city of Moagitty.* The unleashing of death itself, the face of pure murder—the only difference being, he knew, between whitening skeletal remains and these things of crumbling cinder. What he and the other officers of the station had termed an epidemic of murder had been transformed, apothesized, into its own incendiary hurricane, an annihilating firestorm. All to feed McHogue's vaulting ambitions, his embrace of godhood; no doubt he would be ready to boast that he had given these victims immortality as well, incorporated them into the fabric of the world that had burst into existence from the limits of his skull.

"Is there anyone here?" Sisko called aloud, his voice echoing in the high-ceilinged space. "Anyone left alive?" He could hear in his voice the absence of hope, the playing out of his role as the station's commander. A charade, he knew, a performance without an audience, unwatched except by embers inside the blackened eye sockets on all sides of him as he moved forward. He walked carefully, finding an empty space for each footstep.

Outside the entrance to the security office—the doors had pulled away from their surrounding girders, the heat that had passed across them sufficient to warp metal—unexpected motion snagged at the corner of his sight. Sisko turned, his hand reaching to touch a section of bare wall.

The shimmering movement rippled away from his fingertips, as though a stone had somehow been dropped into vertical water. The firestorm that had swept through the Promenade had left the expanse before him smooth as molten glass. A dead thing, as dead as all the rest of the station's structure and those who had occupied it . . .

But alive as well. In some sense beyond Sisko's understanding; he could feel a minute vibration, less than breathing, against his skin.

"Who's there?" he asked, though he already knew.

I remain . . .

A voice, a whisper that brushed against his ear. But one that he recognized.

"Odo?" He turned to look over his shoulder, as though he might find the shapeshifter's human form standing close to him.

Where I have always been. Where I will always be. . . .

The wall rippled again, and became a mirror, one in which he could see his own face reflected; the depths of apparent space might have been made of obsidian, rendered dark as the ashes that surrounded him.

There was another face in the mirrored surface, that Sisko could just discern. Eyes closed, it might have been asleep and dreaming, encased inside a becalmed sea. The slow currents of its words parted the somnolent mouth.

Where I should be . . . where I wanted to be . . .

The voice was drained of all emotion, as though it emerged from narcotized sleep. That was how Sisko knew the face he saw in the glass-smoothed wall was not the real Odo—not the Odo of reality, that place outside McHogue's dark universe— but his echo. From that time when the security chief, taunted by Gul Dukat's hints of secrets to be revealed, had gone into the altered holosuite and found . . . what? Odo had refused to tell anyone; had said, in fact, that he had found nothing in there.

That assertion might have been true, but even then Sisko had doubted the other's words; doubted, but had not pressed him on the matter. The mix of emotions that he had detected in Odo's face and voice—rage and fear and a swirling confusion—had been too close to his own, the product of stepping into the brightly lit nightmare into which McHogue had twisted his son Jake's summer fantasies. Such knowledge was shameful, something to be hidden away, clutched tight to one's own belly; he had too much respected Odo's privacy to order him to reveal what he had found inside the holosuite. If

Odo had found some clue to his origins, the mystery of his created nature, it remained his secret.

But what Odo had left there in the holosuite, left the way that all who had entered McHogue's world left some small parts of themselves behind—the "echoes" that McHogue fastened upon and nourished in the forcing ground of unlimited possibilities, a nursery for insanity and murder—that was something Sisko had known of, but hadn't wanted to think about.

Until now, when he had to confront the results of that process.

He stepped back from the mirrorlike wall, looking up and across its breadth. His vision had sharpened, or Odo—the inanimate yet sentient thing that bore Odo's face and essence—had chosen to show itself more fully. The original Odo, the Odo who had existed in the great reality outside McHogue's skull, had been an entity personifying the notions of *fluid* and *protean*, an embodiment of constant change. The echo of Odo that Sisko now saw before him, an echo magnified and made louder, silently deafening, by McHogue's powers in this world, was both less and more than what the original had been. Whatever the shapeshifter's true nature—and Sisko knew that that might always remain a mystery—here in the CI technology's revealing illusions was the static, frozen development of that nature, a Life-in-Death like that encountered by so many other travelers in uncharted realms.

Sisko could see now how far Odo had been subsumed into the fabric of *Deep Space Nine*. The mirror wall that held the sleeping face was Odo, as were the heat-twisted girders stretching overhead; they rippled with the same in-place motion, stone dropped in water, as Sisko's gaze passed across them. And farther: the metal flooring held the blackened corpses, as though they were cradled in Odo's protective embrace. As far as Sisko's vision could reach: walls against other walls, and the twisted doors within them. Even the space between them, the stilled air; everything locked into place, eternal and unmoving.

"Constable . . ." Sisko reached out to touch the sleeping face behind the mirrored surface. "What have they done to you?" he murmured.

Another face was discernible, behind the closed eyes of Odo's visage. Sisko drew back his hand, his fingertips having encountered only smoothed glass; he could feel the other watching him, a thin smile already forming. When the whispered voice came again, he heard the other's words seeping through.

You should be glad for me, Commander . . . this is what I want . . . what I've always wanted . . .

He stepped back, looking above himself, as though he might spot McHogue hovering like a puppeteer deity, invisible strings radiating from the outstretched fingers. He saw nothing there; he dropped his gaze again to the image whose barest rudiments had filtered through Odo's, as though they were antique photographic transparencies laid one on top of the other.

You see? The words sounded different. *What a generous sort I am, to let people find out what it is they desire, and then to give it to them. To cause it to be. Odo so loved the station—his only home, his only real family—and now he's part of it. Just as he wanted.*

"But it's not him," Sisko spoke aloud, his voice tightening with contempt. "It's a lie—there's nothing here of Odo."

Nothing but the truth, whispered McHogue's smiling voice. *That's the risk everyone took when they stepped inside here. That they would see things they might have preferred to remain hidden.* The mocking smile showed in the wall's depths. *That they might become things . . . the same way.*

"You've left the truth behind; you wouldn't know it if it did find its way in here." He shook his head. "There's no one here but you now."

Ah—brave words, Commander. The voice and image began to fade. *Perhaps you should be on your way . . . and see what you find.*

He was alone again, the images gone from the mirror before him. The water motion rippled through the wall and its connecting girders, then was stilled. Only the dead, and the not alive, surrounded him.

His path lay outside the Promenade. He turned and began walking.

Something was moving—something was alive—where no living thing should be. She raised her tear-wet face from the knees she clasped close to herself; from where she sat huddled against a corridor bulkhead, she turned and looked over her hunched shoulder. Rage, an all-consuming fire, blossomed in her heart, rolling through her veins to the ends of her fingers, like the blazing force that had scoured the station clean of all that she loathed. Her knuckles were white bone where her hands clutched together, her wrists pressed tight against her shins.

She uncoiled herself and stood up, staying crouched in the corridor's shadows. The distant sounds of footsteps and breathing, even the soft tap of a heartbeat, jostled against her keen hearing; the anger they evoked notched higher at the base of her throat. She could taste it, like warm salt pooled under her tongue.

The sounds indicated that the intruder was not the station's other occupant, the thing that flowed in and out of the walls and ceilings, the only creature that had remained after the purifying fire she had unleashed. That thing had once had a face, something she could have remembered and put a name to; no more. She could barely tolerate its presence, and that only because it had made itself no different from the station, a necessary component. It knew its place in the new scheme of things.

Cautiously, she moved down the corridor, staying out of any direct line of sight. She wanted to see the intruder first, before it could have any warning of her approach. That was always the best way; her knowledge, her skills, in the proper eradication of enemies, came from a long time back. From another world, one where events and consequences had never worked out as satisfyingly as they had in this one. In some future time, she knew—a time when she was able to think again, and not just sense and react—she would have to consider that entity who had made such glory and justice possible.

She halted when she perceived a shadow stretching along the gridded floor; a dim overhead light silhouetted a human figure from behind. Drawing back into herself, she made ready.

The figure stopped, as though it had sensed her presence. She ground her teeth together in fury, nails digging into the flesh of her palms.

Into another small pool of light, the figure stepped forward. She recognized his face—or knew that at one time she had been able to. Faces and names didn't matter now, though; in this cleansed world, there were only two categories beyond herself. The enemy . . . and the dead.

"Kira?" The figure stooped and peered toward her hiding place. "That's you, isn't it?"

A moment of wonder, a fragment of the emotions that she had purged herself of, stayed her wrath. She spoke from the shadows. "How do you know my name?"

"Why wouldn't I?" He took a step closer. "Don't you know mine?"

She laughed in scorn. "Don't know, and I don't care." She felt her hatred turning toward her own gut like a thorn, for having been tricked into having words with the creature, whoever he was. As if there could be any question as to what he was. She closed her hand into a fist and saw white sparks leak between the fingers.

"But you're not Kira . . ." The figure shook his head sadly. "You're just a little piece of her. One that he's changed and made into a mockery of everything you were." His gaze become one of pity. "Just an echo; that's all you are. From when you stepped into his world, and left a bit of the real Kira behind."

Her fury rose inside her, but was stifled by the other voice that sometimes spoke for her. "Oh no, Commander," she heard herself saying. "This is the truth revealed, just as the one before had been."

"What did you do to her?"

"Can't you see?" The voice in her mouth drew blood with a needle rather than a knife blade. "Such a nice, *strong* echo—all I had to do was cut away the soft, weak parts, and expose the diamond at the center of her soul. Don't tell me, Commander, that you didn't know such a thing existed there all along. Didn't you consider yourself to be her friend? Didn't you *know* how badly she had been hurt, how many terrible things she had seen, and how she thirsted for revenge? Such a purifying emotion, I think." The voice was laughing behind its words; she felt dizzied for a moment, as though each syllable was about to hammer through her brow from the inside. "All I did, Commander, was give her the chance to . . . *go* with her precious feelings. To expand upon them, as it were. And you might be surprised at how well she did, given the opportunity."

The face of the figure standing before her turned grim. "I think I'm finally beyond being surprised at anything that happens in your little world, McHogue."

"Good for you—" The voice lost its laughing edge. "Then you won't be surprised at what a pure instrument of murder our Kira has become here. Pure, in that she no longer needs to make a distinction between the oppressor and the oppressed, between the strong and the weak, between those who inflict suffering and those who meekly receive it. She's found a better way, Sisko; I've shown it to her."

"You've shown her nothing; she doesn't even exist here. All you ever do, McHogue, is talk to yourself."

No longer laughing, and with an anger rising to match her own. The voice was like broken glass at her lips as it spoke. "Once again, Commander, you've managed to annoy me. I really don't like that kind of talk—especially here. This is my *home*. I won't have it."

"Why?" The figure looked around the corridor as if searching for someone, before returning his gaze to her. "Because it's the truth?"

"Truth, Commander . . ." The voice had started to fade, to fall back from where it had come. "I'll give you truth." Then it was gone.

She raised her head and looked into the gaze of the figure standing before her. He said nothing . . . but he didn't need to. She saw the worst thing possible in his eyes.

Pity.

Her anger burst forth, unstoppable. Her throat tautened as her head was flung back. Fire leapt from her heart.

She had been born in fire. She remembered that moment, when she had risen into the sky above Bajor, above both the weak and the strong in the refugee camps. A burning angel, rising on wings of coruscating radiance, looking down upon all who deserved her wrath, who deserved death and ashes in their unfleshed jaws. She had risen above what she had thought was a dream, an illusion . . . a lie. And what she had realized in that perfect moment was the truth, the world that was more real than any other, because it had battered free from the most secret chambers of her heart.

Even now, she felt the ceiling of the corridor burst open, torn by the thrust of her shoulders as she mounted higher. Far above the figure that had confronted her, that had dared to say it knew her, knew her name, dared to say that she had any name other than vengeance.

She let her hands spread wide, a white-hot sun in each palm. The firestorm rolled like a churning tide through the corridor, washing away the puny thing that had stood before her. The face that she had almost been able to recognize tumbled away from her. The arm that had been lifted across his eyes to shield them was already ashes, the bone inside crumbling like a charred branch.

Above the fire she had unleashed, above the dead like other dead, she stepped higher, heart singing with a fierce joy, tears turning to steam against her own flesh.

He awoke in pain. Made blind by the brilliance of the light flooding what had been his eyes; his nerve endings were heated wires, exposed from beneath the tatters of his skin.

"That's enough of *that*—"

As soon as the voice spoke, the wind died, the wind that had carried him helpless in its swirling grasp. His spine had shattered against one of the bulkheads, limbs wrenched from their sockets. A storm, in the space between one scalding breath and the next; there had not even been time in which he could have wished to die.

"I apologize for letting things become quite so rough on you." McHogue's voice spoke out of the darkness above him. "But sometimes people just won't learn any other way. Most unfortunate—but necessary."

Sisko rolled onto his knees, pushing himself up from the floor with his hands. The pain had ebbed out of his body, leaving him weak and dizzy, but able to open his eyes. He could see his undamaged forearms; balancing his weight with one hand, he touched the flesh beneath the uniform sleeve and found it whole and unscarred.

A few meters away, the image of McHogue leaned back

against the bulkhead. Sisko could feel the amused gaze resting upon him. "Where . . . where is this?" He lifted his head and looked about the space. "How did you . . ."

"Really, Commander. And after all your boasting about how nothing could surprise you anymore. Once more, I'm disappointed in you." McHogue shook his head sadly. "Did you really believe I'd let Kira—*my* Kira—just blow you away like that? Like a dead leaf at the end of summer? I didn't even find it all that amusing to watch. I hope *you* learned something from it, though."

"Nothing . . . that I didn't know already." Stiffly, he managed to get to his feet. Sisko reached behind to steady himself against the nearest girder. "It's all false. These things here . . . these echoes . . . they're all just you wearing different masks."

McHogue shrugged. "That's partly so, I admit. But again, a matter of necessity. And didn't I tell you that I dealt in truth here? It's not as if all those who have entered my presence, both here in the station and below in my city of Moagitty, haven't derived some substantial benefit from their transformation. There's a certain matter of immortality, for one thing; with their essences incorporated into mine, they shall live forever. My victories will be theirs; the universe I create is my gift unto them." His smile returned, but without any trace of mockery. "As I've maintained so often before, I am a *very* hospitable entity."

"Is this why you brought me here? To boast of your powers?" Sisko leveled his gaze at the other. "You'll have to pardon me if I'm still not impressed. You can parade around in your little world all you want, and go on talking to yourself . . . and it will mean nothing."

"Somehow, Commander, I knew you would still doubt me and my accomplishments. But I didn't save you in order to carry on this running argument. My generosity knows no bounds; you came here, whether you knew it or not, to find something, and it's my wish to make that discovery possible for you." McHogue made a sweeping gesture with one hand, toward the distant end of the corridor. "Continue, my dear Sisko. You're not done yet."

He was alone again; the smiling image had vanished, like a candle flame snuffed out between two fingers. Another light spilled along the passage, from the open doorway he could see farther on.

Empty, lifeless space spread before Sisko as he stepped onto the Ops deck. The instrument panels showed their monitoring of the station's continuing functions, the unconscious maintenance of DS9's homeostasis. Slowly, he turned where he stood, his gaze searching . . .

And finding.

He had perceived that he was the only living creature there. He was not proven wrong, when a chair before one of the consoles swung about revealing the figure that had been sitting there.

An image with his face.

His voice: "I've been waiting for you." A smile formed on the face of Sisko's own echo. "For a long time."

He nodded slowly, acknowledging its existence. He knew he should have expected it.

"That's right," said the echo. It stood up from the chair. "But you forgot, didn't you? Because you didn't want to remember. That you had left something of yourself behind, just like all the others, when you first came into this world. That bright summer place . . ." The echo looked around the Ops deck. "Very different from here. But . . . the same as well. In its essence."

"Because it's you, isn't it, McHogue?" Sisko regarded the seeming mirror before him. "Everything here is you."

"A metaphysical conceit, Commander." The echo's voice changed slightly, letting the other's seep through, as though from behind a mask. "I'm afraid I don't see the point in discussing it any further. Why should I make any distinction between myself and this universe? The question that should be asked isn't whether *you* exist here, my dear Sisko, or any of the others, for that matter; the question is whether *McHogue* exists anymore!" The mask of Sisko's voice turned radiant with triumph. "I've *become* the universe!"

"This universe," said Sisko. "This little, shabby world inside your head—that's all."

The echo looked pityingly at him. "You still don't understand, do you? You never realized the agenda I had from the beginning. No one did—not General Aur and the Bajoran provisional government, nor that fool Gul Dukat and the rest of the Cardassians; none of them. And certainly not you, Commander. Otherwise, you would have known that this isn't the limit of my ambitions. There is no limit." The voice had shed all pretense of disguise, becoming openly that of McHogue, a cry that echoed against the space's circumference. "With every tiny scrap of life that I've taken in and added to myself, even down to an insignificant, broken creature such as Ahrmant Wyoss—with every one, this universe has grown and become greater. And now it's time to go from inside here"—the image smiled and tapped the side of its head—"to out there." It turned and pointed to the stars visible in the central viewport.

Sisko looked up at the vista of worlds beyond counting, then back to the image that bore a mockery of his face. "It's not your ambition that knows no limits, McHogue. It's your madness that does."

"You doubt, Commander, because the process of transformation is not yet over. There are so many more lives that I need to bring inside my own, their little souls to be added to my great one. It will take a long time, I know. Or no time at all, perhaps—in the twinkling of an eye, as it was once said. Already, eons are as microseconds to me. When time itself ceases to exist—because I have abolished it—you shall see, as others have already seen, that this waiting, this mere gam that you have called your existence, was but an illusion all along."

"Spare me the mystical claptrap." Sisko hardened his heart, let the cold rigor of his thoughts become an armor against the other's words. But there were things McHogue had said that he knew were true. A dire process had begun: McHogue had both his city of Moagitty on Bajor and *Deep Space Nine* as part of his world; the stable wormhole and all the treasures onto which it opened would continue to be an irresistible magnet for all the intelligent entities, humanoid and otherwise, of the galaxies. *They'll all pass through this sector eventually,* thought Sisko. And they would all experience the effects of the CI technology; there will be no escaping it. And then inside each one of them will be a little piece of McHogue. A seed of this new universe—he could see it, like a speck of infinite darkness. And another time would come, when McHogue was greater than the universe that had been his progenitor. Then the transformation would be complete, Sisko knew. Another reality would have supplanted the old; the unreal would have become the real. And all that exists— all that could exist—would be there, inside the head of the smiling figure that had stood before him.

The face behind the mask had faded, along with McHogue's voice. Sisko watched and said nothing.

"It's a shame you won't experience that, Commander." McHogue's voice had become almost a whisper from some distant point. "In your case, I'm going to make an exception. You've reached the limits of my hospitality. I'm afraid that it's time for you to cease existing . . . in this universe or any other."

The last trace of McHogue disappeared from behind the echo. Sisko found himself gazing into the image of his own face again, with no other force inhabiting it.

His face . . . and behind it, something that he could still recognize, something that was yet a part of him.

"There can't be two of us here. That's not possible." The echo's voice came from deep inside, as though the words were the result of long brooding. "You'll have to go." The image's hand lifted and reached for Sisko's throat.

His strength had been depleted by the rigors of his passage through this world; he found himself unable to struggle, to tear loose the grasp that choked away his breath. Both his hands tugged futilely at the echo's tautened forearm.

Even as Sisko gasped for air, his knees buckling beneath him, he could look into his echo's eyes. And see what this part of him had become.

The echo's face—Sisko's face, transformed but still the same—was an emotionless mask, cold and inhuman, divorced from all feeling. Behind the dead eyes, no concern existed for his son, for Dax or Kira or Bashir or for any of the DS9 crew members; for no other living thing. There was only the desire, the will to command, to control, to bend reality to one's own inexorable will.

"That is right," whispered the echo, watching life dwindle in his hand, the last spark dying. Sisko could hear the words spoken in his own voice. "Now you know the truth at last. The truth that you kept hidden even from yourself."

A wavering shadow swept across the echo's face, through which its cold gaze burned toward him.

"The truth," came the voice to his ears. "That I am what was always inside you. When you searched for murderers, you looked everywhere but in your own heart."

No . . .

He could not speak aloud. A vise of iron clasped shut upon his throat.

In that world, in the universe that had collapsed to the width of a man's hand . . . a world that had already turned lightless, without air . . . he closed his eyes. Looking for something in that darkness . . .

Something that he found. That had always been there, just

as the other, his echo, had told him. But not in his heart. But somewhere else, as real and unreal as the other's fist locked upon his mortal flesh.

That didn't matter. In a world without time, there was no need for breath. In the eternity between one heartbeat and the next, he opened his eyes.

His echo no longer stood before him. But a door, that slid open, spilling bright, false sunlight against his face. He walked slowly toward it, letting the sharp-edged radiance slip through his open hands . . .

Leaving behind that part of him that was dying, lungs and brain struggling against the stopped flow of oxygen . . .

He stepped into the sunlight; the door closed behind him, and he was once more in that small, limitless world. That McHogue had created . . .

For his son.

Sisko turned, looking about the fields of yellowed grasses, the darker shapes of trees at the horizon; the sky blue and unclouded, as though no storm could reach into this perfect sanctuary.

Go, he told himself. *Do what you came here to do.* He knew that this world's eternity was an illusion; that time inched forward in another world, where his hands had risen, gripping the echo's wrists in futile struggle. *You don't have forever.* He started walking again, the tall, brittle stems tracing against his legs.

"What are *you* doing here?" A child's voice spoke. A child's face, scowling with suspicion, turned to look at him. The child's eyes were dark pieces of a starless night. "You're not supposed to be here. Not anymore."

Water rippled against the glistening rocks. Sisko shaded his eyes against the sun, the better to see the boy kneeling on a rounded perch in the middle of the stream. The fish that had been the target of the boy's attention splashed and darted away.

"I came here . . . to see you." The wet, pebbly sand grated beneath the soles of his boots.

"Why?"

This was the boy that his son Jake had come here, into this world, to be with. A boy . . . and something more.

Without turning around to look, without stepping away from the stream's bank, he knew that bones whitened beneath the trees' heavy shadows.

He kept his voice low, even kindly. "I came to tell you," said Sisko. "That it's time for you to go home."

"What?" The boy gazed at him in mocking disbelief. "You're crazy. *This* is my home."

"No . . ." Sisko shook his head. "It can't be. Not anymore."

"You're crazy. You don't know what you're talking about." Anger darkened the boy's face. "Get out of here! I killed you once before, already—" The boy's voice turned sullen. "I can do it again."

"No, you can't." He could see even more clearly, when the boy's eyes deepened and hollowed, the face of McHogue before him. "You can't do what you want here, anymore."

"Huh?" The boy crouched on the rock, head lowered to watch his confronter. "Why not?"

"Because . . ." There was no way he could keep the words from sounding sad. "Because it's not your home now."

That was the truth, that Sisko had come so far to discover. The world that McHogue had created—this little part of it had come to exist inside his own mind. When he had stepped inside here, so long ago, to find where his son had gone so many times before. And had found his own lifeless eyes gazing up through the trees' interlaced branches. McHogue's world —McHogue's universe—had come inside him then. A piece of it . . .

And that was enough. To make it his own, in ways that even McHogue could not have known about.

To reclaim it.

"You're crazy." The boy's voice, taut with rage, broke into his thoughts. "Go away!"

There was no need for any more words. Sisko bent down and touched the water's surface. The tips of his fingers penetrated the cold, silvery currents.

"No!" The boy's voice was a scream now, more fear and surprise than anger. "Stop—don't—"

There was no water now. The bed of the stream was dry ground, cracked where the mud had begun to crumble into dust.

He straightened up, turning to see the other changes that he had willed to happen.

"No . . ." The boy moaned in terror.

Brown leaves scattered from withered branches. The wind twisted them, a lifeless flock, across the mottled sky. Clouds incapable of rain tinged the sun to a dimming sulfur.

The sweep of Sisko's thought moved across the fields. Blighting the thick stands of grass, the stems curling black and skeletal, as though scorched beneath an unseen fire.

Dust trickled from the gaunt flanks of the false world's bones, the exposed rocks splintering in turn. And below those . . . there would be nothing, he knew. He turned away; there was not much time left.

The boy was silent now, huddled into a ball on the rounded stone. Silent but for his broken and uncomprehending tears.

And even those . . . Sisko closed his eyes again, not wanting to see what happened next . . . even those would be gone soon.

Perfect silence. He opened his eyes, catching just a glimpse of something that looked like tattered rags, swirled by the wind to vanish with the leaves from the dead trees.

Slowly, he nodded. In a dead world; mercifully dead. So that the other world, the real one, could have life.

"No," he said aloud. "You don't understand."

There had been no need to step back through a door, from

the false bright world to this one. He had always been here. And in that time, from one heartbeat to the next, breath had rushed back into lungs.

His echo gazed at him, with the same uncomprehending wonder with which the dying boy had. And in the same death.

Another transformation, the final one, had taken place. Sisko opened his hand, releasing the throat of his echo, the thing with his face broken in sudden confusion.

"I don't . . . understand. . . ." Its eyes flooded with tears.

Sisko watched as the echo's image slowly crumpled to the floor.

"How . . ." It lay in agony, the last of its false life seeping from its body. "I don't understand. . . ."

Pity moved inside Sisko. It was still a part of him, however terribly changed.

"McHogue lied to you." He knelt beside the echo. His own voice became gentle now. "Or else he never knew. There was one element that he couldn't take into account, in all his plans."

"What . . ." The echo's eyes had begun to flutter closed.

"The CI technology—its operations are all based upon the users' experiences, memories, perceptions of reality." Sisko kept his voice level, though he had the disquieting sense of watching a part of himself die before him. "The CI modules extrapolate from the real world—the real universe—to form all their hallucinations and fantasies. That was how McHogue made his universe—from pieces of the real one."

"But you . . ." The echo nodded feebly. "There was something more to you . . . to *us* . . ."

There was no time left; he could sense the last of the echo's life dissipating.

No time, and no possibility of explaining. What he had only now come to understand.

Prophecies and blessings . . .

The Kai had known. That there was another part of him,

that no longer had its origin in the real universe. So long ago—a span beyond centuries, it seemed—he had gone into the wormhole, and had encountered things there beyond all knowing, beyond any universe's concepts of space and time. They, the ones whose very existences were mysteries beyond comprehension, had shown him only a little of what they knew.

But that had been enough to change him. Forever. To place a seed within, beyond all sentient reality. And beyond the reach of McHogue.

The echo died. Sisko laid his hands upon the sleeping image of his own face, and drew the eyelids shut. He stood up, looking over his shoulder as a noise of metal intruded upon the silence.

A jagged fissure ran through the bulkhead like a stroke of empty lightning. He could feel the illusory station tremble and shudder beneath his feet. An inanimate groan became a cry of agony as the buried girders began to separate from each other.

He turned, seeing black webs shatter across every surface. The ceiling broke apart above him, but the crumbling pieces didn't fall. Light and gravity had ceased. Spun from his balance, he raised his arms to protect himself as his shoulders struck and splintered open the wall behind him.

The last he saw was stars rushing in through the razor-edged shards of the viewport.

"We've got to get out of here—"

She didn't know what had happened. There would be time for explanations later.

"Come on, Benjamin." Jadzia wrapped her arm around the commander's shoulders, bearing his weight against herself. In the few seconds that he had been gone, struck from existence by McHogue's hand, his strength had been drained from him; he could barely stand upright.

"Where . . . where's McHogue . . ."

She half-carried, half-dragged him toward the runabout. "I don't know." That much was true; the smiling, black-clothed figure had vanished as abruptly as Sisko had. "It's not important right now—"

Overhead, the sky had darkened with the return of the storm clouds; their first winds rushed through Moagitty's broken walls. The inlaid marble floors, spattered with blood, trembled from upwellings deep beneath Bajor's surface.

The runabout's door slid open, and she managed to dump Sisko sprawling into one of the seats. There wasn't time to strap him or herself into the restraining harnesses; she slapped the pilot controls, readying the thrusters for maximum force.

Sudden acceleration was enough to pin her against the seat's back. Without having plotted a course, Jadzia manually aimed the craft for the only opening she saw above them. Only when the *Ganges* had broken beyond the planet's atmosphere did she throttle back on the engines' force.

They were beyond the reach of something else as well. She felt something inside her, filling a hollowness as wide as her heart.

Welcome, child. The symbiont didn't need words to speak, its thoughts becoming her own again.

Beside her, Sisko stirred, his eyes dragging open for a moment. "Where are we . . . where are we going . . ."

Dax glanced over at him. "Home, Benjamin. We're going home."

He thought it to be a most peculiar thing. Where was everybody?

There had been so many of them here . . . and now they were all gone. McHogue looked around himself, wondering what had happened.

So many, and only one that wouldn't fit, that had to be gotten rid of. He had done that, out there on the station that was the other part of his world, and had come home to Moagitty. And found it empty.

Very peculiar . . .

Other changes had taken place in his absence. The broken walls had seemed to heal themselves, the domed ceiling again arching overhead. That was a good thing; he took a definite pride of ownership in the place. But none of his guests remained, none of his people, the lives that he had taken into his own and transformed into glory. No gamblers at the Dabo tables, the banks of holosuites all unoccupied; no one.

The odd thing, it occurred to him, was that there was no other place they could all be. This was the only world there was; there could be no other. He had seen to that.

He called out, voice echoing down the empty concourse, but there was no answer. So he would have to go find them. They had to be around somewhere.

McHogue started walking. The empty corridor stretched out before him, seemingly infinite. He realized he had no idea of how big it actually was.

He kept walking. He'd already decided that he would go on walking, for however long it might take. . . .

A FEW LAST
QUESTIONS

CHAPTER
18

Major Kira Nerys stepped into the center of the Ops deck and gazed about herself. For a moment, it seemed to her as if she might still be mired in the dreaming that had accompanied her long sleep. The fatigue had drained from her at last, but had been replaced by a measure of guilt and surprise at discovering how long she had been out.

She looked with deep suspicion at the calm, orderly activity surrounding her. The last time she had been here, the very atmosphere had been electrified with the sense of crisis and impending disaster.

One of the comm technicians passed close by; she reached out and grabbed the tech's arm. "Did I miss something?"

In the commander's private office, Chief of Security Odo reviewed the statement that had been received from the Cardassian ruling council.

"Gul Dukat's formal apology—" Commander Sisko pointed to the words on his desk's computer panel. "The line they've taken is that it was a rogue group of their scientists who had developed the new cortical-induction technology and supplied it to McHogue. Naturally, everyone involved will be severely punished."

Odo looked at the text on the screen with a cold eye. "In Cardassian society, failure is always accompanied by punishment. Its just a question of who receives it."

He watched as the commander nodded and blanked the panel. There had been other accounts, of measures taken and fates decided. The most satisfying had been the word received from Bajor, of the collapse of the Severalty Front and the reestablishment of the previous provisional government. At last report, the disgraced General Aur, chastened by experience, had resigned all positions and entered one of the contemplative religious orders that had formerly been headed by the Kai Opaka.

"Oh, and Dukat appended a personal message." The commander leaned back in his chair. "Seems that he intended to tell us about the trapdoors, the whole system of surreptitious access, when we first took over the station. It just slipped his mind, is all."

"The Gul's memory can be . . . convenient when necessary." Odo had firsthand knowledge of that. "If there's nothing else, I should be returning to my duties at the security office."

"Yes, of course, Constable; I didn't mean to detain you. Though I noticed, when I passed through the Promenade, that our friend Quark seemed rather upset about something. I would have thought that he'd be feeling pleased now, what with the effective eliminating of his competition."

Odo shrugged. "The Ferengi does not easily let go of any grievance. Something occurred a few shifts back, something not quite to his liking, and he requested my assistance in determining absolute proof of the culprits involved. So he could press for damages from certain, shall we say, *responsible* parties."

"Oh?" The commander raised an eyebrow. "And what did you tell him just now?"

"I told him that absolute certainty, at least in this existence, was not to be acquired. He would just have to do the best he could, with what knowledge he did have available to him." Odo gazed up at the office's ceiling, as though contemplating the tiresome sins of the universe's sentient species. "I'm afraid, Commander, that this is something you're going to hear more about."

He had been idly tossing up a baseball and catching it with his fielder's glove when his father came into their living quarters. Jake looked up at him.

"You look kind of tired," he said.

His father managed to raise a smile. "A little more than usual, I suppose."

For a moment, his father regarded the wooden crate that still sat in one corner of the room. Jake still wasn't sure exactly what was in the crate; he'd been told that it was stuff that had belonged to the Kai Opaka, down on Bajor. His dad would have to do something about it all, eventually.

But not just yet.

Weighed down with fatigue, his father sat, slumping into the couch with his eyes closed. Jake wondered if he was going to fall asleep right there.

He didn't. One eye opened, regarding Jake with an alert, sidelong gaze. "I have a question for you." As Jake watched, his father drew himself upright; he took out his data padd and turned its small display panel around. "Could you tell me why Quark would send me a bill for two dozen broken items of assorted glassware?"

Jake gazed at the laced spheroid sitting in the center of his glove's padding. "I can explain. . . ."

"You know," said his father, "I really don't think you have to." He set the data padd down on the low table before them. "Quark will just have to realize . . . that it's one of those games where anything might happen." He plucked the baseball from Jake's glove; with a quick snap of his wrist, he side-armed it down the living quarters' long hallway. It could be heard crashing off unseen objects.

Jake grinned. "Nice pitch, Dad."

His father slouched back against the cushions, already looking less tired. "About as good as one of yours, judging from this." He held up Quark's bill on the data padd.

"Hey—" That remark brought a protest from Jake. "I wasn't pitching; I was at bat."

"Indeed?" His father raised an eyebrow.

"Well . . . yeah. Kind of." Jake realized that he had just been caught out. "Anyway, it's not exactly easy, you know, trying to practice inside a holosuite. *And* all by myself."

"What about your friend Nog?"

Jake snorted. "I don't think you're going to see any Ferengi in the big leagues soon."

"Well . . . you present a very reasoned argument." His father flexed his hand. The toss of the ball had been nothing, a literal throwaway. But Jake knew that his father had a pretty decent fastball; maybe the kinetic memory was still locked inside there, somewhere inside his dad's arm, through his elbow and all the way up into his shoulder. "Tell you what—I could use a little practice myself."

"You sure?" Jake regarded him with a mixture of hope and skepticism. "I mean, you've been busy a lot . . ."

"Only with things that don't even exist." His father closed his eyes again, rolling his head back against the sofa cushion. A different tiredness, a better kind, visibly moved through him. "And . . . they can wait."

Jake watched him for a moment longer, then slid off his fielder's glove and set it down on the sofa cushion between them. He stood up, glancing back over his shoulder as he headed to his room, leaving his father to his long-delayed rest.

"It could have been much worse."

She knew she didn't have to tell Julian that; as the chief Starfleet medical officer in this sector, he had been in charge of evacuating the ruins of what had been Moagitty. There had been more individuals left alive than they had initially expected, enough to overwhelm DS9's own emergency facilities; hospital ships and personnel from the closest navigational sectors had been routed here and into orbit above Bajor. Dax had observed, at first with a degree of surprise and then with a growing admiration, the organizational skills that the doctor had brought to bear upon the problem of coordinating the rescue effort's varied elements.

"Believe me, I know," replied Julian. His around-the-clock labors had left him looking more unshaven and ragged-edged than Dax had ever seen him before. He leaned back against the lab bench, kneading his brow. "It's bad enough as it is. If everybody had been found dead down there, we could've just performed a few regulation autopsies and been done by now."

Dax made no reply; she was aware that he was merely trying to get a reaction from her with a bit of gallows humor. She knew him better than that; he wouldn't be working himself to the point of exhaustion if his heart wasn't in perfect synchronization with the demands of his profession.

"I'd better be getting back." Bashir took a deep breath, letting his shoulders drop with its exhaling. "To the infirmary . . . the last few cases should be arriving . . ."

"No, Julian; you should get some rest." She forced a stern tone into her voice. "They can do without you for now— you've set things up well enough, for the others to carry on."

He shook his head slowly. "I don't know . . . there's so many . . ."

"Then it won't help anyone, will it, for you to collapse in

the middle of it all. Julian, let the other medical personnel take care of things. The best course of action for you at this time is to go back to your quarters and get some sleep."

"Maybe you're right . . ." He pushed himself away from the lab bench. "Don't say any more." He held up a hand to ward off any further argument, managing a smile behind it. "Your diagnosis is, of course, correct. *And* the prescription." Julian turned and headed for the lab's door; he stopped there and looked back at her. "Perhaps later, when everything has finally settled down—perhaps we can talk then. There's a lot you haven't told me about yet."

As the door slid shut, Dax turned again to her own work. The matters that Julian wished to discuss with her, the question that he had left unspoken but that she knew he wanted to ask—the time for all of that might never come. Because she didn't know—or understand—the answers herself. Not entirely.

She looked across the instrument readings displayed on the computer panel. The station's remote sensors indicated no subspatial anomalies in this sector; the dark, shifting processes that the CI modules had unleashed, the erosion and collapse of the universe's underlying structure, had ended. Something had happened, something that Benjamin—in that brief, chaotic moment that had followed the strike of McHogue's fist—had accomplished. An act of Benjamin's will, a blow surer and more telling than McHogue could have defended against. But one that her own eye had been unable to see . . . and that Benjamin himself had been unable to elucidate to her.

The sensor readings only confirmed what she had sensed to be true, even as the *Ganges* had returned to the station. After a last, near-apocalyptic fury, the atmospheric storms had already begun dying out on Bajor's surface; in space, the runabout had encountered none of the turbulence that had made Benjamin's rescue flight so dangerous. There had been time, a respite of calm on their journey home, for Benjamin to attempt telling her what had happened. What he had done.

Benjamin had lain back in the seat beside her, as she had piloted the runabout back to DS9; he had looked exhausted from the rigors of his confrontation with McHogue. In a low voice, he had spoken of things at the limit of her scientific understanding. Language itself was inadequate for the purpose.

He forgot, Benjamin had whispered to her. *McHogue forgot, that the world he'd created . . . it was inside our heads as well. In our thoughts and dreams. Because he'd put it there. That was where it was real . . . or as real as it could ever be.*

That had been how he had defeated McHogue. The true backdoor that McHogue had left behind, an entry into the secret workings of McHogue's *idios kosmos,* his private universe.

All that had happened, the lashing storms on Bajor and the deeper, more threatening disturbances beneath the fabric of space itself—it hadn't been an effect caused only by the CI modules' operations. *We made it real,* Benjamin had told her. *Just as we make . . . this universe real.* He had raised his hand to point toward the runabout's viewport. *It doesn't just happen out there. It happens in here as well.* Then Benjamin had tapped the side of his head with a single fingertip. *And what McHogue had made real . . . inside our heads . . .* Benjamin had closed his eyes, smiling faintly. *Then we could make it unreal again. If we just knew how . . .*

In DS9's research lab, Dax reached out and shut off the computer panel's display. The scroll of numbers and graphs, the vital signs of the universe, indicated nothing now, other than that her old friend Benjamin had indeed known how. Even if he couldn't explain it to her in any terms that her rational mind didn't push away as being just too mystical.

The older part of her, the symbiont inside, was equally rational—but wiser; it reserved its judgment on these matters. It had known Benjamin Sisko longer than she had; long enough to assure her that he had indeed changed, in some way both profound and subtle. It had something to do with what had happened to him in the wormhole; what he had found in there . . . and what he had found of himself. Whatever it had been—and he had only made the most cryptic comments about it to her, allusions to mysteries even greater than what had happened to McHogue's real and unreal worlds—it enabled him to speak of the connection between the universes both inside and outside the humanoid mind, and as more than just metaphor. The return of the remote sensors' readings to normal levels proved that. Whether she wanted to believe that or not. Or whether she even could.

It was a bit too much to think about now. Dax rubbed her own eyes. She knew she should take the advice she had given Julian, and get some rest herself. It had been a long shift, with longer ones before it. Whatever sleep there had been, for anyone aboard the station, had been filled with dreams more arduous than anything encountered while awake.

The lab door slid shut behind her, as she headed for her quarters. She doubted if there would be any dreams at all, in this long-delayed night.

Sleep would claim him, if he let it. He only had to close his eyes and lean back against the cushions of the sofa.

But not just yet. Sisko turned his head slightly, to regard the wooden crate that still sat in one corner of the room. Next shift, he promised himself, he would have it taken away and sent back down to Bajor. The objects inside, the mementos of the Kai, could be more properly taken care of by her own people. He had no need of them. He had his own memories of her.

Prophecies and blessings, thought Sisko. More than anyone else knew; more than he himself had known. So much had been changed within him, in ways that he was only beginning to understand.

The need for rest weighed heavily across his shoulders. He knew why he put it off, why he tried to forestall its inevitable approach.

When he had been down there, in Moagitty . . . in that city and world that McHogue had created . . . there had been the smallest possible glimpse, as he had passed through the doorway between one false universe and another. A instant that had been both remembrance and eternal non-time: for just that flash of consciousness, he had seen again that which had been shown him, so long ago, inside the wormhole.

He closed his eyes, willing himself toward that memory again.

He had seen his wife, Jake's mother, inside there. In that time, in that lost universe, when she had still been alive. She had turned toward him, one hand reaching back to his, smiling as if she were about to say something. . . .

There hadn't been time enough to hear what her words would have been. The vision of her face had gone as quickly as it had appeared; he hadn't even been conscious of it when he had found himself wandering in the corridors of a nonexistent *Deep Space Nine*. Only now, when he could allow his thoughts to sort themselves out, had he remembered what he had seen. What had been granted to him.

He wondered what it meant. Perhaps nothing; perhaps a gift, a blessing. He slowly shook his head, smiling in rueful acknowledgment. It would have been just like the Kai, to have given him something like that, something that would enable him to go forward and accomplish what he had to.

Falling now; he let himself fall. Toward that bright world, the other one inside him. Where he might yet hear those tender words that had been—and always were—about to be spoken to him.